Romantic Suspense

Danger. Passion. Drama.

K-9 Alaskan Defence
Sarah Varland

Uncovering the Truth
Carol J. Post

MILLS & BOON

K-9 ALASKAN DEFENCE
© 2025 by Sarah Varland
Philippine Copyright 2025
Australian Copyright 2025
New Zealand Copyright 2025

First Published 2025
First Australian Paperback Edition 2025
ISBN 978 1 038 94058 2

UNCOVERING THE TRUTH
© 2025 by Carol J. Post
Philippine Copyright 2025
Australian Copyright 2025
New Zealand Copyright 2025

First Published 2025
First Australian Paperback Edition 2025
ISBN 978 1 038 94058 2

This is a work of fiction. Names, characters, places, and incidents are either the
product of the author's imagination or are used fictitiously, and any resemblance to
actual persons, living or dead, business establishments, events, or locales is entirely
coincidental.

Published by
Harlequin Mills & Boon
An imprint of Harlequin Enterprises (Australia) Pty Limited
(ABN 47 001 180 918), a subsidiary of HarperCollins
Publishers Australia Pty Limited
(ABN 36 009 913 517)
Level 19, 201 Elizabeth Street
SYDNEY NSW 2000 AUSTRALIA

MIX
Paper | Supporting
responsible forestry
FSC® C001695
www.fsc.org

Cover art used by arrangement with Harlequin Books S.A.. All rights reserved.

Printed and bound in Australia by McPherson's Printing Group

K-9 Alaskan Defence

Sarah Varland

MILLS & BOON

Sarah Varland lives in Alaska with her husband, John, their two boys and their dogs. Her passion for books comes from her mom; her love for suspense comes from her dad, who has spent a career in law enforcement. When she's not writing, she's often found dog mushing, hiking, reading, kayaking, drinking coffee or enjoying other Alaskan adventures with her family.

Books by Sarah Varland

Love Inspired Suspense

Visit the Author Profile page at millsandboon.com.au.

Now unto him that is able to do exceedingly abundantly above all that we ask or think, according to the power that worketh in us, unto him be glory in the church by Christ Jesus throughout all ages, world without end. Amen.

—Ephesians 3:20–21

To my family, who has faithfully supported every dream I've ever had. I'm so blessed. And to God, whose dreams are even better and bigger than my own.

Chapter One

No matter how fast Lily Peterson ran, it was never quite fast enough. Her feet dug into the soft dirt of the Alaskan mountain side trail, winding along the ridgeline. The view in front of her was a study in contrasts, wilderness that gradually gave way to houses, then the city of Anchorage ahead in the distance. So many buildings. So many lights.

She loved the beauty of it from up here, running with her German shepherd, Timber, but she was thankful to live twenty miles north of the city. The town of Silvertip Creek, named for the brown bears who frequented the area, offered her the solitude of the wilderness that she needed. Especially after everything that had happened this past year.

Her pace quickened inadvertently, and Lily felt the welcome burn in her muscles that always came when she pushed herself. Timber kept pace, like she always did. Lily couldn't have asked for a more faithful companion, even though Timber really had never been meant for her...

She took a deep breath, tried to clear her mind, and ran faster and faster until she finally had to stop for air. Timber stopped beside her, and Lily reached down and petted her in between gasps.

"Good dog." With a long inhale, she began to stretch, looking out at the view where Cook Inlet met the rocky shore. In the land of the midnight sun, there would be light for hours yet since it was only eight o'clock at night. But she and Timber both needed dinner, so it was time to head back.

"Ready to go home?" she asked, expecting the dog's ears to perk like they usually did at the word. For a German shepherd who'd been trained as a police dog, Timber was quite a fan of relaxing on the couch and generally staying close to home. These mountain trips were more for Lily than Timber, though she had a feeling the dog viewed it as her duty to take Lily for runs.

This time, though, Timber continued to stare off into the distance, farther down the jagged ridgeline, past any real trail. There was a look of focus in her eyes Lily had never seen before.

She felt her own breathing slow as she listened. Her heart still pounding, she leaned closer to Timber, trying to see what the dog saw.

Everything seemed to her to be the same as it had been moments before, but Timber was clearly picking up on something Lily wasn't. It shouldn't be surprising—the dog had been born, bred and trained to work. Until an attack a year ago had nearly taken her life and left her with an injury that led to her early retirement. She'd been sent to live with Lily, as a sort of condolence for the fact that Timber's handler, Lily's fiancé, hadn't survived.

"What is it, girl?"

Timber whined, shifting uncomfortably. Lily's shoulders tensed, and slowly she started to reach for Timber's collar. The dog usually hiked off leash, but she was behaving strangely. There could be a moose, a bear...

Timber took off at a full sprint.

"Timber, no!" Lily leapt to her feet and took off after her.

Muscles that had been so glad to get a break began burning anew with the sudden increase in activity. "Timber!"

The German shepherd ignored her, something that would have been unthinkable moments before. Timber's recall was bombproof—a remnant of her former job. Lily had never had trouble with her before. This was terrifyingly out of character.

Lily picked her way farther down the ridgeline, unable to run in some places where the trail hugged the side of the mountain or where jagged rocks jutted out. How Timber hadn't lost her footing, Lily didn't know. The dog was extremely athletic and in good shape, but her back leg had never been quite the same after she'd been shot.

She kept her eyes on Timber as long as she could, praying she'd be okay, but then Timber leapt over a rock and out of sight. Lily bit back her scream to avoid startling the dog even more and hurried after her.

She noticed the smell first, dense and reminiscent of iron. Reddish brown blood soaked the mountainside foliage, staining the ground around the body of a motionless man.

Timber sat beside him, whining and pawing the ground. If Matt had told Lily details about Timber's training, Lily couldn't remember them. It seemed to her as though the dog had found the person. Or...the body? Was Timber trained to do that?

Willing herself to keep it together, Lily started forward. Only to be knocked sideways by a blurry force.

She screamed as she slid down the scree on the mountainside, her hands fighting for something to grab, anything that would keep her from plummeting farther. Out of the corner of her eye, she could see the drop—it was much too far to fall and survive. She twisted her body to fall back onto the ridge, looking around wildly to figure out what had hit her.

A figure crouched nearby—a man, she guessed by the size and build—wearing black sweats, a black hoodie and a black ski mask over his face. He was reaching for her, rough hands grabbing her wrists, when Timber growled and launching herself at the man.

She couldn't lose Timber, not with all the other things she'd lost in the past year. She also knew she couldn't fight off this man alone. He was too big, too strong, and she'd already almost fallen. Even with adrenaline coursing through her veins, Lily wasn't sure she could sustain another attack.

Timber bit down, and the man released Lily, his scream ripping the air. Every muscle in Lily's body tensed, and panic tightened her throat. She hurried out of arms reach, toward the body Timber had found, trying not to think about the gruesome scene behind her. Instead, she watched as Timber let go of the man's arm and jumped at him again, growling.

The man kicked at her, but Timber clamped down on his other arm. He threw her off violently, and Lily watched in horror as Timber flew toward the knife-edge of the ridgeline. She ran to her, heart in her throat, as the dog fell just inches away from the drop-off.

With Lily's eyes off her attacker, the man turned to run away. Timber's body tensed to chase after the man, but Lily left no room for argument in her tone. "Stop, no."

Timber stayed. Lily waited, crouched at her side, until she could no longer hear the man's feet crashing through the brush.

The danger had passed, at least for now, but her heart still pounded in her chest. Why had the man attacked her, whoever he was? Why had he hurt the man behind her?

Was he even still alive? She had to check.

Moving slowly, she approached him carefully and knelt down beside him. His eyes were closed. She glanced along the rest of his body, then looked immediately away. He had to be dead. No one could lose this much blood and not be... She felt for a pulse at the man's wrists and waited.

Nothing.

She moved her hands to his neck.

Still nothing.

Exhaling, she felt defeat press against her, hating the idea that she'd been unable to help. She stepped away from the body and threw up the little lunch she'd eaten earlier. When she finally managed to get her nausea under control, she pulled out her phone and dialed 911 to report what she'd found. Talk about another layer of trauma—police officers were the last people she wanted to talk to today. A memory flashed in her mind, a police car in her driveway, a knock at her door.

Lily took a slow, deep breath. Held it. Let it out.

She couldn't do this. She absolutely couldn't face the police alone. Not today. She glanced back down at her phone. But did she dare not? There was no one else to call. Heart still pounding, Lily scrolled through her contacts, finger hovering over the one number she never thought she'd have a reason to call again.

Travis Beckett had broken her heart years ago, and she'd been less than thrilled when she discovered he was her fiancé's partner at the Anchorage Police Department. Having him back in her life in any capacity was something she didn't want.

But she didn't know anyone else connected to law enforcement who might be able to brace her for the storm she was afraid was coming. A man had died, the violent wounds puncturing his body speaking of rage. Intention.

A criminal was out there right now, loose. He could come back any minute.

Refusing to overthink it anymore, she pressed the screen. Waited. "Travis… It's Lily. I need you."

Hearing from Lily Peterson wasn't something Travis would have expected to happen in this lifetime. Their last link had been broken when Matt died. But he'd recognize her voice anywhere, had known it was her as soon as she said his name, though he hadn't had her number saved in his phone, and then she'd said she needed him…

The protective feeling that welled in him surprised him.

She hadn't finished explaining by the time he grabbed his keys and started for his truck.

She was far up the ridgeline of Avalanche Peak, but he still had his trail runners on from the short run he'd taken after work. He guessed police officers probably brought up bad memories for her; the last time she'd been around many of them, she'd been hearing the details of her fiancé's death. He'd call them when he'd reached Lily, to make sure she didn't have to talk to them alone.

The trail was hard beneath his feet as he ran to the location she'd described. Finally the smell hit him. Blood.

And a body. Nothing she'd said could have prepped him for the sight of that much blood on the ground. Lily knelt beside the man, sobbing into her hands. Timber was pressing against her as though for reassurance.

He'd missed that dog. The department had offered her to Travis after Matt died and Timber's injury forced her into early retirement, but he hadn't felt right about taking her. Not when Lily was alone, her future decimated by one person's bad choices, her fiancé in the wrong place at the wrong time.

Travis should have been the one in the line of fire. He'd been a second too slow. Now he was alive, and Matt was dead, and Travis had wrecked Lily's life…again.

How was she? He'd wondered many times over the past year since the shooting. One year ago today. He'd finished out the next few months after that with the Anchorage Police Department and then resigned, moved from his apartment in the city back to Silvertip Creek, where he'd lived growing up. He was helping his brother at his hardware store while he tried to figure out what he wanted to do with his life. All Travis knew for sure was that he was ready for a job that involved fewer homicides and drug cases and more small-town things.

His days were slower now. Easier.

Still too much time to think, but there wasn't much a job

could do about that. One of these days that was probably an issue Travis was going to have to solve himself.

"Lily, you okay?" A stupid question, he decided as soon as it left his mouth.

Her pale blue eyes were red rimmed from crying. She blinked but didn't answer him.

"How's he?" He nodded toward the body on the ground.

"I think… I think he's dead."

"And Timber?"

Lily turned to the dog and scratched around her ears. Travis thought he saw the tenseness in her shoulders soften. Good, that had been part of the idea with Lily adopting Timber.

"She seems okay. She found him. Completely ignored me when I called her back, just took off, and then I found her here." Her face was wrinkled into a frown. "Is that, you know, normal? Like is that something she's trained to do?"

"Possibly." He didn't know the degree to which he should go into Timber's training with Lily. She was trained for search and rescue and was able to sniff out narcotics, contact a suspect on command and deliver a bite, among other things. She'd been an incredibly promising police canine, only three when she'd been shot, which was a shame.

So much about that incident was.

"Did you notice anything else here? Anyone else, evidence that says someone else was here?"

She hesitated. His stomach tightened.

"Someone attacked me."

It was like someone had hit him square in the chest. He fought to catch his breath and breathe normally again. "Tell me what happened."

She did so, detailing the attacker's large build, his scream, Timber's attack and his retreat.

"You're okay?" He stepped closer to her, scanning her for signs of injury.

She held out her arm. "Bruises, but I think that's all."

The harsh purple of the bruises against her light skin made him want to find the guy himself.

"Why were you way up here, past the regular trail?" He tried to keep the judgment and frustration out of his tone. The idea of Lily taking chances like this grated at him. She was supposed to be in her coffee shop in Silvertip Creek, where it was safe, not on mountainsides risking her life discovering dead men.

Even as he thought it, he realized his error. Lily was free to do what she wanted. Always had been. She'd made that clear when they were both in high school, when they'd been dating for over a year and graduation had been approaching, and Travis had thought their futures might be together...

Forget what he thought. He'd been wrong.

He looked at Lily, who was watching him. Dang it, he'd never been able to hide his thoughts from her. If he wasn't imagining it, her face had softened slightly, when she should have been defensive at his unreasonable question. Could she still sense his lingering feelings for her, whatever they were? Not romantic feelings, certainly, but caring? Too much caring for someone who was essentially a stranger now.

"Timber needed a run."

"There are other trails." Travis said. His eyes were drawn back to the body and a familiar clenching feeling tightened in his stomach.

He'd seen bodies like this too many times, was altogether too aware of the ways people hurt each other. It was why he'd left police work after the death of his partner. He'd tried to stick with it for a couple of months, went to the counseling the department had mandated, but none of it seemed to work. He despised the job he'd once enjoyed, and there didn't seem to be anything he could do that would change that. So he left, joined his brother in the hardware store business and avoided reminders of what his life had once been like.

Today was a jarring reminder, in so many ways. Lily's pale

face. A situation that felt impossible. The tension as they realized someone would not make it out alive. Just like last year.

"Travis." Lily's voice was tense.

He whirled to face her. She'd walked back to the ridgeline where the dead man had been. She was staring at a tiny piece of paper on the ground, stark white against the brown of the blood-soaked earth, immediately beside the body, against his hip like it had dislodged from a pocket.

"He dropped something. Could that matter?"

"For what?"

"Finding out more about who he is, why he was attacked…"

"That's the police's job."

"But you're…"

"I'm not anymore."

"Oh." She stopped, looked away from the paper and up at him. "Since when?"

"Not long after."

She nodded. She clearly knew what he meant. For once in their lives, they probably understood what the other was feeling better than anyone else. Lily and Matt had been engaged for months before he was killed. Travis had been his partner at work, handling Timber together, investigating together… Each of them had lost a chunk of themselves when they'd lost Matt.

He saw emotions chase across Lily's face as she seemed to realize that, too. Again, he watched her face soften.

"You asked me why I was up here," she said.

"Yes."

She shook her head, and he thought he caught a flash of disappointment in her eyes. "Don't you know what day it is? It's one year since he died." She reached out a hand and pointed. "See that spot on the mudflats right there?"

He did. And suddenly he understood why she'd ventured onto this ridgeline. From anywhere else, the view of that place was blocked. But from here?

She could see the place where Matt had drowned in the relentless Alaskan tide and her dreams for the future had been lost forever.

Chapter Two

Lily almost couldn't believe she'd pointed that out to Travis, the place where Matt had died, or that they were talking about this thing that she didn't talk about with anyone so casually. But Travis probably understood how she felt better than most people would. He didn't understand losing a loved one, of course...

She slammed the door on that thought almost as soon as she'd opened it. Technically speaking, maybe he did know what that was like. Not losing to death, perhaps, but maybe to the other person's choices.

"The counselor I was seeing told me I had to figure out a way that worked for me to mark the days, whether that was to do something special or just somehow remember him." She shrugged.

"I think that sounds wise."

A minute of silence passed, and then Travis shifted beside her, and she felt his glance on her. He wanted to ask or say something, she was fairly certain. Finally she looked his direction. "What is it?"

"Hmm?"

"What's on your mind? You seem preoccupied and not

with…" She didn't have the energy to talk about it, so she motioned with her hand instead. "This."

"It's you."

She turned to him. Waited in a heavy silence as their eyes met. Her heartbeat quickened ever so slightly.

"I'm worried about you," he clarified. "You said the guy attacked you."

"Oh." She shook her head, scattering thoughts of the past. "Not badly. I mean, I'm okay. Bruised, but…" She trailed off, looked down at her arms.

Travis moved closer, and his fingers brushed against her arm as he reached to look closer. Just as quickly, the contact was broken as he snatched his hand away.

"May I?" he asked.

She nodded and held her arms out to him.

There was no reason for her to react this way to Travis's touch. However, while any romance between them had ended years ago and badly, it appeared she hadn't entirely forgotten the connection they'd once had. Goose bumps chased down her arms.

"I hate that you're hurt. Maybe you should get these looked at?"

Already, she was shaking her head.

"At least clean the cuts well. It looks like you got scraped." He motioned to a spot on her forearm.

Lily glanced at it. "Probably from when I fell."

"You fell up there?"

"Yeah, when we were struggling, before Timber fought him off."

Timber seemed to almost materialize beside her, and Lily smiled as she reached down, scratched the dog between her ears. When she looked up again, Travis was staring down the sheer drop-off along the ridgeline.

Lily looked away. She didn't want to think about what could have so easily happened.

He took a deep breath and turned back to her. Apparently he didn't want to think about it, either. "So this paper." Travis walked over to where it lay, and Lily followed. The corners of the paper were edged in deep brown, as though it had soaked up some of the blood.

"From his pocket, you think?" she suggested.

"Best I can guess. Hardly anyone hikes back here." He nudged it with a foot.

"I've got some thin gloves in my backpack. I could pick it up with those?"

"Better than nothing. I'll do it, though."

She slung the small runner's pack off her back and dug out the gloves, then handed them to Travis. The gray gloves lined with hot pink fleece looked funny stretched across his hands. She watched as he bent and picked up the folded paper carefully. There was a torn piece of scotch tape on the back side of it, dirtied by the ground, its stickiness long gone.

Travis stood beside her as he unfolded it. The words written in black ink stood out against the white of the paper.

742 Aspen

Her heart skipped.

It had been almost a year since Lily had experienced what she was feeling right now. Her chest felt tight. Tighter. Tighter. It was a normal fear reaction, she tried to remind herself even as her world seemed to narrow. *Breathe in. Breathe out.*

She glanced at Travis, but his world seemed unshaken. He was frowning but in confusion. "Why would…" he started, but she interrupted.

"It's my address."

If he'd been glad before that Lily had called him, he was extra thankful now. His mind raced. Why was her address on this paper? Who was the dead man she'd found in the wilderness? Was she meant to have found him, was it some kind of trap? Regardless, the body had some connection to Lily.

The wilderness around them no longer held its usual benign feeling, but rather one of threat. Even the clouds looked darker to his mind now.

The danger had just increased past his comfort level.

"We need to get out of here. I'll call the police on our way down so they can come for the body, and I'll swing by the station to give them the note. I don't want to leave it in case the killer comes back for it."

"No, the tape. What was taped to the letter?"

She was right, the tape. Better to investigate that now than wonder later... Investigate? What was he thinking? He was a former cop, emphasis on *former*, and she owned a coffee shop. Neither of them had any business investigating anything.

Except Travis wasn't comfortable leaving her safety to the police, no matter how competent they were. He knew how busy police departments got. There was a chance a case like this could get set aside once progress on it stalled, and he couldn't afford for Lily to be in danger during the interim.

"We can look for a few minutes and then we're out of here. This might be some kind of trap."

"Don't you think I'd be dead or hurt worse or something by now if it was?"

Travis didn't answer. He was already crouching to look at the ground. He'd shoved the paper with the address into his back pocket. Probably there weren't any usable prints on it, but you never knew for sure.

Out of the corner of his eye, he saw Lily bend down to search, too. Timber still sat near her, watching.

Man, he loved that dog. She was one of the best he'd ever worked with or had the pleasure to watch work. On one hand, it was a shame she'd had to retire early because of her injury, but on the other, he was glad she was with Lily.

"I found a key." Her voice sounded strangled.

"Are you okay?"

He watched as she swallowed hard and shook her head slightly. "No. I mean, yes, I will be, but..."

"Let's get off the mountain. Now."

A wind picked up and chilled the air as they hurried back across the ridgeline. Travis felt his heart in his throat every time he watched Lily traverse one of the knifelike edges carefully, arms out to grab on to something in case of a fall.

Finally they were back on the main trail. Almost without thinking, he looked out toward the inlet. Sure enough, he couldn't see the spot where Matt had died from here. But how had Lily known there would be a view of it?

He asked her as much, partially out of curiosity and partially to give them something to talk about to make the time go faster until she was safely away from this place. As far away as he could convince her to get.

"Matt and I used to come up here. You know he loved trail running."

Travis nodded. He'd never seen why someone would want to run up in the mountains when he could walk, take in the view, really be present and enjoy the moment, but he knew his friend had loved it.

"He took me up here once, not long before he died actually, and I just remembered the view."

"But you don't go on that trail often, right?" He feared for her safety if she did, and was also concerned if her movements were predictable. Could someone have assumed that she'd find the dead man?

"I don't. I haven't been back since."

Travis nodded. They continued picking their way down the trail, which angled toward the base of the mountain. His car was parked at the trailhead, and he assumed Lily's was, too, though he'd only noticed a couple other cars in the lot. The trailhead led to several different places and was fairly popular, but it was a chilly day even for Alaskan summer, so not as many people were out.

"Where's your car?" he asked.

"I walked."

He didn't know that there was anything to say to that. It was completely reasonable that she'd have walked here a few hours ago. But now, with what had changed… Why did a dead man have her address? Was she in more or less danger now because he was dead?

And why—his mind finally wrapped itself around asking— why had the dead man looked familiar? Something chased around on the edges of his mind, the shadows of a cobwebby idea. He'd have to get back to that later.

"How far is it to your house?"

"Less than a mile."

"Is there anywhere else you could go for now?"

She raised her eyebrows and said nothing. It was answer enough.

"Listen, I know I don't have a right to tell you what to do anymore."

"Never did, actually."

"Right, but…"

"Could we talk about this at my house?"

"Fine. Lead on." He blew out a breath of frustration that he knew wasn't fair to direct toward Lily.

This was a situation he never could have imagined finding himself in, being back in Lily's life in any capacity. He struggled to wrap his mind around all the implications of it as he followed her down the narrow trail. She followed Timber, whose body language didn't seem to indicate any particular threats at the moment. Travis had been watching her for a while for any signs that there was something particular to be concerned about.

"Here it is, just up here…" Lily turned off the main trail onto a much less traveled trail. Travis had known there were a few houses up here on the edge of town, up against the mountains, but hadn't known Lily was one of them. She rounded the corner. Stopped.

The tiny cabin in the clearing was cozy, welcoming, exactly what he would have pictured her in.

It was also on fire.

Timber whined and shifted uncomfortably.

"Timber, stay!" Lily yelled and then sprinted toward the log cabin and the flames.

"Lily, no!" Travis shouted and chased after her until he lost sight of her in the smoke and flames.

She was gone.

Her house. Her books. Her photos—why couldn't she just keep them on her computer like other people her age? Her coffee mugs from places she'd visited. Her favorite rug. She thought of all of them as she sprinted up the hill into the clearing where her house was in flames.

Mind somehow still working, she pulled her phone out of her pocket and dialed 911. "My house is on fire! Help!"

"I'll get someone there as soon as I can. What's your address?" The calm, neutral voice of the dispatcher almost made her angry and more panicked. This was urgent, didn't she know that? Of course Lily realized it was their job to sound like that. Maybe it steadied some people. It did nothing for her.

"742 Aspen," she said as fast as she could, then hung up, despite the woman's insistence she stay on the call. She had to do something. Her house was on fire.

The hose was on the side of the house opposite most of the fire. Of course sometimes fire could be in the walls—she'd probably read it in a book somewhere, but the random fact chose now to present itself in her mind. If she hurried, could she put the fire out by herself?

She heard Travis yelling. Of course he wouldn't want her to fight the fire herself. But it wasn't his house.

"Lily, stop."

"No."

"They're just things." He reached for her arm, and she shrugged away from him.

"I said no! It's all I have, Travis. I won't lose my house. I won't."

With a quick glance backward to make sure Timber was staying put—she was, though the look on her face made it clear this wasn't her preference—Lily grabbed the hose and started to fight.

At first, the steam rising was her only result, and the effort seemed pointless. Then finally she thought she saw the flames lessening. They hadn't gotten to the roof yet, as if content to feed on the hand-hewn log walls. Little by little the fire retreated, until Lily heard the sirens approaching. At that point, she gladly stepped back and let the professionals take over.

She called Timber to her side and watched as the Silvertip Creek Fire Department fought to finish saving her little cabin. At some point, Travis came and stood on the other side of her from Timber. Somehow his presence made everything a little better.

When the last of the smoke was extinguished, one of the firefighters walked toward her. He removed his face mask and nodded in her direction. "You're the homeowner?"

Well, she had been. "Yes. Lily Peterson."

"I think we've got it out at this point. It's possible there could still be hot spots. We're going to walk around and make sure that it's out. Once we've confirmed it's safe enough, you can get a few belongings out of the house, but you won't be able to stay here for a few days."

She felt her face scrunch into a frown, and the fireman noticed. "The chemicals. Fires release them, you know."

She hadn't known. "But…" She felt Travis's hand on her arm and stopped. Nodded. "Thank you."

"You did a great job with the hose. Probably saved the house, to be honest. We just finished up what you started."

Lily tried to smile but only managed a sort of half smile as the firefighter walked away.

Was the fire entirely unrelated to finding the dead man? On one hand, it seemed too coincidental that two things with so much gravity and drama could happen in one day. On the other…how could they possibly be related? She didn't know who the man was, she'd found him entirely by accident.

And the fire?

"Will they be able to tell how the fire started?" she asked Travis. Maybe he'd had experiences with fire investigations as a police officer.

"To a degree, yes. They'll know if there was an accelerant that helped the fire spread, or if it was intentional or because of bad wiring…"

"Why would someone do this? I really don't understand. Is it related to the paper with my address?"

Travis shook his head. "I just don't know."

Neither did she. That was the problem.

The firefighter called her over to the house. The door of the cabin was intact, though it had been sprayed down. He eased it open for her and motioned her inside. In a fog, she went through.

The entryway was normal, though she could smell the smoke. The farther she went inside, the more damage she could see. Some of the walls were charred even on the inside. It appeared that overall the structure was intact, though.

"It all looks pretty good except this back corner." The fire-fighter motioned to the room that had been her study.

Oh, not her study. Her books…

She did her best to brace herself as they eased the door open.

It was better than it could have been. That's what she kept repeating to herself over and over. By her side, Timber seemed to tense up, probably mirroring Lily's own anxiety. The dog whined, and Lily reached down to pet her for reassurance.

The bookcase that was built into the outside wall was completely destroyed. It wasn't entirely burned up, but the damage was likely irreparable.

"This room is the reason you're going to need to let the house air out for a couple of days before you try to move back in."

Lily nodded, ran her hands along the spines of some of the books that hadn't been damaged. She looked up. The ceiling had some holes.

"My roof…" She trailed off. "Is it still intact?"

"From the outside it looked okay but you should have it checked out thoroughly by a contractor. I can give you the number of a guy I've seen do wonders with restorations like this."

She nodded. What else was there to do?

Her safe in the corner appeared to have taken some damage, too, but it was fireproof. She opened it, confirmed that her documents and other things she kept in it were unharmed, then shut it again.

"Matt helped with this room," she mumbled under her breath.

"What was that?" the firefighter asked.

"Nothing," Lily said, unwilling to repeat herself or explain. One year without him, and now…all of these things were happening. It couldn't be a coincidence. A chill ran down her back. Was she in some kind of danger?

She hurried to gather what she wanted for the night, necessities like spare clothes, pj's and toothpaste, but also the book she'd been in the middle of reading, some snacks, and a notebook and pen.

When she got back outside, Travis was still standing in the yard, waiting. Not that she expected him to have gone anywhere. He'd made it quite clear he was taking some kind of protective role, or trying to. The question was, did she want that?

"You okay?" he asked when she stepped outside.

"I have no idea."

"Want to come to my house? I've got a small cabin on my property that I usually rent out to tourists in the summer but it's empty for the next couple of weeks. You could stay in it until you're allowed back in yours? I can plug the address into your phone if you want."

She ran through her other options. Her best friend, Terina, was out of town. She could probably stay there, but it would involve pet sitting for Terina's tiny Chihuahuas, since she'd be displacing the pet sitter. While Timber was well enough behaved, as a rule she didn't seem to enjoy time spent with the smaller dogs biting at her ankles.

"I appreciate that," she said at last. "I'll meet you there?"

"Sure. And, Lily?"

She turned around, met his eyes.

"Be careful."

She felt the weight of his gaze even more than his words. In that moment, Lily realized that she hadn't overreacted. She hadn't been wrong to somehow link the events of this day together: the one-year anniversary of Matt's death; the discovery of the dead man; her burned cabin.

She was in danger for some reason. And with no idea where the danger was coming from, she would have to be alert to all possible sources of trouble if she had any hope of keeping herself safe.

Chapter Three

Travis had just climbed into his car when he saw the Silvertip Police Department patrol car pull into Lily's driveway. An officer who looked vaguely familiar slid out of one them. She was probably in her midthirties, with reddish hair.

Travis put his own car back into Park and got out, walking over to join her. He stuck out a hand to introduce himself. "Travis Beckett."

"You were at APD for a while, right?"

So she had looked familiar. He raised an eyebrow, prompting her for more information.

"I'm Officer Keller. Emily Keller. Zach Keller who works at APD is my brother."

Travis nodded. "Of course, makes sense. Nice to meet you." He could see the resemblance now. He hadn't thought about Zach in months, though the two of them had been close once. Maybe that was a possibility for keeping close to the investigation—it wasn't uncommon for police officers to keep each other posted. He was still technically post certified, so it wouldn't be any kind of violation.

"I'd like to ask Lily Peterson about what happened," Officer Keller went on. "It looks like the report is still pending in the system, but she called 911 earlier today on a ridgeline and found a body is my basic understanding?"

"I'm Lily Peterson." Lily walked up from where she'd been packing her car. She gave Keller a bit more information, then reached into her pocket, with a glance at Travis.

He nodded slightly, in case she was asking his opinion on sharing the note with the police. Anything would help, and the police needed to know everything they knew if there was going to be any kind of hope of solving this case.

"We found this at the scene." Lily handed Officer Keller the note and waited while she looked at it.

"That's this address. Your address."

"Exactly. And there's more." Lily handed the officer the key she'd found. They'd put it into a small plastic bag Lily had in her pack. "I don't know if you guys can get fingerprints off things this small..."

"You'd be amazed at what we can get prints off of."

"Well, I hope it helps. I don't want..." Lily trailed off, not seeming able to articulate more about how she felt.

"We don't want this to drag on. It's disconcerting," Travis finished, glancing at Lily who seemed to give him a small smile of approval.

"As you know," Officer Keller addressed Travis, "we can't promise anything in an investigation. Our latent print department, along with the rest of our tiny crime scene team, is pretty swamped, and the state crime lab is backlogged also. It may be a while before we get anything definitive from these."

Lily nodded. "Thank you, though, for looking into this."

"You're welcome. Anything else happens, call me or Officer Wilkins. He's the one up on the mountain right now recovering the body."

Officer Keller handed Lily a business card, then walked back to her car and drove away.

"You okay?" Travis looked over at Lily.

"Exhausted. I'm just exhausted."

"Let's head to my house. I'll feed you."

It was all he needed to say. She hurried to her car, and Travis did the same.

As he drove the five miles to his house, which was on the other side of Silvertip Creek from Lily's cabin, Travis went through the facts as he knew them. It was a habit he'd developed in his law enforcement days, a way to process through events.

First, Lily had called him, in trouble because Timber had run off and found a man who was dead. He needed to look into what degree had Timber alerted; how much had she performed according to her search-and-rescue training? K-9s were interesting—you could train them, but they were still living creatures with their own minds. They had some of their own decision-making skills, which some departments let dogs use more than others. It may not be relevant to this case, but he still wanted to know what had really happened to the best of his ability.

Second, someone had set Lily's house on fire. Did they intend to destroy it? Destroy something inside the house? Hurt or kill her? Scare her? Motives were too varied for him to make any kind of guess.

Third, this was the one-year anniversary of Matt Davis's death. Was that related? Coincidence? Travis didn't believe in coincidences.

Ironic that he wished his friend was here to bounce ideas off of. Matt had always been smart, incredibly so. He didn't come across as an intellectual by any means, but he had a mind for puzzles and if anything qualified, this did.

Of course, if Matt were alive, things might be different. He and Lily would have been married by now, for one thing.

There was something Travis didn't want to think about. The idea of Lily as another man's wife made his stomach feel hollow in a way he wished he could ignore. Surely after all these years he was over her. Wasn't he?

He pulled into his driveway and tried to see his house like she would. How much did she think about the past? Would she imagine what life would have been like if they'd stayed together?

He certainly wouldn't have imagined himself in the house he had now, in a quiet mountainside neighborhood, downright quaint with its weathered logs and A-frame structure. But Matt's death had changed Travis's priorities, as well as his dreams about the future. It had changed him.

He doubted Lily ever gave him much thought at all. It had been years, he reminded himself, and she'd been engaged since then. A real engagement with a real ring and a wedding date, not a class ring and some sincere but flimsy promises.

Climbing out of his car, he did his best to put the past back in his memory where it belonged. In the very back of his mind. She'd called him today as a friend. He had no business getting caught up in the land of what-if and risking that trust. What she needed now was a friend, someone to talk to, someone who would feed her, like he'd promised.

He waited in the driveway until Lily's car pulled in, and then he ushered her inside of his house, making sure to lock the door behind them.

"This is it." He shrugged.

"Wow."

If he'd imagined how she would react, instead of just wondered, he wouldn't have pictured her utterly delighted wide-eyed stare. "Your house is beautiful. It's so peaceful here."

"Thanks." He smiled, remembering every day he'd spent remodeling the house, ripping out old carpet and refinishing long-forgotten hardwood floors. His goal had been to blend the inside of his house with the outside, making it fade into the forest in a way. Having Lily notice and appreciate it warmed a part of himself he hadn't realized was cold.

"Want the grand tour first or dinner?"

Her stomach growled, and she looked down, embarrassed

for half a second, and then she looked back up at him with a smile. "Dinner, apparently. Thanks."

They headed to the kitchen, where she ran her hands appreciatively over the countertop. "Nice."

"It's functional."

"Oh, come on, it's so much more than that."

Travis shrugged. "I wanted it to be more than that."

"Well, you succeeded. You really did."

Something in her voice caught his attention, and he looked at her, their eyes meeting and holding for one second. Two.

He looked away first. She was hurting, he reminded himself. She needed a friend. Food. Not some boyfriend from her past confusing her when her life was in chaos already.

"How does beef stew sound?"

"Perfect. Want me to make something? Biscuits maybe? Do you have milk and flour?"

He motioned to the fridge and pantry. "Be my guest."

They worked side by side, the rhythm feeling more natural than it should have as they danced back and forth between counters and pantries and stove.

"That smells so good." Lily said with an appreciative sigh.

"Thanks."

Before long, they were sitting down at the table to eat. "Mind if I pray?" Travis asked.

"Go ahead." Lily replied, but there was something in her voice he couldn't quite identify. Matt had never been much for praying, or faith for that matter. Had that rubbed off on Lily or was he reading too much into her reaction? Hard to say.

After they prayed, they started to eat.

Lily paused. Closed her eyes. "This is so good."

"Self-defense. It was either learn to cook or starve."

She laughed, and he'd forgotten how much the liked the sound. "Well, you did a great job. This is delicious. I haven't eaten in hours."

The furrow between her brows returned, stress etching itself into the edges of her face.

"Well, you're eating now, no worries."

She seemed to appreciate his response. It earned him a smile at any rate. He kept eating his stew.

"I wonder how long this investigation is going to last." Lily said.

"Could we just set all that aside for tonight? You need to relax, get some rest."

"I can't just forget it about it."

"Well, no."

"Can you?"

Forget the idea of her being in danger, being powerless to stop it, utterly in the dark as to who could be after her in the first place? Hardly.

His expression must have answered for him, because Lily's mouth curved up at one end into a tiny smile and then she said. "Exactly."

"So if you don't want to forget about it—"

"I didn't say that, I said I couldn't."

"Right, sorry. If you can't forget it about it, then what do you want to do tonight? Would you rather be left alone? I can show you the guest cabin after dinner. Or better yet, you can sleep in here, and I'll sleep in the cabin."

It wasn't that the guest cabin was less safe than his main house, it was just slightly more isolated. It sat behind the house, farther from the main road. Although that could be a good thing, too...

"I'm not kicking you out of your house, so it's the cabin, or I go back to mine."

Had he forgotten how much fire this woman had? Lily was not one to do anything easily.

"The cabin, then. I'll show it to you after dinner. Do you want to try to sleep, or we could try to talk through today, see if there are any avenues to investigate?"

Her eyes met his almost instantly. "Investigate?"

"Well, yeah."

"You said you weren't law enforcement anymore."

He felt the tension grow as she waited for an answer, and he waited to try to figure out exactly what he was going to say. "I'm not working as law enforcement right now," Travis confirmed. "But I'm still post certified."

"Which means?"

He shrugged. "I could go back to work if I wanted to."

"And why don't you?"

"Today sums it up pretty well. Would you want to run into stuff like that most days?"

He'd put it as gently as he could have, Lily felt, but the gist wasn't lost on her. No, she wouldn't want memories of people dying, covered in blood, haunting her dreams every night. It was hard enough that she'd had the few experiences she'd had with such things.

Well, really, just today's. Matt was the first person close to her who had died, but there had been no graphic violence, no terrifying scene to confront. Just uniformed men standing on her door and the absence of someone she cared deeply about.

There had been cracks in her and Matt's relationship, of course, but every couple had their differences. Faith, for example. Lily had been raised to cling tightly to hers and Matt's approach to life had been less oriented toward such things. She'd found it somewhat insulting the way he patronized her a bit when they discussed faith, as though he was more intelligent for not believing... But besides that and some small squabbles, they'd had an ideal relationship. Smooth sailing.

Nothing like her and Travis. Fire and water if there ever was...

"Lily?"

She blinked, fighting to bring her mind back to the present conversation. "Yeah, I see why you wouldn't want to do that. Every day, I mean, or any day…" She shook her head. "It was awful."

"You should talk to someone about it. That's a lot to carry on your own."

"Who do you talk to?"

Travis hummed. "My oldest brother. He's a counselor, so does that count more than just talking to a normal brother?"

Lily smiled. "Maybe it does. Maybe I should. For tonight, though, yeah, let's talk about it together. For the case, I mean, if that's okay."

Travis nodded. "Sure, for the case."

It was normal that she still felt a little drawn to him, wasn't it? That he was the first one she'd thought to call when she was in trouble? Surely that was to be expected, even with the years looming between now and when they'd been close. People didn't just forget a relationship.

The truth was, the way she felt for him was making her a little… Well, it wasn't making her nervous at all, and *that* made her nervous. He was taking care of her, keeping her safe. It was like no time had passed, yet Lily felt like she'd lived several lifetimes since then. How did that make any sense?

As she tried to untangle her thoughts, it occurred to her that, honestly, she shouldn't try to quantify any of it. Travis was trying to keep her from being hurt or killed, and she appreciated that. Whatever she could tell him that might help him toward that goal, that was all tonight was about.

When they were finished eating, she helped him clear the dishes from the table and then washed them, much to his protest. Timber sat beside her on the kitchen floor, watching. She'd eaten her kibble when their dinner was cooking, though she did seem to be harboring some kind of hope that Lily might feed her scraps from dinner if only she looked cute enough.

Well, she wouldn't feed her too many, Lily thought as she tossed Timber a small bite of beef.

"Hot chocolate or coffee?" Travis asked from behind her, where he stood holding up two mugs.

"Hot chocolate would be great." Maybe it was a strange favorite drink for someone who ran a coffee shop, but there was nothing like hot chocolate, in Lily's opinion, to help you wind down after a stressful day. Or just enjoy the wrapping up of a good one.

It wasn't until he headed to the stove with a pot that she realized he meant to make his own.

"Wait, it doesn't always have to come from a packet?" she teased, and he laughed at her.

"You own a coffee shop, I'm pretty sure this comes as no surprise to you."

"Sure," she admitted, "but even I usually use chocolate powder with the sugar already added. This is next-level commitment."

"It's one of my favorite things. Still."

Oh, that was right. Her love for hot chocolate had developed in high school when she was dating Travis. Maybe it even developed because of him? Another bit of their past she'd forgotten or shoved to the back of her mind, maybe intentionally.

The silence as he made the hot chocolate wasn't companionable; it was awkward, and Lily knew it was her. Since they'd gotten to Travis's house, everything had been natural and cozy, almost too much so. Lily's emotions were too tumultuous to sort them fully, but if she felt so strongly connected to Travis still, was she being disloyal to Matt?

On the other hand, Matt was gone. Moving on would be expected. Healthy, even. But was it moving on if you were moving backward?

"You okay?" Travis handed her a mug of hot chocolate. "Careful," he warned as she took it, "it's hot."

"Thanks. Actually..." She trailed off, then cleared her throat. "I'm pretty tired. Maybe you could show me the cabin? I may need to call it a night pretty soon." She took a sip of the hot chocolate. It was so good she felt herself wishing she could sit down and savor it. But tonight was proof that she needed to be on her guard, not just for her physical safety but also for her emotions around Travis.

Not that he wasn't safe emotionally. He was. Too safe. That was the problem. Being around him made her feel like there was someone she could fully trust, someone she could open up to. Share her burdens. But she and Travis didn't have that kind of relationship anymore. Frankly, they didn't have *any* relationship anymore. He'd been the only one she could think to call. He apparently didn't want to see her hurt, and that was all.

On the trek across the lawn between his house and the cabin, Travis had to turn and wait for her a couple times. "You're good, though?" he asked. "Besides being tired?"

Lily quickened her pace, aware of the dense woods on the edges of his property. It wouldn't take much for someone to hide there, lean against a tree, watch them... To what end, though? Lily didn't know of any reason she should be in danger.

But she also didn't know why anyone would have tried to burn down her house. Could someone truly be watching her now?

"I'm, uh..." She meant to say, yes, she was okay, then lock herself in the cabin and try to sleep. But try as she might, Lily didn't seem to be able to put on a face and pretend everything was okay today. It was like a full year of pretending to have everything together had finally caught up to her, and her expressions simply weren't willing to lie for her anymore.

"It's going to be okay." He started to reach for her hand, as if on impulse, then stilled, and he turned back to the cabin.

Of all the people she could have called for help. But who else was there? She and Matt had gotten so caught up in their whirlwind romance that her other friendships had sort of dropped away. She'd been busy. Distracted.

"This is it." Travis motioned to the cabin, and Lily took it in. The A-frame was classic, like something straight off social media. It was the type of place you'd go for a relaxing retreat. A bright red door was set into a wall of solid logs, adding a layer of warmth and playfulness. The attention to detail continued to surprise Lily as she eased the door open at Travis's invitation and stepped inside.

To her left was a small kitchen, an efficient style that she'd always pictured in tiny European cottages. There was a small table with two chairs beyond that, but most of the open space was a cozy living room, anchored by a fireplace on the back wall. Large windows on either side of the fireplace took full advantage of that view of the woods. There was a door off the living room.

"There are blinds." Travis motioned to the slim built-in blinds she hadn't noticed.

Lily felt herself relax a little. "Thanks, Travis. For letting me stay here and the hot chocolate and everything." Could she have chosen more inadequate words? He'd walked into a literal murder scene for her today, and all she could do was thank him for the hot chocolate and *everything*?

Still, when she forced herself to meet his eyes, she didn't see any kind of judgment. Instead his brown eyes were warm, like the cocoa they'd shared. He didn't touch her, didn't even reach for her hand, though somehow she felt her body warm as though he had.

"It really is going to be okay, Lily."

When he said it, she almost believed him.

Chapter Four

The sky wouldn't fully darken at all in late July, but Travis still found himself looking out the window, watching the shadows of the woods grow longer on the lawn, his eyes darting to the cabin entirely too often.

Was Lily really safe out there? He had second-guessed himself more than once since his return to his house. As safe as she was anywhere, he supposed. At least here she was close by. He'd have preferred she stay with him, but that hardly seemed appropriate to offer.

Stepping away from the window, he shoved a hand through his hair, then went through the motions of shutting the house down for the night. Dishes done. Counters clean. He turned off lights, then finally sat back down in a chair.

The silence should have been soothing, but it felt empty, heavy. It pressed against him, the blackness almost a tangible thing.

He sat with his eyes closed. Thinking.

If someone was specifically after Lily, there had to be a reason. Earlier, he'd satisfied himself that there was no way it was random. So why, then? It had been a long time since he'd investigated anything, and any good police officer knew that being emotionally invested in a case changed the angles they looked at. Being objective mattered.

Stepping back was an option, he supposed. He could just call the police department, follow up, make sure it stayed in the front of people's minds.

But realistically speaking, he knew how stretched thin law enforcement was in an area as geographically big as Alaska. He'd experienced it firsthand. When he knew he could help her, shouldn't he?

At the same time, how was he going to help? He didn't even know where to start.

He opened his eyes, now adjusted to the darkness, and sat, looking around and thinking. The man who'd been killed... who was he? Maybe he was the best place to start.

He pulled his phone out of his pocket to make a call, then realized how late it was. Tomorrow. He'd call tomorrow, get the guy's name, start there...

Even as he slid the phone back into his pocket, though, he realized he didn't need to call to get the name.

He knew it.

The man's height. Build. Last-seen location.

Which was the boat where Matt had gone to arrest a ring of narcotics smugglers. That man had shoved Matt into the inlet.

The man who'd had the key and Lily's address in his pocket...was Arnold Harris, the one who had killed her fiancé.

Until Timber's whining woke her, Lily hadn't even been aware that she'd fallen asleep. She wasn't even in the bedroom of the small cabin, but in the living room—blinds closed, thank goodness—on the couch.

She'd fallen asleep with a notebook in hand, brainstorming everything she could about any reason someone might have for attacking her. So far the list was...nonexistent. She simply wasn't someone who gathered a lot of enemies. Last week

SARAH VARLAND   41

someone had complained about having too much foam on a
latte? But that hardly seemed worth killing over.

It made more sense that this was coincidental—maybe she'd
found the body, and then someone had been scared she'd seen
something up on the ridgeline and somehow figured out where
she lived and set her house on fire to scare her. Except…then
why had the dead man had her address in his pocket? That
ruled out any flicker of hope in a coincidence.

That might have been about when she'd leaned back and
closed her eyes, just to clear her head. She must have fallen
asleep entirely.

Timber whined again, and Lily looked over at the dog. She
was standing near the front door, eyes on one of the front
windows.

Her phone. She needed her phone. Lily felt in her pockets
and came up empty, fumbling around until she found it on
the floor beside the couch. She must have dropped it when
she fell asleep.

She texted Travis to let him know Timber was on alert and
something might be wrong. She waited a couple seconds, her
pounding heart threatening to beat out of her chest, then finally decided she was going to have to call.

Timber's hackles rose.

"Timber, come," Lily whispered in the most authoritative
tone she could manage.

The dog obeyed immediately, and Lily was off the couch
and moving toward the bedroom as quickly as she could. Or
would it be better to go out the back door?

None of her options seemed particularly good. Barricad-
ing herself inside the cabin, even with Timber for protection,
seemed naive. But running outside defenseless without a clue
as to what she was facing didn't seem smart, either. The bedroom seemed like the best plan. She could go out the window
in a pinch.

Her heartbeat quickened, and Lily fought for control over

her emotions. She went to the bedroom window and tried to move the blinds aside just enough to see outside.

Beside her, Timber continued to growl, low and intimidating. Was it possible the dog was reading the situation wrong? Lily didn't think so, not with the way Timber had performed on the mountain. A police K-9 wouldn't simply forget all their skills just because they'd been injured. It was like having an extremely high-performing car when all she was really prepared for was a Honda Accord. Lily probably couldn't comprehend all that Timber was capable of. But it was clear that the smart, beautiful shepherd was not to be underestimated.

Because of that, maybe Lily could relax a little. Timber had this under control.

Once upon a time, she would have found comfort in believing that God had this under control. But that was ages ago. More than a year. Matt's death had changed things.

That wasn't true. She'd stopped asking God for things even before that, if Lily was honest with herself. Matt had always rolled his eyes at her faith, and then she'd started to think maybe it was childish of her to go to God with everything. She still believed in Him. It seemed incredible to her that some people didn't when evidence of Him was everywhere. Though she did think that He probably didn't want to be involved in her life quite as much as the church she used to attend had taught.

Travis had gone to that church, too. He'd believed that God was involved in all the details. Did he still feel that way? Or had he also changed as he got older?

Attention on the window, Lily was sure she was alone until three things happened at once.

Timber whirled around, hackles up—she heard one footstep—and then there was the weight of a hand on her shoulder.

A scream built in her throat, and she opened her mouth to let it out when a hand clapped over it. Fighting with everything she had, it took at least three seconds to realize that the voice saying "it's me, it's me" belonged to Travis.

"What…" She scooted away from him, against the wall in the corner of the small bedroom. "What on *earth* are you trying to do? Kill me yourself?"

He rolled his eyes. "Obviously not. You texted, remember? So I came to help."

What she wanted to do was argue with the idea that every time she needed help, he came running, but hadn't it been true? For years, she'd told herself that Travis had broken her heart by asking her for something—marriage—that she hadn't been ready for, but the truth was he'd done everything for her. She just hadn't been able to give him the commitment he wanted.

Maybe she'd broken his heart?

"Okay, sorry. I'm sorry," she whispered. "But someone's out there, and I thought…"

"That I was whoever it is?"

"Exactly."

Timber had relaxed when she'd seen Travis, as though his presence took some of the weight of responsibility off her shoulders, but now she was eyeing the window again.

Then, just as quickly, she stopped. Turned to the bedroom door.

"I don't get it."

Travis shook his head. His jaw was tense, and she could practically see the storm clouds in his eyes.

"How did you get in?" she asked.

"Back door."

"No one around out there?"

"No."

Even though she'd been jolted awake, fatigue still pressed in on her. How she could be so tired with everything going on right now?

Timber stopped growling.

Frowning, Lily looked at Travis. "What's going on?"

But the way he shook his head, she could tell that he didn't know, either.

They waited like that for several more minutes, but nothing else happened. Had the danger really passed?

"Travis…" she started, but he interrupted her.

"Listen, there's something you have to know."

"Okay."

His tone was serious, and she found herself studying his face for some sign of what he was about to say.

It was strange how familiar his face still was, though time had matured it. His jawline was more defined than it had been when they were in high school—it coordinated nicely with the broadening of his shoulders. His eyes had always betrayed his emotions, but to Lily, they were even stormier and more full of feeling now.

"The guy who you found dead?" he continued finally.

She waited.

"It was a guy named Arnold Harris, the man who's wanted for Matt's murder."

He hadn't meant to startle her with the information, but though the immediate danger seemed to have passed, he wanted her to be prepared for anything.

He wasn't sure what to think about that fact that the prime suspect in Matt's murder was dead. The man's death had been murder, for sure, it didn't matter what crimes he'd committed—Travis didn't condone any kind of vigilante justice. But who had killed him? Someone seeking revenge for Matt's death? Had his own gang killed him as punishment?

Travis would have guessed that execution-style killings were more the speed of this particular gang, though. They were one of the largest operations in Alaska, and it struck him that they'd have been less…passionate about the man's murder. Multiple stab wounds? That belied entirely more emotion than what a gang like that would do.

She spoke after a few moments. "How do you know?"

"I remember his face. So many wanted posters, I can't believe it took me this long to remember it."

"And you called someone currently at the police department to confirm?"

"Not yet, I figured in the middle of the night they had more on their minds. But I will."

Lily nodded, seeming to take it in. "What does this mean? What does it change?"

For her? Nothing. Her life was still in danger, and he had no clear ideas as to why.

But it might change things for the police department. "Chances are good it'll be bumped up in priority," he began. "Not that you weren't important, but now it's part of an open investigation where resources are already directed, which might make things move faster."

Her face seemed to say that she understood. He watched her for a minute as she sat without saying anything. Then she moved to stand.

"Where are you going?" he asked.

"The danger has passed, right? So no need to stay sitting on the bedroom floor."

She was right. He just hadn't quite managed to think past telling her who the dead man was. He followed her out into the living room.

"So what do you think?" she asked. Her tone was a little hesitant, he thought, but that made sense given the circumstances.

"About?"

"Tonight. Do we go outside? Try to find whoever it was?" She sounded about as doubtful about that as he felt. It didn't seem like a good plan in the middle of the night.

If he was on this case in an official capacity, yes, he'd go outside, try to find evidence of whoever had been lurking and see if they'd left anything behind that could be used as evidence, forensic or otherwise. Cases were often solved by the smallest details.

But if he were investigating this officially, he wouldn't have Lily with him. The chances of her staying put inside while he went out were slim, he assumed. He could tell her to stay, and maybe she'd listen, but Lily had never been big on taking orders.

"Will you stay inside?" he asked. He really had no business ordering her around anyway.

She looked at him for a second or two, then nodded. "Yeah, I'll stay. How long will you be gone?"

Already moving toward the front door lest she change her mind or he lose his nerve—it had been awhile since he'd done this—he answered, "Not long. If you haven't heard from me in half an hour, probably better call someone."

"Like the police?"

"Yep, that would be good. Lock the door behind me." He looked at Timber. "Stay." While he'd have sworn the shepherd rolled her eyes, she at by Lily's side as he reached to shut the door.

"Wait."

Lily's voice was enough to stop him in his tracks.

"Take her with you. You know you need her. She'll find things faster."

She wasn't wrong.

"Timber, come."

And just like that, the dog was at his side, as she'd been so many times in the past. She'd been Matt's K-9 partner, technically speaking. But Travis and Matt had worked together so much that Travis had worked with Timber almost as much as his friend had.

Shutting the door behind him and waiting until he heard the reassuring click of the lock, he gave Timber the command to search. Off leash, she searched for the trail that anyone nearby would have inevitably left. Very little of the scent would have dissipated in such a short time, so Timber should be able to tell him exactly where they had been hiding out—and whether they'd been preparing to come inside.

What had their goal been? No shots had been fired. There actually didn't appear to be anything amiss, at least to his eyes.

Timber ran from the front door and swerved to the right, toward the woods that sheltered the side of the house.

Travis always found so much peace in those woods but now he saw them as a liability, making it more difficult to see if someone was back there hiding. Waiting. He didn't hear anything, and looking at Timber, he didn't think she did, either. But she sure smelled something.

The dog continued determinedly into the woods. Then her pace slowed. Had she lost the scent? Or was she simply being cautious?

He called her to his side, petted her shoulder. Stopped. Looked. Listened.

People called it gut instinct, intuition and any number of other things—Travis suddenly felt like he wasn't alone. It wasn't anything he could pinpoint exactly, not like he'd heard a noise or anything. No movement caught his eye. Absolutely nothing seemed out of place in the dark woods.

Timber's body language had relaxed beside him. Travis thought about the way they moved in the woods, weaving here and there, almost in a circle, away...

Away from the house.

Chills chased down his arms. "Timber, come."

He didn't care about being heard now, didn't care if someone started shooting at him. Let them, at least then he'd know they weren't shooting at Lily. Right now, he had no such reassurance.

Travis had messed up. Big time. Leaving her alone and taking the dog...

It had made sense on paper—Timber was the most reliable way to search for evidence—but it had also been the most predictable course of action. And whoever was after Lily had predicted it. Law enforcement? Search and rescue? Someone who was just good at putting himself in other people's shoes?

He almost muttered a word he hadn't said in a good five years as he ran through the woods back toward the cabin, calves burning. He was sprinting in boots, not really his first choice, but he had been in a hurry when he'd left the house, focusing on getting to Lily as quickly as possible, and not considering a possible foot chase.

That was two mistakes tonight, both possibly big ones. If he was going to do this, he needed to help Lily, not get her hurt due to his negligence. He used the anger to push himself faster and was entering the clearing for the cabin before he knew it.

Everything looked the same. His human eyes simply couldn't gauge how concerned he should be. Instead, he looked down at Timber. She had easily kept pace with him and had the audacity not to be the slightest bit winded. She was alert, ears slightly forward, nose up.

Hackles raised.

He had not imagined this danger, had not jumped to the wrong conclusions.

"Easy," he told her as they moved toward the cabin. The front door was still shut, but Timber headed instead toward the back of the house. Travis followed.

Suddenly, the dog sprinted ahead, like a spring that had been released. She dashed around the house and straight through the back door that had very much not been open when they'd left.

Travis's chest squeezed with the most fear he'd ever felt—even more than yesterday. Now he knew how deeply they were entangled in a criminal case that had already cost the police department one of its best. He ran inside.

He heard Lily scream before he could see anything, and the sound terrified him. Vision adjusting, he saw Timber stopped in the doorway to the bedroom, looking like she was assessing her next move. Beyond her, he could barely see figures—Lily and someone else, someone larger.

Travis shouted the command for attack.

Timber leaped into the room, and he heard a man gasp in pain at the bite she delivered. If he'd still been law enforcement, he'd have had to warn the man that it was coming, but because he wasn't, the dog could bite without warning.

He dashed into the bedroom and saw Lily on a blood-smeared floor, and he could see blood, but couldn't tell how much or from where. He could hear her shuddered breaths, though, like she was holding back tears or trying to manage pain, so he knew without a shadow of a doubt that she was alive. Injured...but alive.

Chapter Five

Lily wasn't even sure where the pain was coming from, only that it was intense. Her arms felt bruised from the struggle, and the man had had something…a knife? She couldn't think about it yet—not when her dog and Travis were both in danger. Because of her.

That thought stung nearly as much as the bruises on her upper arms.

Fighting against the pain and the fear sliding around inside her, she crawled toward where Timber and Travis were both fighting with the attacker. She called Timber off and in the split second after the dog moved, Travis delivered a kick to the man that seemed to hit its mark.

"You all right?" Travis asked quickly, scanning her.

Out of the corner of her eye, she saw the man with the mask stumble to his feet and pull his arm back.

"Travis, watch out!"

Her warning came soon enough that Travis wasn't knocked down by a full hit. Instead, the punch glanced off his nose, and Travis closed his eyes instinctively with a yell.

Before the attacker could press his advantage, Lily told Timber to attack. This time, the man seemed to have had enough—

he ran for the door, but not before he kicked out behind him, connecting with Timber hard enough for the dog to yelp.

"Timber!" Lily tried to crawl toward her, but the pain in her side made her double over. What was that? A rib? Something else?

Timber was already up and sprinting after the masked man. Was he seriously going to get away again?

The pain in Lily's side told her, yes, he was. She certainly couldn't chase after him, and Travis appeared to be regaining his bearings after taking a punch to the face.

"Timber!" she yelled again, but the dog ignored her, as if driven by a desire stronger than the one she usually had to please Lily.

"Lily, stop," Travis said, dropping to her side and breathing hard. "Don't go after him, it's not worth it."

She knew he was right. All she wanted was to find her attacker and kick him in his own ribs, which probably wasn't the right way to handle things, but he'd threatened her life more than once. She wanted him gone, put away in jail. She didn't want to know that he was out there, waiting. Next time, he'd probably do worse.

She had a feeling this had all just been a warning so far. Surely if he'd been trying to kill her, he would have?

It hurt her mind to even think this way. Why would a human want to harm another? She couldn't fathom what could be of this much importance. If she somehow had something they wanted, she would gladly give it back. Nothing was worth this.

This was why the world needed men like Matt, like Travis, who were willing to take risks and make sure people like that were behind bars instead of terrorizing others.

Why on earth had Travis quit? Not the time to ask, she knew, but she did want to know. One day, maybe it was a subject she could broach with him.

"Are you all right?" she asked him. "What can I do?" She

felt a little silly, because clearly she wasn't in much of a position to help.

On the floor beside her, Travis rubbed his face and looked
over at her. "Me? What about you?"

"I'm…" She trailed off. Ultimately she couldn't lie to him.
She was not fine, and she was not in any position to pretend
otherwise, not when moving made her wince.

"You're in worse shape than I am, I think," he told her. "I
shouldn't have taken my eyes off him."

"You were checking on me. It wasn't like you just weren't
paying attention."

"Mistake number three," he muttered.

Lily didn't ask but noted his frustrated tone.

Timber ran back into the room, panting, but otherwise okay.
Lily checked her over carefully, noting the tightness of her
muscles but not seeing any broken skin or signs of blood. Nowhere that seemed overly tender. She felt some of her own
tension leave her shoulders.

As soon as Timber had come back, Travis had gone out
into the cabin's living area. He came back into the bedroom
now, face looking slightly less tense. "Doors are locked. He's
gone. And based on Timber's behavior, I think for real this
time. Want to sit in the living room? I called 911, they're sending an ambulance."

She frowned at him. "I'm not going anywhere."

"Fine, but they're at least checking you out."

"Just right here, no hospital?"

It wasn't as though he could force her to go; she was an
adult. So he nodded. "Just let them see how you are."

They sat in silence until the EMTs got there.

"Looks like there's some serious bruising developing." The
EMT gently palpated her ribs, and Lily gasped as pain radi-
ated through her midsection.

"It hurts." The understatement wasn't lost on her.

"You've definitely done some damage but I don't think anything's broken. Just bruised." As the EMT stood, he looked down at her and frowned a bit. "Even so, I'd really feel better if you came in."

"I'm fine."

Much as it was clear this wasn't his preference, he didn't argue with her, instead giving her a regimen of drugs and rest that was good enough for Lily.

Travis walked him to the door, locked it and returned to where she sat on the couch.

She watched as Timber followed him back to her. "How did whoever is after me get past her last time?"

Travis's face looked serious, and he glanced down at Timber. "Hard to say. She was tracking a scent, but the woods are thick with scent, and sometimes it's difficult to differentiate..."

Was it her imagination or had his voice trailed off? She waited.

"And I don't know," he finally went on, settling into a chair opposite her. "I guess maybe she seemed a little off? She's trained, very well trained, but this isn't what she's trained for. This is more personal protection, with some searching thrown in. She knows the commands, she knows the skills, but contextually that could be affecting how she behaves, at least a little."

Only some of what he said made sense to Lily, but she thought she understood what he was trying to say. Timber was extremely smart and knew what to do, but the weirdness of this situation, her being retired and then suddenly being asked to work by both of them... It wasn't quite what Lily had expected out of life, either.

Maybe people weren't the only ones who had to adjust their expectations. The thought almost made her smile. It definitely made her feel a little less alone and even more connected to her dog than she'd felt before.

She reached over and petted Timber, then sighed, closed her eyes and leaned back against the couch. How had life turned so complicated? Yesterday morning, she'd been a woman trying to heal. She'd been grieving, yes, but working on healing. She enjoyed running her coffee shop, coming up with new scones to sell, exploring outside. Overall, she was pretty happy.

Immediately her conscience gave her a gentle nudge. Happy? That was overstating it. Lily felt…not unhappy. A little empty. Sometimes frantic to find something to fill the space in her heart and mind. Lonely.

And as much as she did miss Matt, at least the happier times they'd had—things had been stressful there at the end, but she didn't like to dwell on that now, it didn't feel fair—she missed even more how her life had been simple and uncomplicated.

Maybe the emptiness was just part of getting older.

Or maybe Lily missed the innocent faith she'd had as a child, the way she would talk to God like He really heard her.

She swallowed hard, then looked over at Travis. He seemed to be studying her. Did he know, could he tell that she'd mostly walked away from what they'd both believed, at least functionally speaking?

Lily somehow hoped he didn't. The idea of disappointing him didn't sit well with her, and she knew he would be disappointed.

"What are you thinking?" he asked.

She froze. Then decided they'd gone long enough without talking.

Maybe it was the lateness of the hour and her defenses were down, but suddenly being honest with him felt like the right thing to do.

"About faith…" She trailed off, and Travis felt like she was choosing her words with more care than she would have at one point. Delicately. That was how she treated them now.

"Yeah?" He made himself relax his shoulders a little, even as his insides tensed.

"I just don't know anymore, Travis. I mean, do you? You've

seen stuff now as a police officer that surely you couldn't have fathomed before."

"So what are you saying?" What did she not know?

"Matt believed in God and all of that, but Matt also thought that He's not so involved as we like to think He is, you know?"

If she was looking for agreement, she wouldn't get it from him. Travis was far from perfect, but if there was one thing he was sure of, it was that God was even more present in their daily lives than they realized, not the opposite. "So Matt's beliefs influenced yours?"

"I think he just helped me see what I hadn't wanted to." She stopped, as if waiting for him to speak, but when he didn't answer, she continued, "That God is real but I need to stop bothering Him."

"You're not bothering Him."

"He's busy, Travis. Keeping the world going and all of that?" She shook her head. "Anyway. I was just thinking about what I used to believe."

"I can see why the topic would be on your mind." Now it was his turn to pick his words with intention. The last thing he wanted to do was push Lily away, but this was so far from what they'd been raised to believe, from what she'd used to cling so tightly to.

She shrugged, and he thought she looked a little more tired than she had earlier. And it didn't seem like just a middle-of-the-night sort of tired. Maybe her exhaustion wasn't just from the stress, but from the weight of trying to carry everything all alone?

He found himself praying without even thinking about it. *Help her, God. Be with her, bring her back.* If she wasn't going to talk to God for herself right now, Travis could at least bring her to God in prayer. It wouldn't be the same as having her own relationship, but it was what he could do right now.

"Yeah. That, the past… All of it. I never meant to disappoint you, Travis. With this, or…you know, before."

They were going there? Right now in the wee hours of the morning on this couch, still unsure who was after her and why?

"You could never disappoint me." His words were firm.

"That's not true."

"Of course it is."

"I disappointed you before, you know I did."

No. She'd hurt him and made him wish... Well, he wasn't sure what he wished. Was there something he could have done differently?

Not really, but he did wish maybe that their love had been enough, ridiculous as that sounded. He wished he'd been enough for Lily, but she'd had dreams she wanted to chase, and her fear of never realizing those dreams had overshadowed what they had.

"You didn't. Maybe just broke my heart a little." He said it with a smile, figuring if she was going to be honest, he owed it to her to be honest, too. Besides, it was better than her thinking she'd disappointed him.

"I'm sorry about that," she said.

"I know."

She didn't say anything else, and Travis was content to sit there in silence. He watched from his chair as Lily leaned her head back against the couch and closed her eyes. One hand was on Timber's head, which was resting neatly on her paws where the dog was curled up on the couch.

Moments later, Lily jerked, like she'd fallen asleep and woken up.

"I'm not going anywhere," he told her quietly. "Just go to sleep."

To his surprise, that was exactly what she did. It didn't take more than a minute or two for her to nod off again. This time, she didn't fight it.

His heart ached as he watched her, both for how much physical pain she must be in and also for her spiritual state. For her to have stopped believing that God really cared was heartbreaking to him. How hard it must be for her to live that way. He tried to imagine what it would be like, but it was too much to consider. He wasn't any kind of perfect person, not the kind of guy people would label as *saintly* by any stretch of the imagination, but he was very aware of his need for God. Travis talked to Him throughout the day. Living that way was almost second nature at this point.

Once upon a time, Lily had had that, too. While Travis was aware there was some kind of agreed-upon code never to think badly of someone who had died, he did have to resist the urge to think of all the ways Matt had failed her.

Yeah, his friend hadn't been able to control getting killed in the line of duty, and he'd been a hero. But Matt hadn't been there for Lily emotionally before he'd died, at least not to the degree that Travis felt like someone should support. He'd tried hard not to pay attention to their relationship—it made working conditions too weird between him and Matt—but he'd heard the tail end of enough phone calls in the months before Matt's death to know there had been trouble in paradise.

He also found himself angry at the way Matt had effectively led her away from her faith, at least to some degree. It was useless getting upset with a dead man, though, and a complete waste of energy. Instead he tried to turn his attention to praying for her, asking God to help them get through this and quickly find out who was after her. He begged God to keep her safe.

Then he looked over at her while she slept, noting the way her hair fell softly across her forehead, the way her lips parted just a little when she fully relaxed. And he debated whether or not he was brave enough to pray for a second chance with her. Was that something he was even prepared for? It would be a risk for him, too, as he'd not walked away unscathed the last time…

Her coming back into his life was the most dangerous thing for him. Not only would he walk in front of anyone threatening to harm her, but he was fully ready to try again with their relationship, if he was honest with himself. He felt like he should have hesitations—he certainly saw the logical ones that were there—but in his heart, he had none.

Just give me wisdom, please, God, he prayed. *Help me to know if this is something I need to pursue, maybe when things are safe for her again, and she's not a target anymore.*

He found himself looking around the room, imagining the last few hours and the terror Lily must have felt when she realized she was alone with a killer.

Help me to be wise. I have a feeling I'm going to need that. Whoever this is has the advantage in almost every way, but God, You're on our side. Help us figure this out. Help her to stay safe.

Another glance at Lily.

And God, help me to win her heart again if that's what You want.

Travis stood and did a circuit of the cabin, listening for anything out of the ordinary. Satisfied all was well, he went back to the living room, watched Lily sleep and smiled.

He was going to help her. He was going to make up for all the ways he'd failed her before. And maybe...

Maybe then he was going to try again.

Chapter Six

She'd never felt quite so relieved to walk through the back door of her little coffee shop, partially because she'd missed it, and partially because she'd had the uncomfortable feeling in the parking lot that she was being watched. She felt herself relax as she locked the door behind her. The shop smelled like rising cinnamon rolls that Hannah, her baker, had come in to make earlier, and like coffee beans. Always the smell of coffee beans. Initially she'd planned to roast her own coffee beans on-site, but when she'd discovered that the smell of freshly roasted coffee and the smell of roasting coffee were quite different, and that there were plenty of local roasters who made better roasts than she did, she decided to stock local things and focus on her favorite aspects of the business.

One of those favorites was the ambiance itself, the idea of creating a space for community where people could be comfortable. She'd spent long hours choosing details about the flooring, the light fixtures—industrial-style Edison lights, some with wire cages for dramatic emphasis, hanging over individual tables, and strands of Edison lights all across the top of several other walls. The warmth of the room was undeniable, even before she'd lit the fireplace.

She lit it now, and while she'd intended to go right to work, she found herself sliding into one of the booths.

All of this had been…a lot, to put it mildly. She'd come to work today thinking it might be good to keep something in her life consistent, and she was sure now that it had been the right choice. So much had changed since she impulsively called Travis.

How could someone go from being such a huge part of her life to not being in it at all, then back in it again? Maybe she needed to spend less time thinking about this, but try as she might, Lily was finding Travis a huge distraction.

Reliving the past had its consequences. She had slept well enough last night, but she'd dreamed entirely more than she would have preferred. Mostly about Matt, some about Travis and some about being alone in a dark room. All of the dreams had tangled into a nonsensical swirl. She vaguely remembered tossing and turning.

Resting her elbows on the smooth wooden surface of the booth's table, she took a deep breath.

The bell over the door chimed, and she looked up to see Hannah, the baker.

"Morning, boss." Hannah smiled in her direction.

"Very funny." Though it was true that Lily was Hannah's employer, the two of them had been friends for years.

"Everything okay? The message you left was kind of vague."

Lily had left Hannah a hurried voicemail early in the morning, attempting to explain why she might be late today, but Lily was sure it hadn't made much sense. She hadn't wanted to worry her unnecessarily.

"Yeah, I think so. Mostly." The less Hannah knew, the better. The last thing Lily wanted was to put her friends in danger.

"Sitting with your head in your hands like that doesn't really give that impression, just so you know."

A solid point. Lily attempted a smile. "It's…it's a lot of things."

Hannah was kind enough not to press her, and the two of them fell into their usual morning routine of getting ready for the day. Her customers started coming through right on time, and Lily let herself be distracted for a few blissful hours. Even though she knew she could only ignore her own life for so long.

Timber seemed as though she was staying on alert. Usually she slept soundly on the floor of the coffee shop at the end of the front counter, but today one ear was always perked as though she was merely napping and ready to snap into action if the occasion warranted it.

It was just before four, almost time to close, when the door chimed. Hannah let out a low whistle. Lily turned.

It was Travis, dressed casually in jeans and a long-sleeved plaid shirt. He looked exactly like what she would expect to see if she Googled handsome man who works at hardware store.

Should Lily feel butterflies in her stomach at his presence? Nothing the least bit romantic had happened between them recently. But he'd been so easy to talk to and hadn't judged her for the way her faith had changed. Travis always had been a keeper. Maybe she'd been foolish not to keep him.

On the other hand, how could she question her past choices when those choices had led to her standing in the coffee shop she owned and seeing her dream come to life? She'd chased her dreams *without* destroying anyone else's life. If only her own mother had realized how badly she wanted to pursue her dreams before she'd made other choices.

Then again, Lily might not be here if she had.

"Travis, hi," she finally said, shifting her attention to the person currently in front of her and away from her mother, who might as well be a figment of Lily's imagination. "How was your day?"

"Good. Yours?"

She heard the uncertainty in his voice and smiled, hopefully in a way he would find reassuring. "It's been fine. Boring, even."

"Nothing suspicious?"

"Not in the slightest." And it was true. People had been their normal selves, she'd sold various coffee drinks, Hannah had baked and helped run the front. Timber had not once alerted. It was like it had all been a dream. Not entirely a bad one—Lily was finding it was nice to be on speaking terms with Travis again—but a dream she was ready to see the end of anyway.

"Did you learn anything?" she asked, and he hesitated, his eyes flickering toward where Hannah was cleaning up behind them.

Finally he nodded. "Later. My house for dinner?"

"Yeah, I guess we'd better. I still haven't heard from the fire department about mine."

"I'll stay while you close up if that works for you."

She didn't mind terribly, though she was hoping it hadn't come to that. Then she thought back to that morning and how she'd had a slight sensation of being watched as she walked into the coffee shop.

"You didn't follow me to work and watch me this morning, did you?" she asked.

Travis shook his head.

A shiver ran down her spine. So either she'd imagined it entirely, or it had been someone other than Travis. Neither option was reassuring.

Telling Hannah good-night once the shop was properly closed, Lily locked the door behind her and started walking to her car. Travis walked with her, looking both ways intently. Lily thought that if she was going to keep this on the down-low at all, he was going to have to look a little less like a bodyguard and a little more like a friend who just happened to stop by.

Then again, it was a small town. People were going to talk either way. But after the news articles that ran after Matt's death and having people talk about "poor Lily" all last year… Lily just wanted to fly under the radar for a bit. For once, she'd like not to be the woman with the story that demanded pity.

Once they arrived at Travis's house, he wasted no time telling her what he'd learned, which was very much like him.

"The man was definitely the one we believed was responsible for Matt's death," he began.

"Wow." Lily shook her head. "I know you told me that was likely but knowing for sure..." She'd felt so bad about not being able to help him. Did she still feel that way, knowing he'd killed Matt? She'd like to think she wasn't the kind of person who believed in vigilante justice. Still, it was eerie. Especially when she considered that the day the man had died was the one-year anniversary of Matt's death...

It was too coincidental.

"It's weird," Travis said slowly, almost like he could read her thoughts.

"It is, yes. What do you think? Any idea who could be behind this?"

"With what we know?" He inhaled deeply. "I really think it's someone from the narcotics group that Matt was investigating when he was killed."

It wasn't something Matt had talked much about. But Lily had known in the days before he died that he'd been fairly deep undercover, working with a narcotics group in the hope of bringing to justice. She was aware of how drugs had left their mark on the Last Frontier, leaving so many Alaskans homeless and hopeless, destroying lives, families and more. The work he was doing had seemed worthwhile, though it had taken a toll. At the end, he'd been even more short-tempered than usual. He'd told her he was fine, but the dark circles under his eyes had said he wasn't sleeping well. Lily hadn't known how to help him, and she'd felt them drifting apart.

Then he was gone, and it was like her future had been stolen from her the night his was stolen from him.

Honestly, she was only just starting to feel like maybe she could move on. She didn't know about falling in love again, but in most ways she could move on. And now…what? She was going to just step right back into the nightmares of her past?

Deciding she should get clarification before she went into full panic mode, she asked, "And I'm guessing the only way to figure out who is behind this is to look back at Matt's case, see who was involved and do a little investigating of our own?"

Much as she tried to keep the anxiety from her voice, Travis still knew her better than that, and she could feel his concern as he studied her. Attempting to look unfazed, Lily stayed silent under his scrutiny.

"I think that's what will help lead us to our suspect the fastest, yes," Travis said, not doubting his own words for a second. "But I'm not sure that's what's best for you."

What did Lily even know about that case? He doubted she'd seen anything like the case records, as there would be no reason to let those leave the police department. He could probably get his hands on a copy of them, or at least a chance to look at them, with his connection to APD and his post certification. But Lily had probably just been told Matt was killed in the line of duty and then left with only questions.

"What's best for me is for this to be over." She was shaking her head, her eyes closed. "Or better yet, for none of it to have happened in the first place."

"The second would be my vote, but we don't have that option."

Her face said that she knew he was right, and Travis wasn't surprised. Lily had never been much for playing the victim. She'd rise to the occasion, he knew she would.

But how far would she go to solve it? He still had concerns that it would be too far. And Lily couldn't possibly know what that was, she'd never poured her heart and soul into solving a case and then watched it slowly take over. She hadn't spent hours contemplating the worst of what humanity was capable of.

"I need to be able to move on with my life," she said. "And I can't do that if I'm looking over my shoulder all the time. Someone wants…" She shrugged. "Wants something from me. To hurt me? Scare me?"

"Someone wants to kill you, most likely."

"Doesn't that seem like an overreaction? I mean, I didn't see anything except the body. Okay, we found a key and an address on him, but the address was to my house. It's not like I stumbled upon some new place."

She had a point, but it still made no sense. She was clearly in danger, but what did the person after her have to gain by scaring her? This was the part of police work he'd hated the most, the need to climb into the mind of a criminal and guess what they were thinking. As a sane individual who liked to stay on the right side of the law, Travis didn't want to be able to imagine what they were thinking, not really.

"I understand you want to be able to move on with your life," he began, shifting on his living room sofa, "but this is going to be tough."

Her eyes flashed when she turned to him. "I think I can handle something tough."

A couple seconds of silence. "Look," he said at last, "I didn't mean it like that. Of course you can handle it."

She was already shaking her head. "No, I appreciate that you don't want me to have to handle things like this. That's what you meant, right? Not that I can't?"

No matter how many years had passed, she clearly still understood him. Once upon a time, they had barely needed words to communicate, they'd been that in sync with each other.

"That's what I meant, yes." Then he admitted defeat. "If you really want to do this, let's get in my car. I'll drive us to the police department and get the records, and see what we can work through."

She smiled. He gathered his keys and headed toward his car

with Lily and Timber following to join him. They drove toward Anchorage, swinging through a coffee stand on their way.

He ordered his typical triple shot Americano and started to order Lily's latte with sugar and whip when he realized he didn't know her anymore.

When he paused, she smiled. "Same coffee. Same as it always was."

That was the problem, wasn't it? Some things did seem like they were the same, but Travis knew in his heart they were both different people. Right?

"Just like we used to do," Lily said when he handed over her coffee.

"Yeah, just like." Was it? How different were they now than they had been back then?

"I'm sorry…" she began.

"Listen, I appreciate that we aren't trying to dance around the past, but we were both young. No need to rehash everything, right?"

"Sure, right." She stumbled over the words.

Fearing that more conversation would take them down a road he just wasn't braced for, he kept driving.

Silvertip Creek was only about twenty minutes north of Anchorage, a bedroom community much like Eagle River or Chugiak, but the twenty minutes seemed to drag as they'd exhausted all safe topics. He kept his hands on the wheel, his eyes on the road. He wanted to pretend like the years that had passed meant something, but his heart had been in his throat when he thought she might be killed yesterday, when he'd realized that the intruder had intentionally led Timber on a wild goose chase through the woods…

Wait. Intentionally.

"What?" she asked.

"The man intentionally led Timber on a wild goose chase and covered the scent trails so he could double back to the house."

"Right, you said something…"

"Intentionally," he emphasized. "Otherwise it's almost too coincidental. Which means this is someone who knows how search dogs work, or police dogs."

"Dramatically narrowing our field of suspects."

But something still nagged at him. He frowned, an uneasy swirl developing in his gut. "So someone who works with dogs..."

"Why don't you seem happy? Doesn't this make it easier?"

Easier and harder at the same time, Travis thought. "The thing is," he said slowly, "we already narrowed it down to someone likely within the narcotics gang."

Lily's eyes met his, and he saw in their clear blue the same understanding he'd just come to. "No," she said quietly. "Someone involved in the case?"

"Someone investigating it, probably. Or at least close to the investigation." Travis shrugged. "I can't guarantee it one way or another, obviously."

"Sure." Her voice betrayed her discomfort with the idea. Who liked the idea of a dirty cop? Or a search-and-rescue worker who went bad? No one. Travis had turned off more than one movie because of a similar plot line.

"Whoever it is, Lily, we're going to figure it out. I promise." He meant it. He'd started off intending to keep her safe, but she needed more than that. She needed to know this threat was gone and that she could go back to living her life.

And Travis was determined to give her what she needed.

Chapter Seven

What struck Lily most about the trip to the Anchorage Police Department was how glad everyone was to see Travis. When he told her he'd changed jobs, she knew it hadn't been for any kind of job failure. Travis was too good a man and too good at what he did for that to be a concern. But she had wondered if there was any kind of weirdness at work that made him not want to be there. It wasn't something she could picture any more, though; from the time they walked into the glass-and-metal building, the whole department treated him like a long-lost hero.

"Travis Beckett!" An older man beamed at him from behind the front desk. "You're back!"

"Only for a couple of questions."

A shadow cross the man's face. "Narcotics case?"

Travis nodded. "And yesterday's victim."

"I figured. Officer Knox is working it. I'll show you back."

For the first time, the man seemed to notice Lily. He opened his mouth and stuck out his hand as if to introduce himself, then paused as if he recognized her. Lily didn't know how. It wasn't like she'd come to the police office; Matt had kept his personal life and work life very separate.

Besides the fact that he was coincidentally engaged to his police partner's ex-girlfriend. Besides that.

The man showed them down a hallway that looked like it belonged in any kind of office building. But Lily knew behind some of those doors were interrogation rooms, behind others shelves and shelves of evidence.

Police work was fascinating to her, probably because it had been Travis's plan since high school and he'd spent so much time talking about it. Had that been part of what attracted her to Matt? Maybe. She hadn't known he was Travis's partner, though, or she'd never have agreed to go out with him at all. By the time she found out, she was already involved with Matt.

"Here you go." The older man paused at a door. "It's good to see you, Beckett. Don't be a stranger." He patted Travis on the back and was gone.

Lily barely had time to process the interaction when the door, opened almost immediately to Travis's knock.

"Hey!" an officer exclaimed happily. "About time! Back to get a job?"

"Definitely not."

"You can't seriously be enjoying small-town life?" He laughed. "Or maybe you are?" His eyes moved to Lily. "Who is this?"

It was clear the man thought there was something between them. Not sure how to proceed, Lily waited for Travis to handle it.

"Knox, this is…" Travis trailed off, and who could blame him? How to encompass what they were to each other in a sentence or two? "My friend Lily."

She found her shoulders lowering with relief. If he had only defined her as Matt's fiancée… Well, she didn't want that. She wanted Travis to think of her just as her. Or maybe in the context of a woman he cared about. Which was terrifying. Should she be getting close to him again? What if he hurt her?

Or worse, what if she hurt him again?

Dragging her attention away from the past, she tried to focus on the police officer standing with them.

It wasn't the first time she'd heard the man's name. Matt had spent plenty of evenings frowning, muttering about Officer Knox. He'd seemed extraordinarily stressed when his name or any others from the case—names she'd forgotten now—had come up. The longer he worked the narcotics case, the more his behavior had changed. He hadn't spent as much time with her, and when they were together, it was like she wasn't actually there. Or maybe it was like he wasn't there?

Matt had seemed like another person on that case, she realized. Would the same thing happen to Travis? For the first time, she took his warning from earlier seriously, that it was going to be tough if she wanted to dive into this more deeply. But what other choice did she have? She couldn't live like this.

Attempting to ignore the knowing feeling in her stomach, she listened to the men talk.

"You sure you want to wade back in?" the officer was asking Travis.

"I'm sure I have to." Travis motioned toward Lily. "She found the victim yesterday. Her and Timber."

It seemed she wasn't the only one with hesitations. Lily wasn't sure that made her feel any better. If anything, it made her feel worse.

Timber had waited in the car with the window down. As much as Lily hadn't wanted to leave her, she understood Travis's point that it might be strange for Timber to walk back into the building when she didn't have a job there anymore. Lily hadn't wanted to put her through that confusion.

"I can give you what we have on it, most of it." The officer was already sitting back down at a desk, pulling things up on a computer.

Lily always forgot that police records were digitized now, she liked to picture them in a dim basement room somewhere, lining the gray walls and containing all sorts of intrigue. They lost something on the computer, at least as far as atmosphere went, but hopefully the files would still reveal what they needed to know.

"Thanks," Travis responded.

She listened as the two men discussed some of the case's details. At one point, Travis alluded to Matt's death and Officer Knox cleared his throat and nodded as if to point out that Lily was there.

"She knows already," Travis admitted, finally disclosing what Lily wasn't sure she wanted him to. "This is Lily Peterson, Matt Davis's fiancée."

The other man didn't say anything that indicated a change; it was the way he held himself. Because she wasn't a random civilian, he seemed suddenly less guarded, with a slight bit of…what? Respect? Awe? Lily hadn't done anything heroic. She'd loved someone and then lost them in the line of duty. But she'd noticed several people treat her like this. Like she was different now.

And while she unquestionably was, she was getting awfully tired of being treated like it.

"I'm sorry for your loss," the officer said.

Lily had heard the words before more times than she could count. "Thanks. I appreciate your help now."

He nodded, then hit a button on his keyboard. "This should be good." A printer whirred and started spitting out sheets of paper. "Anything else you need, let me know."

As she watched the copied files stack up in the printer, with more words about this case than she'd have thought possible, Lily found herself hoping that maybe this was enough. They'd not solve the whole case, obviously, not when police had been working it fruitlessly for years. But if they could just find enough in those records to tell them who had killed the drug runner, get that person off her back and turned in to law enforcement where they belonged…then maybe she had a chance of having her life back.

It was funny. She'd fought so hard to have her own life that she'd even turned down Travis's proposal when she had loved him more deeply than she'd loved anyone, Matt included. But now she didn't fully know why she'd wanted that freedom so badly. She had her coffee shop, yes, a dream come true, but right now she couldn't even stay at her own house. She was the very definition of not free.

Hopefully something in these files would have the power to change that. Lily wanted another chance to live her life with something more like true freedom. And maybe make some different choices this time.

Her gaze darted to Travis. Did she believe in second chances?

She didn't know, but she wanted to get this case solved, get her life back and have a chance to find out.

Since Lily still hadn't heard from the fire department about when her house would be safe, they went back to Travis's. Lily offered to cook, but he told her he had it under control. Working with food all day at the coffee shop didn't seem likely to lend itself to her wanting to prep dinner after work. Besides, it was his kitchen, and he knew where everything was.

While Lily sat at the counter flipping through the police department files, he prepped chicken Alfredo and salad. Mostly, though, he was watching her, seeing the emotions chase across her face as the details of the case were revealed to her.

"So he was undercover for a lot less time than I thought." Her mouth was scrunched a little into a frown.

"About six months, right?"

Lily nodded. "That's what this says."

As she flipped from page to page, Travis found himself imagining where she was in the whole saga.

"Why did you think he'd been undercover for more than six months?" he asked as he poured the noodles into the boiling water.

She answered without looking up. "I really thought he told me he was going undercover earlier than that? He definitely was harder to reach, more stressed, for longer than six months. I don't know, maybe I'm just remembering wrong."

Except Lily had always had an excellent memory. Her memorization skills were part of the reason she'd done so well in school, along with her natural intelligence. Travis had a hard time believing she'd mix up something like that. On the other hand, trauma did funny things to people, and losing Matt the way she had was bound to impact her mind, wasn't it?

She rubbed at her eyes. "There's so much here. This is ridiculous."

"It's a lot."

"We're never going to find whoever it is, are we? Not if they're buried in a case file thicker than the last book I read."

He figured that was a slight exaggeration, but due to the extensive nature of the narcotics ring Matt had been investigating, she was right that it was an extremely thick file. He walked over, flipped through some of it himself and laid the most important pages in their own stack.

"I'll comb through the rest of it when I have a chance," he promised.

"You have a full time job, too, though," she pointed out.

He appreciated that, though to him there was a difference between her dream job running her own business and him helping his brother out at his store. Police work had been his dream, but what if it had been the wrong dream? He just didn't see how he could keep doing that kind of work. And here he was, stepping into it again. Just a glance at the documents had confirmed his discomfort. Victim. Body. Quantities of drugs, lives destroyed and lost.

Why wouldn't it stop? Why couldn't he just walk away from it all?

Something within him knew that this would all go on whether he was in police work or not. At least in that capacity, he could battle against the darkness, not just ignore it. Not that he thought people who weren't in law enforcement were ignoring anything, not at all, but Travis knew deep in his heart that he had been hiding.

"I can handle it," he told her, hoping what he said was true in several ways.

Lily seemed to take him at his word. She shifted in her seat and started to focus on the smaller pile he'd left. As he set the table, she kept reading.

"So? What do you think?" he asked when the food was ready and on the table.

"I think I'm overwhelmed."

"Dinner, then?"

She nodded and moved to the table. He thought he saw the tension on her face ease when she saw the meal. "Wow," she said, "this looks amazing. Again. You really can cook."

Half wishing her affirmation didn't matter so much to him, he shrugged, but he was more thankful than she'd ever know that she thought his food was worthwhile. There wasn't much he could do for her. Sure, he could offer her a place to stay, but he couldn't actually offer her safety, which was what he really wanted to do. Food like this and maybe a few minutes to relax were the best he could do right now, and he liked that she seemed to appreciate it.

As he served them each food, she went on, "I still can't believe you did this. Do you cook like this when it's just you?"

He'd eaten sandwiches for the past two weeks straight. And not restaurant-quality sandwiches, either, but ham and cheddar with a little bit of mayo. He raised his eyebrows, and she laughed. Apparently she could tell what his answer was.

They ate in silence for a little while, and then Lily brought up the case files.

"So if I'm understanding correctly, this group is based in California, but has a…branch up here now?"

He had to hold back a laugh. He'd never really thought of

drug-running operations in terms of branches—that sounded so businesslike—but Travis supposed there was some truth to the idea. This was a massive organization, albeit an illegal one. These weren't meth heads cooking drugs in a shed in the woods somewhere. These people were very intentional about the way their business ran, and yes, they'd expanded to Alaska.

"That sounds right," he admitted. "Anchorage PD had asked Matt to look into it…"

"Do you guys usually get asked? I mean, I always assumed you were just assigned things."

"They tend to ask when it comes to undercover assignments. If an undercover officer has too much going on personally, or just shouldn't be in that situation for whatever reason, it can turn bad really quickly."

"Is that what happened to Matt?"

"It shouldn't have been. I don't think so."

There was too much in how he'd died that was inconsistent with that idea. His cover hadn't been blown, really. It had only been that last day, when he'd gone to the boat to arrest Arnold Harris, that things had turned and Matt had been killed. Surely if the drug ring had any inkling that he was working for the police department, they'd have gotten rid of him before that. He'd been able to report all kinds of information to the department—the types of narcotics being smuggled, who might be involved, though he hadn't gotten any top names—it didn't make sense that they'd have willingly let him have all of that if they suspected he was really an undercover officer.

Matt had put himself at risk and paid the ultimate price for it. Travis wished he'd been able to do more, but when Matt had been undercover, he'd been in charge of searching different locations with Timber, trying to stop the drugs as they came into Anchorage in various ways before they ended up leaving the city and infecting smaller towns and villages.

"Travis?"

Her voice had the tone of a person who'd been calling someone's name without being heard. He wasn't terribly surprised he'd gotten lost in his own head. It had been a rough case, and he was still working through it mentally. Judging by the emails he still got from friends at APD, and the references to the mandatory counseling some of them were still going through, he wasn't the only one who was having trouble moving on.

"What? I'm sorry, I was distracted."

Her face softened, like maybe she understood how hard this was to walk through again. He'd known it would be, he hated being reminded of all the ways people hurt each other, but he hadn't counted on being so overwhelmed by feelings of guilt. What if he could've done more, could have seen more, discovered more? Should Travis have been the one undercover? But he'd never been as good at it as Matt was. Matt had nerves of steel.

He wasn't sure that he was comfortable with the way she was studying him.

"Are you okay?" she asked, sounding more unguarded than before.

"Not really." What harm was there in answering her honestly? It wasn't like any kind of judgment she could have for him would impact their closeness now. She'd broken up with him once—surely by definition that meant they were not close. But at the same time, he knew that he was always honest with her about how he felt, and so was she.

Maybe that was a weird foundation, but it's what they had.

"I will be fine," he rephrased. "I think, one day."

"It couldn't have been easy standing back, not being the one to go undercover."

"It wouldn't have been easy to go undercover, either. Nothing about that job is easy."

Lilly nodded as if pondering this. "So what did happen to Matt? I mean, I see the facts here."

He heard the unspoken words. The files were just facts, not explanations. Had she expected that these facts would answer questions she'd had, maybe give her some kind of closure? He didn't blame her, but he could have told her that wouldn't be effective.

"But you want to know what really happened," he filled in for her.

She nodded.

Travis took a deep breath and began.

Chapter Eight

"July 8 last year, we thought it was all going down. The meeting was set for midnight, when it would be mostly dark, and that seemed fitting for a case like this. Everyone was excited, I guess, because we had been chasing this narcotics ring for so many months, and from what Matt had told us, this was going to be the night. He had enough to take them down, but he hadn't reported much of it yet. He was so deeply embedded that he didn't feel like he could without getting caught."

That made sense to Lily. The last two weeks of Matt's life, she'd barely seen him. In fact, she'd been planning to have a conversation with him about their future and whether this was what she could expect, but she'd never gotten the chance.

"I was one of the ones who went with him. Me, Chief McDowell, Officer Knox. We were positioned at various points near the drop site, which was along Knik Arm, almost to the valley, near Chugiak. I was the closest to the boat."

As he spoke, she could hear his voice tightening as he thought of what was coming next in the story. Of course Lily knew also, but it didn't make it any easier to brace herself.

"The first sign that everything hadn't gone according to plan was that there was only one person on the boat that came to meet Matt. He'd taken a small craft to the beach and was waiting, and from the way he'd talked, half of the gang was supposed to be on this boat. But it was just one guy."

"The man from the other night," she filled in, and he nodded.

"Yeah." He took a deep breath. "They started to argue. We didn't want to ruin Matt's cover, so we'd been told to wait until we were sure it was time to make the arrests. I couldn't hear their argument well but the body language implied there was some kind of disagreement. Then there was the shouting. The other man threw a punch. Matt deflected it. Punched him. The guy took a second to recover, then punched Matt again. And he went over the side of the boat and into the inlet. Timber started to attack, but he shot her and she went overboard, and somehow managed to make it back to shore."

Lily felt the emotional impact like a fist to her own throat, robbing her of breath. She could imagine the scene, the darkness of the sky and the even darker water. The splash as Matt went over, maybe the struggle to stay afloat in the murky, silty water. Or maybe not, maybe he'd been knocked unconscious immediately and hadn't had a chance at all. Either way, the image was clear of the water just swallowing him up, and the Alaskan tide carrying him away and out to sea never to be heard from again.

It was wrong, that was all there was to it. Even if maybe their relationship hadn't been the best, even if they'd had problems. Everyone did, right? And no one deserved to die like that. No one.

A sob welled up and escaped her throat, and unexpected tears made their way down her face.

"Lily?"

Travis's concern was appreciated, but it was almost too much. She felt overwhelmed, her head building with the pressure that was all her emotions swelling together inside her. "I... I wanted to know, thanks. I'm just thinking."

Thinking. Thinking. Thinking. She'd done entirely too much of that, and now here she was, stuck again on a July night an entire year ago when her life had changed.

Or had it changed then? Had it changed before, when Matt suggested she spend less time with friends and more time with him? Or had it changed when he told her the faith she'd been raised with was silly?

No, it was ridiculous not to remember the good times. The way he'd made her laugh. His smile. He'd died in the line of duty, died a hero.

Still, it was too much all threaded together in knots that Lily hadn't been able to untangle yet, no matter how many therapy sessions she'd been to, how many lattes she drank, how many positive social media posts she looked at.

Matt and her relationship had been deeply flawed.

He'd been murdered.

She mourned his loss every single day.

She mourned the loss of who she used to be, both before she lost him and even before their relationship.

"I think... I need a run. I think that'll help." She scooted her chair back from the table.

"I'll get my shoes," Travis said, moving quickly.

She shook her head. "No need, I don't think. Nothing weird happened at work today. Maybe he's given up."

Not that she believed that. Who would? She just couldn't fit one more thing in her mind right now, and she knew without a doubt that she needed to run, to feel the physical release of some of this tension. Besides, Timber had spent her day on a dog bed in the coffee shop, so she needed exercise, too.

"I'm coming anyway."

She thought she heard him say it, but like a sleepwalker, she barely registered his words. She simply moved toward the front door and outside.

It still wasn't too late, and there was plenty of daylight.

See? She'd be fine. Never mind that daylight hadn't kept her safe yesterday.

"Timber, come." She looked around the clearing for anything out of place, but seeing nothing, started to run, Timber beside her.

Almost immediately, she could breathe easier, and her chest started to loosen. How was she supposed to explain her agony to Travis if he asked? Would he understand that it was possible to miss someone who had maybe hurt you?

Well, of course the answer to that was yes, she realized as soon as she wondered, but her situation was different.

Therapy had helped her understand that her relationship with Matt was not the healthiest, but she'd started to more fully accept that now that she was spending all this time with Travis, subconsciously comparing them. Was that fair to Travis, though? Or to Matt? How could she hold anything against someone who wasn't here anymore? And why did grief have to be such a complicated knot?

There wasn't a distance she could run that would make this simpler, Lily knew that, but somehow she had to try. Or at least try to calm herself down as much as she could.

She wanted to take the trail in the woods behind Travis's house, but it didn't seem wise. She was foolish to venture out on her own at all, she was realizing as her head got clearer, even if Timber was a good protector. But she wasn't foolish enough to run on the dark, narrow paths back there. Instead she ran alongside the road, which did have some houses on it, though most appeared to be tucked back into their own little patches of woods.

She glanced behind her but didn't see Travis anywhere. Just when she'd started to hope that he had followed her against her wishes.

Didn't that just sum everything up? Did she wish Travis had pursued her even when she told him they were finished all those years ago? That would be absurd, she knew, but maybe part of her had hoped that.

It would have saved her from all the failure that had happened in the intervening years. That stupid list she'd had of dreams she wanted to chase before she got married... She thought of it now and wondered if Travis realized that of all the dreams she'd left their relationship to pursue, she'd only actually accomplished one. She had her own coffee shop. Everything else... Well, dreams were for kids, that was what Matt had told her when she'd tried to push him away with the list, telling him a relationship wasn't on the list until last.

At the time, it had seemed romantic that a man was willing to say, *Hey, but what about me?* And so she'd ended up with Matt. When really she'd missed Travis the whole time.

Lily sped up her pace. What was wrong with her?

She slowed slightly when she saw that Timber was panting. "Sorry, girl. I have a lot of feelings, I guess."

Timber's dark eyes were empathetic but also seemed to imply that she appreciated the slower pace.

Taking a deep breath, Lily slowed all the way to a walk, took a deep breath in and let it out, and relaxed her shoulders. She needed to go back to the house and explain all of this to Travis. *All* of it, because what was the worst that could happen? He could reject her? She'd already done that to him. Maybe it was fair to even the playing field, let him experience what it was like.

The annoying fact was, she probably still loved Travis, definitely more than she loved herself. But she hadn't wanted to hurt him, because of that.

Her mom had hurt her when she left.

Definitely not something Lily wanted to dwell on. Her mom's abandonment of their family when Lily was in middle school had escalated her dad's drinking problem, and it had showed Lily that if you had dreams to chase, you'd better do it before you got married and had a family, because otherwise what if you just…abandoned them?

She hadn't wanted to do that. So she'd broken it off with Travis. She'd never really been able to explain to him why.

Picking her pace up again, she decided she should tell Travis that, too. Again, what was the worst that could happen? Maybe it was time for unguarded honesty.

Enjoying the stretch of her muscles, Lily turned back toward the house, narrowing the distance between herself and Travis with Timber at her side.

Then she heard the first gunshot.

Even with all the danger yesterday, her first thought was that a car had backfired. Something, anything besides a gunshot.

But then the gravel of the road flew up about ten feet in front of her. There were woods on either side. Someone was… shooting from the woods?

Being out in the open was now an awful feeling.

Her stomach churned. Which way was the shooting coming from? Left or right? She sprinted forward, praying for the first time in years and hoping that God was actually paying attention to her. Travis seemed to still take that for granted, like a fact, and he was an adult. Maybe that was another one of those things her relationship with Matt had changed that she needed to change back.

Either way, God seemed to be her only option at the moment.

"Please help me figure this out. Please don't let Timber get hit, or me, either," she muttered under her breath as she ran, trying her best to be aware of her surroundings.

The only way she'd be able to pinpoint a location any better would be if they shot again, though she certainly didn't want…

Another shot. This time, judging by the way the gravel shot up, she was fairly certain they were on her left. The side of the road Travis's house was on.

"Timber, ready?" She gave the dog the signal that a command was coming, then dove off the road and rolled down the slope into the woods. She darted through the trees, glancing down now and then to make sure Timber was still with her. The dog's demeanor seemed to have changed, as if she could sense that something was wrong.

Lily heard another shot. So they were following her. She'd still have to run, and somehow she'd have to get back to Travis.

"Really, God, I'm going to need Your help here, I think," she admitted out loud as she ran. "If You're really involved, please, please show up here and keep me safe. I'll try not to do anything stupid after this if You do."

And Lily ran, praying and hoping beyond hope that she'd get to tell Travis all the things she wanted to say.

Travis didn't understand why Lily hadn't waited for him. He'd watched the emotions chase across her face and understood that she was probably feeling more than she was ready to admit. Should he have pulled punches a little more, tried to ease the blow of what had actually happened that night a year ago?

He didn't think so. It gave him no pleasure to know that he'd said something to hurt and overwhelm her, but he cared too much about Lily not to treat her respectfully. To him, that meant telling her the whole story.

He ran faster than he would prefer along the trails in the woods. No sign of Lily. He'd been running about five minutes when he wondered if she'd have gone along the road instead. She always preferred trail running, but like he'd been trying to remind himself, people did change. He reversed his direction, passed by his house and went out onto the main road. He couldn't see her, but the way his road twisted and turned, he probably wouldn't be able to.

He'd been running for over a mile when he heard what sounded like a gunshot. Forget *sounded like*—it was a gunshot.

Resisting the urge to scream her name, knowing that could

put her in even more danger, he sprinted ahead. Another shot. A third.

They weren't close together, he comforted himself with that. It wasn't rapid-fire as though someone was being gunned down. More like a hunter had been lying in wait for something and was finally taking his chance. The fact that there had been more than one shot was good, right? Probably Lily hadn't gone down with the first? And Timber? Timber had to be okay. Lily was his top priority, of course, but he loved that dog.

At times like this, he was thankful that he didn't believe in an indifferent God, the way Lily had talked about earlier. No matter what, Travis knew that God was right there, present with him, extremely involved. He prayed now, believing God would rescue them.

And he ran. If he was going to help Lily, he was going have to catch her.

At first he stuck to the road, and then something urged him toward the woods on the other side of the road. It was illogical. Surely if Lily was trying to get back to his house, the woods on the correct side of the road would be preferable. But on the other hand, if someone was stalking her, having followed her from his house…

Trusting God and his instincts, Travis continued to run. Until he nearly ran straight into Lily.

Grabbing her by the shoulders to brace her as he couldn't slow down, he whispered immediately, "You okay?" He checked her quickly for any signs of injury.

"Yes. You?"

He nodded, then looked down at Timber. "She's all right, too?"

Lily's nod reassured him again.

"We need to get out of here," he said, stating the obvious.

"How do you propose we do that?"

He thought for a second, then smiled. "I've got a plan."

Chapter Nine

Waiting out a shooter in the woods had not been in Lily's plans for the night, but here they were. Travis, being familiar with these woods, knew where there was a thick patch of alders, and they'd gotten down on their knees and crawled into the curtain of branches they provided. It wasn't the sturdiest of hideouts, which made her uncomfortable, but it was better than running through the woods blind, not knowing where the shooter was.

"You doing okay?" Travis whispered. They were both sitting on the ground, their arms brushing against each other. Lily tried to tell herself that she was finding it difficult to breathe because of stress, but she wasn't entirely sure it didn't have more to do with his closeness.

"I'm ready to be inside somewhere," Lily replied nervously.

"It's probably safe to talk, as long as we're quiet and Timber isn't on alert."

Her eyes went to Timber, who was lying on Lily's other side. Lily could just make out her shape in the fading light.

Lily knew Travis was right, that this was a good plan. The sky had stayed daylight for hours and hours, and they'd sat mostly in silence. Now, though, the sky was gradually dark-ening to a denim blue. Soon, they'd be able to move through the woods relatively undetected.

Of course, that meant that whoever was after her would be able to also. Lily reached down and petted Timber, needing to calm her anxiety.

"So..." Lily trailed off. Everything she'd meant to say had seemed like such a good idea earlier, when she was running, and maybe an ever better idea after that, when she'd been afraid for her life and wondering if she was always going to regret the way things had ended between her and Travis. Sitting here beside him now was a little different. He wasn't just a concept from her past, he was a living, breathing person who could...reject her.

It had sounded so much easier when talking had been theoretical.

"So?" he said in return, and it sounded encouraging. Maybe she could do this after all.

"I was thinking earlier... Man, there's so much to say."

He shifted so he was facing her somewhat. Their arms were still touching, but his face was only inches from hers now, studying her.

Lily looked down, then back up at him. "You know my mom left when I was in middle school."

He nodded, and Lily thought his expression may have darkened. The two of them had known each other back then, but they hadn't been anywhere near as close as they would be in high school. "I never really knew why," she went on, "until I was in high school. I found a letter from her when I was looking through my baby pictures for our senior yearbook."

"What did she say?" His voice sounded as tight as her chest felt right now.

"She, uh, she said she had to leave. That she hadn't pursued her dreams before getting married and starting a family and regretted it, so..." The words tumbled out all at once. "So she left us. I guess maybe that's why I couldn't get married.

No, wait." Lily cleared her throat. "I'm not doing this well. I know that's why I was afraid to get married after high school. It wasn't you, or anything you did, it was entirely me. I didn't want to end up like my mom."

He didn't say anything for a couple of minutes. Lily thought maybe it had gone better than she could have hoped. Either way, at least it was over now.

"But you fixed it by doing the same thing."

"What?"

"You did the same thing she did. I mean, it's not the exact same, we weren't a family. But you're saying that you didn't want to hurt me, so you just left to chase your dreams so... what? So you wouldn't do the exact same thing later?"

Never, *never* had anyone compared Lily to her mom. Well, not since after middle school anyway when her mom's name couldn't be said in the house without her dad reaching for the Jack Daniels. And Lily had never wanted to be like her.

How could Travis say that?

Emotions rubbed raw, Lily grappled to even articulate exactly what she was feeling. Frustration? Anger?

Hurt. Deep hurt. From her mom, from Travis.

Why had she thought it was a good idea to be honest with him? Now she saw the situation for what it was. She'd showed him her heart, and he'd shoved her away, pointing out the areas with scars and shortcomings. As if she still wasn't haunted by fears that she could one day end up like her mom, he'd thrown it in her face that she was.

The longer she sat in her quiet anger, the more upset she got.

"Lily? You okay?"

How many times had he asked her that over the past few days? But this time, she truly was not.

"Actually I'm not super great, which makes sense given what you just said to me."

At least one of her thoughts on her run had been true, and that was that she didn't need to care what he thought anymore.

Honesty wasn't just the best policy in this case; it was the only one that made any sense.

She studied his face for any hint of malice or intentional cruelty but found none. Odd since the words he'd said so carelessly had been so effective at shattering her heart.

"I didn't meant to hurt your feelings," he began.

Listening to him fumble through an apology he may or may not really mean wasn't high on her list of things to do. "Just stop. Please."

If anyone could hear them now it would be almost comical, the way they were whispering so seriously. Of course, with the tension between them thicker than the growing darkness, any bit of the comical was welcome, at least to Lily's way of thinking.

"I don't want to walk away from uncomfortable conversations, Lily. We're working together for who knows how long. I don't want there to be stuff between us."

Wasn't there already too much between them for that to ever be true? Their history was half a decade of hurt. So many shared dreams, and then her dreams had ultimately destroyed what they'd had together. It seemed so ironic now, when she considered how few of those dreams she'd left their relationship for had actually come true. She'd had so many big plans and ideas, but life had intervened. At some point she'd met Matt, and he'd convinced her to walk away from the rest of her dreams.

And now here she was. The owner of a coffee shop, which she was very proud of, but also she was very much alone and felt purposeless, like her future was just one endless sea of beige. Where was the adventure she'd longed for? Had she played life too safe? Or…had she taken the wrong risks?

She met Travis's eyes, saw the usual warm kindness in them and realized that no matter how hurt she felt, or how offended she might be tempted to be, he was telling the truth. He truly hadn't meant to hurt her.

"You saying I was like my mom hurt," she finally said. "But I can see why it seemed like that to you. I don't know… I don't know. I haven't thought about that enough." Her voice broke a little.

"I really didn't mean to upset you. I'm glad you told me, honestly. I always wondered why. I thought we were good. Kinda thought we were, you know, the real deal and then…" He trailed off, but she knew how the story ended. She'd lived it.

Maybe she wasn't the only one who was hurt. She should remember that.

Sitting in the grove of alders, the darkness the only real protection they had, Travis's every sense was already on alert. And that was before Lily dropped the bomb that she'd dumped him because she hadn't wanted to be like her mom.

He hadn't meant to hurt her. He'd told her the truth, but he understood why it had hurt. And he was sorry.

Without thinking, he reached over, grabbed her hand and squeezed it lightly, like he'd done so many times through the years.

Only then did his mind catch up with his emotions and scream for him to stop. He'd already been rejected once. If anyone was in danger of getting hurt, it was certainly him.

But now he already had her hand. What was he going to do, pull away? That would invite more questions. Better to play it cool but keep it in his head that Lily wasn't someone who'd be happy with a regular life. She wanted adventures, she wanted the things on that list. And she should have them.

Or maybe she already did? She'd been engaged, which was at the end of her list. That would make more sense.

"So you get all those dreams accomplished?" He tried to keep his voice light and undemanding. Still, he could feel himself holding his breath as he waited for her answer.

But instead of the assured yes he'd been expecting, she tensed beside him, and he knew he'd said the wrong thing again.

"Unfortunately no. Life is weird, right?" She laughed, but it was hollow and humorless.

"You didn't give up on them, did you?"

She shrugged, and he understood immediately that the answer was yes. Somehow without being told, he suspected his no-nonsense partner had something to do with that.

"So what happened?" he asked.

"Everything and nothing. I did open the coffee shop, but then I realized how many of my dreams conflicted. I mean, really? I was going to be a small business owner but also manage to travel and explore new places? I don't know what I was thinking."

Travis remembered the list. He'd been really proud of her in high school when she'd showed it to him and told him about her dreams. Once upon a time, he'd thought maybe he would even help her accomplish some of them, but that obviously hadn't been the case.

"You were a kid, and the sky was the limit."

"So ignorant."

"Hopeful. I prefer to think of it as hopeful," he corrected.

"Anyway," she continued, "nothing happened, I just grew up. And then I met Matt, and we started dating, and when he wanted to get more serious, he pointed out that my idea about finishing this list before I went on with my life was kind of childish. So I thought he was right and…forgot about it."

The way her voice hesitated on the word *forgot* told him that she most certainly had not forgotten about it.

"Remind me what all was on this list."

"Silly things, Travis."

"What else do we have to do right now, though, besides silly stuff?"

She seemed to be weighing her options. "Fine." And she shifted beside him. Closer? Travis didn't know. He'd been distracted by her proximity since they'd climbed into the makeshift natural shelter.

"First, I was going to open my own coffee shop, so I'd have a job."

"Which you did, and it's fantastic."

"Had you been before today?"

He nodded. "Several times. I just—" he looked away "—I used to try to go when you weren't out front working the register." He'd wanted to support her but hadn't wanted to cause any kind of drama.

It seemed like she took a minute to process that and then nodded. "That was really sweet of you."

"What else was on the list?"

She shrugged, laughing softly at herself. "A couple of things, I—" She stopped.

When Travis looked over at her, she was staring at Timber, who was focused on something out in the distance, her body tense.

Sometimes it was frustrating not to have the senses of a dog, because Travis couldn't hear anything. He didn't think Lily could, either, though she had her eyes closed and seemed to be focusing all her energy into hearing whatever her dog had.

Timber lowered her head slightly. For a second, her lip curled back.

Travis felt for the handgun he had in his waistband holster. They weren't defenseless, for which he was thankful, but he knew Lily had already been through a lot. Another shootout wasn't something she needed. He made himself sit still, waiting. Lily did the same.

After one minute, maybe two, which stretched out in a seemingly endless silence, Timber laid her head back down, her muscles gradually relaxing.

It seemed they were safe again, for now.

"Maybe we should go?" Lily whispered.

Travis immediately nodded. It was dark enough to give them cover, and he wasn't willing to risk sitting here waiting for someone to find them. "We'll finish this conversation later."

"We don't have to do that," she protested.

Travis put his hands on her upper arms and turned her gently till she faced him. "I want to, Lily," he said, eyes meeting hers. It felt like there was some kind of bond between them that time hadn't managed to break, not completely. If anything, it was more obvious to Travis now than when he'd been younger that there was something between them, and maybe there always would be.

Thinking of her safety and the unknown threats that could still be lurking in the woods, he made himself look away from her. Nodding in the direction of his house, he said, "Let's go. We need to get you back home and safe."

"I don't even have a home," she mumbled.

"Maybe the fire department will call tomorrow. But you're welcome in my cabin for as long as you need it," he told her as they crawled carefully out of the alders.

As though by mutual consent, once they left the shelter of the trees, neither of them talked. Travis found his senses heightened as he looked between the dark shapes of spruce and birch trees. The sky was a deep blue, not quite black—it still wouldn't be fully dark for long at all this early in July— but the midnight twilight allowed them some shelter to get back to the house.

Timber seemed to understand what they were trying to do, and she kept a steady pace in front of both of them, keeping her nose up and sniffing the air. It was reassuring to know that she was using her skills to scan the woods for them; at least they could confirm that they were fairly safe.

Travis was always thankful that Timber hadn't been killed in the attack that had taken Matt's life, but never more so than now. It was like having another officer at his side, except one who had super heightened senses and didn't hog the coffee.

It didn't take long for them to make their way through the

woods, even at the careful pace they'd set, and soon they were approaching Travis's house.

"Any chance you've got more hot chocolate?" she asked Travis.

He laughed, the tension from the night demanding some release. "You know I do."

"Yeah, I was pretty sure." She hurried inside and into his kitchen.

Travis followed, giving Timber a rewarding pat as she went by him into the house.

Making the hot chocolate was easy enough, he thought, as he topped a couple of mugs with whipped cream and sprinkles. The problem was calming down enough to drink it.

It was all starting to slam into him now. Lily had really been shot at. Her life had been in danger. Again. Then the conversation in the shelter of the trees, in the dark…

Something about talking in the dark made everything feel so much less guarded. Lily hadn't stopped loving him, or at least that wasn't why she'd broken up with him at graduation. There was something deeply reassuring about that; her leaving so suddenly all those years ago had made him question so many things he'd known to be true. This made so much more sense. It didn't change what had happened, but it sure made it easier to deal with.

"You're sure you don't need to get checked out? No bruises, no injuries at all?" He looked her over the best he could in a respectful way, but Lily shook her head.

"He shot at me a couple of times, but it wasn't ever as close as it could have been."

"Bad shot or intentional misses?" he asked aloud, not knowing if he was really looking for an answer.

Lily shrugged. "I'm not sure."

Travis carried the hot chocolates into the living room, and Lily followed, exactly as they'd done the night before. Travis felt that he could get used to this, having a nightly hot cocoa with Lily. Except…that wasn't what she needed, was it?

As he set their drinks down onto the coffee table, it all seemed so clear to him. Matt had encouraged her to stop dreaming, stop pursuing her list; Travis was fairly sure he'd understood that correctly. What Lily really needed was a friend, someone who would encourage her to follow those dreams. Even if doing so would mean she returned to the line of thinking that she couldn't be in a relationship till she accomplished more.

Still, it would be worth it to help her, because he knew it was what Lily wanted. And he really loved seeing her smile.

"Come tell me about the rest of that list. Where were we before we got interrupted?"

He was rewarded by her easy smile. Travis took a long sip of cocoa and waited for Lily to share some of her other dreams.

Chapter Ten

"You're sure you want to talk about this? Like I said, it's silly. Ridiculous even."

"I honestly don't think I'll see it that way," Travis said.

Lily believed him. She hadn't thought it was that bad of a list of dreams until Matt had seemed so down on it. Was it somewhat unrealistic? Sure. But wasn't dreaming part of being alive? Maybe that was why the last year of grief hadn't felt quite as jarring as she'd expected it to. In some ways, she hadn't been fully alive in years, not since…well, not since walking away from who she was in exchange for a relationship.

That had been the heart of the problem with her and Matt, she realized. She had given up too much. And maybe he had, too? But love wasn't supposed to make you change who you were, right? It was supposed to make you a better version, maybe. At least, that was the gist she'd gotten from countless books and TV shows.

"Okay. If you're sure…" She took a breath. "I also wanted plenty of things that didn't make sense."

"Like?"

"I was going to travel a lot." She laughed. "It sounded fun. I wanted to go to Europe, hike around… I wanted to learn another language first, of course, so that I could converse with people."

"Oh, yeah? Which?"

"I was flexible there. French seemed practical. German. Maybe Norwegian. I was also going to learn some new hobbies." She shrugged. "Stuff like that."

There had been more, but it felt strange and oddly personal to talk about. Lily wasn't sure she wanted to go into any more detail. Still, she appreciated that he cared. Looking at him now, it was clear that he had really been listening.

"And you decided you didn't want to get married?" Travis's voice was careful as he asked the question, and Lily could imagine why.

How weird must it be for him to know that she'd walked away from what they had because of this list, and yet she'd agreed to marry Matt? Admittedly, it seemed inconsistent.

"No, it just wasn't on the list because it was assumed. I always wanted to get married and have a family, but I figured I should do the other things first. Get them out of the way, sort of. Have my life together."

Not like her mom. She could tell that he heard the unspoken words, too.

"It just seemed like what was best," she finished.

A heavy silence surrounded them in a way that was impossible to ignore. She'd made her choices, and now she had to live with them. Losing Travis wasn't something that had happened to her like she was a victim. She'd broken them up. She'd made other choices. She didn't have any right to go back on those now.

Even if he did make fantastic hot chocolate and listen to her better than anyone ever had.

She took another sip of the warm drink, letting the liquid warm her throat, her chest, her heart. When was the last time she'd just sat down and talked to someone else like this? She'd missed this kind of closeness. She had liked that about being with Matt—she'd had someone to talk to on a regular basis.

She and Travis had always had this kind of easy relationship, where they could sit and talk and just be together for hours. She'd tried to duplicate it, but no one else had ever been Travis.

The thought was terrifying. She'd never bought into the idea of soul mates and having one person who was right for you, but what if it was true? What if Travis had been her one chance, and she'd messed it up?

Lily's eyes stung with tears she absolutely would not shed. As much as all the things on her list meant to her, she'd always wanted a family and someone to share her life with. Had she forfeited that? She certainly hoped not.

Much as she hated the awkward silence, she didn't know what to say. Out there in the woods, telling him everything had seemed like such a good idea. He knew now, at least, that their breakup hadn't been because of anything he'd done. He'd been the best boyfriend she could have hoped for, and while they'd had their arguments like any normal couple, it had also been so easy between them.

Not able to stand it anymore, Lily stood up. "I've got to do something."

"You just got shot at, don't you think that's enough excitement for the night?"

He had a point, even though his eyes were sparkling... Wait, was he seriously teasing her?

It warmed her chest every bit as much as the hot chocolate, and Lily felt some of her internal chaos relax.

"Was Matt really killed randomly? Could it have been anyone who died that night? Or was he closer than anyone else to figuring out who was involved...or...or something? What if we walked through it all together?" She'd read enough mystery books to throw ideas out, but realistically she knew very little about what would be needed to conduct an actual investigation.

"We assumed it was just because he was involved. Maybe he said something that night that made them realize he was arresting them? There was no way to find out. The trail went cold the second he…"

"Went overboard," Lily finished for him, the words stinging less than they had earlier in the night. There was no driving need to go run this time.

Travis nodded.

"What was the investigation like immediately after? I mean, did APD check out his apartment or…" She tried to remember what had been done at the time. Matt's personal affairs hadn't been hers to handle, since they'd been engaged and hadn't lived together. He'd paid rent months in advance… Was it possible he still had the apartment leased?

"We looked around the apartment. Nothing was out of place. It was extremely clean."

"Huh. Matt wasn't the neatest, but that's good, I guess. Other than that, there wasn't anything useful there?" she asked.

"I think there are photos in this file somewhere." Travis nodded to the stack they'd been going through earlier. "But we can wait, Lily. None of this has to be done right now."

People had said the same thing to her after Matt's death. But the truth was things did have to be done. Sometimes it was easier just to buckle down and get through them.

"I think I'm better now," she said.

Travis stood, got the stack of files from the table and brought them back to the couch. "Mind if I sit here?" he asked, motioning to the spot next to her.

"No, for sure, that's fine." Belatedly, Lily realized that a handful of words spilling out of her mouth instead of a simple *no* probably betrayed the fact that his proximity did shake her up at least a bit.

In any case, he did sit down beside her.

"Yeah, here they are." He pulled a stack of printed photos out of the pile. "Nothing interesting that we found."

No matter how certain Lily had been that she was ready to wade back into this, the photos of Matt's apartment did throw her a little. First of all it was so familiar. She'd spent so much time there when they first started dating. Even if their time together had diminished at the end, probably due to how invested he'd been in the narcotics case, they'd had some good times in that apartment.

She'd watched some of her favorite movies on that couch, listening to Matt mumble about how action movies were better than chick flicks. She'd tried to watch some with him, but her taste in action movies only ran as far as Jack Ryan, a classic hero who never sought out heroism. Matt tended to like the flashier movies. He was more of a Tom Cruise than a Harrison Ford.

Travis was right that the apartment was very clean. Matt had always been more of a *leave his boots in the middle of the floor and get them later* kind of guy, but these photos didn't look like that at all. Even the trash cans were emptied.

"Have you ever noticed before how eerie it is to look at photos of someone's place after they're gone?" Lily turned to Travis to ask.

He nodded like he knew what she meant exactly, and she relaxed, appreciating being understood.

"This isn't like that." Lily continued, "I mean, it is, but in a different way. It just… It doesn't look like he was planning to come back."

Lily looked over at Travis again and blinked as their eyes met. She spoke again. "That's exactly what's weird to me. It was rarely this clean. Do you think he knew it was going to go wrong?"

It had been a year, but she could feel her mind struggling to rewind to the last time she'd seen Matt. They'd argued about something stupid, she remembered. Where to go eat, maybe? Had he given any indication that he'd somehow known his death was coming?

No. Not that she could think of. He'd been off, stressed, shorter tempered than usual, but not depressed or giving any indication that he thought something awful was going to happen to him. No extra-long goodbyes, nothing.

But why was the apartment so clean?

She shook her head. "I hate that the further we look into this, the more questions I have. I keep thinking if I just take a deep breath, focus on it one more time, then maybe I'll understand. Maybe I'll be able to really move on."

"Is it his death that's keeping you from that, though?" Travis asked.

Lily frowned. "What do you mean?"

"Your list, your mom..."

Lily flinched.

"Are you sure you aren't keeping yourself from moving forward? Do you know what you want moving forward to look like?"

It was the stupidest question she'd ever heard. She, who had daydreamed her way through several high school classes and written a to-do list that haunted her in more ways than one, not moving forward? She'd always been able to dream about her future and make plans and now...

Now she had the coffee shop. She dreamed of one day running the shop without the weight of the grief she felt over Matt, but...her dreams were all just focused on getting things back to how they used to be.

What was Travis saying? That she needed a new dream?

Would solving this case somehow help like Lily thought it would, or was Travis right? Was she the one keeping herself stuck?

He'd overstepped, Travis knew it, and he wasn't sure how he was going to get out of this one.

Lily was looking at him, her eyes wide, blinking.

It seemed like it was too late to *put down the shovel* as his mom had always said, so he kept talking. "What do you want, Lily? Like, really, what do you want?"

She stared at him as though he was the answer.

And in slow motion, like her gaze was pulling her toward him, Travis felt himself drawn closer to her. Or was she moving toward him? Either way, it was like an invisible force, slow but determined. Her eyes were still, beautiful pools of blue.

"Lily?"

"Yeah?" Her whisper pulled him even closer.

"I'm going to kiss you if you don't back up." His breathing had quickened, and he could feel his heart beating in his chest. Was he really going to do this? Had he really said that?

She moved closer, and he had his answer for both questions.

Like someone who had returned from a long journey and wasn't sure of whether home was really theirs anymore, he brushed her lips gently with his, another question.

She answered with more pressure.

Travis found him kissing her fully, without thinking, lips moving over hers in a way that was not at all familiar, no matter how many times they'd done this in the past. This was new, fresh. And it meant more to him than the one hundred kisses they'd shared as high schoolers.

Lily was complicated, and Travis knew his life had been simpler before she'd called him just a few days ago, but he didn't need simple. He'd asked her what her dreams for the future were, but he hadn't really been asking himself.

The answer was this.

He ended the kiss far sooner than he wanted to, drawing back just enough to meet her eyes again.

"You. I want…" She swallowed hard. Looked away. "I want you, but… I don't know how to do this. How can you trust me again? How can I trust myself? What about all this, and Matt's death, and…" She stood up and walked across the room, and Travis felt her absence immediately. "What if it's just messed me up beyond repair? I can't do that to you."

He knew she'd changed, but he wanted to know this new version of her. Not just her lips. But her heart. Her dreams. "You're not."

"But how do you know?"

He could see one single tear chasing its way down her cheek. She shook her head again. "I'm sorry, Travis."

His stomach tightened, knowing the rest of that sentence. She shouldn't have kissed him. Shouldn't want him.

Was he really so stupid that he would set himself up for rejection from the same woman multiple times? Part of his mind reminded him that it might not be him she was rejecting. She'd been though a lot. Tonight alone had been overwhelming.

"What's a kiss between friends, right? We're still friends, Lily."

"Friends."

She reached up and touched her lips, and Travis could almost feel the electricity. She knew it, too, even if neither of them was going to admit it. That had *not* been the kind of kiss two friends could share and shrug off. For Travis, that was the kind of kiss he could only experience with the woman who had been and apparently still was straight out of his dreams.

"We can be friends," she said, blowing out a long breath. "But we probably…"

"Yeah, shouldn't do that again," he finished for her. He patted the couch cushion beside him. "Want to come back, look at the file more?"

"Do you mind if we pick this back up tomorrow, after work?" She was already moving toward the back door, toward the guest cabin.

"You're going to need to talk to the police. We should have called them tonight." He'd sent a text to Officer Keller, the woman who'd come by yesterday—had that been only yesterday? He'd let her know that Lily had been shot at but asked if it was possible for her to talk to them the next day.

"Tomorrow… I will, after work. Sure." Lily reached for the doorknob. "Walk me back?"

He appreciated that she at least wasn't completely throwing safety to the wind, but he figured it would be better not to talk about anything serious as he walked her to the guest cabin. Instead he answered her questions about when he'd bought the property, his plans for the cabin, simple things like that. She seemed determined to get them back on level footing.

"Sleep well," he told her after establishing that no one else was inside the cabin. Timber, who had curled up at his house and taken a long nap, seemed alert and ready to be watchful.

Lily smiled back at him, and he felt like maybe they could pull this off. Maybe they could be friends.

"You, too, Travis."

His heart and breath caught at the same time, and he realized the truth. He was probably going to love Lily Peterson for the rest of his life.

Walking back to his house after he'd double-and triple-checked Lily's doors, Travis tried to decide if he had any hopes that she might change her mind about them. After all, she was under an extreme amount of stress, that was for sure.

But for now, he needed to respect her request to back off. Be friends.

What would a friend do?

He sat back down on his couch, wishing Lily was still there, and eyed the stack of papers. He didn't have a lot to offer her. At the moment, he didn't even have his own dreams totally lined up.

Being a police officer had always been it for him before Matt's death had driven him away. It had made him question if the good he could do was worth immersing himself in all the evil he saw on the job. Did good really win? Could evil be stopped?

He knew the answer according to the Bible, but that didn't mean it felt true when you were standing at someone's door telling them that because of someone else's bad choices, their fiancé wouldn't come home.

When he'd seen how much it had crushed Lily after someone had come to her door to tell her bad news, he decided he was never going to do it again. For the months he'd stayed at the department, he avoided it, and then realized that maybe it had broken him, too.

Maybe Lily wasn't the only one who felt messed up beyond repair.

Quitting his job hadn't solved anything, though. Here he was, face-to-face with that kind of evil and pain again, except this time without all the resources he'd had as a police officer.

Travis flipped through the file about Matt's death, reading enough to remind himself of other details he hadn't remembered, like interviews with Matt's acquaintances who reported that the case had been taking over his life. That, connected to the fact that Lily had been so surprised by how clean his apartment had been, bothered Travis. Bothered him enough that he got up off the couch and started doing sit-ups, partly to clear his mind and partly to see if he still could just in case maybe he wanted to go back to law enforcement. Maybe. One day.

Thirty sit-ups in, he'd confirmed his muscles were still in good shape even if his confidence wasn't, and he'd come to some conclusions that bothered him.

Something hadn't been right in that investigation. The signs had been there, but somehow he hadn't noticed, even though he'd been Matt's partner.

Matt hadn't…hadn't been working both sides, had he?

It felt disloyal to even consider. Travis weighed his options. Who could he talk to at the police department who knew enough about the case to be helpful processing it, but who wouldn't immediately take his thoughts as something that was truth? The last thing he wanted was to sully his friend's name after his death.

But what if his friend had been guilty? Didn't Lily deserve to know?

Would she want to know?

He stood up, paced some more, then went outside to patrol the property. He didn't go close to the cabin, not wanting to wake Timber, but he made sure nothing looked amiss.

When he went inside, questions about Matt still taunted him. He wasn't going to get much sleep tonight.

Chapter Eleven

"Can you get that, Hannah?"

The phone had been ringing more than usual today, Lily thought. It seemed like suddenly people she'd been trying to get ahold of for weeks about coffee shop business were all calling her back, making her normally busy workday more hectic than usual. Right now she was in the middle of making a customer's latte, and the espresso machine had been finicky earlier in the morning. The last thing she wanted was to have to repull shots.

Focusing on what she was doing, she was startled when she felt Hannah's gentle tap on her shoulder.

"Sorry, I didn't mean to scare you." Hannah frowned at her. "I guess I understand why you were scared, though, with everything going on."

So she'd heard about that. Lily had been hoping somehow the town was going to be oblivious to what she was going through.

"Anyway, the fire department is on the phone for you."

"Can you…" Lily gestured to the espresso machine where she had paper cups in a line waiting.

Hannah nodded, and Lily smiled an apology at the customer currently in line and walked to the phone.

"Lily Peterson speaking."

"Lily, it's Captain Caldwell from the Silvertip Creek Fire Department, how are you?"

"Fairly well, considering," she said.

"Your house has been cleared." He cut right to the chase. "It's structurally sound, so I don't see why you couldn't move back in immediately. The study where the fire was localized did sustain some damage, but nothing that caused loss of structural integrity. I would recommend you hire someone to clean that room."

Or she could do it herself, which would be infinitely cheaper. It wasn't that she was hurting of money, per se, but this dream of opening her own business hadn't come cheap. She wasn't exactly seeing the fruits of her business in excess yet.

"I can handle that. No problem."

They talked for a few more minutes about logistical details, and the captain left her with instructions that she should call if there was anything at all out of the ordinary when she got home.

It was almost too good to be true. She couldn't quite believe it. She was going home!

A shadow dimmed her excitement. What if the man after her came back, and she was alone? It had been scary enough yesterday when she knew Travis was nearby. She couldn't imagine how terrifying it would be to be farther away from him.

But staying at Travis's house was a nonstarter. She'd still be alone in his guest cabin, technically, and while she knew it was different being so close to him and knowing he could be there any second, she was ultimately still alone either way. And she wasn't willing to be away from home forever.

Mind settled, she texted Travis. She did her best to sound reassuring, even as she wondered if the fire department had really thought this through. Or maybe they hadn't talked to the police department? Somehow she doubted the officers assigned to her case would be thrilled with the idea of her being alone.

Still, though, she was an adult and no one had ordered her to stay at Travis's place or anything like that. She'd go home because that was what made the most sense.

And because she didn't know how she was going to sort out her feelings with him so close.

"Everything okay?" Hannah asked.

This time, Lily couldn't even rustle up a fake smile. "You know...long day."

Hannah raised her eyebrows like she didn't believe her. "What else is going on?"

Besides being hunted by a homicidal lunatic and being kissed so well by her former boyfriend that she forgot everything except the fact that maybe it wasn't too late for a future? With Travis, she didn't feel broken. Not that he *completed* her, Lily didn't feel that way at all, but she did like him and wasn't afraid to admit their attraction was still there. But she felt like a whole person, like someone whose flaws or griefs or struggles did not define her.

She felt safe. She felt known.

It was clear to her that she needed to get out of his house. Had he bought her comment about being friends? In some ways, friendship was the last thing she could imagine when that kiss had been everything she wanted and more. But Lily couldn't trust herself right now. Her emotions were overwhelmed with this case and the threat against her. Travis Beckett had been hard enough to get over the first time—she had no desire to repeat the experience.

"Uh...nothing," she finally said, her mind still a million miles away.

Hannah's expression implied that she knew Lily wasn't telling the entire truth, but she graciously let it go. "I got all those drinks made. I was thinking, do you want me to close up today?"

Usually Hannah opened, and Lily closed. But she would love to go home and assess how bad things were at her house. She needed to see if she could move in tonight or if she would need to pick up some things.

And then there was her plan to go out with Travis and survey some of the areas near where Matt had died, just to see if they could get a clearer picture of what had gone on that night and why. There had to be some detail they were missing.

"I think I'll take you up on that," Lily said at last. "See you tomorrow."

Hannah waved, and Lily grabbed her purse and headed out the door. She was reaching for the handle of her car door when her phone rang. Travis.

"Hey, what's up?" she asked.

"The fire department just called me to let me know that your house was okay."

"They just called me, too. I wonder why they called you?"

"I have a buddy who works there."

Of course he did. Travis was so well connected in the law enforcement/rescue/public service world.

"I want to go over and check it out," she said, "but do you want to do that first or check out the bluffs?"

"Tonight?" Travis asked.

"Well, today, but yeah. I thought I'd leave the shop early."

He didn't say anything for a while, and Lily felt like she was being measured. She stood up straight, as if that would help her project strength through the phone call. Everything in her wanted to ignore yesterday. She didn't want to go over what had happened with the gunshots and being trapped in the woods. She just wanted to move on.

"You're sure you should?" Travis said at last. "I can do this alone."

He didn't sound like he was mocking or even pitying her, which would have been worse, but the words still chafed.

"Yeah, I'm good. I'm fine."

"Okay. I'll meet you at the overlook?"

Lily agreed, got in her car and drove away from the shop and out of town.

The overlook Travis had mentioned was the parking lot at the trailhead that led down to the edge of the inlet. The silty mudflats could be fatal if a person got stuck in them. About once a year, someone would venture into the mudflats and need to be rescued. It was the closet thing to quicksand that Lily knew of. If the texture was just right, it could suck a person in and refuse to let them out.

They'd have to be careful while they investigated. Lily wouldn't be able to forgive herself if something happened to Travis because of her.

Travis hadn't been to the bluff over Knik Arm in months now. In the months after Matt's death, Travis found himself there often, sitting on one of the benches near the parking lot or wandering down toward the water itself, careful to steer clear of the mudflats and the metal-colored water. Some days it was fairly calm, but today he could see the currents churning. The water looked restless.

Travis could relate.

Kissing Lily had been incredible. He should have known she was going to backpedal from it, but it still hurt a little. How could things between them be so perfect and so impossible at the same time?

He climbed out of his car and waited for Lily to pull up. Within a minute or two, she arrived, and he watched as she opened the door of her car. He tensed as she made her way across the empty parking lot, an easy target in the massive open space.

He'd called both Anchorage PD and Silvertip Creek PD today to get a feel for whether they had the manpower to put any kind of temporary bodyguard on Lily. They didn't, as he anticipated, though Silvertip Creek PD thought they might be able to have one of the patrol officers swing by her house more often.

Much as he didn't like the plan, Travis wasn't surprised that Lily was going to move back to her house now that the fire department had given her the go-ahead. Home mattered to her, for one thing, and for another, she didn't like to feel like an imposition.

He wished she felt as at home at his house as her own. He'd done his best to move on, had dated several times since high school, but he'd be lying if he didn't acknowledge that he still had some furnishings that he'd picked out with Lily in mind.

"Good day?" he asked her as she got close. Timber followed them closely behind her.

Lily shook her head. "Too much going on."

"You don't have to go home right away, you know," he tried. "You could hire people to do the repair work, stay at the cabin…"

Lily was already shaking her head as though she'd expected this. She knew him well. "I have to go home, Travis. I can't live like this indefinitely."

There was a massive difference between what was likely to be just a few weeks and *indefinitely*. But he could see her point, especially with Matt's death on the verge of officially becoming a cold case. One year, and they'd learned little that they hadn't discovered in the first forty-eight hours after his death.

Maybe Travis was foolish to think they could uncover more.

"I get it." He reached for her hand as they approached the narrow path down toward the inlet. "It's slick." And he didn't want her to feel like she was facing this alone, but figured the first reason was more acceptable to her.

Lily reached her hand out, and he held it in his, swallowing back emotion as he reminded himself that she wanted to be friends and that was it.

Much of his day at the hardware store had been spent thinking through that, in between helping customers. If she wanted to be friends, he could do that, but how could he be a really good friend to her? The question had circled his mind all day, and he'd finally landed on her list.

Could he help her complete it, at least somewhat? Maybe she couldn't travel the world, but could she travel around here?

He hated the idea of her feeling her life was incomplete, with something inside her begging to do more and see more, and her shutting it up just because society implied it was time for her to settle down. If Matt was alive, Travis would give him a good shove for talking Lily into thinking her dreams were silly.

Did Travis wish those dreams hadn't come between the two of them? Yes. But maybe now the best thing he could do for her was help her fulfill them.

"So where were you that night?" she asked when they were halfway down the narrow trail. Grass and other plants grew along the sides, but the middle was mud, worn down from use. No matter how often people were told the mudflats were dangerous, they held a special allure. And this particular spot, where Matt's meetup had happened, was where the river was most accessible for people who liked to push the boundaries.

Everything looked different in daylight, especially a good six months after he'd been here last. That had been an oppressively gray winter day when he'd felt like hope was a concept that wasn't quite reachable. He'd come here, sat for a while in his grief with no real conclusions and then realized that sometimes life meant going on even without wrapping up the last chapter.

And he'd tried. Maybe even succeeded. Being here now felt like a step back and a step forward all at once.

"I was…" He looked around at the tall vegetation, the shape of the slope, the way the inlet angled below them where it cut into the bank. That was where the boat had been. Travis had had a nearly perfect visual, though he'd not been able to hear anything other than the rise and fall of voices. "There."

He pointed to a spot up ahead, on the left side of the trail. He'd spent time before what should have been the drug bust finding the best spot to hide and still be close enough to take quick action.

Travis walked toward where he'd been hiding but didn't go into the thick brush. Lily stayed beside him.

Timber's ears perked up.

She'd been with them that night. She'd stayed back with Travis while Matt boarded the boat and prepped for making the arrests. Travis had watched her flinch at a loud voice, though she stayed down as instructed. Together, they'd watched the scene unfold. Timber wasn't a stranger to this place, either. Perhaps she also wasn't a stranger to the grief that accompanied it.

Still, whatever reaction he'd been expecting from her, it wasn't this.

The fur on her scruff stiffened, and her eyes focused on the brush.

"Timber, stay," he said firmly.

Ignoring him, Timber crept forward.

Immediately Lily turned to him. "What is she doing?"

"I have no idea." He'd worked with Timber for years, and she'd been so reliable. This entire case was confusing—she wasn't behaving in a predictable way. Police dogs were supposed to be all but bombproof, always able to take commands. But this wasn't the first time it felt like Timber was operating entirely on her own. Travis struggled to find an explanation for her behavior, but nothing made sense.

She moved forward, not at a run, but purposefully.

"Let's follow her," he told Lily. They both trailed along behind the dog, making their way through the brush.

She was taking him right back to the spot he'd used as cover when he'd watched Matt's death go down one year ago.

How? Why?

His heart pounding, uncertainty roiling in his stomach, he followed her.

Chapter Twelve

Lily had never understood all that Timber knew and was capable of, but it had struck her as strange how often Timber was running away from them. She was usually so obedient.

Now if she wasn't mistaken, Travis looked shaken up, too. Timber was trotting through the brush, near the direction where Travis had told her he'd hidden that night a year ago.

She hadn't considered what it would be like for him to come here. Was he okay? Or did it bring back memories in a way that overwhelmed him? Somehow she doubted that even if he did he would run off when someone was after him. She was able to see now how foolish that plan had been.

Up ahead, Timber stopped. Lily hurried to where she was and looked down at the ground.

It was still more cleared out in this spot than around it, though the brush seemed to have grown up somewhat. In several places, though, the earth was disturbed, and dirt was piled haphazardly, like someone had been digging for something.

"Did you…did you have to dig out a place to hide or something?" she asked, frowning. Timber eagerly nosed the dirt.

"No." His voice sounded strained.

Lily watched as Timber continued to sniff the ground, then put her nose up.

"I don't think we're alone here."

Lily looked up at Travis. His face was serious, with no hint of a smile. His body was tense, his shoulders slightly higher than a relaxed pose.

"Who else would be here?" she asked. The person after them? But no one had come down the trail after them, and Lily had even done her best to pay attention to see if any cars had followed them to the lot. She was sure that Travis would have done the same. So if there was someone else here, they would have arrived before she and Travis did.

But who else knew the significance of this particular spot?

"I have no idea. Not very many people." Even the way he said it showed how doubtful he was also feeling about this situation.

She and Travis knew this was where he had hidden. Matt had known, obviously, but he was dead. Could the narcotics gang have somehow found out an officer had been hiding there that night? But even if they had, what could they want with the old hiding spot now?

"You don't think it's someone, you know, from the police department," she asked. "Do you?"

Travis didn't meet her eyes. Finally he blew out a breath. "I just don't know."

He knelt beside Timber and started to push the piles of loose dirt around. As Lily watched, Travis shifted enough dirt aside to reveal a hole, about six by twelve inches.

"Something was there," he muttered, digging some more.

It looked to Lily like something out of a novel. The fully exposed cavity was rectangular, with fairly smooth sides. It hadn't been a rushed job to bury whatever had been here.

And now someone had to come to retrieve it.

"What, though?" she asked aloud, but Travis just shook his head.

Beside them, Timber whined, pawed at the ground and started to sniff again.

"You okay?" Lily frowned. She moved to check the dog for old injuries like the vet had shown her shortly after APD had given Timber to her. Right now, she was clearly uncomfortable in some way, but Lily couldn't find any obvious signs of injury—no part of the dog flinched when Lily ran her hands over her. "I don't understand what's wrong with her."

Timber laid down. Whined again.

"She's alerting," Travis said. "Sort of. Nothing she's doing is following the playbook exactly. But she smells something, clearly."

"Do you know what?"

Travis frowned but didn't answer. Lily didn't know if he was avoiding her question or if he really didn't know.

Suddenly coming here didn't seem like such a great idea. She had somehow felt reasonably safe on this trail, even with the way it was such a dark part of her past. Apparently she wasn't safe.

Maybe she wasn't safe anywhere.

The urgency to find out who was behind this rose in Lily's mind. This was not a sustainable way to live.

Timber stood and continued to sniff and track something, Travis followed her.

Lily watched Travis. He was a natural in this situation, reading the dog's body movements. "You're really good with her," she said at last, hoping saying so wouldn't interrupt him.

"I used to work with her all the time."

"Wait, you did?" Had Lily known that? She'd thought only Matt handled Timber.

"Yep."

Had she made that assumption because Timber had gone to her when she retired? As far as she understood, protocol usually dictated that a retired dog would go to a handler to be a pet. "Then why do I have her? I mean, did you not want her after…"

Travis looked in her direction. "I didn't want you to be alone."

Oh.

He'd given up Timber for her? She didn't know what to say to that or how to convey her thanks, but she appreciated it.

She had more questions but knew now wasn't the time. For one thing, was he planning to go back to police work? The way he paid attention to every detail, his eyes easily moving across the landscape, spoke to how good he had been at his job. Lily couldn't imagine him doing anything else, really. He seemed like he was made for it.

She stood still, looking around now and then to make sure there was no obvious threat nearby. She saw nothing, but then would she if there truly was anyone waiting for them out here? So far she'd been taken off guard every single time. It was distressing but true.

Finally, Travis walked back to where Lily was standing. "Something's wrong here. I think we should go."

Lily nodded. Her eyes went to the mudflats in front of them, just a bit farther down the hill, and out to the water. For what had to be the thousandth time, she imagined what it had been like for Matt.

How the events of his death could have anything to do with her in a way that made someone target her, she had no idea. If someone connected to that case was after her…why? And why now, after a full year had passed? It didn't seem reasonable to her at all—they would have come after her immediately if she was a target because of the case, she was almost sure of it.

But it was only her connection to Matt that tied her to it at all. Lily couldn't make sense of it.

She and Travis hurried back up the hill, not talking, but as he walked her to her car, she finally told him all she'd been thinking.

"You're right that someone trying to hurt you because of Matt seems strange," he agreed.

"Is it just related to me finding the body? Maybe that's the only part that involves me?"

"Your house was on fire as soon as you got down the mountain. How did your attacker know where you lived?"

That was something she hadn't considered. Lily frowned.

"Oh, unless it was because of the note? Maybe...yeah, I've got nothing."

"Stuck again there, too," Travis said. "Why was your address on a piece of paper to start with? If you aren't tied to the case at all, that makes no sense."

Lily hated this. Ending up in her own personal suspense story was not a life goal, and it was something she'd really like to change.

"I just don't know," she finally said. "But I've got to drive to my house. I'm planning to call a contractor on the way home and figure out what's going to be necessary to repair the damage in the study."

"Mind if I come over?"

"You don't trust me alone?"

"I trust you fine. Do I trust whoever is after you to leave you alone? Not at all."

Lily appreciated that he cared, but it rubbed a little that he felt like she needed constant supervision. "You're not overreacting?"

"Did the gunshots last night not answer that question?"

Okay, so he had a point. But she was still moving back home. If she wasn't safe anywhere, she at least wanted to be somewhere familiar, around her own things, have some home field advantage. As nice as Travis's house was, it wasn't hers. She needed something of her own around her right now.

She tried to explain that to Travis, but either it was just a way that they were different or it was a man thing, She could tell that, much as she tried, he just didn't get it.

Calling Timber toward her, she opened the door of her car, let the dog jump in and then climbed in after, bracing herself for whatever she was going to find at home.

If anything had convinced him that there was something more sinister going on here than they were aware of, it was Timber's behavior today. Travis couldn't stop thinking about it as he drove toward Lily's house.

Nothing about how she'd reacted was typical, and all of it concerned him. Her behavior along with what they'd found made him uncomfortable.

Someone with a connection to the police department had almost certainly been involved in the narcotics ring. And not in a way that involved investigating it. Someone had gone bad.

He hated bad cops, hated storylines with bad cops. He rejected the narrative that law enforcement was somehow more likely to "go bad" than other professions. But none of his personal preferences or feelings made what they were dealing with now any less true. Someone had gone to the other side.

As he pulled into Lily's driveway, he breathed a sigh of relief to see that everything looked normal. Her car was parked neatly and not like she'd been in a hurry. He didn't see signs of anyone else being there. Nothing was on fire.

He walked to the front door and knocked, feeling like he'd gone back in time. The idea of knocking on the door where she lived was as familiar to him as his own face.

She opened the door after only a few seconds. "You're here."

"Everything okay?"

"Yeah, it's just creepier than I anticipated." She shuddered, then looked down at the dog who was faithfully by her side. "If it weren't for Timber, it would be so much worse. At least I have her. Thank you for that, by the way."

She smiled at him, and he'd have given her the dog over and over to see that smile. He nodded. "So how does the study look? What's the damage like?"

She led him through the house, which he admired as they walked, to the back corner of the house. It was the most isolated spot of the house, he noticed. Was that why it had been the target? Just because it was least likely to be caught in time? Or had there been a specific reason to start the fire in that room?

"What did the fire department say?" he asked.

"The structure is safe, if that's what you're wondering."

"No, I mean the cause of the fire. Do they know what it was yet?"

Lily nodded. "I called them back when I got here and realized they hadn't actually told me that. It was human caused. Arson."

Arson. Had the person responsible expected Lily to be home? Attempted murder? Or had it been meant as a warning?

As they entered the study, Travis tried to notice the details of his surroundings. This was a nice room, very much the kind of study he'd have imagined for Lily. The bookshelves were made of a warm medium-toned wood, packed with books. None of that appeared to be damaged, which he imagined was a relief to her. The ceiling was charred, and the logs on the outer wall had sustained smoke damage. It appeared to all be cosmetic, they'd caught it in time, but it wasn't pretty.

"Nothing is too bad besides that wall."

"I noticed that, too." Lily sighed. "I put that in. Well, me and Matt."

"Yeah?" He didn't love thinking about her with another man, but he was still curious about the details of her life and besides, he couldn't guarantee that didn't have something to do with the case.

"Yeah, I really wanted some traditional kinds of details in here and fell in love with these log accent walls. They're hollow, so they're not as heavy as regular logs. They're wood but not entirely natural, I think? I don't know, Matt found them online, and I loved them."

"Did he spend a lot of time here?"

"He didn't live here, if that's what you're asking me not so subtly. Honestly, Travis, just because I started to think maybe God didn't care about every single detail doesn't mean I abandoned absolutely everything I was taught."

Her exasperated look couldn't dim the relief he felt at hearing that. It wouldn't have changed his feelings for her, but he'd hated to consider that she and Matt may have lived together. Lily deserved to be treated better than that, for one thing. For another, she was right, they had been taught differently.

"He wanted to," she finally admitted. "But I wasn't comfortable taking things that far, in any capacity. But he did hang out here a good bit, and like I said, we spent some time renovating this room, putting a backsplash in the kitchen, just general stuff like that to make it look better. Personalize it a bit."

"You must really like the house."

Lily shrugged. "I do. But I could move. It's been a good house, but it's pretty isolated. I'm seeing how that can be a bad thing."

Her lack of neighbors was somewhat concerning. Set on the side of a mountain, it was a fantastic retreat for solitude. But there was no one really close enough to know if Lily needed help, which was part of Travis's hesitation about leaving her alone.

"Do you have someone in mind to do the work for you?" he asked.

"Yeah, I called a contractor already, someone Hannah from work used in the past. He's supposed to come tomorrow."

Travis nodded. "Good."

The conversation lulled. Travis's mind was packed full of details about the case, Timber's strange behavior, his realization someone he knew personally had to be involved... So many questions.

"So...do you need to go right away?" she asked. "Or we could try to sort more things out? I'm assuming you have that case file of Matt's somewhere? I feel like you've rarely been without it."

Her voice was teasing, but he could tell that the heaviness of the day and the entire situation was starting to weigh on her as well.

"I can stay for a while." He didn't have any other plans for the night. His only current issue was not wanting to leave her alone, but he'd called the police department to confirm that they'd be upping patrols in the area for the time being. That was going to have to be good enough.

"We could eat first? I've got frozen pizza. I know that's not quite the same as the home-cooked meals you keep feeding me."

"It's good enough."

They headed into the kitchen, as Travis wrestled with how much he should tell her. He only had suspicions. Part of him didn't want to pass those on to her when they left him feeling so discouraged. But if it were him, he'd want to know absolutely everything he could about the situation.

As Lily preheated the oven, he decided it was better to tell her some of his thoughts, even though they were incomplete, than not.

"I'm convinced at this point that someone from the police department was involved." There was no cushioning the words. He felt the impact they had on her.

"What?" She shook her head as though clearing her mind. "I heard you. And I've heard you mention it as a possibility but I dismissed it I guess. I just can't... So you think someone who knew Matt—" she frowned "—set him up?"

He hadn't gotten that far into the tangle of this yet, but yeah, that was all that made sense.

"I want to find whoever this is. Really badly." Lily's face darkened. Abruptly, she reached into the pantry and handed him two paper plates from a stack. "Set these on the table for me?"

Once the pizza came out of the oven, they were quiet for a while as they sat down and started to eat.

"Maybe we should make a list of all the names who were even sort of connected to Matt's death," Lily said at last. "Ignore motive for now since there's not a single motive involving me that makes sense."

Travis nodded. It was a good idea and something he'd already planned to do tonight. "I think we should."

Once dinner was finished, they headed into the living room. She pulled out a piece of paper, took a deep breath and handed it to Travis.

More than anything since Matt's death, this was going to hurt. He didn't want to consider that someone he knew could be capable of murder, but he didn't see any other explanation.

"Ready?" he asked Lily, and she nodded.

He picked up his pen and started to write.

Chapter Thirteen

"I guess Officer Knox should be on there." Travis said aloud as he wrote the name down. "Though, frankly, I can't see it."

Lily didn't think that meant much of anything. It was awful to contemplate anyone doing what the person behind all this had done, much less someone Travis was acquainted with. "Can you imagine anyone you know being involved?"

"No." He shook his head. "Definitely not."

"So just write the names. Everyone connected to the case. Who else?"

"Me. Matt."

Lily made a face. "I think we can safely rule the two of you out."

"I'm just writing anyone with any connection at all. We qualify." He wrote those names and then looked back up at her, as though waiting for her agreement.

"I mean, I guess."

He wrote for another minute or two, adding names aloud, but none of them meant anything to her.

"More people from the police department?" she asked.

"Mostly. A couple search-and-rescue workers, though that seems far-fetched with Timber behaving in such a strange way at the inlet today. It seems more likely it's someone who was directly involved with the investigation."

"How do you think she was reacting?" Lily asked. "I mean, I could tell she was acting strange, but what are your thoughts on it?"

"For one thing, I think she was confused. I don't know what about, but a lot of her behavior reads to me as confusion. Her mixed signals, alerting but only partially or incorrectly… Something isn't making sense to her about all this."

Lily reached down to pet her. "I get that, girl." She looked up at Travis. "Okay, what else?"

"She acted like she *wanted* to alert to something. Whatever scent she was catching, she seemed really interested in it."

"Should we take her back there?" Lily was still petting her, but Timber hadn't looked up. She seemed exhausted.

"I don't think so. Not anytime soon, anyway. She's too shaken up."

Travis fell silent then, and much as Lily had hoped they could brainstorm more, she felt like maybe she'd hit a wall for tonight. "Want to give it up for now?" she asked him.

"And do what instead?"

She shrugged. "You can head home if you want. I'm probably okay here." She did her best to ignore the fluttering in her stomach. Overactive nerves, nothing she needed to pay attention to.

"I'd rather stick around a bit longer, if that's okay."

"Watch a movie?" she offered, reaching for the remote control. They'd loved watching movies together back in the day, especially old John Wayne movies no one else had ever heard of.

The grin on his face warmed her inside. "Sounds good."

As they set up the movie and started to watch, Lily felt her shoulders relax for the first time all day. She was back home. The damage from the fire was bad, but not something she couldn't handle. She had a friend…

Her eyes went to Travis.

She'd insisted earlier that was all they could be, friends, and Travis hadn't argued with her. But Lily was second-guessing herself now. Sure, she still had many things left on her list to accomplish, but did she really want to risk losing him from her life again?

As they watched the movie, the thoughts danced in her mind, twisted and tangled. Maybe that was why almost without thinking, she reached over and took his hand.

The touch of his skin against hers startled her even though she was the one who had initiated it. It was as though being connected even in such a small way, holding his hand, was reminding her how much she cared about him. How much she loved...

How much she loved him?

She'd loved him once, she tried to tell herself, but that didn't mean she loved him now.

Even though he came the second she'd called him. Even though he didn't push her at all and put others above himself and always had, the entire time she'd known him.

Lily's heart beat faster, and she found herself paying less and less attention to the movie and more to Travis's hand. He'd shifted so it was enveloping hers. He was so solid and dependable, but if those were the only qualities she cared about, she had Timber, too. But he was giving and intentionally put her above himself.

Her reasons for breaking up with him seemed thinner and thinner.

"Travis..." She looked up from his hand—their hands— to meet his eyes. She tried to figure out what he was thinking. Should she wait for some kind of clearer indications of his feelings? But it hardly felt like a time for playing it safe, with danger surrounding them. This one moment of quiet in the midst of it all might be their only chance to be like this.

Lily didn't break eye contact. At the moment she was fully

aware of the fact that she'd been the one to break the kiss the last time, she'd been the one to apologize for it, and yet she was the one who was seriously contemplating a repeat.

When she moved toward him, he didn't back up. Slowly, she let her eyes go to his lips, then looked back up at him. "Remember how we used to just sit and talk?"

He laughed softly. "Yeah, we talked for hours."

"I miss that."

This time, Lily was pretty sure he was the one who moved closer.

"You know how I said earlier we should be just friends?" she asked. "I don't know anymore."

"What do you mean?"

"I mean... I think I want to kiss you."

She moved her lips within a breath of his, swallowed hard and waited.

He didn't move.

Lily kissed him gently. Fully. Slowly.

When he pulled away, she started talking. "What do you think, Travis? I know I said let's be friends, but... I mean, do you think you could even forgive me for...everything?"

"I forgave you years ago," he said, his voice barely louder than a whisper. Lily closed the distance between them even more. Their noses were almost touching. "But..."

Something was holding him back. She'd been able to tell even in the kiss. For once, she felt like she might be ready to really take a risk. She'd thought her list was risky, brave, adventurous. But maybe sometimes just living normal life was the real adventure.

"What is it?" she asked, half afraid to breathe as she waited for his answer.

"You didn't want this. Friends, remember?"

She looked away for half a second, then looked back at him. "What if I've changed my mind?"

She waited for his answer for what seemed like minutes.

"I just…" He moved away from her and stood up. "Let me think, Lily. I don't want to hurt you. I don't want anyone to get hurt."

"But I won't… I'm not…"

"It's late. Can we talk about it tomorrow?"

She felt her eyes sting, but she blinked the tears away and nodded. He wasn't asking for anything unreasonable. The logical side of her knew he was right, it was late. It was understandable that he didn't want to say anything or commit to anything that he might regret in the future.

So why did it still feel suspiciously like rejection?

"Sure." Lily stood, too, and walked toward the door to see him out. "No problem. I'll, uh, see you tomorrow after work?"

"Sounds like a plan. I'll work on figuring out how we can best spend our time and what we need to focus on."

Lily nodded along with him, barely hearing what he said, desperate for the night to end so they could just start over on less awkward footing tomorrow.

He told her good night and walked outside, and she locked the door behind him.

Lily knew that he hadn't said anything definite, but she was pretty sure she knew his answer. She'd had her chance. And Travis wasn't taking another one on a relationship with her again.

Nothing was going to help him sleep tonight.

First, Travis had paced the floor of his house, suddenly understanding why fictional characters in movies liked to pace so much. There was something about it that made him feel slightly better, but it didn't come close to untangling his mind.

The case had to remain his top focus. He was worried that he was going to get Lily hurt, or worse, if he let himself be distracted by anything and that included a relationship with her. At the same time, he knew that her admission tonight had cost her. Her eyes had shone with something—he didn't dare call it love, that seemed too optimistic—maybe vulnerability? Then they'd flickered with some kind of hurt when he left without much explanation. But he hadn't wanted to get any more carried away by the trip down memory lane.

He liked her. More than liked her, he loved her. He had for years, and that wasn't going to change now.

He just wasn't sure about the timing. More than he wanted to see the two of them back together, he wanted them safe. His responsibility was to keep her safe more than anything else.

He walked into his kitchen and went through the motions of making himself a cup of coffee. He had just poured it when he heard a noise in the yard. He crept to the window and looked outside into the dimness. It wasn't yet dark enough to take away visibility. Was that…someone near his cabin? Creeping around in the dark?

There was no other explanation. He started to the door, then stopped, realizing he didn't have any kind of weapon on him. Tracking the intruder without one would be foolish and dangerous. He hurried to his bedroom, opened his gun safe and pulled out his handgun. He grabbed a gun belt with a holster already on it and fastened it quickly.

He opened the door slowly, making almost no noise. But getting the gun had taken some time, and he didn't have a visual on the intruder anymore.

The temperature had dropped since he'd gotten home. He shivered in the nighttime chill as he moved softly in the direction of the guest cabin.

Did whoever it was know that Lily wasn't there anymore? Or had her attacker come back to try to finish what he'd started the other day?

Even though Lily should be safely in her own house, dread sank into the pit of his stomach anyway. The situation was truly desperate, the threat against Lily terribly real. It frustrated him that no matter how hard he tried to get away from the sometimes oppressive lack of hope in police work—the uncertainty, anxiety and reminders of the darkness in the world—he'd been pulled back in.

Was ignoring it the answer? Should he continue working with his brother? Or was it time to go back?

Strange that this was the second time that question had crossed his mind in as many days. He didn't quite know what to do with that. Even if he was supposed to go back, he'd have preferred to figure it out in some way other than Lily facing danger. He didn't want her hurt, and he was terrified that he was going to mess up.

Right now, though, she wasn't here. And the situation in front of him had to be dealt with. One hand on his weapon, he moved toward the front door of the empty cabin.

Walking into the darkened cabin felt like going back in time several years, but he took only a second or two to let his eyes adjust before he kept moving forward. Standing still could be deadly in situations like this; hesitation could kill.

Although, so could crashing into something you weren't entirely prepared for.

His ears registered the sound of movement just as something slammed into his shoulders, missing his head only by inches. Desperately trying to remember everything he'd ever learned about hand-to-hand combat, he fought back.

The man was strong, Travis noticed immediately. He'd thought when the man bested him last time that it was just because he hadn't been paying enough attention, but he was just flat-out outmuscled.

But he wasn't giving up. He punched and blocked to the best of his ability.

Then, as quickly as the man had appeared, he turned tail and ran.

Travis blinked for half a second. Why had he sprinted away in the middle of the fight? He sprinted after the man, but when he reached the front yard, he was gone. Again.

Travis kicked the ground. He moved slowly around the

cabin, his eyes open, guard up. No sign of the attacker. The ground didn't yield anything trackable.

Why had he come here? To target Lily? Had he just not noticed she wasn't here? Travis was surprised. It had seemed like whoever was after her was better at tracking her movements than that.

Or had the man been looking for something? But what could it be? Even Lily seemed not to know why she was in this situation, so figuring out what she may or may not have would be difficult.

Catching his breath and doing his best to bring his heart rate back to a normal level, Travis walked back to his house. The night had grown even darker, but his senses were sharp and ready to spot trouble at the first sign. However, all was quiet as he headed back into the house and locked the door behind him.

He'd been in such a hurry earlier that he hadn't locked his own door. While he doubted that the man was waiting for him when he'd been in such a hurry to get away, Travis planned to be careful. Methodically, he cleared every room in the house.

Nothing. No sign of any intruder.

Travis went back to his coffee on the counter. Cold. Which made sense. He dumped it out, made himself another cup, then walked to his bedroom, set the coffee on the bedside table and eyed the bed. He couldn't see himself sleeping anytime soon. Instead, he moved to the chair in the corner and sat, sipping at his coffee.

Should he call Lily?

What was the point? She knew someone was after her. What had happened here tonight didn't directly affect her at this moment, he didn't think. Besides, Travis couldn't imagine that she was having any more luck getting to sleep and hated to be the reason she lost any more.

He took a deep breath and tried to relax. It was over, at least for tonight. The chances of anything else happening were slim. Their attacker would need to regroup, replan.

He took another sip of coffee, felt himself start to nod off and didn't try to keep himself awake.

Chapter Fourteen

The stillness of the night was too quiet for Lily to have any sort of peace. Maybe it was the chemistry between her and Travis earlier, then his subsequent semi-rejection and her mind's confusion about that whole situation. Or maybe it was because, much as she tried to put on a brave face, the idea of staying somewhere entirely alone when someone still wanted her dead was overwhelming and scary.

Should she have gone back to Travis's guest cabin? It was probably too late for that now. Maybe not? She could call him, and he'd probably answer. He always did, didn't he?

All the more reason she should tough it out, at least for tonight. She'd inconvenienced him enough.

Lily turned over on her pillow and opened her eyes. Outside it was dark, so it had to be around two in the morning. There weren't many hours this time of year when the world was fully dark outside.

She could do this. She could fall asleep and wake up in a few hours and sort out all the things going on in her life that weren't going well.

Something inside her whispered that it would be easier if she let God help her work things out, but she resisted it. She didn't need God like that anymore, did she? Matt had been sure she didn't.

Then again, Matt wasn't here.

Travis was just as independent, proud and capable as Matt, if not more—though thinking that felt slightly disloyal. Yet he believed that he needed God every day, all the time.

It was more than Lily could sort out right now.

She closed her eyes and willed herself to sleep.

When she opened her eyes again, the world outside was slightly lighter with hints of dawn creeping across the Alaskan sky. Lily relaxed and blew out a breath. Today she'd talk to Travis and tell him she was willing to look into other accommodations. It didn't have to be his guest cabin, but being alone seemed like a terrible idea. Last night wasn't one she wanted to experience again.

Strongly, she felt colder than she had earlier. Lily patted the bed beside her, where Timber always slept. Nothing.

Where was Timber?

Doing her best not to panic, Lily sat straight up in bed and blinked until it felt like sleep had absolutely no hold on her. She swung her legs over the side of the bed and slid into her slippers, partially for warmth and partially to muffle the noise of her movement. She grabbed her phone from the bedside table, though she didn't text Travis. She was tired of bothering him. Timber had probably wandered off to get some water, or maybe patrol the house.

Although it was unusual for her to do either. Typically Timber came to bed with her, got up maybe once right at the start of the night to do a lap around the house, then slept soundly. Lily didn't know what to think about the dog not being there when she woke, but it didn't seem good.

Heart pounding, Lily waited for her eyes to adjust to the nearly dark room—some light was making its way in through the window now but the sky outside was still a dark early morning blue. Not nearly enough light to actually see by. But enough to know for sure that Timber wasn't anywhere in this room. Lily felt her breathing quickening even as she tried to find more logical reasons for Timber to be gone than the one that haunted her brain.

What if someone was in the house? What if Timber had gone after them?

What if something had happened to Timber?

The what-ifs tormented her as she walked into her bathroom. No Timber there, either. Taking a deep breath, she moved toward the bedroom door, then hesitated. She pulled out her phone and sent a quick text to Travis.

Sorry to wake you. Something weird is going on, I can't find Timber. Maybe it's fine? I feel silly texting.

Lily hesitated before pressing Send, but finally hit it. Maybe he wouldn't notice. Or maybe he'd come right over, which was something she wanted more than she was willing to admit. She moved to the door of her bedroom and eased it open.

Walking out in the main area of the house took more courage than anything Lily had attempted in a while. The living room had fewer windows than her room, and she could barely see. After a minute of struggling against the darkness, she stopped. She would do what she'd seen Timber do many times and just listen. Maybe she'd hear something she wouldn't otherwise.

Freezing in place, Lily waited. Her ears didn't tell her anything, though. There was just silence.

Which actually did tell her something. Something was wrong with Timber.

Lily's imagination sped up, running over all the awful situations the dog could have found herself in. Surely someone wouldn't have…

It took every ounce of self-restraint she had not to yell out Timber's name as panic rose within her. Lily was wide awake now, and she moved through the living room, doing her best to scan every piece of furniture, every inch of floor.

She shivered, anxiety chilling her, then stopped in the middle of the room. She looked to the left, toward the front door.

It was standing wide open. And on the floor in front of the door was Timber, lying still in the moonlight.

Lily almost screamed, so great was her horror, but she knew if anyone was still in the house it would alert them to her location.

Rather than search the other rooms, she hurried to Timber's side, placed a hand on her soft fur and waited. Seconds passed. Then—

Up. Down. Up. Down.

She was breathing. She was alive.

Relief wrestled with panic as Lily worked to shove her hands under the dog's heavy body. She pulled Timber close to her chest and moved toward the bedroom, pulling the door shut behind her, latching it and locking it as quietly as she could.

Her heart was still pounding. Someone was in her house. Someone had hurt her dog.

She called 911, explained the situation to them, then called Travis, who didn't answer. She left a voicemail, trying to stay calm.

And then Lily sat on the bed beside her dog and waited.

As she sat, the urge to pray seemed to well up inside her until she couldn't ignore it anymore.

Had she prayed at any time lately? Or had it been years? She couldn't even remember anymore. All she knew was that more than anything right now, she wanted to know that Travis was right, that God really would show up and help.

I feel like I might have messed up. I don't know, God, who is right and who isn't between Travis and Matt, but if Travis is right, and You do actually care, please save my dog. I don't deserve it or anything, but I don't want her to die. I want her to be safe and me, too.

She squeezed her eyes shut to stop the tears that were threatening to come. Somehow she knew, though she hadn't been sure only minutes before, that God had heard her. Travis was right. She thought. Wasn't he?

As she sat on the bed, petting Timber and waiting, she kept praying, kept listening. She didn't hear anything.

But someone had clearly been in her house.

Why? They'd poisoned Timber, most likely. She was no investigator, but it seemed pretty obvious that Timber had been incapacitated somehow. But she'd have expected that whoever it was would come after her, take advantage of the fact that she was sleeping and kill her.

But they hadn't. Why?

A soft knock at her bedroom door startled her enough that she jumped. Then Lily felt for Timber's ribs again, confirmed that she was breathing and walked to the door. Her hand was on the knob, about to unlock it, when she froze.

Was this Travis coming to help? Or had the intruder come to finish the job?

Speaking of breaking in, how had the door been opened? She hadn't noticed any damage, but she hadn't investigated closely because she was focused on Timber.

Deciding that the risk was worth it, she eased the door open and met Travis's eyes through the crack in the door.

Something inside her broke.

But in a good way, like it needed to be broken.

Tears streamed down her face for the first time that night, and Lily cried, something in her feeling like she finally could. As though because Travis was here, she didn't have to be strong for Timber anymore.

If Timber even knew she was here. The dog seemed entirely unconscious.

"I'm so glad you're here," she said, wiping a tear from her face that somehow didn't embarrass her. Matt had made her feel bad for her tears, for any kind of large show of emotion really, but with Travis she could just be herself. She could feel how she felt.

"What's wrong?" Travis asked in a rush. "What happened?"

"Didn't you see the door?"

"What about it?"

"It was wide open, someone... I guess someone was in the house?"

Travis hesitated. "It was closed. The door was closed."

Lily blinked. She was sure she hadn't imagined the door being open. She'd seen Timber on the floor in the moonlight. And Timber was unconscious on the bed right now, which proved that she hadn't made it all up.

"I believe you, I mean," Travis clarified quickly, which she appreciated. "But it was shut."

"So either someone left or wants us to think they did."

"One of those probably. Strange." He frowned. "And Timber? What's wrong? Wait, she's not..."

His voice trailed off, and Lily reached for his hand without thinking. She squeezed it quickly before letting it drop. "She's alive. But I don't know what's wrong."

Travis walked over and examined Timber, opening her mouth and looking at her gums. He turned back to Lily. "I think she's going to be okay. She seems drugged? Honestly she seems like she's been given a sedative. This is exactly how they described it in one of the trainings we had."

Lily nodded, though her face pinched into a frown. "How long until she wakes up? Should we take her to the vet?"

It was so easy to include him in her decision-making processes. It felt right.

"I think she'll be okay. Let's give it a little time." He ran his hand along the length of Timber's body, then looked up at Lily. "Someone probably drugged her so they could get in without worrying about her."

It gave more weight to their idea that it was some type of first responder involved in Matt's case.

Lily felt a heaviness settle over her. Even though they had no other leads, it felt wrong that someone who had worked with Matt could be trying to kill her now.

They had to solve this. For her own peace of mind, they had to.

Lily didn't look like she'd slept. Of course, he could hardly blame her. The amount of stress they were both under, with the case and trying to figure out...well, whatever they were trying to figure out about the two of them.

Timber had started to stir not long after he'd told Lily his suspicions about her having been sedated. They offered her some water, which she accepted gratefully. Still, he thought it was a better idea that she rest. So Timber was locked in Lily's bedroom while he and Lily took a look around the house to see what had been disturbed.

He should have let Lily know about the intruder breaking into his house. Clearly he'd been bent on finding something, whether it was Lily or something he thought she had.

"Do you have any idea of anything he could be after?" Travis asked her. "Some kind of object, or evidence from the case..."

"You said it was a narcotics case, right?" She turned to him with raised eyebrows. "Since I don't have any narcotics, I'm going to have to go with no on that one."

He smiled a little at her attempt at middle-of-the-night humor, but persisted, "Seriously, anything you can think of, no matter how weird it sounds. Anything related to the case, Matt, anything."

"You think Matt himself could be the reason I'm a target, not just the case?"

Travis truly didn't know. He was grasping at straws at this point, but there just wasn't time to waste doing anything else. Every moment that passed with them walking around in the dark like this was another moment with Lily in danger. That was unacceptable.

"I think anything you have that's related to Matt is worth investigating," Travis said at last.

It felt odd to talk about Matt, especially Lily's relationship with him, but it was possible that something between them had value to the narcotics gang. Wasn't it?

Nothing made sense.

Lily moved through the house, commenting on little things here and there. Matt had given her that bench, they bought it from someone in the area who made furniture out of Sitka spruce, did that count? Travis thought no, though it was a nice bench. But the chance that someone had broken into her house in the middle of the night to get it were slim.

The truth was that Lily shouldn't be a target. Her house was meticulously organized, there were no unkempt piles of paper anywhere that could hide useful documents and she didn't have any of Matt's personal belongings since they'd never been married, and he'd had his own house. Who knew what had become of those after his death.

Finally, they made their way into the study.

"I don't think Matt gave me anything in here. Except labor, I mean. Lots of labor."

"He put the logs up, you said?" Travis nodded to the accent wall with its heavy fire damage.

"Yes," she affirmed. "And built in the bookshelves. We spent the most time in here, probably. I'd read a book, and he'd work."

"Work?" Travis frowned. Most police work, even paperwork, was done at the department itself. It wasn't something that got taken home.

"Like I said, that undercover case seemed to keep him pretty busy."

Something still felt odd about that, but Travis wasn't sure if it was just the fact that undercover cases always left something of a bad taste. Deception never felt good, even when it was for a good cause.

Or maybe there was a reason that thought made him uncomfortable. How busy could Matt have been really? But with the doubt, there was once again the uncomfortable feeling that he shouldn't go looking too deeply into a dead man's secrets. Especially when he was falling for his ex-fiancée. It felt petty.

"This room." Lily stopped. "Something is weird in here."

They searched all over. Books out of place? No, Lily said. Any furniture moved? No.

Travis saw no help for it. "Let's get Timber. If she's better, I'll have her sniff around."

Easing the door to Lily's room open, Travis tried to be quiet in case Timber was sleeping off the drugs still. If she was, he didn't want to wake her. But when he stepped inside, she wasted no time jumping up on him. She looked much better, her eyes sharp.

"You're okay, aren't you?" he asked as he petted her.

Her eyes seemed to answer *yes*.

Travis turned to Lily. "Let's bring her out and see what she notices in the house. We won't go right to the study. It could be that there's something in another room we missed, but I also don't want to bias her against a particular room."

Lily nodded and opened the bedroom door.

Travis turned to Timber. "Timber, search."

The command included anything out of the ordinary and could turn up anything from a person to hidden drugs in a normal police investigation. Travis wasn't expecting to find either of those, but it would be interesting to see what she would come up with.

Timber ran first to the front door and whined.

"That's where I found her," Lily said, anguish clear on her face. That had to have been hard.

Travis put a hand on her upper arm, and she smiled at him.

Maybe everything wasn't messed up after last night. Maybe they could figure this out after all.

Timber moved around the living room, clearly on alert but not keying in on anything. The same went for the kitchen. And the guest bathroom.

She ran to the study last. Stopped in the doorway. And whined.

The noise immediately made Travis's chest tighten with anxiety. She sounded exactly as she had the day before at the inlet where she'd seemed confused.

Even Lily seemed to notice. A frown stretched across her face, and she glanced over at Travis. "Is she doing it again?"

Timber moved into the room and sniffed with her nose in the air. She whined and looked back at Travis. It wasn't quite an alert, but it was something. More than just *something*. It was concerning and unnerving.

What smell was upsetting her so much? Why was she acting like she didn't know what she was supposed to be doing?

Her retirement had purely been for physical reasons. She'd been shot the night Matt had died and hadn't been able to go back into the field as a police K-9 because of that. Otherwise, she was fine. Her abilities, her intelligence, all of that remained unchanged.

So what was with her odd reaction?

Nothing about this felt right. And it felt entirely too much like her behavior earlier by the inlet to be coincidence.

But what did these two places have in common?

Chapter Fifteen

Lily stood in her study and watched her dog and Travis, waiting for him to explain to her what all of this meant.

"Something isn't right," Travis said at last.

That much was clear to her already. Lily threw him a look, hoping that thought was communicated.

Her cell phone rang.

"Hello?" She stepped out of the room, since Timber's whining was loud enough to be distracted on a phone call.

"Lily Peterson?"

"Yes."

"This is Officer Keller. Could you come down to the Silvertip Creek Police Department? We need to talk about some of what we found."

Lily glanced back into the study, at Timber who was still out of sorts. Was Travis right that the drugs hadn't affected her? Or should she be seen by a vet?

"Uh…" She glanced at her watch. "Okay, I'll come down. It might be a little while? You know it's only 5:00 a.m.?"

Officer Keller laughed. "Sorry. I couldn't sleep. Came in early and had news waiting." Her voice sobered. "You definitely need to come in as soon as possible."

"Okay. I'll be there soon." Lily hung up, frowning at the phone. That call made about as much sense as Timber's behavior.

She relayed the news to Travis.

"We'd better get down there then," Travis said. "That's really unusual."

Was there anything about this case that wasn't?

They called Timber out of the study and shut the door. That seemed to help, though she still seemed a little anxious even in the rest of the house.

"If I had to guess, I'd say whatever smell it is that's causing her to react that way is concentrated in the study," Travis said. "But there's enough of it in the rest of the house to make her somewhat upset."

"I guess I could see that, but what is it? Drugs?" Lily asked. It was the only thing that made even little bit of sense.

He was shaking his head. He didn't know.

She could feel his frustration and wished she could reassure him that everything was okay, but the fact was it wasn't. They both needed answers, and nothing about their situation was okay.

"Maybe whatever the police found out will help," she muttered and moved toward her bedroom. "I'm going to get dressed. I'll meet you back out here? That is, if you want to go together to the police department. I didn't mean to assume."

Travis reached out and squeezed her hand.

Lily looked down at where their hands were touching, then back up at him.

"I'm going with you," he said. He dropped her hand to motion quickly toward her bedroom. "Hurry. A phone call at five in the morning? I'm half afraid of whatever they're going to tell us."

"But it's good, right? Progress?"

"It's good," he confirmed. "Almost certainly. Any information is helpful. But I'm concerned that this early in the morning and wanting to tell you in person, whatever they've got is going to be earth-shattering."

Feeling anxious, Lily closed her bedroom door and started pulling out pieces to wear today—jeans, a long-sleeved T-shirt, a vest. The forecast called for rain today, which always cooled the temperature way down. It was amazing how cold fifty-five degrees without sunshine could be.

She hoped that whatever Travis was worried about didn't happen. He was reminding her a little of Timber right now. He seemed upset, but she didn't know if he could exactly articulate why.

Still, she was excited about whatever they might find out. Whatever it was, it had to be better than not knowing.

The drive to the police department was somewhat quiet. Lily looked out the window. Travis wondered what she was thinking about. His own stomach was churning as he drove.

"Mind if we make a quick stop?" Lily asked.

Travis shook his head. "That's fine, where to?"

"Swing into my coffee shop, if you would. I desperately need a cup of coffee and one of Hannah's cinnamon rolls."

He turned into the shop's parking lot. The Open sign was off, as he'd expected, but the lights inside were still out. "I have bad news, but I don't think your shop's open. Maybe the owner had a crazy night and isn't at work yet."

She laughed at his completely awful joke. "Maybe. But Hannah's here baking already in the back. Come on." She climbed out of the car and motioned for him to follow. Timber trotted along beside her.

They walked up to the front door, and Travis watched as Lily pulled out a key. She eased it into the door and motioned for him to go in before her. She followed, and he glanced back to make sure she locked the door behind them.

"You sure about this?" he asked. "I don't mind buying somewhere."

Lily laughed. "Seriously, what good is owning a coffee

shop if I can't go in and get coffee on what has so far been a rough morning?"

He couldn't fight her there.

Lily walked confidently through the front of the shop, flipping on a small lamp. The massive glass windows in the front were a security risk, he realized. If this dragged on for much longer, he'd want to talk to her about making her workplace less vulnerable. Or maybe talk her into taking some time off work.

Though he could imagine what the response to that would be.

"Morning, Hannah," Lily said as she walked into the kitchen. Sure enough, a woman was already back there baking.

"Good morning." Hannah barely looked up. "Cinnamon roll?"

"Please. Two."

Travis was only too happy to take the cinnamon roll that Lily offered him, and the coffee she'd made like it was nothing. "You're really good at this." She laughed off his compliment as they walked back to the car, so he tried again. "No, really. You're very good at this. You were onto something with that list."

Lily's face fell instantly, and he opened his mouth to backtrack, but she held a hand up and cut him off. "I really still feel bad. I don't think…"

He shook his head. "You had dreams, I get it. You don't have to keep apologizing."

She stopped in the parking lot, and he stopped beside her. "What if they cost me another dream?" she asked.

He didn't have to be a genius to know she was talking about them.

They were words he'd waited for years to hear, really, and hearing them hit him every bit as hard as he would have expected. But once again it was like something inside was slowing him down, telling him to wait.

He reached for her hand and squeezed it. "Let's deal with all this first."

He was ready for a happily-ever-after, but in his experience, nothing worth having came this easily.

They climbed back into the car, and Travis drove them to the police department where they parked and walked inside.

This building was much smaller than the Anchorage Police Department's impressive structure, very small town. But it was adequate for the level of crime that Silvertip Creek usually dealt with, which wasn't much.

The entry was well lit, almost friendly. Again, fitting for a town where the police were typically called on for things like search and rescue or neighborhood patrolling to discourage the occasional small crime.

A murder discovered on one of their mountain ridges wasn't typical for Silvertip Creek at all.

For half a second, Travis pictured himself working here and didn't hate the idea. Maybe police work wasn't something he had to be entirely done with after all? Just because he was done with the pace and tension of Anchorage didn't mean that he had to be done entirely, did it?

Officer Keller met them in the lobby, looking relieved. "Thanks for coming down," she said immediately, then seemed to eye Lily carefully. "We have something we need to talk about."

Lily nodded. "No problem."

Travis didn't like the way Officer Keller seemed so cautious around Lily. Again, the sense of foreboding he'd had earlier haunted the edges of his mind. What had the police discovered?

"We have results back from the note and key you found at the scene," Officer Keller said at last. "We found the fingerprints of several men on it. One is Arnold Harris, the man you found on the ridgeline."

Lily looked over at him, and Travis fill in the other blanks. "The man accused of killing Matt that night."

Officer Keller cleared her throat. "And…well, Matt."

"Matt Davis?" Travis clarified. "The police officer?" He glanced at Lily. "So Arnold had that note for…"

Officer Keller was already shaking her head. The uncomfortable pit in Travis's stomach deepened.

"We investigated the murder scene on Avalanche Peak carefully," she said. "We were able to find the murder weapon and run prints on it, too." Her gaze shifted between Lily and Travis and back again. And then she said the words that Travis had been dreading and yet somehow expecting ever since Timber began acting strangely at the inlet.

"The prints on the murder weapon—which was a knife— also belong to Matt Davis."

Silence had never felt so violently loud.

Travis didn't know whether to reach for Lily's hand or give her a minute. The expressions crossing her face told him the words were still sinking in. Being rejected. Denied.

"Wait, but Matt… He's dead," Lily said at last. "He was an officer, but he's…"

"He's not dead." Officer Keller didn't sugarcoat the words at all, and they fell on the room with the gentleness of an anvil. "And he is now wanted for the murder of Arnold Harris."

He is now wanted for the murder of Arnold Harris.

The words echoed in Lily's mind, which seemed empty of all else. Matt wasn't dead. Matt was alive. Matt was a killer.

Every terrifying moment she'd experienced over the last few days shifted and darkened with new perspective. The man in her house? Matt.

Shooting at her in the woods? Matt.

The man who'd created the gruesome scene she'd stumbled onto on the mountain ridge, who had tried to push her off the mountain, who had burned part of her house?

Matt?

A wave of nausea crashed into her, and she reached her arms out, feeling for a wall, Travis's arm, a chair, anything that could steady her. Although was there anything that could steady someone who had been caught so off guard?

Travis' arms were around her, bracing, gentle. But her panic went too deep.

"I need a minute," she was able to say at last. She looked up at Travis, whose face spoke of something very much like pity. Maybe it was just kindness.

She'd thought it was bad before, having people think of her as the woman who had lost her fiancé in the line of duty. Now that life, that identity, was nothing more than a lie.

Matt's lie, which she had bought.

Matt, a killer?

The news seemed too strange to be true. She'd seen him be harsh to others, though Matt was nice to her, but still, a killer? She'd never have agreed to marry someone she could think capable of that.

The memory of the bloodstained ground around Arnold's body on the mountain ridge made her chest feel tight.

"I don't understand," she gasped.

"We don't, either," Officer Keller spoke up. "That's all we know. Usually this is the kind of thing we wouldn't release immediately to the public, but you both need to be aware as it changes how you act."

Both Travis and Lily looked at Timber.

"That's why she was acting so strange," Travis said.

"She smelled Matt." Lily shook her head. It was too much. She didn't even know what to think, what to feel. Her immediate instinct was to never trust her instincts again—hadn't she almost ended up married to a murderer?

Why had he wanted to marry her anyway? Surely he hadn't really loved her, not if he was willing to kill her now that... now that what? She was in his way somehow?

"Our working assumption is that Matt must have been involved in the narcotics case beyond his official duties," Officer Keller explained. "I've got a call in to Officer Knox at APD, but he's not in the office yet."

Well, it was 6:00 a.m. That seemed logical. How much longer would they have to wait? This changed everything, she was sure. Lily was not going to work today, that was clear. They had to be close. They knew who was after her now, and while the situation was even more dangerous, it had to put them closer to finding him and stopping him.

Didn't it?

But Officer Keller's next statement urged caution. "This could last days, weeks, longer. The man has been presumed dead for a year, and somehow gotten away with it. He knows how to hide."

Lily looked at Travis. "My house. The logs. What if he hid something there?"

It seemed plausible enough. Quickly, all three of them headed for the parking lot, where Officer Keller got in a squad car and followed Travis and Lily back to Lily's place.

Her house looked different to her now. It was as if the knowledge that a killer had helped her renovate it, had spent time there, robbed it of its peacefulness.

Taking deep breath, bracing herself even though technically nothing had changed, Lily walked through the front door.

At her feet, Timber whined slightly, and compassion for her flooded Lily. How was Timber supposed to reconcile the fact that she smelled an intruder with the fact that the smell belonged to her former handler? Lily reached down and petted Timber.

The German shepherd looked up at her appreciatively.

"You're such a good dog," Lily said with all her heart. One good thing had come out of Matt's deep deception—Timber belonged to her now and couldn't be taken away.

"You said the K-9 alerted in the study?" Officer Keller asked Travis.

He nodded. "Yes. And Lily had mentioned that the log wall was installed by Matt. Chances are good he hid something there." He trailed off at the end. "Could it be whatever had been dug up at the inlet, where Timber started acting strangely?"

Lily's eyes widened as she realized exactly what Travis meant. "What if both men were after whatever was buried there? Otherwise why would Arnold and Matt both have been on that ridge?"

Officer Keller looked surprised, but Travis just looked impressed.

"Let's take a look at the logs first," Officer Keller suggested at last. "Let's see what we've got." She led the way into the study.

It hit harder emotionally to be in a room that had once symbolized so much happiness between Lily and Matt. She glanced down at Timber; the dog was still clearly confused. How would she react around Matt if he did ever see them in person again? Would Timber actually attack someone she'd once worked with? Or would Lily no longer be able to count on her to help protect her? She wasn't sure.

Lily watched as Travis bent down and talked to Timber. She couldn't quite hear what he was saying, but he ran though several exercises with her, having her sit, spin, run under his legs, lie down. After a few minutes, she'd noticeably settled down.

"Now let's see what she can find," he said, and Timber started to sniff.

They watched, waiting for what she would discover.

Chapter Sixteen

"There. She's alerting."

Timber was pawing at one of the logs in the wall that had been damaged by the fire. It was a few logs up from the bottom on the right side of the wall, and looked exactly like all the others.

"What is she alerting on?" Lily asked.

Lily spoke as if she was in a sort of trance. It had to be surreal to learn that Matt was still alive and a criminal all in one instant.

"Not sure." Travis knocked against the log Timber was focused on. It sounded hollow, but Lily had said they all were. He frowned. If something was stored in it, wouldn't it sound less hollow? He knocked slowly, over and over, down the length of the log. Then finally came to a spot that sounded slightly different.

He could tell as he looked around at Lily and then Officer Keller that they'd all heard it.

"Do you mind if I cut it open?" he asked Lily. "I could be wrong…"

"This room has to be redone anyway because of the fire." Her face was tight, her eyes anxious. "Yes. Just cut it."

It took a few minutes to find the right tool for the job, but Travis emerged from Lily's small garage with a saw after a few minutes. Without fanfare, he started to saw into the log.

Slowly, sawdust piled up on the floor. Travis's arms started to burn with the effort, which was mildly embarrassing.

The wood finally cracked. He stopped sawing and wiped sweat from his forehead with the back of his arm.

"Keep going." Lily was staring at the log, fixated.

He understood. Whatever they were about to find might finally hold some answers, answers she'd wanted for over a year now, though she hadn't known exactly what questions to ask.

Travis knew when this was all over, it would hit him hard that a brother in arms had gone bad like that. He liked to pretend it never happened, that everyone who entered the profession was honorable and true, but people were people in every job. Always some bad apples.

This one just seemed a bit more rotten than usual.

As the wood cracked, Travis poked at it with his fingers, trying to pry the gap wider. If this was why Matt had been in Lily's study, it was no wonder he hadn't gotten whatever was in here out yet. It wasn't a quick job or a quiet one. Maybe that had been the purpose of the fire, to destroy this wall...

In that case, whatever Matt was after should be in a fireproof safe.

The wood splintered against his hand as he jammed it in with too much force. Still not enough room, and not enough leverage to snap it. Wincing, Travis pulled his hand back out. "Almost there." He continued to saw.

Finally, he shoved his hand into the gap, at first feeling nothing but empty space.

Lily and Officer Keller were both watching, neither speaking. He felt their anticipation, the hope that this wasn't just leading to dead ends and more questions.

His fingertips hit something cold. Hard. A metal box.

Just like he'd expected.

Reaching his arm even farther in, he managed to wrap his fingers around the box and pull it toward him. He dragged it to the opening, which wasn't nearly large enough.

"You don't have a sledgehammer, do you?" he asked Lily.

"What is it?" Officer Keller asked eagerly.

"A box."

She nodded. "I'm calling Officer Knox from Anchorage on his cell. He needs to be here."

Travis agreed, tugging his hand out of the wall. He turned his attention to enlarging the opening in the wood enough to get the box out. After a few minutes of wrestling, jamming and sawing, he tugged it out and set it on the floor.

It wasn't large, probably five by eleven inches, maybe slightly bigger. And it was locked.

"The key!" Lily said.

Officer Keller pulled a bag out of her pocket. Travis raised his eyebrows and she shrugged. "I brought it just in case."

Wearing a pair of gloves, she slid it out of the bag and into the safe's lock. It opened without a fight, smooth and easy.

Inside were stacks of papers, folded in half so they'd fit. Newspaper clippings, handwritten sticky notes. Financial statements for Weatherby Enterprises, a company in Anchorage they'd suspected might have ties to the narcotics ring.

He scanned through the statements, finding several lines that would account for illegal activities. Other lines caught his eye also.

"Davis Consulting."

Lily met his eyes. "Matt? Do you… I guess you usually don't get paid by the gangs in undercover ops." She reached for the statement, and Travis handed it to her.

"Maybe." He shrugged. "But we put the funds in a dummy account that the department can access, never in someone's actual personal account, and these—" he ruffled through the papers "—appear to be Matt's statements."

Scrawled on them in someone's rough handwriting were

notes about Matt's guilt—lists, dates, *evidence* that Matt wasn't who they thought he was.

"Someone else wrote these," Travis said.

"Yeah. But he's dead now."

The voice behind them was one Travis hadn't heard in a year.

He used to think of the voice as confident, useful to have with you in tight situations. Matt had never seemed scared of anything, and his confidence had always been inspiring.

Now Travis just heard coldness.

"I'm going to need that," Matt went on calmly.

Timber whined.

Officer Keller pulled her weapon, but Matt pulled his faster. He shot her, hitting her arm. She cried out and fell to the ground.

Lily yanked off her vest and knelt down, immediately pressing it against Officer Keller's wound. She stuffed something into her pocket, too, though Travis wasn't sure what.

Wait, she had one of the papers from the safe! A small amount of relief flooded through him.

Travis's heart pounded as he reached for the sidearm he knew was no longer in his holster. He'd had to remove it before going inside the police department and left it in his car. He was completely unprepared.

They all were.

If Lily had thought she'd feel more pain when she saw Matt's face again, she'd been wrong. Surely there would be a variety of emotions to deal with later, but right now all she felt was disgust. Anger.

His voice was cold and hard, and his eyes barely flickered when she turned and met his gaze. Who even was this man whose appearance she recognized, but whose actions didn't line up with the man she thought she'd known?

"You're not getting any of this." She looked up at him from

where she knelt next to Officer Keller, who was mostly unconscious. Lily tried to say the words with more firmness
than she felt.

Inside, she was shaking. They didn't have a plan from here.

Travis had noticed that something had been taken from the
scene near the inlet. And now there was evidence hidden here
in her house. Why had Arnold and Matt been up on Avalanche
Peak? Was something hidden there also?

Her gut said yes, though it was likely Matt had retrieved
it by now.

What was their best option? She wanted to talk to Travis,
but there was no time. It surprised her how much she cared
about his input.

That had been another stark difference between the two
men, she realized now, looking at Matt's cold eyes. Travis
listened to her, talked to her, communicated with her. Matt
had just told her what to do. She'd not fully seen the difference until now.

But neither man could help her now. Matt was against her.
Travis was stuck in the situation with her.

Her eyes darted to Timber.

"Don't even think about trying to turn her against me. It's
basically impossible. Besides—" he patted the gun he'd put
back on his hip in a slow, threatening way "—I don't want to
shoot her, but I will."

"You poisoned Timber," Lily said suddenly. Of course she
knew the dog had been given something to knock her out, but
it hit so much harder realizing that someone Timber trusted
had done that to her.

"It's hardly poison." He rolled his eyes. "I could have hurt
her if I wanted to."

She supposed he was right, though it was hardly reassuring. Lily felt sick, every part of her feeling betrayed. Not hurt
like she would have expected, though. It turned out any kind
of connection she'd had with Matt that could hurt her on a

deeper, more personal level had been severed. If not with his death, than with her realizations over the past few weeks and months about the ways in which their relationship had never been healthy. He'd never really seen her, only who he wanted her to be, and it had showed in the way he treated her.

She glanced at Travis, who was still holding the safe, which he'd closed back up. She looked down at Officer Keller. The bleeding had slowed, it seemed. Maybe the shot had only grazed her, and she'd passed out from shock or pain?

They had to get the information Travis was holding to the police department, or everything they'd endured would be for nothing.

Officer Keller was out of commission. Hopefully Officer Knox would arrive soon and call her an ambulance...

But Lily and Travis still had plays they could make. They were not stuck.

Maybe that was the most amazing realization from this whole ordeal, from her list to her failed relationship with Matt. She realized now that she didn't have to be stuck, and she could change her mind. Her list wasn't foolish or silly, but if she didn't want to pursue it and chase a new dream instead— her eyes went to Travis—then she could do that.

She had options.

And she was going to use one of them now.

Her eyes flickered to Travis again. She angled herself with her back slightly to Matt, so that he wouldn't be able to read her lips. She whispered quietly, "I'm going to run. Get the records to the police."

His eyes widened, and she thought he might have been about to shake his head, but she didn't wait to find out. Instead she stood, sprinted out of the room and yelled, "Timber, come!"

And she was out into the daylight alone.

She didn't have a destination in mind, but she hadn't grabbed her car keys, which limited her options. She hadn't thought through this plan beyond desperately needing to make a way for Travis to get Matt's records to the police.

All but the one she had in her pocket. Either way, they each had evidence that Matt was a crooked cop.

Her only other thought as she ran was that Lily wanted to keep Travis, herself and Timber safe.

If he'd wanted to, Matt could already have shot Travis and her for the records, she realized now as she sprinted away from her house toward the mountainside trail that she'd run up days ago when all of this had started. Hopefully her running away would throw Matt off enough that he wouldn't shoot Travis but come after her instead.

It might have been a bad plan. But it was the only one she had.

With Timber at her side, she ran up the mountain to where this all began. And where, she hoped, it would end.

With something approaching a happy ending.

Chapter Seventeen

The scream of rage that came from Matt as Lily left the room chilled Travis to the core. He'd expected the man to stay and try to get the safe from him, but he ran from the room after Lily.

Glancing down at Officer Keller, Travis hesitated. He hated to leave her defenseless.

At that moment she started to stir. "He shot me? I haven't been shot before." She looked up at Travis, blinked, then looked back down at her arm.

Travis pulled out his phone, dialed 911 and left it with Officer Keller. "I've called 911. They should be here soon, but…"

"Where's Lily?" She seemed to be gaining alertness.

"I've got to go after her." He unlocked the safe, pulled out its contents and shoved them into an inside pocket of his vest. When he ran from the house, he hesitated for a second in the driveway when he saw her car.

Why had he thought she would have driven away? But of course, she may not have had her car keys on her. He glanced down at the ground, willing himself to see footprints or something to indicate where she'd gone, but the ground was grassy and dry.

After a moment's thought, he didn't think he needed any signs like that. The only place he could think that she would have gone was up, back onto the mountain.

Anger and fear coursed through his veins, fear the stronger of the two at the moment. Why had she run somewhere even more isolated? The mountain trails and ridges felt familiar to her, he supposed, but they were familiar to Matt, too. She'd have been better off staying low.

The thought of Matt reaching her intensified Travis's terror. He'd looked almost crazed as he left the room following Lily, and while Travis already knew he was dangerous, this was a different level.

He hadn't been sure how his former friend felt about losing Lily to his faked death, but now Travis wasn't sure he'd considered it correctly. Matt seemed to take Lily's presence for granted, despite the fact that he'd tried to kill her multiple times in the past week. Or had he only been trying to scare her with the gunshots?

It was impossible to say.

Travis hurried up the trail, keeping an eye out for any sign of Lily, Timber or Matt, but he saw nothing. He was alone.

What-ifs taunted him. Matt could have caught up to Lily already. Then what? Horrible fears taunted him, and he did his best to push them away.

God, be with her, he prayed. As saddened as he'd been when Lily had told him she didn't pray much anymore, he certainly hadn't been praying as much as he usually did. Had he subconsciously picked up a little of that false belief? That God didn't care? Why else wouldn't he talk to God?

As he kept hiking and his lungs and legs burned, he probed his mind for an answer. He only managed to come up with one: he'd just thought he could handle this himself.

After all, he was former law enforcement, capable of taking on this unofficial investigation. And maybe that was right, but even it was, God had given him the gifts to be able to do that. Attempting to do it on his own without God's help and strength? That was a recipe for disaster.

Forgive me, God, he prayed as he hiked. *I want to do this with You. Not alone.* And he meant it.

The morning was chilly, especially since Lily had ditched her vest back at the house. She thought of Officer Keller and hoped she was okay. And Travis…

Surely he understood that she'd run because she wanted this to end, right? She hadn't meant to abandon him, she'd just known they were backed into a corner. Running had been her only thought for what to do.

Although, wasn't that what she'd done in high school, run from Travis?

This was a different situation. She'd like to think of her list as bold and risky, but didn't running away feel safe for her? Her mom had run away. And Lily never wanted to be like that.

Pushing away those uncomfortable thoughts, she kept going. In this case, running seemed to be the right thing. Although she was conscious of the fact that she couldn't run forever. And Matt was probably faster than she was.

Matt. The idea of facing him made her chest tight.

Lily kept running.

When she came to the trail she'd taken only a few days ago, the one that went up to Avalanche Peak itself, she'd stopped and cut left instead, around the ridge to a rocky face of the mountain. She'd come here once during a rainstorm and found some rock formations that had let her hide from the downpour. Was it possible that she might be able to hide from Matt there?

Lily thought it was possible.

Reaching down to pet Timber, Lily carefully picked her way around the mountainside. Her shoes had decent traction, which was good. A glance to her left confirmed that if she slipped, the scree would likely carry her down several hundred yards. If she didn't crash into a boulder first.

This was definitely a time when balance mattered, so she went slowly. Carefully. Using her hands to help her, she felt her way around one large rock formation, then another. On the third, she didn't think she was going to be able to pass. Her left foot slipped, and she tightened her grip with her hands, closing her eyes against what felt like her inevitable fall.

But she didn't.

Breathing a deep sigh, Lily took a minute to catch her breath and regain her confidence. Her hands and arms were starting to shake now, pumped up with blood. She was exhausted. Had she slept last night? She almost couldn't remember anymore, but yes, she'd slept a bit before she woke up and discovered someone had drugged Timber.

Not just someone, she reminded herself. Matt. *Matt* had drugged Timber. Killed a man. Shot at her.

She never would have believed it without the fingerprints. Why had he left them on the knife? Had he wanted to be caught?

It wouldn't surprise her. It seemed like the kind of power move Matt was capable of. In his mind, he was above the law, so the idea of him taunting them by intentionally leaving fingerprints wasn't entirely surprising.

He'd been so nice when she first met him. Maybe a little controlling. But not like this.

How much of his true personality had he hidden? Was some of it drugs? Could he be taking the drugs he'd been helping to sell, all the while "investigating" the people selling them?

Travis knew Lily was somewhere up the trail along with Timber and Matt, and the knowledge made him creep cautiously upward. He was unwilling to draw attention to himself, unless Lily needed him to do that to keep her safe.

He should have grabbed a gun before he ran out of the house and up the mountainside, but his only thought had been to close the distance between him and Lily. Dumb. Another mistake.

As he climbed, he let his thoughts wander. Mistakes took him back to the police department and his time working there. He considered Matt. Should he have seen that his partner was crooked? It would have been useful.

But realistically could he have?

Now that Lily had mentioned several times over how busy and distracted Matt had been, it was unsurprising that he'd been too involved in the narcotics ring. At the time, though? Travis wasn't sure there was anything he could have done differently. His friend had been in deep cover, and Travis had bought it.

Now, though, the mistakes he'd made on this informal investigation.

This was the other reason Travis had left law enforcement, besides the desire not to be around evil and death so often. Any mistake was high stakes, could hurt someone else. Travis didn't want to live with that kind of stress, yet here he was again. He felt out of control, and he hated that.

Maybe you were never in control in the first place.

The words came across his mind. Like a reminder of something he knew was true. Travis stopped for half a second, then stumbled forward again.

Travis believed in God, believed in the power of prayer, but he could count on one hand the times he'd had such a clear impression of what God wanted him to know. It made his heart rate rise, and all his senses sharpen. He kept listening, but there were just those two impressions.

He wasn't in control. He needed to give this to God.

He quickened his pace. He had to hurry. Lily needed him. Didn't she?

Like puzzle pieces coming together, Travis saw that maybe that was true. But it was also true that he could only do so much. He wasn't God. He wasn't fully in control of the situation. And God loved Lily more than Travis did.

Travis had been forced to let her go for years. Now that he

had her back, everything within him wanted to be the hero she needed.

But maybe Lily didn't need that. Maybe she needed God more. And for God to be her ultimate hero.

He blew out a breath, kept up his pace but whispered back, "Okay, God. She's Yours."

And continued on.

God was going to be the hero here, Travis saw that now. But that didn't mean he couldn't do his best, too.

Another crunch on the rocks. Lily's stomach tightened. She didn't think she and Timber were alone on this mountainside anymore. Was it possible Matt had gone on the other trail and was now up above somewhere, unaware of where she was hidden? Or was he lying in wait?

The second wouldn't surprise her. Now that she had a full picture of who he was, nothing about him would surprise her. He probably had never loved her. It hit her hard, somewhere inside where she preferred to think that people were basically good and not capable of this kind of evil.

It made her need for God even more evident. She couldn't believe she'd almost let Matt talk her out of that belief. How had his smooth talking almost made her turn from the beliefs of her childhood? Thank goodness God was forgiving and loving. She had a feeling it wouldn't be the last time she'd need a second chance, but she had full confidence He would always give her one.

Thank You, she whispered in her heart. *Thank You for never leaving me. Even now. You're here, aren't You?*

And He'd given her Timber. It was going to be okay, wasn't it? No matter what?

With tendrils of fear still curling around her, she petted Timber. Tried to breathe in and out. Not long now, and it would be over. Travis may already have delivered the evidence to the police department. Matt was going to be in jail for years, if not forever. Lily just had to hang in there a little while longer.

Carefully, she scooted back even farther.

"Lily. I know you're up here."

Matt's voice was low, almost taunting. She felt herself tense but said nothing in response.

"You were stupid to run, you know. Not that I'm surprised. You've never been very smart, have you?" His laugh was without humor, his voice low. Cold.

She heard more crunching against the rocks. It was still impossible for her to pinpoint where it was coming from. Should she stay where she was, or try to creep farther back into the cave-like formation? Her innate sense of self-preservation told her to move back farther, so she did.

"It's time to let this go. Give me that paper you took from the safe. Apologize for what you did wrong. Let's start over."

Wait, apologize? Start over?

He was crazy. And she didn't use the word lightly.

"You're nothing by yourself, you know."

It was as though he'd compiled her worst fears, her deepest hurts, and was using them against her as weapons. She supposed he was. *Why* hadn't she seen how unhealthy this relationship was when she'd been in it?

She wasn't alone, though. She wasn't. She dug her fingers deep into Timber's fur.

"Timber, come."

His low voice hadn't diminished in its menacing quality.

The warmth beside Lily evaporated as Timber moved away from her. Moved toward the voice. Toward Matt.

Wait...no.

She wanted to cry out. Had Matt been right? Was it impossible for Timber to switch loyalties? She was a good dog, but she was a dog, after all, unable to reason or understand things like crimes committed, promises broken, lies told.

She was out of sight now.

Lily really was alone.

Chapter Eighteen

Panic tightened its grip on her, and Lily struggled against it. It was a lie, she knew that. She was stronger than this. She was not alone.

But without Travis, without her dog, without any clear hope of how she was getting off this mountainside… Lily was afraid this might be the one time when positive thinking wasn't going to help her at all. Was there a time to admit defeat?

She didn't know. Couldn't think anymore.

So with Matt's voice still calling hurtful things, taunting her, she laid her head down in her folded arms and cried.

"Something wrong?" The too-sweet voice chilled her to her core. It echoed at the entrance to her little cave.

She looked up.

Matt looked almost feral, his hair longer than he'd kept it before, somewhat shaggy. His smile was wild, hollow. "You always were exceptionally whiny." He rolled his eyes. "I don't know why I put up with it at all."

His words would have hurt before, but they didn't now. Now Lily felt…fear. Loneliness.

Help, God, she prayed.

"But I did put up with it. Don't forget that." He stepped closer. "And this is how you repay me?"

She wanted to shudder in disgust but held herself still, tensing all her muscles. "You were dead, Matt. We all thought you were dead."

"We. You and my idiot partner? You guys have a thing going on now?"

She didn't want to talk to him about Travis. That relationship was too important, too special to expose to this kind of evil and ridicule. Matt could never understand something like what she and Travis had.

Instead she said nothing. Which seemed to make him even madder.

"And then you have the nerve to try to expose me?" He shook his head. "Don't you know I've already won, Lily?"

She flinched at the sound of her name on his lips. Still didn't reply.

"I see the dog abandoned you," he continued. "She won't be loyal to you, you know."

She heard the implied taunt: no one ever would be.

She'd never specifically told Matt about her mom. She'd never felt close enough to him for that, even when they had been engaged. But somehow he'd picked up on all the vulnerability and sensitivity she had around it. And now he was using it against her.

"It wouldn't do you any good if you did have her," he continued, "because she would never attack me. I was her handler. Her master."

She flinched at the term. "She trusted you," Lily said, hearing her own bitterness creep into her voice.

"You know who I trust? Myself. Maybe the rest of you have to learn that lesson the hard way. Now, you know what's going to happen? You're going to give me the paper you have in your pocket. Then you're going to get out of my way, and I'm going to go find your little boyfriend and get the papers he has."

"There are more up here, aren't there? Papers? You hid things in my house, at the inlet overlook and up here, right?"

He stopped moving toward her and cocked his head to the side as though she was fascinating to him. "Well, you at least figured that much out. I suppose you realized that's why Arnold and I were both up here?"

"Yes." Her voice was still hesitant, but she felt her confidence growing. "I figured he must have decided to reveal that you weren't dead for some reason."

"He didn't want to keep taking the fall for my 'murder.'" Matt sounded disgusted. "As though I wasn't enough of an asset to their organization to make up for that. So he came up here to get the papers, but I figured out what he was up to. He'd been acting strange. I followed him up. Got him out of the picture the day you saw me, then came back another day to find the documents here. Too bad I couldn't get the ones at your house. The fire did more damage overall than I'd counted on, but not enough to easily access the safe."

Everything lined up with what they'd suspected. "Why try to kill me, though?"

Matt shrugged. "I needed you out of the way. If you were dead, getting to the safe was easier. And I knew you'd figure it out eventually, and I didn't want you to turn me in."

As he talked, Lily tried to figure out if there was any way she could escape. He was coming closer and closer to her as he spoke. She could smell his breath now.

She leaned back.

"Something wrong, Lily? You never minded if I was close before."

The reminder disgusted her. The idea of kissing him now was repulsive.

"Wait. Stop. I…" She trailed off. There had to be something else she could ask to slow this down.

"I'm done talking. You're out of chances to get away or whatever you're planning."

Sunlight coming through the caves caught the metal of his gun. He raised it now, bringing it closer to her face. She felt on the ground, grabbed a rock.

"Don't even think about it." Matt brought the gun level with her eyes.

Lily watched in horror as his fingers started to tense.

Then, behind him, Lily saw a flash of something.

Timber!

Her brown body streaked through the air as she launched herself at Matt. She knocked him sideways, and he fired wide. The sound was explosive in the small space, but it didn't hit Lily.

"Timber, no!" Matt yelled, but the German shepherd didn't listen. As though he was the suspect and she was back with the police department working a case, she went after him exactly how she'd been trained. Lily watched in amazement as Timber pinned him to the ground.

Matt struggled against the dog, reaching for his gun.

"No!" She knew if he grabbed the gun now, he wouldn't hesitate to use it on Timber, now that she'd turned into the flesh of his arm with her teeth. Lily couldn't let anything happen to Timber. Instead, she launched herself forward, toward Matt and everything she feared, and grabbed the weapon herself.

"Timber, no!" Matt threw her off, but Timber was not to be deterred. She bit down hard on his arm once again, and he screamed in pain.

"Leave her alone!" Lily screamed, hands on the gun.

"Or what? You'll shoot me? You wouldn't."

"She might not." A new voice echoed through the cave. "But I sure would."

Officer Knox stood in the mouth of the cave, his service pistol drawn.

Travis, looking out of breath, stood beside him.

"Timber, come," Lily commanded.

The German shepherd came to her at once and curled up beside Lily as though to reassure her.

"You wouldn't really have left me, would you?" Lily whispered in her ear, realizing now that Timber must have left to find Matt and stop him from harming Lily. To keep watch, essentially. What an incredible dog.

Timber gladly accepted the scratches behind her ear.

"Matt Davis, you're under arrest for the murder of Arnold Harris. Among other things, I'm sure." Officer Knox's dry voice echoed as he cuffed Matt, whose arm was bleeding from Timber's bite. "You have the right to remain silent..."

"I know the speech," Matt said.

"Yeah. I guess you'd remember that from when you were a cop." Travis looked him up and down. "Pity you didn't remember the part about protecting and serving."

Matt tried to lunge at Travis, but Officer Knox pulled him back.

"That's enough from you." Officer Knox turned to Travis. "Come down later to give a statement?"

Travis nodded.

Officer Knox turned to Lily. "You, too."

"I'll be there," she said with a small smile.

And then Matt and Officer Knox were gone, and it was just Lily and Travis. And, of course, Timber.

"I didn't know if I'd ever see you again," Lily said to Travis with a smile.

"You going to come out of there?" he asked, and when she reached her hand to him, he helped her out. Moving carefully, they walked out of the cave and onto the mountainside.

"I knew I'd see you again," Travis said.

"Oh, yeah?"

"Yeah," he said, stepping closer. "You're strong. I knew you'd be okay."

"You looked a little out of breath and nervous for someone who knew I'd be fine the whole time," she teased, but she was smiling.

"I'm glad you're okay. Do you want to talk?"

"I'm okay, really," she said again.

They stood there together in the morning sunshine, face-to-face.

"I think I was wrong," Travis said finally.

Swallowing hard, Lily stepped back.

He laughed, then pulled her gently forward by her shoulders. "Not about that. Actually, yes, about that. I think I was wrong that we should just be friends."

It was almost too much, in a good way. God had shown her that He was really all she needed. But that wasn't even all she'd been given. She had Timber. She had friends. And maybe she had Travis as more than that?

Lily waited to hear what he had to say.

"I love you, Lily Peterson," he said at last.

"I love you, too." She barely got the words out before he captured her lips in a kiss.

Maybe Lily wasn't like her mom. Actually, she was sure she wasn't. She didn't have to give up her dreams for love, but neither did she have to give up love for her dreams.

And God was with her, either way. No matter what.

As they stood on the mountainside, Lily felt contentment flood through her. She didn't need a list.

She had everything she could ever dream of right here.

Epilogue

The sun was shining bright on the mountainside when Travis stood with several friends and waited for Lily to walk down the trail that would serve as their aisle. He was amazed by how quickly the year had gone, and how blessed he was.

Was it really only a year ago they'd stood on this mountain before? God had redeemed this place, just like He'd redeemed so many things in their lives.

After they'd sorted out all of the details at the police department, Travis and Lily had talked for the entire night. They talked about the past and the future. And Lily had told him that he meant more to her than any list ever could. Before morning came and Lily drove back to her own home, Travis had told her that one day he wanted to marry her on that mountainside. He'd figured it made sense to make his intentions clear.

Five months later, beside the town's Christmas tree at the lighting festival, he'd asked her to marry him. And she'd said yes.

Now he watched her move toward him, her white dress fitting her perfectly, her hair spilling over her shoulders. She was beautiful. The way she handled difficulty was beautiful. And he loved her.

"We're gathered here today to celebrate the marriage of Travis Beckett and Lily Peterson…"

She faced him there on the trail, and Travis knew every dream he'd ever had had come true. It was funny, they had talked a lot about dreams over the past year, and both of them had come to the conclusion that God's plan was even better than any dreams they could come up with on their own. Even if Travis would have left out some parts of their story, like fearing for Lily's life, he couldn't deny that God was better at being in control than he ever was.

Travis heard little of the pastor's message. He was too distracted by Lily, and with the knowledge that after years apart they'd been given a second chance and would soon be husband and wife.

"You may kiss the bride."

Sharing a smile with Lily, Travis moved forward and kissed her.

And it was even better than he could have dreamed.

* * * * *

Don't miss the stories in this mini series!

K-9 SEARCH AND RESCUE

MILLS & BOON

Uncovering The Truth
Carol J. Post

MILLS & BOON

Carol J. Post writes fun and fast-paced inspirational romantic suspense stories and lives in the beautiful mountains of North Carolina. She plays the piano and also enjoys sailing, hiking and camping—almost anything outdoors. Her daughters and grandkids live too far away for her liking, so she now pours all that nurturing into taking care of two highly spoiled black cats.

Books by Carol J. Post

Midnight Shadows
Motive for Murder
Out for Justice
Shattered Haven
Hidden Identity
Mistletoe Justice
Buried Memories
Reunited by Danger
Fatal Recall
Lethal Legacy
Bodyguard for Christmas
Dangerous Relations
Trailing a Killer

Canine Defense

Searching for Evidence
Sniffing Out Justice
Uncovering the Truth

Visit the Author Profile page at millsandboon.com.au for more titles.

Therefore if any man be in Christ,
he is a new creature: old things are passed away;
behold, all things are become new.
—*2 Corinthians* 5:17

Thank you to my wonderful sister, Kim Coker—
my plotting partner, my research buddy
and my all-time best friend.

Thank you to my editor, Katie Gowrie,
and my critique partners, Karen Fleming and
Sabrina Jarema. Your amazing insight
always makes my writing better.

And lastly, thank you to my husband, Chris, for your
encouragement and support. If I had it to do over,
I would do it all over again.

Chapter One

The overstuffed backpack landed on the scuffed counter with a thud.

Alyssa Anderson rolled her shoulders and rang the bell. Five minutes later, she was still alone in the motel lobby. Granted, this wasn't the Ritz-Carlton or even a Holiday Inn. But someone ought to at least be manning the front desk.

"Hello?"

Moments later, a young woman came from the back and stepped up to the counter, looking a little harried. "Sorry to keep you waiting. How can I help you?"

"I need a room for the night." Maybe more than one night, depending on how long it would take the mechanic to get to her hunk-of-junk car.

"Sure thing." She made several clicks of the mouse, squinting at the computer screen.

The clock on the wall behind her said almost four thirty. Alyssa shifted her weight to the other foot. Her mother's graveside service would have ended an hour ago. More than a decade had passed since she'd been killed, and she was finally getting a proper burial, her death, the mourning it deserved.

The service had probably been beautiful, with friends and

family members remembering a life well lived but cut short. The words spoken over the casket had likely included the 23rd Psalm and other verses of comfort.

Alyssa wouldn't know. She hadn't made it. One more reason for her sisters to judge her.

It wasn't that she hadn't tried. She'd left Atlanta in plenty of time to make the five-hour trip to Pensacola. She'd only gotten as far as LaGrange when the old Tempo had made a sound resembling an explosion and started rattling as if trying to shake off all four fenders.

The clerk straightened and met Alyssa's gaze. "I'll put you in room 106. That'll be $54.88 with tax. How did you want to pay?"

"Debit card." She hesitated. "On second thought, I'll pay cash."

She was probably being overly cautious. Maybe even a bit paranoid. No one had access to her bank account, so there was no way for anyone to follow her trail through her banking transactions.

Regardless, she pulled two twenties, a ten and a five from her wallet and laid them on the counter. If there was anything she'd learned over the past decade, it was how to take care of herself.

After printing a receipt, the clerk slid the room key into its sleeve and wrote 106 on the outside. "Checkout is at eleven."

"Thank you." Alyssa folded the receipt then palmed the room key and slipped both into the back pocket of her jeans.

She hoped she wouldn't have to extend her stay. Even if the mechanic didn't get her car fixed until late tomorrow, she'd do what she'd done today. After having her car towed, she had spent seven hours riding public transportation, roaming the LaGrange Mall and strolling the park to pass the time until check-in.

She hadn't bothered to call either of her sisters. One of them would have driven from Pensacola to pick her up as soon as the service was over. But she didn't want charity from anyone, least of all her uppity sisters.

She dragged the backpack from the counter and slid an arm through one of the straps. The pack was remarkably light considering it held all of her worldly possessions. She heaved a sigh. She was pretty pathetic—twenty-five years of life and all she had to show for it fit into a space the size of a carry-on.

After walking out the door, she turned left and made her way along the front of the building. Her room was six doors down.

Her burner phone rang before she'd even made it halfway. She fished it from her pocket and eyed the 706 area code. Her pulse kicked up speed. Maybe the mechanic already knew what was wrong with her car. Now if she could just get it fixed without having to wipe out her entire savings.

Whatever happened, going back to Atlanta wasn't an option, not if she hoped to escape the latest mess she'd gotten herself into. And since her mother's graveside service was over, there was nothing for her in Pensacola. Nothing except a couple of sisters who would probably rather she not return anyway.

She swiped to accept the call and pressed the phone to her ear. She'd guessed right. The call was from Jim's Garage, where they'd towed her car, and the mechanic had already diagnosed her engine troubles. Not only that, he'd fixed them.

"How much do I owe you?"

"Two hundred dollars."

Was that all? She breathed a sigh of relief. The problem had to have been extremely minor. She would call a cab, try to get her money back from the motel clerk, pick up her car and be gone. The sooner she could get out of LaGrange, the better. Actually, the sooner she could leave Georgia behind, the safer she would feel.

When the cab arrived, she walked out of the lobby fifty-five dollars richer than when she'd gone in. A few minutes later, the driver dropped her off at the garage. Her Tempo was parked out front, next to a Chevy Trailblazer. A Nissan pickup waited along the side of the building.

She stepped into the office area where a man sat at a desk that was covered in papers, a phone pressed to his ear. While she waited for him to finish, she glanced through the door leading into the side of the garage. Another man was leaning forward under the open hood of a Chevy pickup truck.

He straightened, and she wandered in. "Are you the one who repaired the red Tempo?"

He closed the hood and pulled a rag from the pocket of his overalls. "That was me."

"So what was wrong with it?"

He wiped his hands on the rag. "You threw a piston rod. It's a good thing it went into the cylinder head instead of out the side of the block or you would have needed a new engine. As it was, it didn't even damage the crankshaft."

Her breath released in a rush. Finally, good news. For real this time.

Lately, she'd thought everything was looking up. After years waitressing in greasy spoons where tips were often in the form of coins rather than bills, she'd run into a girl she'd worked with years earlier. Rachel's recommendation had gotten her a job at La Maison D'Elise. It was one of those places with linen tablecloths, candlelight and live background music. And patrons who thought nothing of adding a forty-or fifty-dollar gratuity to their bill.

She'd even had a new boyfriend, someone with some class—someone who picked her up in a shiny, new Audi A5 convertible and took her places requiring attire other than holey jeans and a tank top.

He'd been a regular patron of La Maison, a successful photographer, with some high-profile modeling clients. She'd been so sure he was too good to be true, she'd turned him down for a solid three weeks before she'd finally agreed to go out with him.

Then, less than twenty-four hours ago, everything had blown up in her face. Now she had no boyfriend, no job and no home.

Alyssa had seen something she wasn't supposed to have seen and now some bad men wanted her dead. Her ex-boyfriend was one of them.

At least she still had a car and she hadn't needed to wipe out her savings to get it fixed.

"Thank you. I appreciate you getting the work done so quickly."

"No problem. Jim said it was a rush job and put two of us on it."

She thanked him again and stepped back into the office as the man she'd seen earlier was hanging up the phone.

"Are you Jim?"

"I am."

"Alyssa Anderson, owner of the '92 Tempo."

"We've got you ready to go. That'll be two hundred dollars."

She took the pack from her back and removed ten twenty-dollar bills from her wallet. She had hit the ATM on her way out of town and pulled out five hundred dollars. Now her cash was almost half gone.

In the garage, one bay door and then the other rolled down on their tracks, the metallic rumble drifting into the office. The mechanic she'd spoken with earlier walked through the open door.

"'Night, boss." He gave Alyssa a salute. "Safe travels."

"Thanks."

She picked up her pack from the counter but didn't bother slipping her arms through the two straps. When she turned her attention back to Jim, he pulled a handwritten invoice from the top of one of the haphazard stacks on his desk. After writing "paid in full" across the bottom, he rose and handed it to her, along with her car key. "I'm right behind you."

He followed her out and locked the door then disappeared

around the side of the building, probably headed to the Nissan she'd noticed earlier. The Trailblazer pulled from the parking lot, the mechanic at the wheel.

Alyssa glanced down at the invoice as she made her way toward her car. The top line of the description said, "Repairs to 1992 Ford Tempo." The list of what was involved was lengthy.

Far too lengthy for the two hundred dollars she'd been charged.

Her breath caught and her hands started to shake. The garage hadn't discounted the charges because they'd felt sorry for her. They knew nothing of her situation. No, the amount she owed was so low because someone else had paid the rest of the bill. Making sure the repair was affordable with her meager savings was the way to guarantee she would return. Otherwise, she would have abandoned the car and kept running.

She looked frantically around her at the empty parking lot. Nearby, the Nissan's engine roared to life. Then a car shot from the business catty-cornered, across the four lanes of traffic, barreling toward the Tempo.

Alyssa spun and retraced her steps at a full run, still clutching the loop on the top of the pack. She needed to reach Jim before he left.

As she rounded the corner of the building, the Nissan pulled onto the side road, headed away from her. Behind her, the car roared closer. Trees lined the property on the other side of the street. If she could make it across before the car hit her, she might have a chance at escape.

She shot into the road...right into the path of an SUV. The driver braked hard, the squeal of tires setting her teeth on edge.

As she glanced over her other shoulder, the car that had pursued her swerved toward the highway. Relief flooded her, but only for a moment. An arm extended through the open passenger window, and sunlight glinted off the barrel of a pistol.

Two shots rang out as she dove and rolled, tossing the pack. A searing pain stabbed through her left shoulder. She came to a stop in the narrow stretch of patchy grass lining the side of the street, the trees she had targeted only six feet away.

She sat up and grasped her shoulder with her other hand. The bullet had grazed her. At least, she hoped that was all it was. The sleeve of her shirt was already wet. When she drew her hand away, her palm was covered with blood. Her wrist hurt, too. So did her knee. She'd probably injured them hitting the pavement.

When she tried to rise, pain shot through her right knee, sending her right back to the asphalt. *No, not this on top of everything else.* She looked frantically around. The car was gone.

The SUV had stopped—a later model white Land Rover. Its door swung open, and a sneaker-clad foot appeared beneath it. The driver likely wanted to make sure she wasn't hurt. She would tell him she was all right, thank him for stopping and send him on his way.

Alyssa pushed herself upright, hands splayed against the pavement, her weight on her left leg. After snatching up her pack, she again pressed her hand to her left shoulder. There was more blood than she'd initially thought. She'd deal with it later. Right now, she had more pressing things to concern herself with—like staying alive.

She limped toward the Good Samaritan, trying hard not to wince with each step, all the while casting frequent glances at the highway behind her. Still no sign of the car.

How had she even wound up in this situation? The scene had seemed so harmless: four businessmen sitting around a table discussing famous works of art. But what she'd witnessed had had more significance than she had initially thought. Maybe the art had been stolen. Or maybe the paintings they'd been talking about had been copies or fakes and they'd been marketing them as the real thing. The details didn't matter.

Because now some dangerous men were determined to keep her quiet.

She had to get out of there.

* * *

Spencer Cavanaugh slid from his Land Rover, heart pounding. Not only had a woman just run right into his path, he'd heard two pops. Maybe it had only been a vehicle backfiring, but with his windows up and radio on, it had sounded an awful lot like gunshots.

His hand shook as he reached for the back door handle. At his command, a chocolate Lab jumped from the back seat. He was still wearing his service dog vest from their trip to the U-Haul store to purchase more packing boxes.

The woman he had braked to avoid was staggering in his direction, clutching her left shoulder with the opposite hand. When she had run out in front of him, he hadn't observed her long enough to form an opinion of her condition. One moment, the road ahead of him had been clear. The next moment, she'd been darting into his path.

Now, the way she was stumbling, she looked injured. Her long, red hair hung in her face, twigs and leaves caught in the tangles. One leg of her jeans was ripped at the knee, and blood oozed between the fingers of the hand clutching her opposite shoulder. She cast frequent glances behind her, as if expecting an attack.

"Thanks for stopping." She came to a halt about three feet in front of him.

Apollo stood next to him, pressing his weight into the side of Spence's leg, just as he'd been trained to do in tense situations.

Without releasing her left shoulder, the woman raised that hand to fling her hair out of her face, turning toward the main highway as she did. "I'm all right. You don't need to stay."

His jaw went slack. In the final second before she'd turned, recognition had slammed into him.

Alyssa Ashbaugh? The red hair wasn't familiar. The face was—the green eyes, the full lips, the soft lines of her jaw. He'd long ago memorized every feature.

He removed his sunglasses. "You need a doctor."

"No, I'm fine. I have to get—" Her gaze locked with his, and her eyes widened briefly before narrowing to slits.

Eight years earlier, he'd broken her heart. She obviously still hadn't forgiven him. But now wasn't the time to rehash the past.

"You're bleeding. Let me take you to the emergency room."

"It's just a nick. I don't need your help." Coldness underlay her tone. She spun to limp toward the mechanic shop next to them.

In two long strides, he'd reached her side, Apollo trotting next to him.

"Alyssa, don't be stubborn."

"I told you, I'm all right."

"You can hardly walk, and that's too much blood to classify as *all right*." Her sleeve was soaked with it and red rivulets trailed down her arm. His jaw dropped a second time. "You've been shot."

Those pops he'd heard hadn't been from a car backfiring. They'd been gunshots, one of which had found its mark.

She shrugged. "I'm sure it's just a flesh wound."

"Regardless, if someone is out there shooting at people, we need to call the police."

He pulled his phone from his pocket to dial 911. She continued her trek across the parking lot without acknowledging what he'd said. It was empty except for an older compact car that looked as if it had seen better days. Its body boasted at least three colors of paint, one of which was probably primer.

He grasped her right shoulder. She was still using that arm to stem the bleeding on the left. "Hold on, Alyssa. Where are you going?"

She shook off his hand. "See the old Ford Tempo up there? It's mine. I'm going to get in it and leave."

"What about your knee?"

"I'm more worried right now about getting gone before those guys come back."

"That's why we need to call the police." He'd wondered if it had been a random drive-by shooting. Her statement told him it hadn't. Those guys had been gunning for her and apparently weren't going to give up.

She stared at him, features set in determination. "Calling the police isn't going to keep me alive."

"You can give them a description of the car. Maybe they can catch the guys."

"Gold sedan. That's all I know. I was too busy dodging bullets to zero in on things like the make and model of the car."

She turned away from him and limped a few more steps, obviously in pain.

He walked next to her. "You think the bleeding is going to stop on its own?"

"Eventually."

"And you're planning to drive with that knee."

"Yep."

"How do you think you'll do mashing the brake?"

She winced at the thought. "It'll be fine, or I'll use my left."

"You're sure your knee will be fine without care, enough to risk permanent damage?"

She hesitated, lips pressed together. Maybe he was getting through to her.

"And I'm guessing that, whoever these guys are, they know what you drive. You don't think they'll be watching for your car?"

Her steps slowed even more.

"Let me take you to the emergency room. The police can meet us there. The doctors will stitch up your shoulder and make sure there isn't a bullet lodged in there, and figure out what needs to be done for your knee."

After another moment of hesitation, she nodded. "Okay."

"Wait in your car while I bring my SUV over." He didn't

want her to have to retrace her steps all the way back to the side road, but leaving her standing outside wasn't a good option, either.

"Okay."

He turned to hurry back to his truck, trying to disguise his own limp. With all the time he'd spent on his feet today, he wasn't quite successful. Twenty-six years old, and he sometimes walked like an old man.

He glanced over his shoulder, hoping Alyssa wouldn't take off before he could get back. He'd just have to trust her. Confiscating her key would have only ticked her off.

When he pulled into the space to her left a minute later, she was watching him through the side window. After swinging open the door, she slid from her car into his SUV, dragging the backpack with her.

The smile she flashed him held resignation. "Thanks."

"You're welcome." He handed her his phone.

"What's this for?"

"Since Georgia is a hands-free state, and sitting in the parking lot while I make the call wouldn't be the smartest move, I figured you could handle the 911 call while I drive."

When she hesitated, he continued. "Tell the dispatcher what you know and that we're on our way to the emergency room."

While she placed the call, he drove. When she identified herself as Alyssa Anderson, he did a double take. She was married? He glanced at her left hand. She wasn't wearing a ring. That didn't necessarily mean anything, though.

He continued to listen to the one-sided conversation. She couldn't describe the car, other than saying it was a gold sedan, and she had no information about either of the men inside, except that the passenger had a gun.

When she finished the call, she set his phone in the cup holder. "They're going to send an officer to the hospital to do a report, but I won't be able to tell him any more than I just told the dispatcher."

"Any idea who the men were?" Not that he really expected her to tell him.

"Not a clue."

"Do you live in LaGrange?" He'd been there a year and hadn't run into her. But in a town with a population of more than thirty thousand, that didn't mean much.

"No, Atlanta. I was just passing through when my car broke down."

"When did you move to Atlanta?"

"The first time? A year after you left. Then I lived in South Carolina, Alabama, Tennessee and a couple of other towns in Georgia before winding back up in Atlanta."

"That's a lot of moving around in seven years."

"I thought you were somewhere on the other side of the world, trying to be a hero."

He smiled at her description. That hadn't been his goal. At least, not at first. In fact, when he'd joined the army, it had been more for his own benefit than any sense of duty to his country. With all of the stupid decisions he'd made as a teenager, he'd been smart enough to recognize he'd needed to make some drastic changes. The discipline of the military had been the quickest way to that end.

"I'm not sure I can claim the hero title, but, yeah, I was on the other side of the world until a year ago. I did two tours in Afghanistan and then finished in Kuwait."

He'd reenlisted but only made it a few months before having to take a medical discharge. One of his buddies had lost a leg stepping on an IED, and another had lost his life taking an RPG to the gut. Yet, in spite of being in numerous combat situations himself, he'd managed to leave Afghanistan unscathed. Physically, anyway.

Then, after being in Kuwait a while, he'd swerved to miss hitting a kid, rolled the Jeep and shattered his hip. Two surgeries later, he'd been left with some serious metal and a limp he could hide pretty well unless he was really fatigued.

Alyssa nodded. "Now you're back. What made you choose LaGrange?"

"One of the guys I served with was from there."

He'd made a promise. After the grenade had done its damage, his buddy had held on just long enough to ask Spence to look after his wife until he knew she was going to be all right. That was exactly what he'd done. He'd fulfilled his obligation. His friend's widow had even agreed it was time for him to get on with his own life.

Now he was ready to move back to his hometown of Pensacola, Florida. He'd planned to spend the next two days packing. Putting off the move wasn't an option. The lease on his apartment was up in two days. Everything was set in Florida, too. He'd visited Alyssa's sisters a month ago and signed a lease for the other half of the Ashbaugh Charters building. It would house his living quarters as well as the retail space beneath. He was finally going to realize his dream of owning his own music store.

As he pulled into the emergency room parking lot, he retrieved his phone from the cup holder. "I'm going to drop you off at the door and then park."

"Are you coming in with me?"

"I was planning to."

"What about your dog?"

"He can come in with us." With his vest on, he was welcome anywhere Spence went. In fact, he hadn't been separated from Apollo since K9s For Warriors had hooked them up three months ago.

She nodded. "I'd like to get a dog someday. My life just isn't very conducive to caring for an animal right now."

Yeah, it probably wasn't. He eased to a stop at the covered entrance. "We'll be in as soon as I park."

When he and Apollo walked through the automatic doors a

few minutes later, Alyssa was still sitting in the waiting room. He took a seat in the chair to her left, and Apollo lay on the floor between their feet.

"They've checked you in?"

"Yes. She said they'll be calling me back in a few minutes."

He looked down at her shoulder and frowned. She was doing a good enough job of keeping pressure on the shoulder that she wouldn't bleed to death, but the injury had to be painful. Riding in an ambulance would have gotten her into triage a lot more quickly. At least the place wasn't packed. In fact, there were only two other people in the waiting room.

The automatic door slid open, and a LaGrange police officer stepped into the waiting area. His gaze scanned the room until it settled on Alyssa.

"Alyssa Anderson?"

"Yes."

"You reported a drive-by shooting." He took a chair on her other side. "What can you tell me?"

"I was at Jim's Garage, picking up my car. When I came outside, there was a car waiting in the convenience store parking lot catty-cornered from there. I didn't notice it until it shot out of the parking lot and crossed the street, headed right for me. I ran across the side street there, right out in front of him." On *him*, she tilted her head toward Spence. "That's when they fired the shots."

As she talked, the officer jotted notes in his pad. Finally, he looked at her. "Did you recognize the car these people were in?"

"No."

"Can you describe it?"

"It was a four-door, gold, not new but not old, either. I'm not even sure what kind. There wasn't anything that stood out about it, but I was more focused on trying to stay alive at that point."

"Any idea who the shooter was, or why he was aiming at you?"

She shook her head but didn't meet the officer's gaze. "No clue."

Spence studied her. She was lying. At least, she knew more than she was letting on.

After a few more questions, which Alyssa was unable—or unwilling—to answer, a nurse called her back.

The officer stood. "I've got your phone number. If I need anything else, I'll call you."

Spence stood, too. Alyssa didn't object, so he followed her. Apollo walked right next to him, ever alert. The Lab's demeanor always went from relaxed to "on duty" the moment Spence picked up the service dog vest, and it stayed that way until he removed it.

The nurse led them into one of the triage areas and, after Alyssa took a seat on the bed, pulled the curtain around on its track. Spence eased into the nearby chair, and Apollo lay next to him. After she had taken Alyssa's history and her vitals, she left the area.

"How are you feeling?"

"All right. My shoulder's throbbing, but I'm pretty sure a shot is going to take care of that pretty soon. Then it'll get stitched up and be good as new." She put a hand on each side of her right knee and slowly straightened her leg. "I'm not sure about this, though. I'm hoping I haven't done serious damage."

"Me, too." Especially if she was running from someone. "Do you need to let anyone know what happened? Wouldn't *Mr.* Anderson want to know you're here?"

Her eyebrows drew together. "Who?" The confusion cleared. "No, I'm not married. Never have been. As soon as I left home, I ditched the Ashbaugh name. Haven't been back since."

Before he could respond, a doctor walked in and introduced himself. Another nurse wheeled in a rolling table.

The doctor picked up a syringe. "We're going to numb this and see what we've got. If it's just a graze like you suspect, a few stitches should do it."

Alyssa dropped her hand. "Sounds good."

Since Spence was sitting on her right, he couldn't see her injury or watch what the medical folks were doing to tend to her. After the doctor administered the injection, the nurse approached with a sterile cloth and wound cleaner.

So, Alyssa wasn't married. She had changed her name, likely to escape her past. He wasn't surprised. With an alcoholic father, a mother who'd taken off when Alyssa was fifteen, and two older sisters she'd never been close to, she didn't have a lot of fond memories of her family. Maybe he was part of the childhood she was trying to forget.

His chest tightened. He hadn't wanted to hurt her. He just hadn't had a choice.

At eighteen, he'd witnessed a best friend die from an overdose. By then, he had begun to develop his own drug habit. The experience had shaken him up enough to scare him clean. But at the time, Alyssa hadn't been ready to give up anything. Neither had his other friends. Staying in the town where he'd grown up, hanging with the people he'd hung with his entire childhood, the pull of his old life had been too strong.

So he'd walked away from everything—his friends, his dysfunctional family and the only girl he'd ever truly loved—and joined the army. That decision had probably saved his life. The irony still struck him—the thought he'd been more likely to survive Afghanistan than Pensacola.

But that wasn't the only irony. It was while he'd belonged to the US government and his life was not his own that he'd discovered true freedom. During his first tour in Afghanistan, while pinned down by enemy fire, he'd promised God if He would spare his life, he'd give Him whatever time he had left.

God had, and Spence had kept his side of the bargain. He was still keeping it.

Alyssa really needed what he'd found. From what he had observed during their brief encounter this afternoon, she hadn't changed much. The toughness she'd always had was still there. So was the chip on her shoulder.

Regardless of what she had said to the cop about not knowing who had shot at her, something told him she wasn't simply an innocent victim. She'd seriously ticked someone off—enough to try to kill her. Maybe she had outgrown her propensity to find trouble, but it had obviously found her.

As much as he wished otherwise, he wouldn't be in her life long enough to help her navigate her way out of whatever mess she was in. Wherever she was headed, it wouldn't be Pensacola. She obviously wanted nothing to do with her childhood home.

He would stay with her this evening. The doctor was currently stitching her shoulder. Then they would have to do X-rays and possibly an MRI on her knee. But once Alyssa was finished at the emergency room, she would insist they go their separate ways. And he'd never see her again.

With the thought, a sense of heaviness pressed down on him—sadness and regret. But most of all, worry. What had she gotten involved with that had her fleeing for her life?

She needed to tell the police everything she knew. They couldn't go after the threat if she refused to talk. But unless she had changed a lot over the past eight years, that wasn't going to happen. When she had her mind made up, there was no changing it.

How could he protect her when she stubbornly refused help?

Chapter Two

Moans and groans came from the other side of the drawn curtain.

Alyssa looked at Spence and heaved a sigh. They had watched the other patient come in thirty minutes ago, hunched over in a wheelchair, both arms wrapped around her abdomen. She had complained of stomach pain that had begun that morning and gotten more severe as the day had progressed.

Another moan came from a few feet away, rising in volume and ending on a wail. Alyssa rolled her eyes. She wasn't unsympathetic. She was just antsy. She really wanted to get out of there.

The ER doctor had already stitched up her shoulder. The bullet had made clear entry and exit wounds, with a bloody path between, so he was confident it wasn't lodged in the tissue. Now, one shot and eighteen stitches later, she was patched up, the bleeding stopped. The doctor had assured her it would heal fine, but to take it easy for a few days. Without knowing what the immediate future held, she couldn't guarantee how closely she'd be following that advice.

Now she was waiting for the results of an MRI of her knee. Although she hadn't wanted to spend the extra time there, she hadn't argued. She'd tried to put her full weight on the leg while transferring from the wheelchair to the bed when she'd first arrived. The pain that had shot through her knee had almost taken her breath away.

Spence was still sitting in the chair immediately to her right, her backpack leaning against its front leg, the dog lying next to him. Having Spence there had been all right. He hadn't plied her with questions, as she'd feared. Instead, he'd kept up a fairly steady stream of small talk, which was good. She'd seen his look of doubt when she'd told the officer she didn't know who had shot her. Spence obviously hadn't believed her.

But she'd told the truth. She really didn't know who'd been in the car. She hadn't felt the need to admit she'd known who'd ordered her execution. With no idea who she could trust, her best bet was to reveal as little information as possible.

He reached beside him to scratch the top of the Lab's head. "You mentioned you were en route from Atlanta when your car broke down but didn't say where you were headed."

"Pensacola."

At his raised brows, she frowned. "I was going back for my mom's graveside service. Since I've now missed it, those plans are scrapped."

His brow creased. "Your mom came back?"

"She never left."

"Wait a minute. I was there."

Yeah, he had been. They'd just struck up a friendship when her mom disappeared. She'd been fifteen, he'd been sixteen. It hadn't taken them long to move from just friends to boyfriend and girlfriend.

She drew in a deep breath. "Turns out my dad killed her, buried her and had the gazebo built over the site. His secret would have stayed buried forever if the last hurricane hadn't destroyed the gazebo."

"Whoa, that's some heavy stuff."

He raised his right arm to run his palm over the top and

down the back of his head. Sometime in the past eight years, he'd spent time in the gym, evident in both his flexed arm and the way the T-shirt stretched taut across his chest. He'd always worn his dark-brown hair a little on the long side. Not anymore. It wasn't as severe as a military haircut, but it was nowhere near the length he'd had in his pre-army days. She couldn't say she didn't like it. It made him look capable, mature, one hundred percent masculine.

She tamped down the old attraction that had risen so unexpectedly and shrugged. "His killing her was an accident. At least, that's what he claimed."

"I'm sorry."

The Lab rose from his place on the floor beside Spence and approached the bed. Alyssa scratched him on the back of the neck, and he rested his head on her lap. For the past hour, the dog had alternated between lying next to Spence and rising to check on her.

While Spence's presence had been tolerable, Apollo's had been awesome. He acted as if he sensed her anxiety and wanted to offer her comfort. What kind of service did the dog provide for Spence? He'd apparently been injured. Although he seemed to try to walk as normally as possible, there was an awkwardness to his gait, a slight limp. Not wanting to pry, she hadn't asked. At one time, no topic would have been off limits. That had changed.

Another groan drifted through the closed curtain. Alyssa hoped the woman would get some relief soon, for all of their sakes.

Apollo moved away from the bed, but instead of lying next to the chair, he sat and put a paw on Spence's leg.

Spence looked from the dog to her. "I think he needs to go out. Will you be okay for a few minutes?"

"Of course. Bored maybe, but okay. Take your time. The poor boy has been cooped up for a while."

Shortly after Spence and Apollo walked out, footsteps approached and fell silent outside the curtain sectioning her space off from the rest of the room. Apollo and Spence couldn't be back already. They'd left just two minutes ago. Maybe the doctor was there, ready to give her the results of the MRI and send her home.

Fingers wrapped the edge of the curtain. A moment later, it lifted to the side. A man stepped through, and the curtain fell back into place.

This wasn't the doctor, and it wasn't either of the radiology people she'd seen earlier. In fact, she hadn't had any previous contact with him.

"I'm here to give you something for pain."

What pain? Her shoulder was still numb from the injections they'd given her before stitching her up. Lying in bed, her knee wasn't even bothering her, other than a deep ache.

Alyssa swept the length of him with her gaze. Instead of those cotton-type pants nurses often wore, he was dressed in blue jeans, tennis shoes covering his feet. If he had a name badge, it was hidden beneath his zipped jacket. So was whatever uniform top he might be wearing. The jacket was also hiding a lot of bulk, which she guessed was ninety-five percent muscle.

She shook her head. "That's okay. I don't need anything."

He gave her a slight smile. Maybe it was supposed to be reassuring, but it fell short of reaching his eyes.

"The doctor disagrees. He wants you to have this before you leave." He slipped a hand into his jacket pocket and pulled out a syringe.

What kind of nurse carries a syringe in their pocket? She scooted away from him on the narrow bed, her pulse kicking into high gear. She'd always considered herself street smart. Maybe she was paranoid, too. Because something about this man set off every internal alarm she had.

He stepped closer. "Relax. It'll just be a little prick."

"No." She pushed herself into a seated position, her tone emphatic. "I said I don't want anything. You need to leave."

Indecision settled across his features. But it didn't last long. He moved the syringe to his left hand and curled his right into a fist. A split second later, that fist flew toward her face.

Alyssa twisted and threw herself over the side rail of the bed and then hit the floor with a thud. She released a scream, loud and long, and scrambled to her feet. The curtain between her bed and the next slid back, and the woman who had the stomach issues stood there, slightly hunched, mouth agape, alarm in her eyes, her own pain apparently forgotten.

The man with the syringe looked from Alyssa to the woman and back to Alyssa again before darting from the room. There was a clatter in the hall, followed by shouts.

Alyssa looked frantically around, searching for anything she might use to protect herself if he came back. He'd been determined to give her whatever was in the syringe. Since she wouldn't take it willingly, he'd tried to knock her out so he could administer it while she was unconscious.

The sound of approaching footsteps sent panic through her again, and she fell into a fighting stance, fists raised. It was only one of the nurses.

"Are you all right?"

Alyssa lowered herself to the bed, panting, her legs suddenly weak. Now that some of the adrenaline was starting to dissipate, her knee was screaming. She put a hand on each side of her kneecap and gently massaged the swollen joint.

She looked back up at the nurse. "The man who just ran out of here, wearing the jeans and jacket, he wasn't one of your people, was he?"

"No, he wasn't. After knocking a couple of us down in the hallway, he escaped out the emergency room entrance. We've called hospital security. I'm sure they'll want to talk to you."

Yeah, they probably would. But there wasn't much she could tell them. She didn't know who he was or what was in the syringe. But one thing was sure. If he'd been successful in giving her that injection, she'd have left the ER in a body bag.

Spence stepped up next to the nurse, Apollo's leash in one hand. "Is everything all right?" His gaze shifted from Alyssa to the nurse and back again. "The hallway seems to be in a bit of an uproar."

Alyssa pressed her lips into a thin line. "Somebody insisted on giving me an injection I didn't want."

Spence frowned. "What kind of injection?"

"A lethal one, I'm guessing. The guy who shot me apparently decided to finish what he'd started."

His eyes widened. "Apollo and I were heading back when I saw someone run from the building. I'm sure it was the same guy. The doors hadn't even finished opening when he slipped between them and took off. I should have pursued him."

"And both you and Apollo could have been shot." Spence needed to stay out of her business. She had enough problems without having to worry about him going all Rambo on her and getting himself killed.

Before either of them could argue the point further, the security guard stepped into the space. The nurse walked away, leaving the three of them and the dog alone.

The man introduced himself as Tom Atkins and asked the same type of questions the police officer had asked. Alyssa's answers remained the same, too. She couldn't tell them what she didn't know.

And she didn't feel safe telling them what she did.

Throughout the conversation, Spence looked on her with disapproval. From his position in her peripheral vision, that judgment was something she felt rather than saw. But it was there.

Fine, let him judge. Soon she would be out of there—away from LaGrange and away from Spence and the judgment and disappointment in his eyes.

As Atkins was finishing his report, the doctor walked in.
He was wearing a smile.

"I have good news. Your anterior and posterior cruciate
ligaments look good, no tears that we can see. Same for the
meniscus. No fractures, either. Looks like you just have a bad
sprain. Take it easy for a few days. Ice the knee for twenty
minutes every two or three hours. We'll send you home with
an elastic knee brace. If you've got a set of crutches, that might
help, too."

"Thank you."

Relief collided with dread. They were sending her home.
The address she'd given them on the paperwork was where
she'd lived for the past eight months. But it wasn't home. Not
anymore.

Besides having nowhere to go, she wasn't even sure she
could make it back to her car. She could call a cab, but what
if the men who wanted her dead were hiding out in the hospital parking lot or waiting for her at Jim's Garage?

She would call the police. Surely, after two attempts on
her life, she would be able to get a unit to follow the cab from
the hospital to the garage and make sure she got away safely.

At least she wouldn't have to handle the financial end of
things on her way out. Someone had brought the paperwork to
the triage room shortly after she'd arrived, and she'd proudly
provided her insurance card. That great job she'd landed had
actually come with health benefits.

When the doctor left, Alyssa finally made eye contact with
Spence. His jaw was tight, his eyebrows drawn together. Yep,
just what she'd suspected. He was judging her.

He frowned. "You told both the police and the security
guard that you have no idea who's after you."

"That's because I *don't* know."

He leaned forward in his chair and studied her some more,
so intently she could hardly keep from fidgeting.

"What's going on, Alyssa? What did you do?" He released

a sigh heavy with disappointment. That same disappointment was reflected in his eyes.

She hadn't set out to be a disappointment to everyone she cared about, but that seemed to be her lot in life.

She crossed her arms and glared at him. "I didn't do anything."

"So, a random drive-by shooter followed you all the way to the hospital to finish you off. And you have no idea why he's after you."

A nurse walked in with the brace the doctor had promised, sparing Alyssa from having to respond to Spence's accusations. She slipped one foot through and pulled the brace into place over the top of her jeans. No way would it fit underneath.

"What are you going to do now?"

She carefully slid her right foot into her tennis shoe without looking at him. "I'm going to call a cab."

Spence would insist on driving her back to the garage, but this was her battle, not his. If these men decided to take pot shots at her, she didn't want him anywhere in the vicinity. She started to tie the laces and then hesitated. She wouldn't put Spence in danger, but what about the cab driver, possibly a man with a wife and kids? Even with the police following, someone could still be hurt.

Spence heaved a sigh that sounded a lot like one a parent might expel when dealing with a difficult child. It sent a shot of annoyance through her.

The same quality she'd heard in his sigh came through in his tone. "So you're going to walk out of here with no plan and no way to defend yourself."

She finished lacing her shoes and straightened. "And I suppose *you* have that plan."

If he did, she was willing to hear it. Because she was no longer feeling as confident as she had when she'd come in.

"Actually, I do. How's this? I call a friend of mine to meet us here. He radios Dispatch to send some of his law enforcement buddies. They make sure we get from here to the garage and see you safely out of town."

Wow. Someone with connections. Definitely a better plan than hers.

"Where are you going after you leave here? Something tells me you're not going back to Atlanta."

"I don't know."

"You don't know, or you won't tell me? Come on, Alyssa. Regardless of who these guys are and why they're after you, you've got to be willing to accept some help."

A stony hardness wrapped around her heart. "I don't need you to take care of me." She didn't try to soften the flinty tone. "Eight years ago, maybe. But you took off."

He winced and pain filled his eyes.

Guilt pricked her. She half understood why he'd done what he had, but that didn't make it any easier.

He sighed again, but this one held resignation. "You've had two attempts on your life in a span of less than four hours. Do you think these men are going to just give up and leave you alone?"

She drew her lower lip between her teeth. No, they probably wouldn't.

When she didn't respond, he continued. "I was planning to leave for Pensacola the day after tomorrow, but I can go earlier. Come back with me."

He had to be joking. "There's nothing for me there."

"You have family. Two sisters whose fiancés happen to be cops."

What? He'd stayed in touch with Kassie and Kris and neither of them had bothered to mention it?

Alyssa closed her eyes, tamping down the swirling emotions and forcing herself to look at everything logically. She'd lashed out when he'd said it, but Spence was right. If she hoped to get out of the mess she was in, she would have to accept some help.

It wasn't easy. She'd taken care of herself since she'd left home at eighteen. Actually, she'd taken care of herself before then. She'd lost her mother at fifteen. In the years that had followed, her father had climbed out of the bottle just long enough to rake her over the coals for her infractions. Two years after losing her mother, Spence had left. She'd made it one more year, finishing high school before taking off herself.

Now, at twenty-five, having to rely on anybody rankled. Having to rely on Spence really stuck in her craw. And having to crawl to her sisters was almost unthinkable. They'd always judged her. Now that they were both regular churchgoers, they probably thought that gave them an even better platform from which to look down on her. She didn't need them or their faith.

But as much as she didn't want to admit it, accepting help, even if it came from Spence or her sisters, beat the alternative. Because this time, she really *was* in over her head. After walking in on that conversation, she had slipped right back out, but not before the men had noticed. Her boyfriend had promised the other three he would take care of it. She'd managed to escape before he'd had the opportunity.

Since then, Peter and his cronies had come after her twice. They would keep coming until they succeeded. They wouldn't give up until she was dead.

Weapons, lethal injections, thugs to do their bidding—these men apparently had unlimited resources to make that happen.

Spence stood just to the side of the emergency room's automatic glass doors, peering out into the night. Apollo stood next to him, ever alert. Alyssa had walked from the treatment area and, after stopping by the restroom to change out of her bloody shirt, had taken a seat in one of the waiting room chairs.

When she had stood from the bed, he'd offered her his arm. She'd passed, claiming she was going to have to be able to walk on her own. After gingerly putting her weight on her right leg, she'd taken a step and then another. She wouldn't be running any races, but the brace helped. She was at least able to walk.

It had taken a lot of convincing, but he'd finally gotten her to agree to go to Pensacola and let him follow her. He wished he could stay there with her rather than having to immediately head back to LaGrange.

The only other option would have been to keep her with him until he could clear out his apartment and head south for good. Knowing there were men who wanted her dead hiding nearby, that would have been a bad plan. The sooner he could get her away from LaGrange, the safer she would be.

So, he was following her out tonight and leaving her in the care of her sisters first thing tomorrow morning. He wasn't sure about Kassie's housing, but Kris still lived in the family home on Bayou Texar. The place was huge. Hopefully, it would be large enough for the two sisters to share without coming to blows. When they'd all been teenagers, it hadn't been because the animosity between them had been so great. From his brief contact with Alyssa this afternoon, it didn't sound like those relationships had improved much.

Headlights drew closer, and a vehicle stopped under the porte cochere. He motioned to Alyssa. "Here's our ride. To my truck anyway."

Jason wasn't just one of his best friends. He was also a detective with the LaGrange Police Department. He was in his personal vehicle, but he'd assured Spence there would be others, some marked, some unmarked, who would follow them from the hospital to Spence's apartment to Jim's Garage, and well out of town, all the way to the Georgia/Alabama line.

Alyssa rose from the chair she'd been sitting in and limped to the door, which slid back on its track. Spence handed Alyssa the leash and held up a hand. As he stepped out, he looked around. There was activity—two vehicles that appeared to be heading toward the exit, another sliding into a parking spot. No gold sedans. That didn't mean anything. The men could have swapped vehicles.

He opened the front passenger door of Jason's Kia Soul. "Thanks, buddy. I appreciate this."

"Don't mention it."

Spence motioned at Alyssa, and she stepped outside, Apollo next to her. After passing off the leash, she tossed her backpack on the floorboard then sat and swung both legs inside. Once he and Apollo had climbed into the back seat, Jason pulled away from the entrance. Spence made brief introductions and directed him to where he had parked.

Jason eased to a stop behind the Land Rover. "There are a couple of unmarked units here in the parking lot and another at your place. A third is circling the area around Jim's Garage." He glanced over at Alyssa. "Whoever these guys are, we're hoping to get them off the street before you even get away from LaGrange."

Alyssa nodded. "Thank you."

Her gratitude seemed genuine, in spite of the fact that getting her to this point had involved a battle. She swung open her door. As Spence stepped out, she twisted in her seat, preparing to exit herself. When she tossed her hair over her right shoulder, some of the wavy red locks trailed across the side of the bucket seat.

Her natural hair color was a medium brown. Over the years, he'd seen it jet-black and several shades of blond. The red looked good on her.

She looked good. All three of the Ashbaugh girls were short—no more than five foot three or four. But where twins Kassie and Kris had always had sleek, athletic builds, Alyssa had always been curvier. Even their facial features were different, which had led to claims by Alyssa's father that she wasn't his, claims their mother denied.

After once again thanking his friend, Spence walked Alyssa to the passenger door of his Land Rover and instructed Apollo to hop into the back seat. As he turned onto Medical Drive, headed away from the hospital, Alyssa twisted to look at the dog. His tail immediately began to thud against the leather.

Spence stopped at a traffic light. She had twisted a little further but still couldn't reach the back seat. Apollo accommodated her by stepping forward and resting his head on the center console.

"You're a sweet boy." Alyssa scratched his neck and then worked her way down his back as far as she could reach.

Behind him, Apollo's tail continued to thud against the seat. The light changed, and Spence stepped on the accelerator. When he slid Alyssa a sideways glance, she was smiling. It hadn't taken him long to notice that the stiffness she displayed with him disappeared when she interacted with his dog, who now stood with his front legs on the floor, his back haunches still on the rear seat. The position didn't look comfortable. But Apollo seemed to have a knack for recognizing who needed his calming presence.

She looked at Spence. "He's a Lab, right?"

"He is."

"Labs are good dogs."

He nodded. Apollo was the best.

"How long have you had him?"

"Three months." During that time, the dog had brought him out of numerous nightmares and even staved off a few flashbacks. But he'd done so much more. He'd given Spence a new lease on life.

During those months he had waited to be matched with a dog, he'd found himself withdrawing from life. Going out in public had become increasingly more difficult. Soon he'd been ordering groceries and anything else he'd needed online, stepping outside only to bring in packages and walk to the mailbox. Getting Apollo had brought him back into society.

As Alyssa continued to pet and coo at his dog, a heaviness settled in Spence's chest. He'd really hoped by now her life would be on track. She had always had a good heart, had never wanted to hurt anybody. She just hadn't been wise in her choice of friends…or firm in fighting bad influences. Regrettably, *he'd* been one of those bad influences back in the day.

He released a sigh. Whatever she was tangled up in, maybe she would share with him eventually. She used to tell him everything. That sharing had gone both ways.

They'd had a lot in common, the least of which had been alcoholic fathers. While his had tried to whip him into submission with fists, belts or whatever he could put his hands on, hers had simply beat her down with words. Or ignored her altogether. And they'd both dealt with the fallout in the most destructive ways possible.

Spence pulled into the parking lot of his apartment complex and eased to a stop in one of the spaces. Jason's Soul appeared briefly in his rearview mirror as it passed behind him. The other vehicle that had exited the hospital parking lot behind Jason's had pulled in also, selecting a spot two spaces before reaching the Land Rover.

He swung open the door and stepped out. "I'm going to grab a change of clothes and some dog food. Will you be all right staying out here with Apollo?"

"I'll be fine, especially with Jason and the other guys keeping an eye on me."

He nodded. He wouldn't leave her otherwise. He would have made her hobble up with him. He'd have even carried her if he'd had to.

A few minutes later, he headed back down the stairs carrying a duffel bag filled with some toiletries, one change of clothes, two cans of Blue Buffalo and Apollo's food and water bowl. While in his apartment, he'd slid his Glock into the end pocket of the bag. He hadn't been armed today but he would be from here on out. At least until the men after Alyssa had been captured and locked up.

When he reached the parking lot, Jason was standing at the open passenger door of the Land Rover, talking to Alyssa.

Spence slung the bag onto the floorboard behind the driver's seat and removed the pistol. It would ride in the center console.

Jason patted the roof twice. "I'll follow you to the garage. Two or three others will be there, too. They'll escort you all the way to the state line."

Alyssa gave him a grateful smile. "I don't know if this escort service is standard or if I'm getting special treatment because of you and Spence, but please let everyone know I'm really grateful."

Jason tilted his head. "Glad to be of service."

When they arrived at Jim's Garage ten minutes later, her car waited in the soft glow of one of the parking lot lights. Whatever had been wrong with it, he hoped the garage had fixed the problem and no new ones would crop up before they reached Pensacola.

He stopped next to the old car as Jason turned around some distance away, ready to pull back out onto the highway.

Alyssa gave Apollo a couple more scratches on the head. "Thank you."

"I'll be right behind you. I'm not telling you to drive crazy, but the sooner we can get you to Pensacola, the better I'll feel."

"I agree."

She climbed from the Land Rover, dragging her pack with her. As she tossed it into the back of the Tempo and slid into the driver's seat, he glanced around. Jason was still sitting where he had parked. Spence didn't see the others, but according to his friend, they were there. He pulled his phone from his pocket and sent Jason a quick text.

Thanks again. I'll let you know when we arrive.

Alyssa's door closed and he dropped his phone into the cup holder with a relieved sigh. She was safe for the time being. No one would be able to get to her.

But what if while one guy had been at the hospital trying

to administer a lethal injection, another had been carrying out a contingency plan and planting a bomb on her car? Cold dread washed through him. He swung open his door and laid on the horn. Alyssa looked over at him, and he jumped from the SUV. Her face was in shadow, but he could guess what was there—alarm.

He hadn't wanted to startle her, but someone needed to thoroughly check her car before she cranked it, even if it delayed their leaving.

As he moved toward her, a low rumble rose above the hum of the Land Rover's engine. Her car was already running. She had apparently started it the same time he'd blown his horn. And it was all in one piece. He heaved a sigh of relief, gave her an okay sign and got back into his vehicle.

When she pulled from the parking lot, he was right behind her. Less than a block away, they passed a dark SUV sitting at the edge of a convenience store parking lot. It pulled out but stayed several car lengths back.

For the next twenty miles, they would be under the watchful eye of the LaGrange Police Department. Then they would cross the line into Alabama, and it would be up to him.

He had no idea what Alyssa had gotten involved in. But it didn't matter. He would still do everything in his power to protect her. She wasn't his responsibility. She certainly wasn't his girlfriend, because she wasn't even his friend. But he couldn't turn his back on her.

Maybe he was trying to make up for the past. Maybe, after serving his country for the majority of his adult life, the need to protect was ingrained in him.

Or maybe she had never totally vacated that special place in his heart.

After several turns, they merged onto Interstate 85. It didn't take Alyssa long to accelerate to the seventy-mile-an-hour speed limit. The gap between her and a semi in front of her narrowed, and she moved into the left lane. Two more times, she went around slower traffic and returned to the right lane.

Ahead, a sign welcomed them to Alabama. When he glanced in his rearview mirror, the SUV he'd observed earlier decelerated and made a U-turn in an emergency break in the median.

He glanced at the clock on the dashboard. The time was nearing ten. The sky was dark. If the moon was up there, it was hidden by clouds.

Over the next hour, traffic grew increasingly sparse. Headlights approached from behind, rapidly gaining on him. He cast frequent glances in his rearview mirror, waiting for the left turn signal to come on. Was the person behind him a reckless, aggressive driver who was going to wait until the last minute to go around him? Or had Alyssa's enemies found her again?

As the vehicle drew closer, a little of the tension seeped from his shoulders. Those were pickup truck headlights. They were too high to belong to the car Alyssa had described.

The driver did wait until the last minute to change lanes. But instead of continuing past him, he decelerated suddenly to travel next to him.

It was definitely a pickup—a large one, like an F-250 or a Silverado 2500. He jammed on his brakes, sending Apollo crashing into the back of his seat. At the same moment, the truck swerved into his lane. Its right rear bumper caught his left front one, and his back end swung around. Spence overcorrected, sending the vehicle hurtling toward oncoming traffic. For several seconds, his SUV followed a wild zigzag path, headed for the median one second and the tree-lined edge of the road the next. He fought to regain control, his heart pounding in his throat. *God help us!*

The wheel jerked in his hand as the Land Rover left the highway. He bounced over the uneven terrain, praying he wouldn't roll the vehicle and Apollo would come through unhurt. His foot on the brake did nothing to slow his forward momentum. He hit a ditch, and the wheel jerked right then left then right again.

His head snapped sideways, slamming into the side window, and the sharp sound of cracking glass filled the vehicle. Trees loomed large through the front windshield. The crash of metal and the explosion of the airbag happened simultaneously.

His ears rang, an annoying sound that grew louder as darkness closed in from all around.

Then there was nothing.

Chapter Three

Alyssa sped down the road, maintaining a death grip on the steering wheel, a sob rising in her throat. A vehicle had just run Spence off the road. It had to be a truck, a rather large one. Its headlights were quite a bit higher than Spence's.

At the speed they were going, once the Land Rover left the road, it hadn't stood a chance. The uneven ground between the shoulder and tree line several yards away had tossed the SUV around like a toy, headlights making erratic paths through the darkness.

She hit her brakes. As she watched in her rearview mirror, the SUV came to an abrupt stop, lights shining diagonally across the road. Had Spence slammed into a tree?

Now the truck was gaining on her. Of course. They had only attacked Spence because he was with her. Anyone watching them would have guessed they were traveling together. Spence had maintained a distance of about five or six car lengths behind her, and every time she changed lanes, he had, too.

She stepped hard on the gas. Trying to outrun the truck was pointless. The gap closed and it moved into the left lane. Soon it was beside her.

Panic pounded up her spine. There was no one to help her.

The driver of the truck had waited until she and Spence were in a gap in traffic. Although several sets of oncoming head-lights were close, the traffic behind her was too far away for anyone to even recognize her distress. In front of her, taillights were visible far in the distance.

She glanced over in time to see the truck's passenger win-dow lower. An arm extended through the open window. With-out waiting to see what he held, she jerked the wheel to the left and slammed into the truck. The ear-splitting pop of a gun-shot accompanied the sharp crunch of metal against metal.

The impact ricocheted her car in the other direction, send-ing her off the right shoulder. She jammed on the brakes and jerked the wheel back to the left. The truck was ahead of her now, and she was racing toward the center median. A few yards away, headlights moved rapidly in her direction.

A quarter turn of the wheel in the opposite direction sent her back off the right shoulder and bouncing along the un-even ground. Trees sped past, illuminated in the beams of her headlights. Her steering wheel turned sharply side to side, as if controlled by someone else.

Suddenly, a huge pine stood right in front of her, not twenty feet away. She made a hard left just in time to avoid hitting it head on, but not in time to miss it altogether.

The Tempo shuddered as the tree scraped along its side from front quarter panel to rear bumper. At the sudden abrupt stop, her head snapped forward, her face barely missing the steering wheel. There was no airbag. Her car had been made several years before they'd become mandatory.

She sat for several moments, panting, hands still gripping the wheel. Her head and neck hurt, and her skull seemed to be stuffed with cotton. Looking behind her in the side mirror, she could no longer see the Land Rover's headlights. Maybe she had travelled farther than she'd thought.

When she looked ahead, the truck had pulled off the road. Its backup lights brightened as it began to move toward her.

They were coming back for her. If she sat there trying to collect her wits, she would end up dead.

The truck slowed and the passenger door swung open. She jumped from her car and ran around its rear and toward the woods, ignoring the pain stabbing through her knee. As she disappeared into the tree line, two shots rang out. One pinged off a tree just ahead and less than two feet to her right. A spray of bark hit her in the face.

A cold male voice reached her over the rustle of the branches that slapped her as she passed. "I'll take care of her. You make sure whoever was following her isn't going to give us any grief."

Her knees almost buckled, and her stomach dropped like a boulder. They were going after Spence. He was armed—he'd told her he would be. But was he in any shape to use what he was carrying? Was he even conscious? She had to do something.

Up ahead and to her left, something large suddenly crashed through the underbrush. She leaped sideways, away from whatever creature she had startled.

Several shots rang out in rapid succession, and she stifled a shriek. Hand pressed over her mouth, she ducked behind a large tree, molding herself against its bark.

There was more movement, this time behind her. She held her breath as her assailant passed within ten or fifteen feet of where she stood. He was moving at a jog, pistol drawn.

Alyssa slunk around the tree, keeping it between herself and the man who was hunting her. Suddenly, the footsteps stopped, and she peered out from her hiding place. He was looking slowly side to side, weapon apparently following his gaze.

She closed her eyes, afraid to even breathe. *Keep going.* If he continued to follow whatever they had heard, she could double back. Maybe she could get to Spence.

And do what? She wasn't even armed. If he was incapacitated, she would be powerless to help him.

A vise clamped down on her chest. She should never have agreed to allow him to follow her. She should have given him a flat-out no and finagled a way out of the mess she was in without involving him. She'd tried. She should have tried harder. Instead, she had pulled him into her drama. Now he might pay with his life.

There was a rustle deeper in the woods, probably a deer or whatever she had heard earlier.

The man headed off in that direction.

She waited until she could no longer hear his footsteps. If she couldn't hear him, he likely couldn't hear her. Then she turned to retrace her steps. Maybe she could make it back to the interstate and try to flag someone down. Or better yet, get to her phone and call for help.

Alyssa crept forward as quietly as she could, the traffic ahead helping to mask her steps. Finally, she reached the edge of the trees and hesitated. She wouldn't step from their cover until she made sure no one was waiting beside her car.

Of course, they weren't. One of the men was pretty deep in the woods by now. The other had hiked back to the wrecked Land Rover. With his military training, Spence would be a formidable foe.

Unless he was unconscious.

But she hadn't yet heard a gunshot. That had to be a good sign.

The rumble of a semitruck grew louder, and she stepped from the line of trees. No one was standing next to her car or anywhere in its vicinity. She moved closer. So did the semi, the glow of the headlight beams spilling off the shoulder and barely reaching the edge of her car.

She stifled a gasp and froze.

Someone was sitting in her back seat, looking down at something in his lap. Was he going through her things? Looking for a way to get to her through something on her phone?

He would be out of luck there. Since it was a burner phone,

she hadn't saved any contacts, had no social media accounts to link, hadn't sent or received any calls except the one from Jim's Garage.

So how many men were pursuing her?

At least three.

Without taking her eyes from the car, she crept backward, slipping silently into the woods.

If it was two against three, she and Spence weren't badly outnumbered.

But with one weapon between them, they were far outgunned.

Spence peered around a large pine tree, his pistol in his right hand, Apollo pressed against his left leg. Five minutes ago, he'd been oblivious to everything around him. He'd awoken to moans of pain. It had taken him several seconds to realize those moans were his own.

The next thing that had registered was a series of soft whimpers and a wet tongue slurping up his cheek. Through the cracked front windshield, a narrow beam of light some distance ahead had swung toward him then toward the ground, up and down. With the brain fog starting to clear, it hadn't taken him long to realize someone carrying a flashlight was walking in his direction.

He hadn't known whether it was a passerby who had noticed his SUV, pulled over and come back to render aid, or if it was one of the guys in the truck coming back to finish him off.

He hadn't waited around to find out. He'd turned off the dome light to keep it from illuminating when he opened the door and pulled his weapon and Apollo's leash from the console. When he'd discovered the door was jammed, he'd had to fight off a panic attack. After a few blows with his shoulder, it had finally creaked open. Then he and Apollo had slipped into the trees before the man had gotten close enough to see them.

Now he was watching from just inside the tree line about

twenty feet from the back of his SUV. Apollo stood next to him, as he waited to see if the man approaching was friend or foe. He didn't even have his phone. It had bounced from the cup holder and was lying somewhere in the darkened Land Rover.

When the man reached the vehicle, he shone the flashlight through the front windshield and then moved to the side to check the back seat. A stray glimmer illuminated the nickel barrel of a pistol. Spence straightened, face now hidden, no longer peering around the tree. This was no Good Samaritan, a passerby willing to interrupt his schedule to see if a fellow motorist needed assistance. This was someone determined to see Alyssa dead. What had happened to her? Had she been able to escape? Or had the men forced her off the road and shot her?

He hadn't heard gunfire, or any kind of commotion, for that matter. But that didn't mean anything. He'd been out cold. There could have been an all-out war, and he wouldn't have known.

Two vehicles approached, headed south on 85. The man crossed his arm in front of him, the weapon pressed between his left elbow and waist. Then he circled back around the front of the SUV to crouch at its right front quarter panel.

Spence took advantage of the noise of the vehicles to slip deeper into the woods, Apollo trotting next to him. The dog appeared unhurt. Except for a monster headache, he was, too. Both were serious answers to prayer.

When everything fell quiet again, he paused. Someone moved through the woods, not far to his right. He held his breath and waited, heart pounding. Were the footsteps growing closer? He squeezed his eyes shut and listened, trying to pinpoint the exact location of the man pursuing him.

The image in his mind wavered, and trees became desert sand broken by sparse shrubs. Instead of woods, damaged mud-brick houses lined a pothole-marked street.

No, not now. Spence opened his eyes wide, ingesting the

view around him. Not much light came through the heavy clouds. Even less made its way through the branches above him.

But it was enough. He wasn't in Afghanistan. He was in Alabama, his smashed vehicle sitting somewhere along Interstate 85, and his dog leaning into him, further grounding him to reality. He inhaled a deep, silent breath and forced his heart to slow.

He wasn't out of danger, though. He had no phone, no way to call for help. And he had no transportation, no way to drive himself to safety. His vehicle was toast. He didn't have to be an insurance adjuster to make that determination.

The footsteps changed direction. His pursuer was now moving closer. Had he heard something? Had Spence made a sound as he'd fought to stave off the flashback? Or had a small animal moved through the underbrush, and he'd been too distracted to notice?

Now he heard it, a rustle about six feet away. Definitely an animal. Likely an armadillo.

Spence crept silently in the opposite direction, praying he wouldn't step on any twigs or branches. He didn't want to kill someone tonight, but he would if he had to.

Some distance away, another group of cars sped past. When the engine noise faded, the tension fled his body. Whomever he had heard was moving away.

For several more minutes, he waited, listening. Once confident no one was near, Spence backtracked toward the road. He had to check on Alyssa.

Maybe they hadn't been able to get to her. Maybe she had successfully evaded them long enough to call 911. Or maybe they had forced her off the road, and she'd been able to slip into the woods the same way he had.

Alyssa was smart. She'd foiled two attempts on her life in less than six hours. If she'd been conscious and alert enough to escape her car, she could probably remain hidden long enough for help to arrive.

God, please let her outsmart whoever is after her. Please keep her safe.

When he reached the edge of the woods, he looked both directions. His smashed-up Land Rover was twenty or thirty feet behind him. Alyssa would be somewhere up ahead. Maybe.

Instead of walking in the grassy area, he stayed just inside the woods, paralleling the road. Without knowing how many men were out there, he wasn't letting down his guard. The truck had carried at least two. He wasn't sure about the gold car from which the shots had been fired outside Jim's Garage.

He hadn't gone very far when there was a continuous series of loud rustles to his right. He froze, pistol raised. Something large was barreling through the woods toward him. A person, or maybe two people—someone in pursuit and someone fleeing. Judging from the sound, he was right in their path.

He pulled Apollo behind a tree and slipped in behind him, putting the trunk between himself and whoever or whatever was charging toward them. As he peered around it, someone moved into his line of sight, closing in at a limping run. The figure was smaller, like a woman. *Alyssa?*

A shot rang out and his heart went into his throat. But other than a brief zigzag, the figure continued straight for him. Two more shots and she dropped and rolled.

Spence stepped out, spread his legs and squared his body, pistol raised. A second figure came into view, much larger than the first one. He apparently saw Spence the same time Spence saw him. The man raised his weapon and fired a split second before Spence did, but the shot went wide. Spence's was true.

The man crumpled to his knees and fell forward, face-first on the ground. Spence waited to see if he would attempt to fire again. He didn't.

After signaling Apollo to stay, Spence dropped the leash and approached slowly. He hadn't wanted to kill anyone, but the man had given him no choice. It was either take him out or let him kill Alyssa. This wasn't the first time he'd taken a life. War was ugly. But pulling the trigger always left him with a knot in his gut and a vague feeling of nausea.

Only after making sure the other man had no pulse did he slide the barrel of his weapon into his waistband. "Come, Apollo."

They both approached Alyssa. As soon as he helped her to her feet, she threw herself into his arms, almost knocking him backward.

He wrapped his arms around her, and she slid hers around his waist, holding him as if she would never let go. He'd held her so many times, but it had been eight long years. It had felt natural then. Now it felt awkward. They had both changed. Or maybe it was because he had changed and she hadn't.

He rested his chin on her head. Awkward or not, she needed him. She apparently needed Apollo, too, because the dog had positioned himself against both of them.

"It was him." She spoke the words against his chest. "The guy at the hospital. The one with the syringe."

"Do you have your phone?"

She shook her head, something he felt rather than saw. "It's in the car. I didn't have time to grab it."

"Same here. Where is your car?"

"About a mile ahead of where you crashed."

"Let's get it. We need to call for help. There's still a guy in the woods, the one who came after me."

She stiffened suddenly. "There's a third one watching my car. When I eluded the first guy, I went back for my phone and almost ran into him."

He frowned. So there were still two men out there hunting them. At least, that they knew of. There could be more in other vehicles. "We'd better hike to the nearest town, see if we can flag down a police cruiser. Someone might see our wrecked vehicles and call the authorities, but waiting around to find out doesn't seem like a good idea."

"We passed Tuskagee two or three miles back."

"We did. Can you make it?"

"I'll make it."

When she dropped her arms, he picked up Apollo's leash and put one hand through the loop. As he straightened, a rustle sounded some distance away. He held up a hand. "Shh."

For several moments, Spence listened, cocking an ear toward the woods. There was definitely movement, but whether someone was walking their way or parallel to the road, he couldn't tell.

"Let's cross. I think we'll be safer on the other side of the interstate."

As soon as there was a good break in traffic on both sides, she hurried with him across the southbound lanes, through the median and to the opposite side of the lanes headed north. Apollo loped ahead of them, leash gently taut. Then they slipped through the edge of the tree line.

A few hours ago, he'd been headed to his apartment, boxes in the back of his SUV, schedule for the next two days neatly laid out, ready to pack up, clean and vacate his apartment before his lease ran out.

If having his plans wrecked, his vehicle totaled and someone trying to kill him didn't put him in a bad mood, thinking about the dead man he'd left in the woods did. So did not even knowing what any of it was about.

He looked over at Alyssa. Her face was in shadow. The little bit of light that reached them from approaching traffic came from behind, and the starlight filtering through the trees was almost nonexistent.

"Tell me what you took. Who did you tick off?"

She crossed her arms and stared straight ahead, her gait even stiffer.

"Come on, Alyssa. I killed a man. I have a right to know."

"I didn't take anything." She emphasized each word. "You automatically assume the worst about me." She heaved a sigh. "That's why I don't want to go back to Pensacola. I'll get the same thing from everybody there—my sisters, the people I went to school with, everybody who knew me growing up." She uncrossed her arms to throw her hands up. "Even the police. Everyone's got the same negative expectations, and that's never going to change."

"If you weren't acting like you're hiding something, I could probably be a little more understanding."

"Okay, I inadvertently saw something I wasn't supposed to see. Now these guys are determined to silence me."

"Why don't you report it, get the police involved?"

"Because I don't trust anybody. I don't know what kind of connections these guys have."

He studied her as she spoke. He was inclined to believe her. Maybe, for once, the trouble she was in wasn't because of her own doing.

After almost two hours of walking, they reached Tuskagee.

Alyssa was limping worse, but she hadn't complained once. She was a tough one. His own limp was almost as pronounced as hers. He'd passed the point of trying to hide it more than an hour ago.

Tuskagee was a quiet, small city, but at almost midnight, there was no activity at all. Finally, a Tuskagee Police Department vehicle approached, and they flagged it down. An officer stepped from the passenger side, Probst, according to his name tag. They explained the events of the day, ending with how Spence had killed one of the men in self-defense.

After instructing the other officer to put out an APB for the pickup truck, Probst turned back to Spence. "I assume reports were filed about the shooting near the garage and the event at the hospital."

"Yes."

"And you can show someone where we'll find this body?"

"I can."

"If you two and your dog don't mind sitting in the back of the patrol car, we'll give you a ride to the scene and have the Macon County Sheriff's deputies meet us out there." Probst frowned. "We'll need to confiscate your weapon until the investigation is over."

"I suspected as much."

After the officer had donned a pair of latex gloves, Spence handed over the Glock, which went into an evidence bag. At least he had another weapon at home, that one a Colt. If he hadn't, he would have bought one; no way was he leaving Alyssa unprotected.

When they arrived at the wrecked Land Rover, two Macon County Sheriff's cruisers were already there. It didn't take long for Spence to backtrack to where he'd left the man in the woods.

Then he called a tow truck for his vehicle. Once his insurance company opened in the morning, he'd report the accident to them.

Probst took them a little farther down the interstate to Alyssa's car, and as soon as he opened her door, she climbed from the back seat. "I'd like to see if my car is drivable." She limped in that direction. "The doors on the right side probably won't open, and they may leak. But if it's safe to drive, I'd rather not have to rent something."

Spence agreed. The sooner they could get out of there, the safer they would be. And based on the little bit Alyssa had told him, not leaving a paper trail with a car rental company was probably a good idea.

She pulled her keys from her pocket and slid into the driver's seat. "Since the damage is just on the side, I'm hoping the engine and transmission are fine."

The engine cranked on the first try. As she eased forward, Spence watched, the screech and groan of metal setting his teeth on edge. The major components were apparently okay, but that didn't mean pieces wouldn't fall off in transit.

She turned the wheel slightly to the left, easing the vehicle away from the trees. Once clear, she shifted into Park and stepped out.

"I think we're good to go. I wouldn't try any cross-country trips, but as long as it doesn't shimmy and rattle too much, we should be able to make it to Pensacola."

Spence looked at Probst. One of the Macon County units had already left. The other deputies were in the woods, waiting for crime scene to show up. "Can you guys make sure we get away without being followed?"

"Sure thing."

"Thanks." Meanwhile, he'd look for a route to Pensacola using back roads, in case the men would be watching for them along the interstate. If her car stood out before, it would really stand out now.

After Probst relayed the request, Alyssa crossed her arms, frowning. "When I left Atlanta, I made sure I wasn't followed. When I left LaGrange, the LaGrange Police Department made sure I wasn't followed. But both times, some dangerous people found me. How is that possible?"

Probst pressed his lips together. "Any chance you've got a tracking device?"

Spence nodded. "My thoughts exactly." They were probably Alyssa's, too.

He passed Apollo's leash to Alyssa. Then he and the officer dropped to their knees and slowly worked their way around the Tempo, inspecting its underside by flashlight.

Alyssa waited at the back bumper. "I'd offer to help, but I have no idea what we're looking for."

Spence wasn't sure he did, either, but he had enough knowledge of mechanics to know when he was looking at something that didn't belong there.

After searching the exterior, including the bumper and grill,

Spence moved inside. He'd heard the most common place for GPS trackers was under the dash. Dropping the dash took time, longer than he'd hoped, and didn't produce a tracking device.

Officer Probst met him at the open driver's door. "I have one other idea." He looked at Alyssa. "Is it all right if we remove your taillight covers?"

She lifted her brows. "Are you seriously concerned about doing damage to my car?"

He smiled. "I guess not."

Spence climbed from the car and watched him remove the left cover then the right.

"Bingo."

Spence moved closer. A flat, rectangular object had been connected to the taillight wiring and stuffed into the space.

Alyssa shook her head. Even in the dim light, her face seemed to have lost color. "I have no idea when that was put there, but I want it gone." She looked at Spence. "Can you get rid of it?"

"Without making the taillight inoperable?"

"Preferably."

"Maybe. We'll need to cut the wiring going into the tracking device and splice it."

"Can you do it? I need to be able to drive my car."

At 1:00 in the morning, they weren't likely to find an auto parts store open. "I'll give it a shot."

Thankfully, Alyssa carried a well-stocked tool kit in her trunk. Within twenty minutes, he had the tracking device removed and her taillight functional. The brake light and turn signal even worked.

She gave him a crooked smile. "You're good."

"I know a few things."

After they had both thanked Probst and the other law enforcement personnel who had shown up to see to their safety, Alyssa slid in behind the wheel, and Spence and Apollo climbed into the back seat.

He passed her backpack forward. "If you let me use your phone, I'll look for an alternate route."

After she had handed it to him, she pulled onto the interstate, the sheriff vehicles coming out behind them.

"These guys who are after you, do they know where you're from?"

"No. Any time someone asks, I say Florida. If they want to know where in Florida, I say near Tallahassee."

He quirked an eyebrow. She was apparently using the term "near" loosely. Both towns were in the Panhandle, but they were three hours apart. Her secrecy said a lot about the people she chose to hang around with. Maybe that was at least part of the reason she had changed her name.

Alyssa continued. "But don't worry. I'm not planning to stay. As soon as I can figure out a game plan, I'm out of there."

"You know, there are worse places to be stuck than Pensacola."

"Yeah, Atlanta."

Her voice was heavy with meaning. The trouble she'd found was apparently there. But it wasn't staying there. It was following her wherever she went.

"Please don't leave before I get back."

She didn't respond.

"Let me help, please. Promise me. Don't you at least owe me that?"

Maybe that was low, trying to make her feel obligated. But if it would keep her from running before he got back, it was worth it.

Spence had no control over her actions. No matter how badly he wanted to make sure she was safe, he couldn't force her to stay.

But one thing was sure.

This time, he wouldn't be the one to walk away.

Chapter Four

"Alyssa."

Alyssa squeezed her eyes shut more tightly and released a moan. Someone was calling her. It wasn't the first time, either.

"Alyssa, wake up." The voice was deep, but soothing.

"Go away." Her words came out slurred.

Now, a gentle shoulder shake. Why couldn't they just leave her alone?

She opened her eyes. The ceiling was less than two feet from her face. Where was she?

She pushed herself upright, and everything came back to her in a rush. She was in the passenger seat of her Tempo. During their 3:00 a.m. gas stop, she had crawled over the console and allowed Spence to drive. After being awake for a straight twenty-two hours, she had needed a break.

For the next two hours, she had talked with Spence, helping keep him alert until they'd pulled into a rest area along I-10, sixty minutes from her childhood home. At that early hour, she hadn't been willing to call either of her sisters. She hadn't felt like landing on Kris's doorstep at six in the morning, either.

She didn't know what Spence had done, but at that point,

she had reclined her seat and fallen promptly to sleep, staying comatose until—

"What time is it?"

"A quarter till eight."

She brought her seatback into a vertical position. Whoa, she had slept almost three hours. They weren't even at the rest area anymore. They were getting ready to enter a McDonald's drive-through.

Spence pulled up to the communication box. "Did you want anything?"

Alyssa looked at the menu board. She should conserve her cash, but showing up at her sister's house needing to beg for a place to stay was bad enough without having to add, "By the way, I need you to feed me, too."

Spence cranked the window down as a female voice came through the speaker.

"Welcome to McDonald's. May I take your order?" The woman sounded annoyingly perky for seven forty-five in the morning.

While Spence placed his order, Alyssa read the menu choices and settled on a bacon, egg and cheese biscuit. That should tide her over till lunch.

When the woman passed the bag containing their breakfast to Spence, pleasant aromas filled the car and Alyssa's stomach growled. She hadn't eaten since lunch yesterday. During what should have been dinnertime, she'd been stuck at the emergency room. After leaving the hospital, she'd been too focused on trying to stay alive to think about her stomach. Now she was starving. Maybe she should have ordered two breakfast sandwiches.

Once Spence had unwrapped his sandwich and folded back the paper, he pulled onto North Ninth Avenue. A knot formed around the few bites Alyssa had already taken. Her childhood home was only fifteen minutes away.

She'd walked away from her past seven years ago and never

looked back. While planning the trip to her mother's memorial service, she had tried to mentally prepare herself. Her one consolation had been that as soon as it was over, she could hightail it back to Atlanta. That was no longer the case. She would be stuck in Pensacola for an indeterminable period of time.

She squared her shoulders and straightened her spine. It was still temporary. Maybe not as temporary as she had originally planned, but as soon as she could get on her feet and figure out a game plan, she would be out of there.

She finished the final half of her biscuit. Although it still tasted good, each bite seemed to lodge somewhere just before reaching her stomach.

Finally, Spence pulled into the driveway and the old Victorian stood in front of her.

It looked much the same as it had when she'd left, just slightly less maintained. Paint that had started to fade almost a decade ago showed even more signs of age, with the parts exposed to full sun a tone of gray several hues lighter than those areas blessed with shade. The accents that had once been burgundy and slate blue looked more like mauve and a bleached-out blue-gray.

But the Victorian was still grand and elegant. She would appreciate it if not for her past. Besides, it was a whole lot better than some of the places she'd lived over the past seven years, which wasn't saying much. If the shutters were cockeyed, the roof sagging and the porch railing gone, it would exceed that bar.

In spite of its need for a couple coats of paint, the yard looked great. Kris had obviously spruced it up. The lawn was neatly mowed and flowers lined both sides of the curved walk leading from the driveway to the front porch.

Spence killed the Tempo's engine but left the keys in the ignition. "Would you like me to walk up with you?"

"Let me go first."

Her sister wouldn't be thrilled to see her. If she rang the

bell with Spence next to her, Kris might shut the door in both of their faces.

Neither of her sisters had liked Spence. They'd probably felt he was a bad influence on her. He probably had been. But she'd been an equally bad influence on him.

Spence opened the door and stepped from the car. Even though he wasn't walking to the door with her, he still had to let her out. Having the entire passenger's side of her car smashed in was a pain in the neck.

She climbed over the console and, when she had slid from the driver's seat, Spence got back into the car. As she made her way up the curved walk, her chest tightened. Why did coming home feel like making the dreaded walk to the principal's office?

After stepping onto the porch, she turned to look back at Spence. He was watching her through the windshield. When her gaze met his, his lips curved upward. He'd always had an infectious smile—ten percent friendliness, ten percent charm and eighty percent mischief. Now it was one hundred percent encouragement.

She squared her shoulders. She could do this, even without Spence's support. It didn't matter that he was moving back to Pensacola and she was stuck there for the time being. She wouldn't get used to someone she couldn't count on.

She lifted her right hand to press the doorbell. As long as she didn't have to use the left, the shoulder didn't bother her too badly. Ten days from now, she would have to have the stitches removed.

Maybe she could get Kassie or Kris to snip them for her and save herself a trip to the doctor. Or maybe she'd go ahead and put the health insurance she had to good use before she lost it at the end of the month.

The lock rattled and Alyssa stiffened. Preparing for a conversation with either of her sisters felt like gearing up for battle. Maybe they felt the same way about her.

The door creaked back on its hinges, and Kris stood in the opening, a golden retriever next to her. There was no hint of surprise on her face. Of course, she had probably peered out one of the windows before opening the door.

Or maybe Kris didn't recognize her. Her hair was longer and a different color. There were probably other changes, too. Although they'd talked on the phone several times, they hadn't seen each other since Alyssa had left. She hadn't come back and, through the years, Kris hadn't made any attempt to go wherever Alyssa had landed.

Kris's gaze flicked over her. "You're a little late, don't you think?"

Yep, Kris recognized her. There was no surprise, but there wasn't any welcome, either.

Alyssa bristled. The resentment she felt toward her older sisters was nothing new. When their mother had disappeared and their father had dived even deeper into the bottle, twins Kassie and Kris had gone off to college a short time later, leaving fifteen-year-old Alyssa to fend for herself. Things had only gone downhill from there. Two years later, Spence had left and they'd gone downhill even faster.

She glanced at Bella who was staring up at her with big brown eyes. The tail moved slowly back and forth. The dog would give her a warmer welcome than her sister would.

Alyssa lifted her chin. She wasn't going to allow her sister's judgment to beat her down. "I was on my way here yesterday morning, and my car broke down."

And someone tried to kill me...twice.

She left the last thought unspoken. It wouldn't get her any sympathy. Just the opposite. Her sister would assume she'd brought it on herself and have one more reason to judge her.

Kris looked past her and into the driveway.

"I had it repaired." The engine anyway. The body was too far gone. Her insurance company would declare the car a total loss if she had full coverage. She didn't. The best she could hope for was two or three hundred from a salvage yard.

She turned back around to face her sister. "I was planning to spend a couple of weeks in Pensacola and was thinking about crashing at the old homestead."

Kris lifted her eyebrows. "That sounds like an *I need a place to lie low.*"

Kris had hit the nail on the head. How could she do that when they only talked to each other every few months? Her sisters never called her, except for brief Christmas and birthday greetings, and she only called her sisters when she needed help, like when she'd given her roommate her half of the rent and the woman had blown the entire thing on a shopping spree.

Kris crossed her arms. "Is that your boyfriend in the car?"

Alyssa laughed, a hearty belly laugh that took several seconds to rein in. The thought of Peter behind the wheel of her beat-up Tempo was hilarious. The idea that the man currently there would ever again hold the boyfriend title was even more outrageous.

Before Alyssa could answer the question, a little boy toddled into the foyer and wrapped his arms around Kris's leg.

"Mommy?"

She picked him up and propped him on one hip, his legs resting one in front of her and the other behind. His arms went around her neck.

Alyssa smiled at the little boy. "Hi, Gavin." She did the math in her head. Her nephew was two and a half and she'd never met him.

"Gavin, this is your Aunt Alyssa." Her tone seemed to hold resignation.

"Ann Issa?"

Alyssa's heart swelled at hearing the little boy try to pronounce her name. It was her first glimpse of what she might have missed by running away instead of working to have a relationship with her sisters.

As children, none of them had been close. From what she'd gathered during infrequent conversations with Kassie and Kris, the twins had mended bridges and were actually enjoying a closeness they'd never shared as children.

Alyssa patted his back. "Yeah, buddy. That's me. Aunt Alyssa is going to be in town for a little while. I hope we can do some fun things together."

She liked kids. Not that she ever planned to have any. She'd probably mess things up as badly as her own parents had.

Actually, putting the blame on her mother was unfair. She'd spent so many years hating her mom for leaving them that, even though she now knew otherwise, the thought often slipped through before she had a chance to censor it.

Kris sighed. "I'd like to invite you inside but, frankly, I have my reservations. Whatever trouble you're in, I don't want you bringing it here. I'm telling you right now, I will do everything in my power to protect this little boy. If you and your friend need a place to stay for a few days, I'll pay for a hotel room. Kassie will probably chip in, too." She looked into the driveway again, where just the driver's side and front of the Tempo were visible from their perspective. "Wait a minute. Is that...?" Her brows dipped together.

Spence took the cue and stepped from the vehicle.

Alyssa watched him approach, his easy gait and relaxed smile reminding her far too much of the teenage boy she had fallen in love with.

Kris moved forward. "Hi, Spence."

Alyssa turned back to her sister and did a double take. The defensiveness she'd expected to see wasn't there. Instead, everything about her—from her relaxed posture to her friendly tone to the smile that matched Spence's—exuded welcome.

An unexpected sense of annoyance swelled inside her. Alyssa had known neither of her sisters would roll out the welcome mat for her, but she hadn't expected Spence to get an enthusiastic welcome when her own had been somewhere south of *meh.*

Kris stepped back. "Come on in, you guys. Have you had breakfast?"

Alyssa nodded. "We stopped at McDonald's."

Kris closed the door behind them and looked at Spence. "You've made your move already?"

So Kris knew about his plans to return to Pensacola. How much had her sisters kept from her?

"I'm working on it. I'm going back to LaGrange today to finish packing and heading back down tomorrow with a loaded U-Haul."

Kris led them into the living room, the golden retriever trotting behind them. After putting Gavin down, she shifted her gaze between them. "How did you guys get reconnected?"

"Her car broke down in LaGrange, and I happened to be driving past the garage as she was coming out."

Coming out? She almost laughed. Running across the road in front of him, dodging bullets, was more like it. The fact that Spence had left it up to her how much she would tell her sister increased the appreciation she already had.

She excused herself to use the restroom and made her way down the hall. Kris had said she didn't want her bringing trouble there. She had a valid point.

Now that Alyssa had gotten rid of the tracking device, the likelihood of Peter and his cronies following her to Pensacola was slim. But if they did and she was staying in the family home, Kris and Gavin could be caught in the crossfire. It was a chance she wasn't willing to take. She wouldn't even consider it.

When she stepped from the bathroom, hushed voices drifted to her from the direction of the kitchen. As she drew closer, they fell silent. Had Kris and Spence been talking about her? Maybe she'd been premature in the ramped-up appreciation she'd felt earlier.

She stopped in the doorway and leaned against the jamb. "Instead of staying here, I'd like to crash in the apartment over the charter office."

Kris's gaze went immediately to Spence.

What was up with that? He had no say in their family decisions.

After brief hesitation, she lifted her shoulders in a slow shrug and let them fall. "I'll have to talk to Kassie."

"Why? I have as much right to the space as anyone."

The charter company had belonged to their dad. He was now serving time for drug running, with murder likely being added to those charges in the near future. He was also dying. The house, the boats, the business and the building housing it and the one next door would at some point belong to all three of them.

Another glance passed between Kris and Spence.

Yeah, something was going on, something both of them were keeping from her.

Fine. They could talk all they wanted.

As soon as she could get her act together, she'd be gone.

Whatever they said or did then was none of her concern, because she had no intention of ever coming back.

A powerful explosion rocked the ground, bringing the entire convoy to an abrupt stop. A cloud of dust and debris swallowed the lead vehicle.

Spence gripped the steering wheel of the Joint Light Tactical Vehicle and scanned the landscape on either side of him—miles and miles of rolling desert broken by small patches of scrub. Any of those rises could conceal Taliban fighters.

Seconds ticked by before a barrage of machine gun fire rent the silence. Several shots pinged off the right side of the JLTV.

"Take cover." Spence swung open the door and dropped to the ground, M4 clutched in his right hand.

Three others followed him out, making their way in a crouched run to a berm near the edge of the road.

More artillery fire erupted around them, the attackers taking advantage of their increased vulnerability. Beside him, McCarthy shrieked and dropped to the dusty road, legs bent in a way that didn't look quite natural.

Spence stopped and grabbed his arm. "Come on."

"I can't feel my legs." He screamed the words, the high-pitched tone an amalgamation of panic, pain and terror.

Norris took his other arm and together they pulled him off the road and over the berm at its edge, artillery whizzing past.

The gunfire continued, punctuated by more screams.

The small convoy was outmanned, outgunned and outmaneuvered. The road had supposedly been cleared. One IED had obviously been missed. *God, help us all.*

Something wet moved up Spence's face. Now there was pressure against his side. The screams and gunfire faded, leaving only a soft whimper.

He opened his eyes and the images of war splintered. Instead, a furry brown face hovered close to his own. Apollo whimpered again and followed it with another slurp of his tongue across Spence's cheek.

Spence lifted a hand to scratch his dog's neck. His heart pounded against his rib cage, his pulse rate what it would be after a serious cardio session. His breaths came in shallow pants.

He tried to force both his breathing and his heart to slow. There were no mortars, no mines, no men wielding AK-47s, determined to take him out. He was in Pensacola, ensconced in the apartment over the top of what would soon be his long-dreamed-of music store.

He pushed himself upright and wrapped both arms around his dog. "It's okay, buddy. I'm all right."

At least he would be in a few minutes. With Apollo's help, he was always able to bring himself out of the effects of a nightmare pretty quickly. But that didn't mean he'd be getting back to sleep anytime soon.

He rose from the bed and walked to the small kitchenette occupying the back corner of the apartment. He didn't bother to turn on any lights. Enough glow from the street below drifted through the sheer-covered French doors for him to find his way around without bumping into anything.

After taking a bottle of water from the minifridge, he moved toward the couch. His guitar sat in the stand next to it, still plugged into the amp.

He'd arrived in town just before noon. It was a day earlier than he'd planned to make his move, but he hadn't needed the extra time. When he'd gotten back to LaGrange, he'd boxed everything up, and Jason had come over early this morning to help him load it all into the U-Haul.

By six tonight, he had returned the rental and found places for all of his belongings. Not that there were many. He'd known his stay in LaGrange would be temporary and had managed to acquire only what he'd needed over the past year.

He hadn't seen Alyssa. He hadn't seen Kris or Kassie, either. With today being Sunday, Ashbaugh Charters had been closed. Since Kris and Kassie had given him the key when he'd signed the lease a month ago, he hadn't even had to get in touch with them.

He'd told Alyssa he was moving back to Pensacola but hadn't revealed exactly where. If she had known her sisters were his new landlords and he'd be working and living in the space next door to the charter office, she would probably have kept driving rather than stay in Pensacola.

Yesterday, without going into detail why, he'd expressed those same concerns to Kris. She'd agreed to keep his living arrangements secret until Alyssa discovered them for herself.

He sank onto the couch, and Apollo jumped up next to him, laying his head in Spence's lap. After unscrewing the cap on the water bottle, Spence took a long swig. Cold and pure, it tasted good, but it wouldn't do anything as far as relaxing him. One activity would, though.

Without getting up, he reached beside him to grasp the neck of the guitar. From the time he was a teenager, music had been his refuge. Back when he and Alyssa had been together, his biggest dream had been to become a famous rock star. And he'd been well on his way to developing the drug habit to go with it.

Not anymore. Instead of hoping to be the next Mick Jagger or Jon Bon Jovi, he'd spent the past year playing in his church's worship band on Sunday mornings. And alone in his apartment in the middle of the night, trying to chase away the demons of war.

He picked up the guitar, and Apollo moved farther down the couch before resting his head between his paws. He knew the drill.

Spence laid the guitar across his lap, the instrument occupying the space the dog had just vacated, and strummed an E chord. Several beats later, he closed his eyes, shifting his left hand to finger a C-sharp minor chord. He continued to strum, A then back to E, as he started to sing.

It was one of his favorite worship songs, describing how peace is found in the presence of Jesus. It was a truth he felt down to the deepest part of him.

He moved from "I Speak Jesus" to "Holy Forever" without opening his eyes. When finished, he rose to crank up the amp a little louder. He didn't have to concern himself with disturbing anyone. He was downtown, surrounded by businesses. All of them would be vacant in the middle of the night.

He didn't even have to worry about Alyssa. Kassie would likely agree to let her stay in the apartment over the charter office, but she hadn't moved in yet. When he'd taken Apollo out just before bed, he'd checked the parking lot behind the building as well as the parallel spaces lining Government Street in front. The red Tempo hadn't been in either area.

As soon as he sat back down, he began playing the driving intro of Phil Wickham's "Battle Belongs." Halfway through the song, another sound penetrated the music—something like pounding. He stopped singing and laid his right hand flat across the strings. What had he heard?

It came again, definitely pounding. Judging from the volume, there was some anger behind it. Someone was knocking on the doors leading into his apartment from the balcony overlooking the street.

He spun to face the front wall and peered through the sheers hanging over the double French doors. A figure stood there, fist raised, a dark silhouette against the glow of the streetlights below.

What? The only way to access the balcony was through his apartment or the one next door.

Uh-oh.

He flipped a switch, and the light outside came on. Yep, Alyssa had moved in.

After unlocking the doors, he swung one of them inward. She stood on the balcony, hands on her hips.

"Do you mind? I'm trying—"

The words died on her lips as annoyance morphed to shock. Her eyes widened then narrowed.

"You!"

He winced. She was probably angrier over his not telling her where he would be staying than his waking her out of a sound sleep.

She crossed her arms in front of her. "Kris didn't tell me they had this rented, and she certainly didn't tell me their renter was you."

Yep, he'd awoken her. Her hair flowed over her shoulders in wild disarray. She was dressed in her pajamas—a sleeveless top with Bugs Bunny's face over the words "That's All, Folks!" and coordinating bottoms. The playfulness of her attire was at odds with the anger in her green eyes.

Before he could respond, Apollo pressed past him to lean against her leg.

"Hey, Apollo." She dropped to her knees, wrapped both arms around his dog, and then released him to scratch his cheeks. "It's good to see you again."

After petting and cooing at his dog for a couple of minutes, she looked up at him, her smile fading and her eyebrows dipping downward.

"I like your dog better than you right now."

He caught his spontaneous laugh just as it escaped and tried to disguise it with a couple of coughs. Alyssa always said what she thought and never minced words, something he'd appreciated and often found funny.

Alyssa's frown said she didn't see any humor in the situation. She rose and glared at him.

"During those discussions we had about your move back to Pensacola, you don't think you should have mentioned you were renting Ashbaugh property, especially when I talked about staying over the charter office?"

"I thought about it but—"

"But thought it would be best to keep me in the dark and then just surprise me with it."

"If I had told you where I was staying and my renewed connection with your family, would you have come back? Be honest, Alyssa."

She pressed her lips together, and her eyes dipped to the concrete floor of the balcony. A long span of uneasy silence passed.

Finally, she looked at him. "Probably not. I would have tried to figure out something else."

"That's why I did it. I saw your hesitation when I said I was coming back to Pensacola. I didn't want you taking off and trying to deal with this on your own."

"I don't like being lied to."

"I didn't—"

She cut him off with a raised hand. "You didn't outright lie, but you withheld information."

He raised his eyebrows. That was what she'd been doing from the moment they'd run into each other outside Jim's Garage.

Realization flashed across her features, and her lips turned up in a sheepish smile. "Okay. Fair enough."

"You're staying, right? At least for the time being?"

"You're going to keep it down, refrain from middle-of-the-night concerts?"

"Absolutely." He grew serious. "As much as you don't want to, I hope you'll stay until we know for sure you're out of danger. I'm not law enforcement like your future brother-in-law, but I have a weapon, and after seven years in the military, I know how to use it."

Of course, she knew that. She'd already watched him shoot one man. It still bothered him and would for a while.

But he had no doubt. If put in the same situation, he'd do it again.

In a heartbeat.

Chapter Five

Alyssa made her way down the narrow stairway and into the charter office lobby, elastic brace just below the hem of her jean shorts. Her knee was doing better, as long as she restricted herself to flat surfaces.

Stairs, not so much. She'd quickly figured out that leading with the right foot going down and the left going up was the only way she could manage.

Currently, no one was at the desk, but voices drifted down the hall from what used to be her dad's office. Kris was apparently with this afternoon's charter customers, taking care of the paperwork. Kassie was already at the marina with Buck, their captain.

Yesterday evening, Alyssa had had Kris drop her off at the charter office. Kassie had agreed to let her stay in the pseudo apartment above. Pseudo, because it was nothing more than glorified storage space. The dusty old boxes were still stacked against the wall.

There wasn't even a kitchen or bathroom up there. A trip to the toilet in the middle of the night involved navigating the steep, narrow stairway.

At least the space upstairs had a bed, left from when Kris

had stayed for a short time when her own life had been in danger. She'd come out of the experience unharmed...and engaged. The latter had happened the day before she'd arrived.

Alyssa stepped out the front door without disturbing the business going on in the office. The fact that her sisters had even had to discuss whether or not she could stay in the space still irked her. As if she was required to have permission to use something that was one-third hers.

To make matters worse, they'd conspired against her, keeping Spence's living arrangements secret, making her feel like the outsider she'd always been. Alyssa—the black sheep, the one who'd never belonged in the Ashbaugh family.

Of course, Spence had already explained his reasons. He'd been right. She would have tried to go it on her own. In fact, maybe Kris's having to get Kassie's okay to allow her to stay above the charter office had been nothing more than a way to delay her move until Spence was already settled in.

As she stepped onto the sidewalk, she pulled her phone from the back pocket of her shorts and navigated to the Uber app. Yesterday, she had ditched the Tempo.

Maybe she'd been a bit premature. But her first night back home, thinking about her car sitting in the driveway next to Kris's Honda CR-V, an overwhelming sense of dread had kept her awake for most of the night. No matter how many times she'd told herself Spence had found and removed the only tracking device, she hadn't been able to shake the uneasy feeling that Peter would somehow find a way to use the car to locate her.

Her fears weren't far-fetched. There weren't many 1992 Tempos on the road sporting her paint job. There were even fewer with her paint job *and* the whole right side smashed in.

So, yesterday, she'd contacted a salvage yard and recouped the two hundred dollars she had spent at Jim's Garage plus a little extra. Not having a car for the short time she'd be there would be an inconvenience, but if she moved to a large city with public transportation, she wouldn't need one anytime in the near future.

She cast a glance toward the retail space adjoining Ashbaugh Charters. There was a sign in the window that she hadn't noticed last night. Block letters spelled out Cavanaugh Music Center, with Coming Soon in script below.

Spence was sitting at a desk, the only piece of furniture in the large front room. A laptop sat open in front of him, and Apollo lay on the floor next to him. Like last night, he wasn't in his vest. Maybe he only wore it when they went out.

Before she could return her attention to her app, Spence looked up and waved. She made her way to the door and swung it open, even though she was probably going to regret it. She had no interest in getting chummy with her ex.

Chances were good he felt the same way about her. He had changed in the past eight years. He was no longer a youth with no discipline, no direction. Now he exuded maturity, the sense that he'd managed to somehow get his life together when she was still trying to find all the broken pieces of hers.

Yeah, Spence was probably like her sisters—afraid if he spent too much time with her, some of that *worthless* might rub off.

She stepped inside. "Hey."

"Hey, yourself." He flashed her the smile that had always had a way of undoing her.

She refused to be affected. She appreciated everything he was doing for her. Someday she would pay him back for all of it.

She was keeping tabs. So far, she owed him an insurance deductible on his SUV. And a tank of gas when he'd slid his credit card into the slot on the pump while she'd gone inside to pay cash. And any car rental costs he might be stuck with until his insurance claim was over. No way was she going to allow herself to become obligated.

She let the door swing shut behind her. "You look like you're making big plans."

A legal pad lay next to the computer, a pen placed diagonally across it. Several lines were filled with his jagged script, but, from her vantage point, she couldn't make out what he had written. His wallet was also there, sitting on the other side of his computer.

"I am. Right now, I'm ordering inventory."

"For Cavanaugh Music Center."

"Yep. I'm starting out with guitars, keyboards, amps, mixers, mics, et cetera. Maybe eventually I'll even do lessons out of here."

"Wow." He was putting down deep roots. It didn't matter, because she wasn't.

"Sorry I disturbed you last night. When I went to bed, your car wasn't there, so I figured you were still at Kris's."

"I scrapped the car. I had planned to trade it in soon anyway, but my fight with the trees along 85 sped that up a little bit."

His gaze dipped to the hem of her shorts. "How is your knee?"

"Better. I can almost walk now without limping."

"That's good."

"I'm not ready for any long hikes yet. I'm getting ready to Uber to Publix. Kris took me shopping on the way here last night, but now that I've done some meal planning, I have a few other things to pick up."

Spence closed the laptop and stood. "I'd planned on doing some grocery shopping this afternoon, too. How about riding along?"

She hesitated. "You were going anyway?"

He slid his wallet into the front pocket of his jeans. "Absolutely."

"In that case, I'll save the Uber fare."

After locking the front door, he led her out the back and

into the parking lot, Apollo next to them. None of the vehicles looked familiar except Kris's red CR-V.

Spence clicked the key fob, and lights flashed on a charcoal-gray Subaru Forester. He opened the passenger door and Alyssa climbed inside. While he waited for Apollo to hop into the back seat, she looked at him over her shoulder. "Any word yet on what they're doing with your Land Rover?"

"Not yet." He closed her door and circled the vehicle to slide into the driver's seat. "The adjuster is supposed to be looking at it today, so I should know something soon. I'll be really surprised if they don't total it."

"I'm sorry. I feel bad." She really did. He was probably regretting stopping to help her.

"Hey, don't worry about it. That's what insurance is for."

Five minutes later, Spence pulled into the grocery store parking lot. By the time they'd made it through produce, her knee was beginning to throb.

As she and Spence and Apollo started down the soup aisle, two older ladies entered the aisle from the other end. Alyssa recognized both of them as former neighbors. Dorothy had lived across the street, Mildred a few doors down. As they passed, Mildred greeted them with a friendly hello. Dorothy offered her own greeting, but her features were tight.

Alyssa stopped in front of the selection of soups. After placing a chicken noodle and a vegetable beef into her cart, she picked up a can of clam chowder. Dorothy's voice came from the next aisle. "Let's hope they're just passing through."

"Why?"

"Those two were always trouble."

Alyssa clenched her teeth. Did the woman think those shelving units were soundproof, or had she intended for them to hear her?

"That was years ago. A lot of teenagers get off to a rough start then get straightened out once they hit adulthood. I don't know what Alyssa's been up to, but Spence enlisted in the military."

"Well, you know what they say. The apple doesn't fall far from the tree. Bobby Ashbaugh is doing time for drug running. No telling what his kids are involved in."

"Hey." Mildred's tone held a definite hint of scolding. "I babysit for one of those young ladies, so don't be making judgments."

"That would be Kris. Kassie turned out all right, too." Dorothy's voice faded as they moved farther down the aisle. "Those two always kept their noses clean, but with the younger one, I'll believe it when I see it." Any further conversation didn't reach them.

Alyssa glared at Spence. "See why I don't want to stay here? I'll be judged everywhere I go."

"The one lady defended you guys."

"That was Mildred. Of course she's going to stick up for us. She's sort of employed by my sister."

"Don't let it bother you."

That was easy for him to say. His military experience would redeem him in the eyes of everyone who knew his past. She didn't have any acts of heroism to fall back on.

When they finished their shopping, she hobbled to the nearest cashier, Spence behind her.

"You're limping more."

She looked at him over one shoulder. "I know. If I'd had to navigate many more aisles, you'd have had to wheel me around in the cart."

Spence laughed. Whether he'd actually been planning to grocery shop today or had just told her that so she'd accept his offer, he'd made good use of the time. His cart was more than half full.

Hers was a little skimpier, but not by much. She had watched her spending, taking advantage of the BOGOs. The buy-one-get-one deals had saved her about twenty bucks.

She wasn't quite as worried about her money running out. Besides the two thousand dollars she'd squirreled away in recent weeks, she now had a job. Ashbaugh Charters had recently lost its part-time clerical person. Kassie and Kris had agreed to stop their search and put Alyssa on the payroll while she was there. The offer hadn't even come with any sighs or eye rolls. Maybe there was hope yet the three of them would one day be close. She wasn't counting on it.

When they stepped outside, Spence pointed at a table piled high with cookies, set up not far from the door. They'd passed it on their way into the store. "Dessert. Gotta support the Girl Scouts."

Two young girls manned the table, each wearing a vest sporting more than a dozen embroidered patches. One was talking with a customer who had just purchased a box of Caramel deLites. As they approached, the other girl aimed some baby talk at Apollo and then smiled at his two humans. "How can I help you?"

Spence scanned the offerings. After choosing a box of Caramel Chocolate Chip cookies, he turned to Alyssa. "Which one would you like?"

"I'm going to get the Thin Mints."

"I've got it." He took the box from her and handed both of them to the Girl Scout to bag.

She frowned at him. "I can pay for my own cookies."

"Trust me, I'll make you share them with me."

As Spence counted out bills, the other customer turned and started to nod a greeting. Then her eyes widened. "Alyssa?"

"Brandi."

The woman had been one year behind her in school and looked much the same now as she had back then, with wispy blond hair and an open, warm smile that made everyone feel as if they were her best friend. Alyssa had known her well, but it had been Brandi's older brothers who had hung around with her and Spence, along with whatever girlfriends they'd had at the time.

Brandi's smile widened. "I like the red. It looks good on you."

"Thanks. You look great, too."

"And Spence." Brandi waved an index finger between the two of them. "Are you guys…?"

"No." They answered simultaneously, and Spence continued. "We just ran into each other two days ago."

"And who is this?" Brandi bent over but stopped short of petting Apollo.

Spence dipped his head toward his dog. "This is Apollo."

"Is it okay if I pet him?"

"Sure."

After a few minutes of catching up, Spence asked about her brothers.

"Braydon works for Pensacola PD, and Bryson is with Escambia County Sheriff's Office."

What? The Feldman brothers had gotten into even more trouble than she and Spence had. Now they were cops?

Alyssa sighed. And Spence had spent seven years serving his country and was getting ready to open his own music store. Apparently, all of the old gang had made something of themselves.

Well, almost all.

She hoisted the thin strap of her purse up farther on her shoulder. "Are any of you guys married, have families?"

"Nope, and Mom's having a fit. At twenty-four, twenty-five and twenty-six, we were supposed to have given her grandchildren by now."

Brandi pulled her phone from her purse. "I've got to take a selfie. Braydon and Bryson aren't going to believe this."

She dropped to her knees next to Apollo, and Alyssa bent forward behind her. She wouldn't be doing any kneeling for a while.

Once Spence had positioned himself in a squat on Apollo's other side, Brandi handed him the phone. "Here, you've got longer arms."

When he had captured some photos he was happy with, he handed the phone back to Brandi.

Alyssa peered at the screen. "Can you text me one of those?"

"Sure."

A few seconds after Alyssa gave Brandi the number, her phone buzzed with an incoming text, but Brandi was still typing. Finally, she slid her phone back into her purse.

"Now Braydon and Bryson have it, too, along with the message *Guess who I ran into.*"

Brandi's phone dinged with a notification.

Alyssa tensed, dread trickling over her. "Did you just post that to social media?"

"I did. Why?"

"Please delete the post." She didn't even try to keep the panic from her voice.

"O-kay." Brandi pulled her phone from her purse and opened the app. After a few more taps, she looked back at Alyssa. "Done. I'm sorry. I should have asked."

Alyssa sucked in a stabilizing breath, trying to slow the beating of her heart, which suddenly felt as if it was going to pound right out of her chest. "I'm hiding from an abusive ex."

She would never have described him as abusive before. He'd always been just the opposite, spoiling her every chance he got. But since he'd tried to kill her twice—or had sent someone else to do it—the label fit.

She continued. "I deleted my profile, but I'm not willing to take any chances of him seeing a post and tracking me down."

"I understand. If it'll make you feel any better, my phone is set to not collect location metadata, and I didn't tag a location on the post." She smiled. "Single girls can't be too careful." She turned her attention to Spence. "My brothers are going to want to see you. The last we knew, you had joined the army."

"I had, but I'm out now, as of a year ago."

"Can I get your phone number?"

Alyssa only half listened to their conversation, the social media post overshadowing everything else.

It had been up for only a minute. There was no way Peter could have seen it during that brief time, even if he was friends with every one of her former acquaintances. She couldn't even remember if she had ever received or accepted a friend request from Brandi.

After they said their goodbyes, Alyssa walked with him toward the Subaru, thankful an ice pack was only a few minutes away. She had long ago passed the point of needing to elevate her leg. Spence was having his own issues, evident by how heavily he was leaning against the handle of the cart. Maybe someday she would feel comfortable asking him how he had hurt himself.

They each loaded their groceries into the back, and Alyssa climbed into the passenger seat, a vague sense of worry chewing at her peace of mind. For Peter to have seen the post, he would have had to be watching Brandi's account twenty-four-seven. He was far too busy and powerful.

That wasn't any consolation. He was too busy to stare at social media accounts for hours on end, but he had people. Three of them had already come after her. One was dead. How many more were there?

Spence cranked the engine and pulled from the lot. When they reached the parking area behind the Ashbaugh building, he didn't make a move to get out of the SUV. Instead, he turned toward her.

"I know Publix is only five minutes from here, but you haven't said a word since we told Brandi goodbye."

She shrugged. "I've got a lot on my mind."

"I'm sure you do. Maybe it's time to get it *off* your mind. You told me you don't know who is trying to kill you, but you told Brandi you're hiding from an abusive ex. It can't be both, and I'm guessing it's not either."

Alyssa crossed her arms. She didn't need his judgment, and she didn't need him trying to fix her life.

"Come on, Alyssa. I want to help, but you need to tell me what's going on."

"You can't help. I need to just leave. I'm going to buy a bus or airline ticket to a big city and disappear."

Before Spence could respond, Apollo climbed from the back seat to lay his upper body along the length of the console. Then he rested his head against Alyssa's shoulder.

The flesh there was still tender, but she didn't care. She would take Apollo's comfort any time. He seemed to be picking up on her agitation and offering his calming presence. Was that what he did for Spence? She'd assumed the dog assisted him with whatever physical limitations he had from his injuries, because he seemed too put together to need emotional support. But maybe she wasn't the only one of the old gang who still struggled.

She cupped the dog's chin and pressed her cheek to the top of his head.

"Alyssa?"

When she didn't respond, Spence laid his hand on the side of her head. He couldn't rest it on her shoulder because the dog had claimed that spot.

She closed her eyes. Spence's touch stirred her far more than she wanted to admit. She wanted to hate him, or at least to still hang on to the resentment she had carried for the past eight years.

But that resentment had begun fading during the trip to the hospital. In its place, other things had started to slip in, things she didn't want to feel—tenderness, affection, need.

He let his hand slide off her head, catching strands of hair between his fingers. "I just want to see you safe and…" His voice trailed off.

Yeah, he probably wanted to see her happy, too. And settled. "Please let me be there for you."

Because you weren't eight years ago?

She lifted her face from Apollo's head, leaving the words unspoken.

Letting him be there for her sounded pretty good, even though everything within her rebelled at the thought. Somebody she could trust to help her figure this whole thing out and somehow find a way out of the mess she'd fallen into. Somebody who could carry the burden, just for a while, and give her a break.

"I told you before that I saw something I wasn't supposed to see." The words spilled out, slipping through a breach in the wall she had built around her heart. Letting him into her life, even in a small way, felt like waving the white flag of surrender.

"Thursday night, I was out with my boyfriend." *Was it really just four nights ago?* It seemed like a lifetime. "We had gone out to dinner." The restaurant was one of those places where the cost of dinner was equivalent to a week's salary. Her salary, anyway.

"We had just left the restaurant when Peter got a call. He changed routes and eventually stopped at a row of storefronts downtown and told me to wait in the car. I did, for about twenty minutes. After that, I started to get antsy. It wasn't a great part of town, and I was pretty annoyed he'd left me sitting out there alone all that time."

In hindsight, she should have just stayed put, however long it took. It hadn't been the first time impatience had gotten her into trouble. But it had been the most serious.

"I got out and went into the building. The front of the space was vacant, but I could hear voices coming through an open door to a back room. They were talking about famous paintings." She knew some of the pieces—*Henriette de France, Lady Caroline Price, Marjorie In A Yellow Shawl.* "Peter is an art aficionado, and I recognized several of the names they mentioned as paintings he has."

She took in a deep breath.

Spence didn't ask questions and didn't prod her, just quietly listened.

"When I stepped into the open doorway, three men were sitting around a table with Peter, passing photos around. From where I was standing, I couldn't see what they were looking at, but one of the men said, 'This one is exactly what one of Bud's contacts is looking for.' He said to go ahead and make the arrangements, usual drop-off point, all cash."

She shook her head. "I thought they were dealers of fine art until one of the men looked up and saw me standing in the doorway."

The look he'd given her had sent a chill down her spine. Even now, a shudder shook her shoulders.

"The other two looked up then, and Peter turned around. His back had been to me. I knew instantly I wasn't supposed to be there. I apologized for interrupting, told them I was going to use the restroom but could wait. I hurried back to the car, and Peter came out right behind me. While he was taking me home, his phone rang. I couldn't hear the caller's words, but Peter said, 'Don't worry. I'll take care of it' and hung up."

She stopped talking and stroked Apollo's head, which was still pressed against her shoulder.

"He tried to convince me everything was on the up-and-up, that these guys were very protective of their work and I had just startled them." It might have been convincing if she hadn't been so street smart. "Anyhow, he knew I was leaving for my mother's funeral the next morning, so when he dropped me off at home, he insisted on taking me, afraid my car wouldn't make it to Florida."

She smiled over at him. "That concern was legitimate. But I knew in my gut if I got into his Audi the next morning, wherever I landed, it wouldn't be Mom's service. So I got up before

daybreak, stuffed what I could into my backpack and disappeared. Got as far as LaGrange." She gave him a wry smile.
"And, as they say, you know the rest of the story."

Spence released a slow whistle. "You've really landed in hot
water. You need to report what you saw to the Atlanta police."

"And tell them what? All I have is an overheard conversation. There wasn't even any art in the building. I'm sure those
photos they were passing around went with them. Even if the
art they were talking about was stolen, I have no proof."

"How about talking to Jared and Tony?"

"No way." Jared was Kassie's fiancé and Tony was Kris's,
and they were both cops. "Peter is a successful man, with
enough money to wear designer suits, buy expensive cars and
outfit whatever current girlfriend he has in a brand-new ward-
robe." She'd fallen for all of it, hook, line and sinker. "Money
equals power. And power equals connections."

Going to the police was the first thing she'd thought of.
Then she'd dismissed the idea as soon as it had crossed her
mind. "He's likely to have close friends or family members
on the police force."

"These men are just as likely to track you down somewhere
else as here. You're safest where you've got friends and family members watching your back. In the meantime, how about
if we talk to Jared and Tony? They'll be discreet. They'll do
whatever they need to do to keep you safe." He grinned. "They
have extra incentive. If you get hurt, they'll have to answer to
their future wives."

"That may not be the deterrent you think it is."

No, that wasn't fair. Neither Kassie nor Kris would want
anything bad to happen to her. Sometimes they didn't like her,
but they'd always loved her.

"All right. I'll talk to my sisters and have them set up times
for us to meet with each of the guys."

Maybe that was a mistake. But maybe not involving the
police would be a mistake, too.

Staying might be a bad decision. So might running.

Because she couldn't shake the feeling that no matter what she did or where she went, Peter would somehow find her.

Chapter Six

Spence turned into a driveway and killed the Subaru's engine as Alyssa stared through the front windshield. She'd never been here before. Kassie had bought the ranch-style home three years ago. It was much smaller than the old Victorian they'd grown up in right on Bayou Texar. But it was cute, with its red-brick façade and white front porch.

It also overlooked one of the dozens of Pensacola parks, this one in the North Hill Historic District. It had been one of Alyssa's favorites, with its rose garden, concrete paths, porch swing and white gazebo.

Tonight, though, she wasn't appreciating the park. In fact, she didn't even want to be there. She had agreed to have Kassie and Kris line up times for Spence and her to meet with their guys to get some guidance regarding the mess she was in with Peter. But instead of two one-on-one meetings, Kassie had decided it was a perfect excuse for them to all get together.

It had taken three days to coordinate a time convenient for everyone, but now Alyssa would be stuck sitting through a pseudo family reunion. She hadn't been close to either of her sisters growing up. Although two years wasn't a large spread as adults, during childhood, it had meant different activities, a different circle of friends and often different schools.

She looked over at Spence. "Might as well get this over with."

He gave her a gentle shake. "You make it sound like you're headed to sentencing or something."

"That isn't too far off."

In recent years, the distance between her and her sisters had only grown larger. The few times she had contacted her sisters, she'd had no other choice. When her roommate had spent the rent, Kassie and Kris had grudgingly chipped in so she wouldn't end up sleeping in the park. She now had enough socked away to pay them back but was currently afraid to let go of it.

Contacts from either of her sisters were just as rare. Aside from Christmas and birthday wishes, they only called her when there was something earth-shattering to share—the discovery of their mother's body, the details of her memorial service, their father's cancer diagnosis, Kassie's kidnapping. It hadn't seemed to take either of her siblings long to forget how she had jumped in, willing to put her own life in danger to save her sister.

Spence gave her another gentle shake. "Come on. No one's going to judge you. Let's go inside."

She stepped from the SUV as Spence opened the back door for Apollo. Although he was still driving the Subaru, car shopping was going to be in his near future. He'd gotten a call from the adjuster shortly before they'd left home. They were totaling the Land Rover.

Alyssa shut the door and crossed in front of Kris's CR-V. Kassie's Sorento was sitting in the drive, too. If Tony was there, he'd apparently ridden with Kris. Jared's cruiser was parked in his grandmother's driveway next door, meaning he had probably walked over. According to Kassie, he had moved in when his grandmother was recovering from a broken hip, had met Kassie and never left.

Apollo trotted ahead of them and climbed the three steps onto the porch. Alyssa rang the bell and, moments later, the door swung inward. Kassie wrapped Alyssa in a hug that caught her off guard. She couldn't remember ever being hugged by either one of her sisters. Maybe Kassie hadn't forgotten about Alyssa's selfless act of bravery after all.

Kassie released Alyssa and turned to Spence. "It's good to see you again. And this must be Apollo. Is it okay if I pet him?"

"Sure."

She dropped to her knees. "Hey, buddy." After giving him some scratches on the cheeks and neck, she straightened. "Come on in. Everyone's hanging out around the grill."

Alyssa followed her through living room and into the kitchen, Apollo and Spence trailing behind. Pleasant aromas wrapped around her and her stomach growled. Two packs of hamburger buns sat on the counter, a variety of condiments lined up beside them. A covered casserole dish was there, too, next to a bowl. Judging from what she could see through the plastic wrap on top, the bowl possibly contained potato salad. If Kris had brought it, it would have been made from scratch.

The tantalizing scents, though, were probably coming from the backyard. Kris and her fiancé were visible through the nine panes of glass making up the top portion of the door.

Even after seven years, she recognized Tony. He and his family had had countless meals at the Ashbaugh home during the time their fathers had been business partners. It had all come to a screeching halt when they'd split on rather unfriendly terms. Soon the Ashbaugh and Sanderson families would be joined once again, this time through marriage.

When they stepped outside, Apollo followed, looking around at the strangers there. Kris's little boy was running around the yard, a toy airplane in his hand, and a man Alyssa didn't recognize stood at the grill holding a long-handled spatula. That was apparently Jared, Kassie's fiancé.

After introductions had been made, Jared transferred the burgers from the grill to a platter and led everyone inside. The two couples joined hands and then reached across the space to form a circle, unbroken only by Alyssa and Spence. Spence took Kassie's hand in one of his and Alyssa's in the other. Alyssa allowed Tony to take her free hand.

That was a blast from the past. When they were kids, mealtime in the Ashbaugh house had always begun with everyone joining hands and someone saying grace. That someone was usually their mom. On rare occasions, their dad had muttered a few words. Once their mother had disappeared, prayer stopped.

A lot of things had changed that night. Their father, who had never been allowed to drink at home, had spent increasingly more of his evenings and weekends drunk. Kris, who'd always been a bit moody, had been even harder to get along with, and Kassie had spent hours closed up in her room, crying.

Alyssa hadn't been moody or sad. She'd just been angry and had worked out her anger by rebelling against everything her mother had stood for, including her faith. She'd run as far and as fast in the opposite direction as she'd been able. Spence had been happy to accommodate her.

Until he'd decided to take off, too.

The others echoed Jared's "Amen," and Kris moved to the counter to take the lid off the casserole dish. It held baked beans with strips of bacon adorning the top.

After pushing a large spoon into the edge, she peeled back the plastic wrap on the bowl. "Mom's potato salad recipe."

Kassie smiled. "Mom made the best potato salad."

Alyssa would have nodded agreement, but she was too stalled out by the conversation. In the weeks following their mother's disappearance, none of them had spoken of her. Their father hadn't allowed it. When he wasn't around, if they'd spoken of her at all, it hadn't been with affection.

Of course, that had changed when they'd learned the truth, that she hadn't left them by choice. Being several hundred miles away and wrapped up in her own life, Alyssa hadn't had the opportunity to digest everything the way her sisters had.

After dumping a bag of chips into a bowl, Kassie stepped back. "Grab a plate and dig in."

Spence led Apollo to the other side of the room to lie down. He'd already fed him before they'd left. The dog was well-behaved enough to lie there throughout the meal, never once considering begging.

Alyssa picked up a paper plate, glad for the casual, relaxed atmosphere. Not that the evening would be easy, but at least she wouldn't be sitting stiffly, eating gourmet food from her grandmother's china.

After pouring tea into one of the plastic cups of ice, she headed for the dining room. Soon the seven of them were sitting around the table, plates full and conversation light-hearted. Tony and Jared alternated telling stories that could have been taken right from an episode of *America's Dumbest Criminals.* Soon Alyssa found herself relaxed and laughing with the others.

At a lull, Tony looked at Alyssa, now serious. "Kris said you had some things going on and wanted to get Jared's and my input."

Her chest tightened as the dread she'd arrived with swept back over her. She laid down her burger and wiped her hands on the paper napkin in her lap.

"I stumbled on something that has put my life in danger, and I'm not sure what to do about it."

She relayed everything she had told Spence on Monday while her future brothers-in-law listened without interrupting. When she had finished, she leaned back in her chair. "Now they're determined to do whatever necessary to keep me quiet. My first inclination is to run to a big city and disappear, but Spence is afraid that with these guys' connections, they'll find me."

Tony nodded. "I'm inclined to agree. The safest place for you is right here where you've got friends and family, and we can all keep an eye on you."

Alyssa frowned. Those friends he'd mentioned, she had lost contact with a long time ago. And family...well...

She shifted her gaze from him to Kris. Her mouth was set in a straight line, her eyes slightly narrowed. Alyssa knew the expression.

"Don't look at me like that."

Kris lifted her brows. "Like what?"

"Like *Alyssa's in trouble again. Par for the course.*"

Kris's eyes narrowed even further. "I was looking at you with concern."

Alyssa crossed her arms. "I know I haven't always made the wisest decisions, but for once, the trouble I'm in isn't because of poor choices."

Well, maybe Peter had been a poor choice, but it had been a trap anyone could have fallen into. There was a reason she'd thought he was too good to be true. She should have listened to her gut.

Jared cleared his throat. "Based on what you overheard, it sounds like these guys might be fencing stolen art."

Tony nodded. "Or maybe even pushing quality reproductions as the real thing."

Yeah, those were the same ideas she had come up with on her own. Now for what to do about it. "Whatever he's involved in, he's making good money at it." And he wasn't about to let his cushy way of life go. The sprawling home he lived in, filled with expensive art and collectibles, the brand-new sports car, the yacht he'd taken her out on two weekends ago, moored at a marina near Savannah—those weren't cheap. And probably not financed with money he made working as a photographer.

She should have seen through it. She liked to think she was

smarter than that. Not in this case. Going out with Peter had been the worst decision she had ever made.

But beating herself up wouldn't accomplish anything toward getting her out of the mess she was in.

Jared continued. "I know you're concerned about what kind of connections these guys might have, but I think it would be good to get the police to look into the situation. In fact, a guy I went through the academy with now works for Atlanta PD. How about if I talk to him, tell him the situation, let him know your concerns?"

"I don't know." She still wasn't convinced. "I don't really know anything. Not for sure, anyway. And I certainly don't have any evidence."

"You can give them a good starting point for their investigation—Peter and the vacant storefront. As long as this guy is free, your life is in danger."

She heaved a sigh of resignation. "All right. Go ahead and talk to him."

"Will do." Jared rose from the table. "I'm going to have to cut out. My shift starts in thirty minutes, so I've got about fifteen to get into my uniform and grab Justice."

"Justice?"

"My K9 partner."

"What breed?"

"German shepherd."

A pang of jealousy stabbed through her. Kris had Bella and Kassie would soon enjoy Justice's company. Technically, the dog probably belonged to the Pensacola Police Department, but Kassie would get to love on him whenever Jared was home.

Alyssa had always loved dogs, and the more she was around Apollo, the more she wanted one for herself. Someday.

Kassie walked Jared to the door. Their words drifted back into the dining room—Kassie's "Stay safe," followed by Jared's "I will. Love you," and Kassie's return endearment.

Alyssa was happy to see both of her sisters so much in

love, in spite of the sense of longing settling in her chest. She couldn't say she had loved Peter. The relationship had been too new. It had taken her a lot longer than six weeks to drop her guard to the point of handing someone her heart.

A more apt description of her relationship with Peter was that she'd been dazzled by him. He had the kind of exotic good looks that turned heads—strong, masculine features, jet-black hair, equally dark eyes and olive skin. She'd been impressed with his wealth, how he'd carried himself, the way he'd exuded class and confidence. How, whenever they'd been out together, he'd acted as if nothing else mattered.

It had all been an act.

As the front door thudded shut, a phone's ringtone started up somewhere in the house.

Kassie's "Hello?" came moments later. She stepped into the dining room, eyebrows drawn together. "Who's calling?"

Her gaze shifted to Alyssa and stayed there. Alyssa's chest tightened around a ball of uneasiness. Who would be calling her on Kassie's phone?

Kassie lowered the phone and held it against her abdomen. "A Rachel Osborn is trying to reach you."

Rachel, her coworker at La Maison, the one who had gotten her the job. Alyssa's uneasiness intensified. Right before destroying her phone, she'd sent Rachel a text asking her to let management know she wouldn't be coming back after her mother's service after all. But she hadn't indicated where she was going. She hadn't known herself. So how had Rachel found her?

She took the phone from Kassie and pressed it to her ear with a tentative "Hello?"

"Alyssa?" Yep, definitely Rachel. Born in Alabama, she had the heavy Southern accent to prove it. "I can't believe I got a hold of you."

Alyssa closed her eyes as a wave of dread washed over her.

What if Peter was with Rachel? Maybe tracking her down had been his idea.

"I remembered your name was Ashbaugh back when we worked at Joe's Kitchen, and I figured there'd be a lot fewer Ashbaughs than Andersons. But I still contacted a good half dozen before coming across Ashbaugh Charters. You never said anything about your family owning a charter company."

So she'd found her through Ashbaugh Charters; Kassie probably had calls forwarded to her phone. Rachel was the only person Alyssa still associated with who'd known her before she'd changed her name. She should have thought of that.

Alyssa rose from the table, no longer able to remain seated. "Is something wrong?"

"I'm not sure, but I saw something I felt I needed to tell you about. Have you had any contact with Peter since you left?"

Hearing his name sent another wave of dread over her, as if speaking it aloud would somehow conjure him up. She squelched an irrational urge to duck under the table.

"No. Why?"

As Rachel talked, Alyssa walked to the living room and began to pace. Spence followed her, Apollo right behind him.

"He came into La Maison last night. I was the one who waited on him. He was alone, had his iPad with him."

Alyssa stopped her pacing. That had been a regular occurrence before they'd even started dating. Two or three times a week, he would be there for his evening meal, sitting alone, alternating between watching the activity around him, eyes alert, and working on his tablet. Why would Rachel be calling to tell her that?

"Yes?"

"At one point, there was a photo on his iPad—three people and a dog. Looked like a selfie. I just gave it a quick glance, but I'm almost positive the person in the middle was you."

Alyssa sank onto the couch and dropped her head, pressing

her palm over her eyes. *No, no, no.* He couldn't have seen the photo. It had only been posted for a minute or two.

A wet nose nudged her hand away. When she opened her eyes, Apollo's furry brown face was inches from her own. Beyond him, Spence stood, frowning down at her, brow creased, worry lining his face.

Rachel's words cut into her thoughts. "Throughout the meal, he kept touching the pad's screen, like he was doing research or something. Eventually, he waved me down and asked for his check. He was smiling. I told him he looked like he'd just gotten some good news. He said he had, plopped a hundred-dollar bill on the table and told me to keep the change. On his way out, he said he was going to clean up a mess and he might even make some money while he was at it."

An audible sigh came through the phone. "Anyhow, something told me if that really was you in the picture, I should at least try to make contact."

"Thank you." She put a hand under Apollo's chin and scratched his throat. "I can't tell you how much I appreciate it. I…" She hesitated. Could she trust Rachel?

She had no choice. "Please don't tell Peter you talked to me. I stumbled on something last Thursday night and he has sent people to kill me twice."

Rachel gasped. "Oh, my. He always seems so…nice."

"I thought so, too. But I'm begging you, don't let him know you talked to me. If he thinks he can use you to get to me, neither of us will be safe."

"I promise I won't say a thing."

"Thank you." She disconnected the call and rose.

Spence was still frowning. "That didn't look like good news."

"No." She stalked across the living room and back again while Spence waited. "That was a girl I worked with."

"I thought you said no one knew how to find you."

She heaved a sigh "When I said no one knew my real name,

I was wrong. The lady who just called—Rachel—we both worked at La Maison. We also worked together for a short time when I first landed in Atlanta, so she knew me before I had my name changed. Almost seven years later, she actually remembered Ashbaugh."

Alyssa relayed everything Rachel had told her. "She said she just got a quick glance, so it's possible it wasn't even me in the picture."

"Did she describe the photo?"

"Three people and a dog, and it looked like me in the middle."

Spence's frown deepened. "That sounds a lot like the photo Brandi took. When we get back to the apartment, how about if you email it to me from your phone, and I'll pull it up on my computer where we can enlarge it. Even if it's the same picture, there may not be anything that would identify where you were."

"That sounds good."

She walked back to the dining room, still holding Kassie's phone. If there was no location metadata embedded in the photo and no places tagged in the post, even if Peter had the photo, it wouldn't do him any good.

But based on the comment he'd made when leaving La Maison, that *wasn't* the case. He'd apparently had a breakthrough, and she was sure it had something to do with the picture.

The best she could hope for was that Rachel was mistaken, that Peter and his minions hadn't seen the post and someone else was the subject of the photo he'd been studying.

If she was wrong, she was in deep trouble. Peter had put a tracking device on her car. He'd paid to have the mechanic work done so she wouldn't abandon it, and he'd sent someone to shoot at her. When that hadn't worked, he'd managed to obtain something lethal and have someone try to inject her with it. Those weren't the deeds of a man who gave up easily.

But if Peter really *did* have nothing more to go on than that

Alyssa Anderson might have fled to somewhere near Tallahassee, she might have a chance of making it through this latest mess-up alive.

She would hold on to that hope until she learned otherwise.

Spence walked with Alyssa to the back door of what would
eventually be his music store, Apollo trotting ahead of them.

The evening had started out great. Meeting Jared and getting reacquainted with Tony had been good. Letting the two
men in on the situation with Alyssa had felt like shifting part
of a heavy burden to someone else's shoulders.

Jared having a friend working with the Atlanta PD had put
both his and Alyssa's minds at ease. After what she had been
through, she wasn't likely to trust anybody. Spence understood her concerns. Men like Peter often had connections in
law enforcement.

He unlocked the back door and turned on the hall light.
"How about coming upstairs? I've at least got it furnished
with a couch and a comfy chair."

"Sure."

During the short trip from Kassie's to the building downtown, she had emailed the photo Brandi had texted. Internet installation was on the schedule for next week. Tonight, he would
use his mobile hotspot, as he'd been doing since he'd arrived.

He led Alyssa up the stairs and into the large room. The
living area and kitchen were open. A door at the end of the
counter led to a bedroom and adjoining bath.

Alyssa stepped into the space and looked around. "Would
you believe, I've never been up here? When I was a kid, this
was always rented." She smiled at him. "Your space is a lot
better than mine."

"I'm afraid yours never got turned into living quarters."

"It's all right. It beats trying to live with either of my sisters."

"Hey, tonight went well."

"I guess it did, except for my little exchange with Kris."

"Not to take sides or anything, but I think she really *was* looking at you with concern instead of judgment."

Alyssa frowned. "Maybe I overreacted. I'm so used to them thinking the worst of me that I probably read it into everything they do. I'll try to work on that, especially if I'm going to be stuck here for a while."

He waved a hand toward the couch. "Have a seat, and I'll pull up your email."

By the time he had retrieved his computer from the bar in the kitchen area, Apollo had jumped up next to Alyssa on the couch and had his head resting in her lap.

"Okay, stinker. We're going to have a hard time looking at this together with a seventy-five-pound dog between us." He extended an index finger and pointed at the floor. "Down."

The dog obeyed, but there was a lot of reluctance in the motion.

Once Spence had positioned himself next to Alyssa, he patted the couch on his other side. "Come." The dog curled up beside him, head resting between his front paws.

"Now, for this picture." He turned on his phone's hotspot, opened his laptop and navigated to his email. Hers was right on top. After a couple of clicks, the picture filled the screen.

Alyssa leaned against him, studying what was there. Apollo's face filled the lower portion of the photo. Spence was squatting on one side of the dog, Brandi on the other, with Alyssa peering around her, putting her face between them. The Girl Scout table was behind them, colorful boxes stacked on top. Behind that was a blank wall.

A soft sigh escaped Alyssa as she seemed to relax beside him. "There's no way to know where we are from this, no signage or anything."

He leaned closer, squinting at the screen. The right-hand portion of the Girl Scout banner was visible next to Brandi, its message too small to read.

He clicked to zoom in, expanding the photo to a hundred and twenty-five percent, then one-fifty, and all the way to two hundred. His chest tightened. The two lines of block characters were blurred but decipherable. The first was "OOP" with "15" below.

"Oh, no." Alyssa whispered the words beside him.

Spence opened a new tab and did a search for "Girl Scout Troop 115." North Carolina Coastal Pines 1 came up. Troop 215 was based in Carmel, Indiana. Troop 315 in Gainesville, Florida, a considerable distance from Pensacola.

A few more searches and he landed on Troop 715, Pensacola, Florida.

Alyssa stiffened. "If Peter saw this and blew it up like you just did, it wouldn't take him more than a few minutes to have a whole list of locations to check. Since he knows I'm from somewhere in Florida, my guess is he'll start here, maybe Gainesville first. Eventually, though, he's going to land in Pensacola."

She looked at him with wide, fear-filled eyes. "I've got to get out of here."

"When you're gone, do you really think he's going to stop looking for you?"

"Probably not. But wherever I go, there won't be a trail leading him to me."

"Maybe, but you don't know that. From what you've told me, this Peter sounds pretty resourceful. Let's see what the Atlanta police can do. In the meantime, let your family and me protect you."

A long span of silence passed before she finally nodded. "All right. But the first hint I get that Peter is anywhere in the vicinity, I'm out of here."

"Fair enough."

She reached both hands forward in a stretch. "If you don't mind walking me home, I'm going to try to get some sleep."

Apollo lifted his head, suddenly perking up. Whether he'd

picked up on the word *walk* or *sleep*, Spence wasn't sure. Both were favorite activities. The dog often amazed him with how much he seemed to understand.

"Yep, come on. We're going to walk Alyssa home."

Apollo jumped down from the couch, looking from one to the other, tail wagging. As soon as they headed toward the open door leading downstairs, the dog charged ahead of them, his fast, heavy tread echoing in the narrow stairwell.

When Alyssa got to the lobby, she turned to face Spence. "This is a pain when I could just cut across the balcony to get from your place to mine. But no way am I going to leave my alarm off."

"I don't mind going the long way around. And *he* definitely doesn't." He nodded at his dog, who currently stood at the front door, tail wagging so furiously his whole rear end swayed back and forth. "I do have an idea, though. What if we remove the sensors from your balcony doors and install a separate single-zone system. Then you could arm and disarm it without leaving the second floor."

She nodded. "I like that idea. It just doesn't make sense for me to pay a security company to come out and install a new system when my stay here is temporary."

"It would be overkill. I'm guessing we could pick up something at Lowe's for less than a hundred bucks and I could install it for you." He'd always been pretty handy. If something came with DIY instructions, he could usually manage it.

When they stepped onto the sidewalk to head to the charter office entrance, Alyssa pulled the key from her pocket. "If you let me pay for the system, I'll accept your donation of time to install it."

The moment she opened the door, a steady high-pitched tone said the system was armed. She punched four numbers into the control panel and turned to him.

"Thank you. I can't tell you how much I appreciate everything you're doing for me. Eventually, this will be over and we'll both have our lives back."

Spence frowned. If getting his life back meant Alyssa wouldn't be in it, he wasn't so sure he wanted it back. He was getting used to having her around. They would never return to where they'd been before he'd left eight years ago, but he was developing high hopes for a lifelong friendship.

"If you need anything, call me. I want to hear from you if you feel at all scared or threatened." He smiled. "If you beat on the wall dividing our two units, I'd definitely wake up, even out of a sound sleep." Although he hadn't classified his sleep as "sound" for a while.

He wished her good-night and then watched her lock the door and rearm the alarm. "Okay, boy. One more opportunity to take care of business, and then it's bedtime."

Five minutes later, he climbed the stairs to his own apartment. He really needed to get some rest. But that wasn't likely to happen anytime soon, no matter how hard he tried.

Getting to sleep had been difficult for quite some time. Even when the nightmares didn't come, he was plagued with an ever-present tension, as if danger was around every corner, lurking in unseen places, waiting for him to let down his guard.

Now that situation was compounded times ten. Because he didn't just have to fear the demons that took up residence in his mind. There was also the very real threat to Alyssa. He'd feel better if he was sleeping on the charter office couch, downstairs from her.

God, please protect her, especially when I'm not there to do it.

He picked up his guitar and sat in the chair. Apollo stretched out on the couch adjacent to him, and Spence strummed a C chord, keeping the volume low enough to not disturb the other occupant of the building. Then he stopped to listen.

Silence, except for the lingering tones of what he'd just played.

Both the charter office and Alyssa's apartment above were

protected by the security system. Besides that, she had promised to call him at the first sign of danger. He pulled his phone
from his pocket and laid it on the arm of the chair.

Then he closed his eyes and breathed another prayer for her
protection. He transitioned from C to A minor, consciously
slowing his breathing. Then he picked up his phone to make
sure he hadn't accidentally silenced the ringer. Hand once
again on his guitar, he moved to F and finally G before repeating the four-chord pattern. It was a common progression,
one he could play with no thought.

Ten minutes later, he wasn't any closer to sleep than when
he'd started. He heaved a sigh. He was fighting a losing battle.
He would never be able to totally relax.

Not as long as there were men out there determined to see
Alyssa dead.

Chapter Seven

Spence bolted upright in bed, heart pounding out a frenzied rhythm, breath coming in jerky gasps.

He pressed one hand to his chest, the other to his cheek, wet from where Apollo had licked him.

As his breathing slowed, he lowered his hands to cup his dog's cheeks. "Thanks, buddy."

Only two days had passed since his last nightmare. That one had come Thursday night. He'd chalked it up to the disconcerting discovery that the picture Brandi had posted could lead Peter to Pensacola.

The nightmares always started the same, with him riding in a convoy, sometimes part of a route clearance team, sometimes coming through right behind them. Oftentimes the dreams played out exactly the same way the events had in real life. Other times, his mind chose alternate scenarios just as terrifying as the real thing.

The latter was the case with the dream he'd just had. Instead of McCarthy lying in the dusty road with useless legs and bullets whizzing past, it had been Alyssa. Before he could get her behind the berm, a man had appeared standing over them, an AK-47 aimed at Alyssa's head. Though Spence had never seen him before, he'd somehow known he was looking at Peter.

He pressed both hands to the top of his head and then slid them down his moist face. That wasn't just dog slobber. It was sweat.

He looked at the clock: 12:42. He still had another six or seven hours until he needed to be up. Sleep would come eventually, but not anytime soon.

When he tugged on the sheet to throw it back, Apollo jumped from the bed. The dog was used to Spence's routine on nights like this—sleep, wake up in a state of panic, get out of bed and go play for a while. And on the really good nights, actually get a few more hours of sleep.

On his way to the living room, he stopped at the kitchen for a bottle of water. That was part of the routine, too, not that it aided in sleep, but the panting and sweating usually left him thirsty.

He picked up his guitar and sank into the upholstered chair. Apollo took up his usual spot on the couch.

He strummed a G chord and began to sing softly. "Alleluia, alleluia…" It was an old worship chorus he rarely heard anymore, but he liked it and often played it during those lonely hours in the middle of the night.

There were other verses, things like "Thank you, Jesus" and "You are worthy." He often made up his own, each of them cries from the heart: "God, I need you," "Help me, Jesus" and "Lord, I trust you." Any phrase worked, as long as it had four syllables and could be sung over and over.

When he finished, the last strains faded and other music came through the open door of his bedroom. His phone's ringtone. Who would be calling him at this hour?

He laid the guitar aside and reached the open doorway as the music died. When he checked his call log, Alyssa's name was on top. There would be only one reason for her call at this hour—some kind of threat.

He called her back with shaking hands. While waiting for her to pick up, he hurried onto his balcony. Nothing was amiss in front. The alarm next door wasn't going off, either.

After a click and soft rustle, her voice came through the phone. "Hey."

It was just a single word, but it didn't hold any fear or anxiety. His breath released in a rush. "Is everything okay?"

"Everything's fine. I heard you playing, so I thought—"

"You heard me?" *No way.* Annoyance wove through him. If he couldn't even play softly to soothe himself when sleep eluded him, these living arrangements were going to be tough. "Do you have supersonic hearing or something?"

She laughed. "Actually, I put my ear to the wall to see if you were awake. I didn't want to call you if you were asleep." She paused. "Can I come over?"

The irritation he'd felt moments earlier evaporated in an instant. "Sure. I'll meet you on the balcony."

Yesterday, they'd purchased a security system from Lowe's, like they'd talked about Thursday night. Today, he'd gotten it installed. Now that going from one apartment to the other involved just a short walk across the balcony, something told him these middle-of-the-night visits might become a regular thing. He was all right with that.

As he stepped onto the balcony, one of the French doors at the other end swung open and Alyssa stepped out. The bathrobe she wore fell almost to her ankles.

He smiled as she approached.

"No Bugs Bunny tonight?"

"Oh, Bugs Bunny is here. I've just got him covered up. It's chilly tonight."

She was right. By mid-September, nighttime temperatures could get a little nippy.

He led her into the apartment and motioned toward the couch. "Have a seat. Can I get you anything?"

"No, I'm good."

"Are you sure? I have one Caramel Chocolate Chip Cookie left. I'll split it with you."

"You did good. My Thin Mints were gone two days ago."

"I polished off at least a quarter of them."

"That's right. So I'll take you up on your offer to split the last cookie."

As soon as she sat, Apollo jumped up next to her. When Spence returned with the cookie, he sat in the chair he had vacated a few minutes earlier rather than fight with his dog. "How was dinner?"

He'd walked over to the charter office at lunchtime and talked to Alyssa and Kris. Kassie had been taking care of appointments at her hair salon. Kris had told him Jared was working tonight and Tony had a meeting, so the three girls had decided to make dinner in the charter office kitchen and eat together, along with Gavin. Kris had invited Spence to join them, but he'd passed, refusing to intrude on their sister time.

Alyssa smiled. "Actually, it was really nice."

"No friction?"

"Not a bit, even with the three of us bumping into each other in that tiny kitchen. I'm still not holding my breath, but tonight was good. Kris brought a couple of bags of clothes from home, stuff she said she was planning to donate and thought she'd let me go through it first."

She gave him a wry smile. "I know I'm not in a position to be picky, but I have to say every item in there was something that fit me and was a style I'd wear. That tells me when Kris went through her closet, it had less to do with a desire to de-clutter and more to do with wanting to help a needy sister. But this was how she could do it and not make me feel like a char-ity case." She frowned. "Even though I sort of am right now."

"Only because you had to leave everything behind when you made your quick getaway."

"You make it sound much more palatable." She pressed her lips together. "Did you know they still do Gallery Night here?

Kassie mentioned it at dinner. It's next Friday, and Jared and Justice are going to be working it, doing patrol."

He crossed his arms. "Don't even think about it. You three ladies cooked and ate at the charter office to keep you out of public."

"I know. It's just really appealing. If I have to stay cooped up inside for much longer, I'm afraid I'm going to go stir crazy."

"It's just temporary. Once you know you're safe, you can do all the Gallery Nights you want to."

He remembered the event well. The third Friday of every month, thousands would converge on downtown Pensacola for a time of music, art and food. He and Alyssa had gone several times and always enjoyed it. The streets had been packed, the air filled with fun and excitement.

That was then. Now crowds triggered panic attacks. Thankfully, that was something he wouldn't have to face, at least not in the near future. Until Peter and all his cronies were behind bars, being out in public was something Alyssa couldn't even consider.

She leaned against the arm of the couch and curled her legs up, tucking her sock-clad feet in next to her. Apollo moved over to accommodate her. "When I called, you were playing. I'd love it if you would continue."

"Sure." He picked up his guitar and placed it across his lap. After strumming some random chords, he settled on one of the songs he and the worship team had done the last Sunday before leaving LaGrange.

As he played, Alyssa propped her right elbow on the arm of the couch and rested the side of her head in her hand. Her features settled into an expression of contentment.

As long as he'd known her, she had never played or sung. Kassie had been the musical one of the Ashbaugh girls. But Alyssa had always enjoyed listening to him play, something that apparently hadn't changed.

When he finished, she lifted her head. "That doesn't sound like one of our old rock-and-roll songs."

"Nope, I haven't played those in quite a while." Eight years, to be exact. "Most of what I play now are songs I know from church."

"Wait." She sat straighter. "What?"

"Yep. For the past three months, I've played on my church's worship team." That had started shortly after he'd gotten Apollo. As venturing from his apartment had gradually grown easier, he'd transitioned from watching the service online to attending in person, which had rapidly led to helping with the music.

She swung her feet onto the floor. "You play in a worship band? At church?"

"I did until a week ago. I'm going to your sisters' church tomorrow. If they need any help, I'll volunteer."

Alyssa shook her head. "I'm still trying to imagine you *attending church,* let alone being involved. Tell me how that happened."

"I kind of took the roundabout way, but I guess you'd say it started with Steve's overdose."

It had been almost eight years, and the scene still haunted him. The band had finished practicing and had begun partying. They'd all been at Steve's house. Since he was the one with the large garage, practices—and parties—had always been held there.

Spence shook his head. "We had big dreams, the four of us—Braydon, Bryson, Steve and me. We all thought we were destined for fame and glory, looking forward to lives of glitz and glamour, listening to the screams of adoring fans. But no matter how you pitch it, there's nothing glamorous about dying in one's vomit."

Alyssa winced. Although she'd been with him at almost every party he'd attended from age sixteen to eighteen, that night she'd been at home sick with the flu. It had turned out to be a blessing in disguise.

"What I saw shook me to the core. It was enough to scare me straight. But it wasn't until I was in Afghanistan, pinned down by enemy fire, that I cried out to God. Some people say you're not supposed to bargain with God. I'd say if you do, make sure you're ready to come through on whatever you promise. I told God if He would save me, I'd commit the rest of my life to Him. God did, and I honored the promise I'd made."

He strummed a chord and then flattened his hand across the strings. "I hope you'll go to church with me sometime soon."

She frowned. "You're not going to get me into church, especially with my sisters. They're always trying to fix me, and I don't need fixing." She gave him a half smile. "Well, maybe I do, but definitely not by them. I'll fix myself."

"We can't fix ourselves. It took me going halfway around the world to find that out."

"Whatever." She settled back into the position she'd been in earlier, legs curled up, elbow propped on the arm of the couch. Apollo rested his head on her feet. "Don't hold out hope for getting me into church, but you can play for me anytime. I won't even object to your singing those songs."

Those songs would be worship songs. Since she'd given him free rein to sing whatever he wanted, that was what she would get. Sometimes music had a way of touching hearts when sermons couldn't.

After thinking for a moment, he played the intro for "Graves Into Gardens." Every time he sang the song, he felt as if the lyrics had been written for him. He really had searched the world over and hadn't found anything that satisfied. Not until one afternoon along a dusty road in Afghanistan. When all was said and done, he'd had to agree: There really was nothing better than Jesus.

When finished, he made a smooth transition into "I Speak Jesus." Another song with lyrics he hoped would touch Alyssa.

What struggles did she face that needed the Savior's touch? Did she have dark addictions to break? What about fear, anxiety and depression? She definitely needed hope and freedom and peace. He didn't even have to ask that.

As he continued to play and sing, Alyssa slid further down the couch, nudging Apollo out of the way until her head rested on the padded arm. Her eyelids grew gradually heavier and then closed altogether.

And he continued to play, softly, so he wouldn't disturb her. Her mouth was closed, her lips curved up ever so slightly, as if she'd found the peace in sleep that always eluded her when she was awake.

God, please let me have a positive impact on her. Turn her heart toward You.

How different would their lives have been if he had chosen more constructive outlets for dealing with his abusive father, if he'd led Alyssa to church instead of down a path of self-destruction?

They'd probably be married by now, with a couple of kids. Instead, Alyssa still hadn't forgiven him for leaving her and couldn't wait to get out of town. And they both had enough baggage to fill the back of a semitrailer.

He transitioned into another song, Chris McClarney's "Beauty for Ashes." The opening referred to God as a God of new beginnings.

Spence was still waiting for some of the ashes in his life to be turned to beauty.

But he'd found his new beginning.

God, please let Alyssa find hers.

People packed Palafox Street. The crowd was energized, an atmosphere of celebration in the air. Galleries lined both sides of the street, interspersed with restaurants and bars. All establishments were open, inviting guests to view the variety of artwork displayed or to come in for a meal or drink.

Alyssa had almost resigned herself to hanging out on the balcony and looking down Government Street toward Palafox, hoping to catch a glimpse of the goings-on a couple of blocks away.

This was a whole lot better.

She looked over her shoulder at Spence, standing at the edge of the sidewalk, right behind her. Apollo stood beside him in his black vest. Kassie and Kris were to her right, with Tony between them. Jared was somewhere in the crowd. He'd promised to do his best to keep checking on them, but he had a job to do.

Last Saturday night, she'd fallen asleep on Spence's couch and hadn't awoken until three in the morning. During those two hours, she'd slept harder than she had in…she couldn't remember when she'd last slept that soundly. The sense of security knowing Spence was so close and the comfort of Apollo lying on the couch with her, head resting on her feet, had put her in a state of relaxed oblivion.

For the past week, she'd been a mess. Jared had contacted his buddy in Atlanta the day after the cookout at Kassie's. For the next three days, she'd worried that the information on her whereabouts had somehow found its way back to Peter.

More than a week had passed since her conversation with Rachel. The first one anyway. There'd been two since, both initiated by Alyssa. As recently as last night, Peter had dined at La Maison. Whatever photo Rachel had seen on his tablet, he hadn't pulled it up since. At least, not at dinner. She'd been watching, even going so far as to make sure she was his server. She'd been employed there long enough to make those kinds of demands, regardless of how much the other servers wanted his generous gratuities.

Besides the fact that Peter hadn't left Atlanta, there'd been no other signs of anyone looking for her. She'd gradually gone from jittery, expecting Peter to materialize in the charter office lobby, to having such bad cabin fever she was going to hurt someone if she couldn't get outside those four walls.

Having her stitches removed on Monday hadn't even offered a means of escape. When she'd mentioned to Kris that she needed a ride to the walk-in clinic, Kris had volunteered Mildred. She wasn't just Gavin's babysitter. She was a retired nurse. She'd been happy to come to the office with her scissors and tweezers and go to work.

This afternoon, Alyssa had finally demanded to know how long everyone expected her to stay cooped up when there wasn't the slightest hint that Peter even knew where she was. It had taken a lot of convincing, but she'd finally gotten her sisters, both of their fiancés and Spence to agree to let her go out for just an hour, under their watchful eyes, of course. She even felt somewhat disguised, with her hair twisted into a bun beneath an Atlanta Braves baseball cap.

She glanced over her shoulder again, ready to give Spence an appreciative smile. He'd been the most reluctant to acquiesce to her wishes.

Spence wasn't looking at her, though. He was standing straight and stiff, head pivoting from side to side, gaze darting erratically over the crowd. He was tense, hypervigilant. Had he seen something? Danger? Some kind of threat?

"Spence?" She raised her voice over the conversations going on around her and the music pouring from the stage set up a short distance away. He didn't acknowledge her.

She called his name even louder, and when that didn't work, she grasped his shoulder and gave him a small shake. His eyes met hers. They seemed to hold a wildness she'd never seen before.

"Hey, it's okay. Tony and my sisters are right here. Jared's somewhere nearby, too, with Justice. Nothing's going to happen."

He nodded, but the motion was jerky. She grasped his hand. "Come on, let's get a little closer to the band."

She wove through the crowd, pulling him along behind her. Immersing himself in the songs would be good for him. Music had always had the ability to pull him out of whatever funk he was in.

She moved closer, Spence's hand in hers, until they were only about ten feet from the front of the stage. The group, likely composed of local musicians, was performing songs from eras spanning the '70s to present day. She didn't know them, but they were good.

As the current song drew to a close, the crowd erupted into applause with lots of whoops and hollers.

Alyssa turned to smile at Spence. "Isn't this bet—" She swallowed the rest of the word.

In the glow of the streetlights, sweat glistened on his forehead and the sides of his face. His jaw was clenched, and the wildness she'd seen in his eyes earlier was still there, times ten. Apollo was pressed against his leg, but he seemed unaware of the dog.

Realization slammed into her. Spence was on the verge of a panic attack, and it had nothing to do with her.

She leaned close to him. "Let's get out of here."

Spence didn't move. She gave him a small shove. "Come on, let's go home."

He gave her another one of those jerky nods and then grasped her hand and spun. Behind them, the band began its next song. As Spence made his way through the crowd, her hand in his, Apollo's leash in the other, his pace grew faster and more frenzied. Soon he was bumping people out of the way without so much as an "excuse me." In their mad dash, she'd lost Tony and her sisters. Maybe they'd gotten separated when she'd dragged Tony toward the stage.

Just before they reached the edge of the street, a man crowded between them from her right. He was Spence's height, but outweighed him by a good forty pounds. A second pressed in from the left. She glanced from one to the other. Neither of them was looking at her. Were they even aware they had worked their way between her and Spence?

The music behind them swelled, growing more driving, and the crowd roared. The men slowed their pace, holding her back. Her hand slipped through Spence's. A moment later, she lost sight of him.

"Spence!" Even as she shouted his name, she knew it was pointless. He would never hear her over the music and the noise of the crowd.

One man stayed on her right as the other circled behind her. Soon, she was being jostled to the left, farther and farther away from Spence and Apollo. Yes, the men knew exactly what they were doing. Within seconds, they had pressed her out of the crowd and were forcing her toward an alley between two buildings. Parked cars lined one side. No one was milling around any of them.

When she twisted to make her way back into the safety of the crowd, the man next to her grasped her upper arm in a viselike grip. She released a loud scream. A meaty hand clamped over her mouth, immediately cutting it off. The same man wrapped his other arm around her waist, and her feet left the ground.

Panic pounded up her spine. She clawed at the hand covering her mouth and kicked the man's shins. Her feeble attempts did nothing but make him angry. He tightened his hold and gave her a rough shake.

He had carried her past the first parked car. Within moments, they would be too far away for anyone to help her. They probably already were.

As she twisted and fought, she forced her mouth open beneath the man's hand. Once she had pulled her lips back, she clamped down hard on the meaty flesh of his palm.

He released a high-pitched scream that dissolved into a string of curses. The bite had accomplished what she had hoped. The man still held her, but he had removed his hand, which was likely now bleeding. She twisted her head back and forth, shrieking Spence's name, then Apollo's, and then general cries for help.

"Shut up!"

The man dropped her, but the other one grabbed her before she could even think about running away. Now they had passed the second car, leaving Palafox Street even farther behind.

A bark sounded somewhere behind them, muffled by the noise still pouring from the street. The man who held her spun suddenly, swinging her around with him. A chocolate Lab was bounding toward them.

Apollo?

Before she had a chance to ponder it further, another dog raced into the alley, a German shepherd. Both dogs wore working vests. The man who held her released her. The other one had already made it to the opposite end of the alley and was rounding the back corner of the building.

When she landed, her knees buckled. As she crumpled to the ground, a uniformed police officer charged into the alley, weapon drawn. Recognition dawned as pain shot through her right knee. *Not again.*

Jared was some distance back when Apollo reached her. The Lab released a couple of whimpers and then ran his wet tongue up one cheek. She wrapped her arms around him as Justice raced past, gaze focused intently ahead. The German shepherd went airborne, clamping his jaws around the elbow of the man who had just held her. He released a scream and dropped to his knees. Justice held on. The dog probably wouldn't release him until commanded by his partner to do so.

Jared slowed. "Are you okay?"

"I'm fine. Go see to him. There's another man, too. He ran behind the building—that way." She held up one arm.

Jared jogged away from her, talking into his radio as he did. Then he gave Justice the command to release. The dog sat, tense and ready to react as Jared handcuffed the suspect.

One man dead, one soon to be behind bars. How many more were there? Eventually the authorities would work their way up to Peter and his cronies. Only then would she be safe.

She looked back at Palafox Street. Why wasn't Apollo with Spence? "Where is your daddy?"

As if in answer to her question, Spence hurried into the alley, his limp more pronounced than usual. He rushed toward her and dropped to his knees beside her. "I'm so sorry. I let you down. I'm so sorry."

The grief in his voice broke her heart. She cupped his cheeks in both hands. "Hey, it wasn't your fault. Those two guys were bigger than you. And they were *way* bigger than me. They were able to separate us, and there's nothing you could have done differently."

Two more police officers rushed into the alley. One hurried to assist Jared, and the other stopped next to her and Spence.

"Braydon?" They both said his name together.

"In the flesh. Brandi told me she ran into you guys." He slipped right back into professional mode. "Can you describe the other man who attacked you?"

"Caucasian, maybe thirties or forties. It's hard to say because he was bald. Probably six feet. A big guy, muscular."

"Facial hair?"

"A close-cut beard and mustache."

"Clothing?"

"Jeans and a gray hoodie."

Braydon radioed her description to Dispatch and once again addressed her. "They're putting out a BOLO."

"Thank you." She looked at Spence. "I could try to convince myself this was random, but I like to think I'm smarter than that. Peter has managed to track me to Pensacola, and I'm not going to try to convince myself otherwise."

When she attempted to push herself to her feet, Spence rose and held out a hand. She accepted the assistance. The knee was tender, but not much more than it had been earlier tonight. Maybe she'd just irritated it rather than really set herself back.

She started to offer another thank you, but when she looked at him, what she saw drew her up short.

He faced Palafox, where light drifted into the alley and illuminated his face. He looked rough. Though the wildness had left his eyes, his face was several shades of pale, lines of fatigue embedded in his features.

She'd thought Apollo's service was for physical reasons; Spence had obviously been injured. Maybe she was right. Maybe Apollo *did* give him physical assistance.

But that wasn't all. Apollo was there for emotional support. Whatever experiences Spence had had while fighting on the other side of the world, they had left him with emotional trauma. Maybe even PTSD. And that was why he had Apollo.

The realization left her with a hollowness deep in her gut. Spence hadn't wanted to come tonight, and she had pushed him into it. Her sole focus had been on how tired she was of being trapped inside those four walls and how badly she'd wanted to get out, without a single thought for how the event might affect Spence. Maybe her sisters had been right all along. Maybe she *was* selfish.

She didn't deserve the care and concern Spence was showing her, the way he had taken on her problems when he clearly had enough of his own.

This was just one more reason she needed to leave. At this point, Spence might not even try to stop her.

Because, after the events of this evening, he would probably be glad to see her go.

Chapter Eight

Spence walked down the sidewalk bordering East Government Street, the noise of the festivities growing gradually more distant. Alyssa was next to him, Jared and Justice to their rear. The law enforcement team was providing an escort all the way to the charter office. When they'd left the alley, they'd run into Kassie, Kris and Tony, and Alyssa had given them a brief rundown of the attack. Her account had almost made it sound like he hadn't messed up.

Now, Apollo was at his side. In fact, if the dog was any closer, they'd be tripping over each other's feet. Once making sure Alyssa was all right, Apollo had pretty much stayed glued to his hip. The Lab instinctively knew when he wasn't doing well.

This was one of those times. Usually, when he had his incidents, he was alone. Even when he was in public, it never affected anyone else. Tonight it had. He'd almost enabled Alyssa's abduction.

When he and Alyssa had reached Palafox Street and he'd seen the crowds, it had started almost immediately—the anxiety, the hypervigilance, the sense danger was all around them. He'd fought to beat back the panic, using every rational argument he could come up with, and Apollo had done everything he'd been trained to do.

By the time Alyssa had suggested going home, Spence had been at the breaking point. He'd grabbed her hand and turned, ready to make his way back through the crowd. Soon he hadn't been aware of anything except getting away and retreating into the safety of his apartment. At some point, he'd lost his grip on Alyssa's hand. He couldn't even say when that had happened.

But as he'd headed down the sidewalk toward Government Street, Apollo had begun to tug at the leash, trying to pull him in the opposite direction. That had been when he'd realized he'd lost Alyssa.

What a loser. He wasn't only unfit for military duty. He couldn't even protect the woman he... What? Cared for. They had ended their relationship, but he had never stopped caring for her. No matter what happened, she would always hold a special place in his heart.

When they arrived at the charter office, Alyssa slipped her key into the lock. Once inside, she disarmed the alarm system and turned to face him.

"I'm sorry."

He looked at her. "For what? I'm the one who should be apologizing." Of course, he already had.

"I should never have insisted on going out tonight."

He shrugged. "Hindsight's always twenty-twenty. You had no idea you were going to be attacked in the midst of hundreds of people."

She frowned. "Yeah, going out was a mistake in that sense. But that wasn't what I was referring to. You were opposed right from the start. I thought it was just concern for my safety."

"That was a lot of it."

"But there was more. I should have seen that."

"How? It isn't like I've given you much to go on." He hadn't told her anything about the past eight years, other than that he'd gotten out of the army and had been living in LaGrange for the past year.

Could he share his struggles with her? He hadn't shared the details of the horrors he'd experienced—or the psychological and emotional fallout from them—with anyone except the veterans in the Sierra Delta community. But Alyssa had plenty of her own issues. If there was anyone outside of other veterans he should feel comfortable sharing his troubles with, it should be her.

After a few more moments of hesitation, he twisted the dead bolt into the locked position. "How about rearming this and coming up to my place?"

"Sure."

She led him up the stairs. After disarming and rearming the system he had installed, she secured the French doors, and they walked across the balcony to his quarters. When he unlocked and swung open the door, there was no alarm system to worry about. The security company had come out on Wednesday. They'd quoted him a combination price for both installation and monitoring that had included a sizable discount. So he'd ordered the system and signed a two-year monitoring agreement.

Soon, he would have a lot of expensive sound and musical equipment downstairs. In the event someone broke in, he'd wanted the security of knowing the police would be there within minutes to protect his merchandise.

Alyssa sat on the couch, and he took a seat next to her. Apollo hopped up on his other side and laid his head in his lap. The dog sensed he was still needed. Although Spence was doing much better than he had been fifteen minutes ago, the experience had left him with a jittery weakness in his limbs that still hadn't fully dissipated.

He took a deep breath, not sure where to begin, then decided it didn't matter where he started, as long as he got the story out.

"During my time over there, I saw a lot of death and destruction. Not just random, either. These were buddies—guys whose stories I knew, men who had shared their dreams and plans for the future, brothers."

He stroked Apollo's head as he talked, smoothing the fur between his eyes, over the top of his head and down his neck, then back to the top to do it again.

"There was also the constant state of being on edge—the mortar fire that would have us flying out of bed in the middle of the night, the convoys down roads where Taliban could be hiding behind every rise or berm. That feeling of not knowing which of us wouldn't live to see another day."

Alyssa shook her head. "I can't even imagine."

"It took its toll. I thought once I came home, I'd be able to put it all behind me and return to a normal life. That didn't happen. All those experiences I'd thought I was leaving over there followed me home in my nightmares."

"How did you get Apollo?"

"I was dealing with a lot of depression, unable to sleep, spending my days vegging in front of the TV, taking a whole cocktail of medications just to try to make it through each day. I'd tried praying, but it seemed like those prayers weren't getting past the ceiling. I was getting counseling through the VA, and my counselor suggested putting in an application for a service dog through K9s For Warriors."

He slid his hand farther down Apollo's back, and the dog released a sigh. "I didn't want to do it. I was afraid I'd be taking a dog away from a veteran who might need it worse than I did. During one session, my counselor got online and made me start the application process right then and there."

He smiled. Starting that application was one of the best decisions he'd ever made, even though he'd had to be prodded into making it.

"I take it getting Apollo helped."

"It did, more than you can imagine. I waited eight months, which is actually super fast. I think God moved some mountains."

"I'm not wishing sleep problems on you, but it's been kind of nice having company on those nights I was awake."

He grinned. "Glad I could accommodate you. It is getting better, though. The nightmares are a long way from gone, but they aren't as frequent as they used to be. Once I got Apollo, I felt like I might be able to start living again. That's when I started working on my dream to have a music store. I applied for a small business loan, and now here I am. I've still got a long way to go, but at least I'm moving in the right direction."

"I'm glad." She turned her head to look up at him, eyebrows drawn together. "You have a gun. I didn't think you were allowed to own one when you have PTSD." She had watched a movie a while back where a veteran had a flashback while at the shooting range and killed his buddy.

"Depends on the situation. I've never been a danger to myself or anyone else. I *am* smart enough to leave my pistol out of reach while I'm sleeping, though."

"What happened tonight? Did you see something or hear something?" She paused. "If you don't want to talk about it, I understand."

"It's okay. I don't mind." Now that he'd gotten started, it wasn't as difficult as he'd thought it would be. "Large crowds are one of my triggers."

"Oh, man. I really feel bad."

He put an arm around her. "Don't. You had no way of knowing I was going to freak out."

She snuggled against him, resting her head just above his collarbone. He released a sigh. This was contentment—Alyssa nestled against one side, his dog on the other, big, furry head in his lap.

Ever since reconnecting with Alyssa, she'd regularly mentioned her plans to leave Pensacola as soon as she could, emphasizing that her stay was temporary. Each time, it had bothered him a little more than the last time. He'd blamed it on the sense of protectiveness he felt around her, the fact that if she left, he would no longer be there to protect her.

But it was more than that. She had changed since those early days. She was more settled, more mature. And though she was struggling, she was trying hard to make the right choices. He was really intrigued with the woman she had become.

Once Peter and his buddies were no longer a threat, would Spence be ready to let her go? Probably not. What about once her animosity toward him dissolved and they could part ways as friends, without any hard feelings? Probably not.

What if he could influence her to return to the faith of her childhood and find the healing he had found? If he knew she was finally in a right relationship with God, would he want to let her go then? No, he wouldn't.

The problem was, the more time he spent with her, the more he realized the feelings he'd had for her so long ago had never died. He'd carried them all the way to Afghanistan and then Kuwait. Then, instead of leaving them there on the other side of the world, he'd brought them right back home.

He clenched his jaw. He'd buried those feelings before. He would bury them again. When she was once again safe, he would have to let her go. Growing up with an alcoholic father, a mother she'd thought had deserted her and a past filled with wrong choices, she needed someone stable, not someone whose background was as shaky as hers, who had made the same wrong choices and was currently plagued by flashbacks and nightmares.

God had put her in his path. He had no doubt. The reasons were pretty clear. He was to protect her the best he could, try to lead her into a relationship with Him and be a true friend. But not anything more.

A minute or so passed before Alyssa once again sat up straight. "Have you talked to your father since you left for the Middle East?"

"No. I did send him a postcard when I got home, letting

him know I was out of the army and had made it back to the States alive. I never heard from him."

He'd written his return address on the postcard before he'd sent it. He could have written his phone number on it but hadn't been able to bring himself to do it.

Alyssa nodded, lips pressed together. "I haven't talked to mine, either. Every time I think about what he did—killing Mom, even if it was an accident, and letting us three girls believe she'd abandoned us... If I had to talk to him, I don't think it would be pretty. I'm afraid I would hurt him."

"I would tell you that you need to let the bitterness go, that it's probably doing you more harm than it is him, but then I'd have to take my own advice."

She smiled. "It's annoying how that works, huh?" She grew serious again. "Kassie and Kris say they've both forgiven him. I guess they're better people than I am, because I don't think I'll ever get there."

"I will eventually." He would have to. Those verses in the Bible about forgiveness had been haunting him for a while, long before his accident and return to the States. Especially disturbing were the ones that said if he didn't forgive others, God wouldn't forgive him. That was some serious stuff.

When he'd been on the other side of the world, it had been easy to put off what he'd known he would eventually have to do. After arriving in LaGrange, he'd been struggling with too many other issues to deal with that one. But since he'd returned to Pensacola, the still, small voice had been getting louder and more persistent. His argument that he needed to straighten his own life out first was getting weaker and weaker.

"I talk to my mom pretty regularly, though." During his deployments, he'd kept in touch through the mail. Since his discharge, those weekly letters had turned into weekly phone calls.

"Six months after I left, she walked out. Got tired of the abuse. She's now living near my grandparents in Texas."

"I'm glad she got out. No one deserves that." She lifted a hand to cover a yawn. "I might actually be able to get to sleep tonight. I'm ready to give it a try if you'll walk me home."

He tensed at the thought of her alone in her apartment next door. "Do you think there's any chance Peter and his men know where you're staying?"

"I doubt it. If they did, they would have attacked me here rather than in the midst of hundreds of people. My guess is that Peter had Brandi's photo and analyzed it the same way we did. It wouldn't have taken them long to land in Pensacola."

Spence nodded. "And they came out on Gallery Night hoping they would run into you. Even though the likelihood was slim, it obviously paid off."

She frowned. "I'm afraid tonight was my last time escaping this building anytime in the near future."

At least they were in agreement on that. "You really don't want anyone knowing where you are, outside of your sisters and me, in case these guys ask around."

Of course, if they asked around, someone was likely to mention her given last name, which would lead them to the charter office. He needed to come up with a better way to protect her.

He rose from the couch and held out a hand to help her up.

As she rose, she winced.

His chest squeezed. "The men didn't hurt you, did they?"

"When they let go of me, I came down on my knee again. It's just a little stiff. I don't think I undid much of the progress I've made over the past two weeks."

They headed to the back door and then across the balcony, both their limps slightly more pronounced than before. Sitting always made him stiff, especially after a prolonged time of being up. Alyssa seemed to be having the same problem. They made quite the pair.

When she unlocked and opened the door, a steady high-pitched tone said the system was still armed, proving no one could have gotten inside. She stepped into her apartment and, after punching in the four-digit code, turned to face him. "Thank you for sharing. It really means a lot."

"Thank you for listening." That had meant a lot, too. She had listened without judgment, had even seemed to empathize with him. She'd never seen combat, but she'd had plenty of trauma throughout her life. They probably had more in common, even as adults, than he realized.

When he returned to his own apartment, he headed toward his bedroom. Some of the fatigue Alyssa felt was quickly settling over him. After changing into a T-shirt and a pair of gym shorts, he climbed into bed. Apollo landed in the spot next to him with a *whoomp*.

An hour later, he got back up. Hopefully Alyssa had been more successful finding sleep than he had. He walked to the living room, headed for the chair and his guitar. Instead of jumping up on the couch, Apollo walked to the door at the top of the stairs and looked back at him, wagging his tail.

"Seriously? You want to go out now?"

Maybe the dog was bored. Or maybe he really had to go. Spence slipped his pistol into one pocket of his shorts and his phone and a small plastic bag into the other, and then headed for the stairs. Oh, well. It wasn't like the trip was cutting into his sleep.

After slipping outside and locking the back door, he headed into the night, away from the parking area. At this hour, no one was out and about. He'd checked before he'd even stepped fully from the building.

He led Apollo to a patch of grass a little farther down where the dog could do his business, if he really had any to do. After some serious sniffing, the Lab briefly lifted his leg against a shrub and then tugged at the leash to go home. Yep, that was more about boredom than a real need to go. The small plastic bag would return empty.

He shook his head and fell into step behind his dog. As he drew closer to the Ashbaugh building, his steps faltered. Someone was approaching the back of the charter office. Spence hurried silently forward, his pulse in high gear.

The figure ahead of him tried the doorknob. After stepping back, he suddenly raised and thrust his foot outward. The shrill squeal of the alarm spilled into the night. A second later, the man disappeared inside.

Spence pulled out his weapon and broke into a full run, ignoring the pain in his hip. Someone was inside with Alyssa. As he reached the open door, the figure left the hall and disappeared around the corner of the lobby, a silhouette against the glow of the streetlights coming in the front window.

Spence ran down the hall, bursting into the lobby as the man opened the door leading to the stairs. He aimed his pistol.

"Don't move."

The man spun. Shock morphed to indecision in the glow of the streetlights. His right hand slowly moved toward the holster at his hip.

Spence's jaw tightened. "Bad choice. Both hands in the air now, or you'll share the fate of your buddy in the woods along 85."

After one more second of hesitation, the intruder slowly lifted his hands. Something dark smeared his right palm, possibly blood. If that was from a bite, Alyssa had gotten him good.

"Now, on the floor, face down."

When he had complied, Spence stepped closer. Apollo moved with him. The dog had stayed at his side from the moment Spence had stopped in the lobby.

While keeping the pistol aimed between the man's shoulder blades, he pulled his phone from his pocket with his left hand and dialed 911.

As he relayed everything to Dispatch, he cast repeated glances up the stairs. Where was Alyssa? There was no way the man could have already gotten to her. Maybe she was hiding. That would be smart.

Sirens sounded in the distance and grew closer. Soon, blue

flashing lights strobed through the front window. Without taking his eyes, or his weapon, off the man on the floor, he sidestepped to the front door. Before unlocking it, he cast a glance through the small rectangular panes of glass to verify that a cop stood there.

It wasn't just any cop. It was Alyssa's future brother-in-law with his K9 partner. After a quick command for Apollo to sit, Spence unlocked the door and motioned Jared and Justice inside. While Jared cuffed the man on the floor, Spence explained what had happened.

Soon, soft footsteps sounded on the stairs, and Spence looked up to see Alyssa descending in her Bugs Bunny pajamas. Relief poured through him and, when she reached the bottom of the stairs, he had to restrain himself to keep from wrapping her in a hug.

He dipped his head at the man Jared had just pulled to his feet. "I had taken Apollo out and was getting back just as this guy kicked in your back door. I'll secure it the best I can tonight and then fix it properly tomorrow."

"I'm afraid you have another door to fix."

"I do?"

She gave him a sheepish smile, which looked more like a grimace. "As soon as the alarm sounded, I jumped from the bed to run over to your place. When I couldn't get you to the door, I kicked it in." She lifted her shoulders in a prolonged shrug. "Sorry."

Now he did give in to the urge to hug her, but settled for a casual sideways hug instead. "No problem. I'm sorry I wasn't there. You'll have to blame this guy. He convinced me he needed to go out."

As if sensing they were talking about him, Apollo rose and padded over to them, tail wagging. Alyssa bent to ruffle the fur on his neck and back.

Spence watched her with his dog, heart twisting.

Tomorrow he would fix the doors. But it wouldn't be good enough. Alyssa needed to be somewhere safe.

Wherever that was, he wasn't about to let her do it alone.

Alyssa sat at the desk in the Ashbaugh Charters lobby, staring at the computer monitor, one hand on the mouse, her stuffed backpack leaning against her chair.

It was nine in the morning. After the break-in at the charter office, she had slept on Spence's couch. He'd refused to leave her alone. She hadn't argued. Even with the temporary repairs he'd made to the back door and the alarm armed, the thought of staying there terrified her.

This morning when she'd awoken, everything had been so quiet in Spence's room that she'd slipped quietly out the balcony door and into her own place, not wanting to disturb him.

That had been forty minutes ago. Now she was showered, dressed, and her meager belongings packed, ready to once again take off. She'd made her decision last night.

The thought shredded her heart. Over the past two weeks, she'd struggled to keep the walls she had erected so long ago intact. But last night, as Spence had opened up to her, sharing his struggles, the last of those barriers had crumbled. Those moments of total honesty and shared trauma had forged a bond.

When she'd snuggled against him, everything had felt so right. Did they have any chance at all of reclaiming what they had once shared, before Spence had changed and she hadn't, before he'd taken off and she'd let resentment simmer for eight long years? If Peter was out of the picture and she was safe, would she have the courage to even try?

The answer was irrelevant, because Peter wasn't out of the picture and she wasn't safe. Not by a long shot.

She heaved a sigh and clicked inside the first of three boxes on the screen. She was on the Kayak site, looking for the best deals on airfare. So far, she hadn't seen anyone this morning. Neither Kassie nor Kris had arrived. Kris would likely be walking in the door any minute. Kassie had hair appointments at her salon this morning and would then be helping Buck with a charter this afternoon. Maybe she would drop by the office in between, maybe not.

If Spence knew what Alyssa was doing, he would try to talk her into staying. So would her sisters. But she couldn't do it. She couldn't stay and be a sitting duck for Peter and his goons.

She typed "PNS" into the from field and hovered over the next box. She'd begun her time at the computer with putting "Cities with good public transportation" into a Google search. She'd eliminated Portland, Seattle, Boston, Chicago and four others as being too cold. She was a Florida girl. Atlanta was about as cold as she wanted to get.

That had left only San Francisco, at least on the first search. She filled it into the second box and changed "round trip" to "one way." She wouldn't be coming back. Not any time in the near future.

After choosing the date, she scrolled through the options that came up. If she flew economy, she could get out there on less than two hundred dollars. Not bad.

The two thousand she'd had in her checking account had grown to twenty-six hundred, even after paying for food, thanks to her sisters putting her on the Ashbaugh Charters' payroll and the money she'd gotten scrapping her car. That should tide her over until she got a job if she found a cheap enough place to stay.

Maybe she should check the average cost of rent out there before making her final decision. She opened a new tab and typed her question into the search bar.

Over three thousand dollars? O-kay. That was a little more than she'd expected. At least, if she wound up sleeping in the park the first winter, she wouldn't freeze to death.

She clicked back to the Kayak window as the front door swung open and Kris walked in.

Kris wished her good morning and stopped in front of the desk. "What are you working on?"

"Purchasing an airline ticket."

"To where?"

"I haven't decided yet, but I'm leaning toward San Francisco."

"Why?"

"Because it's warm."

Kris crossed her arms. "So is Pensacola."

"No one in San Francisco is trying to kill me."

"How do you know the people trying to kill you here won't follow you there?"

"I don't, but I have to do something." She dragged the backpack onto her lap and pulled out her wallet.

Kris stepped around the desk. "Hold on. Have you talked to Spence?"

"I don't need to. You know the attack I told you guys about last night? That wasn't the only one."

"You were attacked on the way home, with Jared following?"

"No. A little after midnight, someone kicked in the back door. The only reason I'm alive right now is because Spence was outside with Apollo when it happened and saw the guy break in. He got to him just as he was ready to climb the stairs."

She slid her debit card from her wallet and plopped it on the desk. If there was a way to pay cash for her airline ticket, she'd do it.

Kris put a hand on her shoulder. "Just slow down. Your charging off into the sunset without a plan isn't a good idea."

"I have a plan. It's called *Get Out of Pensacola.*"

Kris heaved a sigh and stalked out the door. Where was she going? Probably to get Spence. It wasn't going to do her any good.

Alyssa viewed the options presented on the screen. An early

to midafternoon flight would work. She could arrive at the airport in plenty of time to get through security and make it to the gate well before boarding.

She chose a flight and clicked on Get Deals. After reading what was there, she hovered over Accept Restrictions. One of those restrictions was no changes, likely typical for low-cost fares. Once she finalized the purchase, she wouldn't be able to change her mind. Well, she could, but she'd be kissing almost two hundred dollars goodbye.

By the time her sister walked past the front window a few minutes later, Alyssa had made it to the screen to enter her payment information. When Kris walked in the door, Spence was right behind her, Apollo next to him. He was still dressed in the shorts and T-shirt he'd been wearing when he'd saved her life last night. Judging from how his hair was sticking up every which way, he hadn't been out of bed long enough to even run a brush through it.

While Kris stood back, Spence charged around the desk to stand next to her.

"What are you doing?"

The question was similar to the one Kris had asked, but his tone said he knew exactly what she was doing and wasn't happy about it.

"Booking a flight out of here." She looked up at him, annoyed that *he* seemed so annoyed. "Last night, even you agreed I needed to leave."

"I said you needed to go somewhere safe."

"That's exactly what I'm doing."

"Not without me, you're not."

She heaved a sigh. Decisions would be a lot easier without all these people trying to "help" her. "You can't go with me. In case you've forgotten, you're in the middle of getting a store set up. You've got merchandise coming next week."

"I can put it on hold."

"You think the company that gave you the business loan will let you put those payments on hold, too?"

He winced. Yep, she'd hit on something he wasn't going to be able to explain away so easily.

He frowned. "Trying to go it alone isn't the solution."

"Do you have another one?" She rose from the chair, giving him all of two seconds to answer. "Didn't think so."

Kris finally stepped closer. "With everything you've told us, these guys really need to be behind bars."

"I totally agree with you. But as far as I'm concerned, as long as they leave me out of it, they can keep doing what they're doing. So, some rich person loses a valuable piece of art and the insurance company has to cover it. Do you really think I care? Not to be selfish or anything, but I don't have a dog in this fight. I'm more interested in staying alive."

Kris's eyes narrowed. Alyssa crossed her arms. Ms. High and Mighty obviously didn't like what she'd just said.

Alyssa nailed her with a stern glare. "Be honest. When I'm gone, you and Kassie will just be relieved to get back to your own lives and not have to deal with your wayward little sister's problems anymore."

Kris matched Alyssa's stance. "You know what your problem is? You think you got dealt a bad hand, and now you're mad at the world. Having our mother disappear when we were teenagers was the pits. But you need to remember she didn't leave us by choice. The day she was murdered, she'd planned for all four of us to run away together. You need to step away from what her disappearance did to your mind and try to get your head on straight. It's time to get rid of the chip on your shoulder."

Alyssa opened her mouth to argue but then snapped it shut again. She didn't have a good comeback because, deep inside, she had to admit Kris was right. She just didn't know what to do about it. That chip had been there so long, she'd probably be lost without it.

Spence cleared his throat, likely trying to keep the argument from getting any further out of hand. "Let's come up with a plan. If you were alone in San Francisco, with absolutely no one watching your back, what would you do if Peter found you?"

Her chest tightened at the thought. "I don't know."

"If you stay here, I'll sleep on the couch downstairs. I'll even send Apollo up to sleep with you."

She shook her head. "I can't take him away from you. You need him."

"But he'll alert us both if someone climbs up onto the balcony. We can also get units to drive by, keep an eye on the place." He smiled. "You're the future sister-in-law of two of Pensacola's finest. If anyone can get protection around here, it should be you."

She sank back into the chair and looked at the computer screen. A few more fields to fill in, and she could be on a plane this afternoon, on her way to a new life in San Francisco.

But Spence was right. What if Peter found out where she'd gone and followed her? There would be no Spence to intervene, no Jared or Tony to have her back.

In trying to go where she thought he couldn't get to her, she would instead make it easy for him.

Like handing him her life on one of La Maison's silver platters.

Chapter Nine

Alyssa stood at the stove in the kitchenette in the back of the charter office, two pots in front of her. One held spaghetti sauce, the other pasta. A good meal for a Sunday evening.

More than a week had passed since the two attempts on her life at Gallery Night. Since then, Spence had camped out nights on the couch in the charter office and had only gone back to his apartment or store if either Jared or Tony was with her.

Units had been patrolling the area en force, driving past on Government Street and circling the parking lot behind the building on a regular basis.

The guy Spence had held at gunpoint until Jared could arrive and arrest him wasn't talking. At least, he wasn't giving them what they wanted to know. His claims that he'd been breaking in, looking for money or stuff to pawn, didn't hold water, especially with the bite marks Alyssa had left on his palm when he'd tried to abduct her earlier.

The fact that there had been no threats for almost nine days didn't coax Alyssa into believing she could let down her guard. In fact, it had done just the opposite. Peter was planning something. After so many failed attempts, he would make sure this time, whatever he did, he would succeed.

The timer on the microwave beeped and she turned the burner off under the pasta, ready to drain it. Right now, she was alone, just briefly. Five minutes ago, Spence had received a call from a delivery driver that the truck was sitting in front of his store, ready to offload some merchandise he had ordered.

Not wanting to be tied up in the middle of preparing dinner, she had let him out the front, locked the door behind him and set the alarm. He'd even left Apollo with her.

She removed the lid on the sauce and stirred it. It smelled good. It looked good, too, with chunks of meat, mushrooms, onions and green pepper. Cooking for Spence the past week had been fun. He seemed to love everything she had prepared for him. A few times, they had cooked together.

It had also been difficult, a keen reminder of the future she had envisioned so many years ago—the love of her life at her side, nothing ugly ever coming between them, the confidence that they would always be there for each other, no matter what.

She shrugged off the wistful thoughts. Childhood dreams rarely remained intact through the harsh realities of life. And trying to reconstruct those splintered pieces years later was an exercise in futility.

The mental tough talk wasn't doing anything to tamp down what she was feeling for Spence. The truth was, she was dangerously close to falling in love with him all over again, and her heart was ignoring every rational argument she presented.

Spence obviously wasn't having the same problem. If he felt anything for her beyond friendship, he was doing a great job of hiding it. Throughout their time together, he'd shown concern, even fierce protectiveness. He'd been real about his struggles, sharing things that he had likely shared with few, if any, others. But not once had he offered the slightest hint that he had any desire to step over that friendship line.

Alyssa glanced at the clock hanging on the wall. At a little after seven, it wasn't horribly late, but dinner was ready.

She hoped Spence made it back before the sauce got cold or overcooked.

She pulled a chair away from the kitchen table and sat. Apollo plodded up to her, and she scratched him behind and under the ears. "Daddy's being a slowpoke, isn't he?"

Apollo wagged his tail, and she laughed. "You agree, don't you? We'll have to see what we can do about it."

The cabin fever was back. Knowing she had no choice had made it even worse. Last night, she had half-heartedly talked to Spence about taking her to church this morning. Twisting her hair up on her head and covering it with a baseball cap hadn't worked, but she'd said she would come up with something else, possibly even find a pair of big, gaudy sunglasses that would hide the upper half of her face.

Spence had said, "No way." She hadn't expected any different. But that had shown how desperate she was about going outside.

As a concession, Spence had brought up the live stream of the service so they could watch it on the computer. That wasn't at all what she'd been looking for. She was still trapped inside, and because she had opened her big mouth, she'd been stuck sitting through a church service.

Once it was over, though, she couldn't complain. It hadn't been near the imposition she had feared. She'd enjoyed the music. It was upbeat, and she recognized two of the songs as ones Spence had played and sung for her on those nights she'd had trouble sleeping.

The pastor's sermon had been good, too. In fact, she hadn't even had to poke herself to avoid falling asleep. Maybe it was because the message had hit her right between the eyes.

He'd preached about Saul's experience on the road to Damascus. She knew the story from those years her mother had taken her to church. The focus of this message, though, was change—Saul's life before his encounter with Jesus versus after. In fact, the change had been so great, God had given him a new name. It was no longer just an ancient story that had happened to someone who'd lived almost two thousand years ago. The pastor had made it relevant to today.

Alyssa had seen some of that change up close. Both her sisters had, in recent years, recommitted their lives to God. Kassie had been first, followed by Kris fairly recently. Alyssa had to admit, there was a distinct difference in the women they were now and the girls they'd been as teenagers.

She had attributed their newfound joy and contentment to both of their statuses as fiancées. But maybe it went deeper than that. Maybe they'd found a sense of contentment that transcended present circumstances, whatever those might be. Their attitude toward her seemed different, too. What she'd thought was judgment over the past couple of weeks, in hindsight, she now saw for what it was—concern.

Even Spence, with all of his struggles, seemed to have an underlying sense of peace that hadn't been there before. It was especially evident when he was playing and singing worship songs.

The pastor had invited everyone to experience that change, to move from "before Christ" to "after Christ." It had sounded really appealing, because whatever she'd been searching for over the past ten years, she hadn't found it.

The lock rattled up front and the sustained tone of the alarm drifted down the hall, followed by four beeps as Spence entered the code. A half minute later, he appeared in the open doorway of the kitchen.

Apollo padded over to greet him, and Alyssa rose from the chair "All good?"

"Yep, everything's accounted for and signed off on. That shipment, anyway. I've got a couple more coming this week."

Over the past few days, there had been a lot of changes next door—shelving installed, brackets for displaying guitars and other merchandise, racks for music books, as well as corkboards for hooks that would hold cables, adapters, picks and any other miscellaneous pieces and parts. The security company had finished installing his alarm system on Friday, so all the new stuff he was buying would be protected. He was shooting for an October 14 open date, a little more than two weeks away. It looked like he was going to make it.

"Perfect timing. Dinner is ready." She turned to the fridge and removed two bowls of salad she had made earlier and covered with plastic wrap.

When everything was on the table, he took both of her hands in his and offered a prayer of thanks, for both the food and God's protection. When the danger was over and they each got back to their own lives, having meals together at night was something she would miss.

She would miss his prayers, too. His saying grace before dinner had gone from something she'd tolerated to something she appreciated.

They had just finished eating when the distant squeal of an alarm sent her heart into her throat. She sprang from her chair.

Spence did, too, but held up a hand. "That's not here. It's not loud enough."

He was right. She inhaled some calming breaths, waiting for her heart rate to return to normal.

"It might be at my place, though. Stay here. I'm going to walk up front and check."

When he returned a minute later, the alarm was still squealing.

"Someone broke the window right beside my front door. I don't know if they got inside."

"Aren't you going to check it out?"

"It's monitored, so the police will be here any minute. Everything in there is covered by insurance. Even if it wasn't, there's nothing in there important enough for me to leave you unprotected."

"But you—" She snapped her mouth shut. He'd left her inside with the alarm and his dog while accepting his delivery. But this was different. Instead of an expected delivery, this was a broken window. It could be random, or it could be someone's way to draw him away and leave her unprotected.

"Stay back here. I don't want anyone to be able to take pot-shots at you through the front window." Of course, she'd been doing that for the past week, handling her clerical duties in the back office, only slipping through the lobby to head up-stairs after he had checked to make sure no one appeared to be milling around outside, watching the building.

He stepped into the hallway, where he could keep an eye on her while still having a view of the edge of the front window. Two or three minutes later, the police arrived.

"They're here. I see the blue lights. I know the police will be right out front, but I'm still setting the alarm and locking the door on my way out."

"Thanks." She would clean up their dinner mess and try not to speculate on who had broken the window or why.

When Apollo started to follow him, he held up a hand. "Stay."

The dog turned and moved to stand at her side. As Spence walked to the front, she scooped the leftover sauce into a plastic container and placed the pan in the sink to fill with water.

The next moment, the crack of splitting wood sent a bolt of panic through her. Apollo charged from the room in a frenzy of barking. When Alyssa ran into the hallway, two men were already inside. One held a pole and was trying to work the loop on the end of it around Apollo's neck. The dog protested with growls interspersed with ferocious barks.

The other man had slipped past them and was headed right for her. The alarm next door was still squealing.

She ran toward the front. She would never be able to get the door unlocked and open before they caught her, but maybe she could catch the attention of Spence or the police.

The man tackled her before she could even reach the end of the hallway. She went down with a crash, and he landed on top of her. Pain shot through her left arm, which was trapped under her. She released a scream, but a large hand cut it short.

The weight on her lessened and disappeared altogether. Then an arm slid around her waist and lifted her from the floor. Just before being spun around, she caught a glimpse of the front window. A police officer was framed in its left-hand edge. He was standing in profile to her, oblivious to her predicament.

The alarm outside fell silent, but it was too late. The hand over her mouth was firmly in place, thumb and index finger pinching her nose so she couldn't even breathe. Biting him was impossible, too. He'd cupped his palm. Maybe he'd learned from the other guy. Or maybe he was smarter.

As he carried her down the hall, she kicked and fought as hard as she could, desperate for air. Her struggles did as much good as they had in the alley. Peter's thugs were far too strong for her.

At the end of the hall, angry barks came from behind the closed bathroom door. The second man waited at the door, his hands now empty of the pole he had held earlier.

When her abductor stepped outside, a white cargo van was waiting in the parking lot, back doors open. Rather than being pulled into a space, its rear end faced the building. The engine was running, the driver in the front ready to take off.

The man tossed her inside and hopped in after her. She sucked in several frantic gasps of air and then released another scream as the doors slammed shut. Moments later, the front passenger door opened, and the man who had restrained Apollo climbed into the seat. The van took off before he even got the door shut.

Alyssa pushed herself into a seated position, fighting against the lurching of the vehicle. It squealed from the parking lot and then turned away from Palafox. The glow of streetlights shone through the windshield and the two front side windows. The cargo portion of the van was windowless.

Her gaze landed on the driver's face, framed in the rear-view mirror—dark eyes, tanned skin, masculine features bordered by black hair.

Her heart almost stopped.

She was looking at Peter.

"Alyssa!" Spence ran through the charter office, Braydon right behind him. They'd just heard a scream. It had sounded as if it had come from somewhere behind the building.

He hadn't taken the time to unlock the door. Instead, he'd kicked it in. He would deal with that later.

The hopes that the scream he'd heard had nothing to do with Alyssa died with his first glance down the hallway. The back door was wide open, leaning against the hallway wall at an unnatural angle.

Muffled barks came from the back, along with another sound—running water. Ignoring his dog, who was currently closed up in the bathroom, and the water running in the kitchen, he shot out the back door and into the parking lot.

A total of four cars occupied the spaces. All of the vehicles were vacant. No one was standing around in the lot or even walking past. He spun to run back inside and almost plowed into Braydon.

"They've got Alyssa. We need to call it in, put out a BOLO."

While Braydon radioed the dispatcher, Spence paced. The officer's description was spot-on. Thick red hair, waist-length, about five-four, medium build. When he gave her name as Alyssa Ashbaugh, Spence didn't correct him.

Braydon lowered the radio. "Any idea what kind of vehicle we're looking for?"

"No." He couldn't even say for sure they'd taken her away in a vehicle. "Can we get people checking the area, seeing if they notice anything unusual?"

It was a long shot. Knowing police were standing right out

front, the likelihood of the men dragging her away on foot was nonexistent.

Braydon finished the latest request, and Spence looked around. "What about security cameras on the surrounding businesses?" Cameras on Palafox wouldn't be any help. The suspects would have avoided that route. But maybe on Church Street behind, or one of the side streets.

Braydon nodded. "We'll get business owners to check the footage and see if there were any suspicious vehicles, or anyone that appeared to be leaving in a hurry about five minutes ago. It might give us a starting point."

When Spence turned back toward the building, the barks coming from inside finally registered again, reminding him his dog was trapped in the bathroom. Poor Apollo was probably beside himself, knowing Alyssa needed help and he couldn't get to her.

Actually, Spence needed help himself. A lead weight filled his gut, and his chest was so tight, he was finding it hard to breathe. He'd thought Alyssa would be safer tucked away in the back of the office than standing out front in full view of anyone driving past.

He'd been wrong. The broken window at his store had been nothing but a decoy, a way to distract him so he would leave Alyssa unguarded just long enough for them to move in. Now Peter's goons had her, if not Peter himself.

He had almost reached the damaged door of the charter office when Jared charged out with Justice.

"I heard the call. I've let Kassie know. She's going to call Kris and Tony. The authorities are doing everything they can to find her, and Kris and Kassie will be on their knees. Tony will be praying, too, but I'm guessing he'll be putting himself back on duty."

"Good. I've got to let Apollo out."

Jared followed him inside. "I'm guessing it was Alyssa's

kidnappers who locked him in there. I'm surprised he allowed it."

Actually, Spence was, too. Apollo wasn't a trained guard dog, but the Lab had always been protective of him. Lately, he'd displayed the same protectiveness toward Alyssa.

When he opened the bathroom door, Apollo sprang toward him, dragging an aluminum pole with a metal noose at one end. That noose was around his neck.

"Poor boy." Spence cupped his dog's face in his hands and then tried to break the noose.

Jared stepped up beside him. "Here. Let me help."

He slid his hand up the pole. Upon finding a slide release, he gave it a sharp pull. One side of the noose fell away and Apollo was instantly free.

Jared then stepped into the kitchen and shut off the faucet. Alyssa apparently hadn't stopped up the sink. There was no water overflowing onto the floor.

Braydon walked inside, giving Jared a brief nod before addressing Spence. "One of the officers is trying to reach business owners in the area to view security camera footage. We've got units patrolling, looking for anything suspicious. Surrounding counties are being alerted, also."

Spence swallowed past a large lump in his throat. Police were patrolling but had no idea what they were looking for. Having Alyssa's description didn't do them much good in the dark. Unless the driver did something careless, there would be no reason to stop him.

The hopelessness of her situation bore down on him. He needed to do something.

"I'm leaving to go look for her."

Jared lifted his eyebrows. "Where are you going?"

"I don't know, but if I just stand around and wait for word, I'll go crazy. I'm going to get on I-65 and drive toward Montgomery. Maybe the men who abducted her are headed back to Atlanta to turn her over to Peter."

"That sounds like a good plan."

No, it didn't. It was a long shot. But since no one had any better ideas, that was what Spence would go with. That and lots of unceasing prayer.

After grabbing his weapon and Apollo's leash, he headed for the door. "Apollo, come." On his way out, he cast Jared a glance over one shoulder. "Please keep me posted on any developments. Kassie and Kris both have my number." They'd collected it when he'd signed the lease on the store.

He moved toward the Forester at an uncomfortable jog, favoring his left leg. Apollo trotted in front of him, excitement rippling through him, as if he sensed they were headed out to find Alyssa and bring her back.

As soon as he opened the SUV's back door, Apollo jumped in, not waiting for the command. The dog was as anxious as he was.

He pulled from the parking lot and drove toward Interstate 110. That would take him to I-65. He would keep his eyes peeled for anything suspicious and stay in touch with the police through Jared. Maybe one of those security cameras would actually let him know what he was looking for.

Why had the men taken her? Were they going to kill her in the vehicle and dump her body? Or were they waiting until they got far enough outside town that there wouldn't be any witnesses?

Something didn't add up, though. If all they'd wanted to do was kill her, shooting her inside the charter office would have been a lot faster and less risky than kidnapping her.

Maybe they had other plans for her.

A sense of dread pressed down on him. One man was dead, and two others were behind bars. Peter and his cronies probably weren't happy. If they decided Alyssa needed to pay for making things so difficult for them—no, he wouldn't even allow his thoughts to go there.

God, please protect her. Please let someone find her before it's too late.

Chapter Ten

Alyssa sat on the floor of the van, propped against the driver's-side wall. She wasn't comfortable. The floor was hard and what she was leaning against offered no support for her back. But she had no choice. Both rear seats had been removed.

The men hadn't bothered to tie her up. They probably hadn't seen the need. There were three of them and one of her. Peter was occupied with driving, but it wasn't any consolation. Before they'd even reached the interstate, he had taken a weapon from his side and laid it in a cubby in the dash. It was close enough for her to see, but not close enough for her to grab, even if she knew what to do with it. She didn't.

As far as the other two, either of them could have smashed her like a bug. They were both as big as the guys who had accosted her at Gallery Night.

Currently, they were on Interstate 10, headed west. They had passed into Alabama some time ago and had to be nearing the Mississippi border by now. Since leaving Pensacola, they had entered plenty of wooded areas where they could have stopped, marched her through the trees and shot her.

Instead, Peter had kept driving. What plans did he have for her?

Not knowing was about to make her crazy. For the past hour, her brain had been concocting all kinds of scenarios, ways Peter could make her pay for the inconvenience she'd been to him. How many men had he sent after her before he'd finally decided to deal with the situation himself?

He was probably furious. Except, he was hiding it well. Actually, she had no idea how Peter displayed anger. She'd never witnessed it. Something told her he was too controlled to fly into a rage about anything. His anger would be much more dangerous—cold, hard and lethal.

Another wave of fear swept through her. She couldn't stand it anymore. She leaned forward to look at him in the rearview mirror.

"Where are you taking me?"

His gaze met hers. That brief eye contact told her he knew the question was for him.

His attention shifted back to the road. Seconds stretched into a half minute or more, the silence broken only by the rumble of the van's engine and the noise of the road beneath her.

Frustration took the edge off some of the fear. "All the effort you and your men have expended in the past couple of weeks is ridiculous. I walked in and heard you guys discussing paintings. Do you think I care? I don't even care if you and your buddies are fencing stolen art."

More of that exasperating silence. Why didn't he say something?

"Look, you probably know me well enough to realize I'm not one to play the hero. You know the strong sense of justice that makes certain people think they have to right everything wrong in the world? I don't have it. Never have. My causes are things that impact me directly. Like trying to avoid trouble, keeping out of other people's business…staying alive."

Still no response. If she climbed over the console and tried to shake him, he'd probably shoot her.

Maybe she could appeal to whatever feelings he might have

had for her. "What about all the things you told me? How I'm different...how you've never met anyone like me?"

"Everything I said was true. You *are* different. You didn't seem that impressed with me. As my waitress, you were friendly but had just enough attitude to make things interesting. You turned me down for a solid three weeks before you would even agree to let me buy you dinner. I've never had a woman do that."

Yeah, he probably hadn't. It wasn't just his looks or even how he exuded success. He had a magnetism about him that drew attention wherever he went. She'd seen the looks he'd received when they'd been out. Instead of jealousy, she'd felt pride and amazement that she'd been the one to land such a prize. Right now, she'd gladly trade places with any one of those women.

"If you think I'm special, then why don't you let me go?"

"My associates would never go for that."

"They don't have to know. I was looking at airline tickets this morning, ready to choose a big city where I could get lost in the crowd. I'd keep my mouth shut and you'd never hear from me again."

"No go. You'd always be a loose end." He shook his head. "You should have stayed in the car like I told you."

"I know that now, but it's not like I can go back and change the past."

"No, you can't."

Despair settled over her. There was no talking Peter out of whatever he was going to do. She was right back where she'd been before she'd begun this conversation—scared half out of her mind, wondering where he was taking her and what he planned to do with her when they got there.

Alyssa heaved a sigh. "Then why don't you just kill me and dump my body?"

"That was my plan after you walked in on our meeting. I'd already put the tracking device on your car and sent requests to all of your friends on social media, just in case something like this happened. Even though you weren't very active and hadn't gotten around to changing your status to 'in a relationship,' the fact you were a mutual friend was enough to get quite a few of them to accept my request. Brandi Feldman was one of those."

She waited for him to continue. He'd said that *was* his plan. Apparently, it wasn't any longer. What was it now?

When he didn't continue, she prodded him. "You said killing me *was* your plan. It isn't any longer?"

"With one man dead and two others arrested, my buddies and I decided death is too good for you."

Too good? What could be worse than death?

God, please help me. Right on the tail of the silent plea came the thought that God wasn't even listening. After all, why would He? She hadn't paid Him much mind *before* her mother had disappeared. Afterward, she'd turned her back on everything her mother had tried to pass on, including her faith.

But when Spence had cried for God to save him, God had come through. Spence had said he wasn't sure if it was all right to bargain with God. It had turned out all right for him. Better than all right.

God, if You help me get out of this, I'll... What? Spence had promised to commit the rest of his life to God. He'd picked up his guitar and used his talents by serving on his church's worship team.

Was she ready to go that far? Music was out of the question. Kassie was the only musically gifted one in the family. What about nursery duty? Teaching Sunday school? Cleaning toilets? Spence had said if someone did decide to bargain with God, they'd better be prepared to come through on whatever they promised.

Before she could ponder it further, the van gradually decreased speed. Her pulse did the opposite. Was Peter getting ready to pull over? Maybe exit the interstate? Why?

She sat straight and craned her neck. The turn signal came on, and her heart pounded harder. The van continued to decelerate. An exit sign sped past the passenger window. After a stop and a couple of turns, Peter pulled under a gas station canopy.

It wasn't a Pilot or Love's, or one of the other large stations. In fact, based on what shone through the front windshield, it wasn't even that well lit.

The passenger door swung open, and Peter handed the man a wad of bills. A few minutes after he disappeared, she heard the sound of the pump nozzle being inserted into the fuel filler behind her. Within a few minutes, he would be finished and they would once again hit the road. This might be her only chance to summon help.

She looked at Peter in the mirror. "I need to go to the bathroom."

"You'll have to wait."

"I won't make it much longer. I drank a bunch of tea with dinner." When he didn't respond, she continued. "I don't know who this van belongs to, but they might have a problem with you returning it with stains or unpleasant odors."

Peter turned around to look at the man who had ridden on the floor opposite her. "Go scope it out."

The man gave him a salute and climbed from the back. When he returned a minute later holding a long, thin piece of wood with a small chain and key dangling from one end, her heart fell. There would be no chance of whispering a plea for help to another occupant.

The man raised the hand holding the stick. "The restroom is around the side. It needs a key to get in."

"Go ahead and take her. Make sure she doesn't try anything."

She climbed from the van and, before he allowed her to step from between the two open doors, the man patted her down.

Then he pulled a switchblade from his front jeans' pocket. At the press of a button, the blade burst from the end.

After a quick glance at the license plate, she walked toward the building, silently reciting the combination of six letters and numbers over and over. She looked around her. She'd been right. The station was small, even smaller than she had guessed. The canopy wasn't much bigger than a residential carport, with one double-sided pump where a maximum of two vehicles could fill up at any time. Currently, the van was the only vehicle there.

The cashier manning the tiny convenience store watched them through the front window as they approached. He was a young guy, probably around her age. Under the bright fluorescents, his features held alertness.

Alyssa's thoughts raced as she tried to figure out a way to signal that she was in trouble. She had just started to mouth the word *help* when he turned away.

At light pressure against her lower back, she stiffened. The man behind her leaned close. "If you even think about trying anything, you'll feel this blade in your right kidney."

She picked up her pace, dismissing her previous thoughts of escape. She wasn't giving up, though. She would just have to think of something else.

After continuing past the first door marked Men, the man unlocked the second one and held it open while she stepped inside. She wrinkled her nose against the odor of urine, thankful she had no intention of using that toilet.

Once the door had swung closed, she turned the lock. Since the man guarding her still had the key, the action wouldn't accomplish anything except possibly buy her a second or two while he fiddled with the lock.

She looked frantically around the space, patting her pockets. They were empty. Of course they were. The man had already patted her down and found nothing. She had no lipstick or pens. Not even a coin to scratch a message in the paint covering the concrete-block walls. A toilet occupied one corner, a small, overflowing trash can next to it. On the opposite wall, a sink and countertop sat atop a two-foot cabinet. There was absolutely nothing she could use to fashion a cry for help.

Or maybe there was. She pulled a long length of toilet paper from the roll and tore off individual squares. The next step was to roll each of them into strips for use in forming letters.

She couldn't lay out her message in the middle of the floor. The man waiting just outside would likely see it as soon as she tried to exit. But there was about a two-foot space in the back corner, hidden from the view of the door by the sink cabinet.

Clutching her rolled-up sheets of toilet paper in one hand, she squatted and started laying them out. The first four formed a *W*. Next to that, she placed two vertical sheets and laid a third horizontally between them, forming an *H*. Next was a *T*.

At a loud knock on the door, she had to stifle a shriek.

"Hurry it up in there. We don't have all night."

"I'm almost done." She flushed the toilet.

Hopefully, the next person who walked in would recognize her abbreviation for *white*.

"Washing my hands. I'll be right out."

After turning on the water, she squatted again and spelled out *VAN* below the other three letters. Next would be the tag number.

She rose again and turned off the water. "Drying my hands now." She pulled two paper towels from the dispenser before squatting again.

She had gotten only the first three characters of the tag number spelled out when the knock came again, louder and angrier than before.

The lock rattled. "Time's up. I'm coming in."

She threw the last pieces of toilet paper against the wall and sprang to her feet. As the door swung open, she wadded up the paper towels she had torn off earlier. He took a step toward her, one arm extended, ready to grab her.

"I'm coming." She had to keep him from stepping any farther into the bathroom. If he saw what she'd been trying to do...whatever would happen, it wouldn't be good.

She hurried to the open doorway, throwing the wadded paper towels in the trash on her way past, hoping he wouldn't notice they weren't wet.

As she stepped outside, he grabbed her by the arm. "Lock the door."

She twisted the lock.

"Now, you're going to hold my hand while we walk back to the van. That guy inside was watching us a little too closely for my liking. We're going to get rid of any suspicions."

He grasped her hand, intertwining his fingers with hers, and she suppressed a shudder. Instead of taking her to the back of the vehicle again, he walked her around between the van and the pump, and opened the side door. After he had shut her inside, he disappeared again and returned a minute later without the bathroom key.

As Peter cranked the van, she closed her eyes. *God, please let someone see my message and call the police.* It likely wouldn't happen until tomorrow. The dinky, out-of-the-way place surely wouldn't be open twenty-four hours. The likelihood of someone else stopping to get gas tonight was slim. It was even less likely someone would ask for the key to the ladies' room.

Maybe one of tasks on the clerk's list of closing responsibilities was to check the bathroom. The time had to be after ten. The station would likely be closing within the next hour.

Peter put the van into gear and pulled away from the pump. Instead of going out the way he had come in, he circled around behind the station. She could guess what he was doing. He was making sure the clerk couldn't read the tag number from inside the store.

The way back to the interstate involved more turns than the trip to the station. Soon, Peter was accelerating up the on-ramp. "No more stops till we get there." The statement was stern and seemed to be aimed at all of them.

So they were headed somewhere specific. Where exactly was "there"? By now, they had to be getting close to Mississippi.

Finally, Peter pressed a cell phone to his ear. "I'm headed your way with an Irène Cahen."

Alyssa looked around the van, all the while knowing she wouldn't find any paintings in there. The entire cargo area was empty except for herself and the man who had taken her to the restroom.

She was familiar with the painting Peter had mentioned. *Irène Cahen d'Anvers*, a Renoir. Peter had it. She'd seen it in his place. Actually, it was a quality reproduction. The original would be well out of even Peter's price range.

Peter laughed before continuing. "A lot of spunk."

Huh? He could tell that from a painting? The girl looked sweet and demure with her hands folded in her lap, her long, red hair flowing over her shoulder.

Long. Red. Hair.

The three words punched into her. *Dear God, no.* She shook her head, trying to rattle loose the realization that had lodged itself in her mind.

Long, red hair. Young, though not nearly as young as the real Irène Cahen D'Anvers. Peter and his buddies weren't fencing stolen art. They were involved in human trafficking. All art aficionados, they made a game out of naming their victims based on famous portraits of women.

She was the Irène Cahen Peter mentioned.

She put her face in her hands, hopelessness washing through her. She had a longtime history of choosing losers. She had thought she'd finally done well for herself. Instead, she'd made the biggest mistake of her life.

Suddenly, Peter jerked the wheel to the right and braked so

hard she had to thrust out one arm to keep from rolling across the floor of the van.

The man on the floor with her did the same. "Whoa, dude. I thought you said no more stops till we get there."

"The overpass about a half mile back, there were a bunch of police cars, lights flashing. They may have been headed to the interstate. Unless Alyssa pulled something at our last stop, it's not likely they have anything to do with us, but I'm not taking any chances."

The man across from her grinned. "That's why we work for you."

Alyssa closed her eyes again as cautious hope trickled through her. Peter was right. Those police cars may have had nothing to do with them. But there was also a chance someone had seen her message, and every agency in Alabama or Mississippi or wherever they were, was searching for a white van with a tag number that began K6J.

Over the next few minutes, Peter made several turns. Finally, he stopped and killed the engine. Judging from the scarce light finding its way through the windows, they were in a neighborhood, or possibly a business district where everything had shut down some time ago.

Peter once again put the phone to his ear. "We've had a little delay, but we'll be there with the merchandise before morning."

His words put a knot of dread in the pit of her stomach, knowing she was the merchandise. Whether the police cars had anything to do with her or not, the delay had to be a good thing. Maybe someone would question the van sitting alone in the dark and call the police to check it out.

God, please send someone.

She leaned her head back against the side of the van, and the minutes ticked by—fifteen minutes, a half hour, longer. Maybe. With no way to judge it, her time estimates were just that—estimates.

Her eyelids began to feel heavy. There was no way she

would sleep. But she could rest. The events of the evening had drained her, and she still didn't know what lay ahead.

Her thoughts grew erratic, and she had the sensation of floating...drifting...

Reality slammed into her, and a startled gasp escaped. The man sitting across from her snickered.

Peter made another phone call. "We're getting back on the road now. We'll be at the port within the hour. Don't ship out the rest of the merchandise until I arrive."

He ended the call and dropped the phone into the console. Two words from his short conversation echoed in her mind: *port* and *ship*.

Alyssa had thought it couldn't get any worse. It just had.

By morning, she was going to be on her way to another country with other trafficking victims to be sold into slavery.

Peter was right. The fate she was facing *would* be worse than death.

Chapter Eleven

Spence sped along I-10, praying harder than he had ever prayed. Apollo lay in the seat behind him and whimpered. The whimpering had been happening off and on for the past two hours.

So had his occasional attempts to climb over the console and get into his lap. Just what he needed—a seventy-five-pound dog in his lap while driving down the interstate at seventy miles an hour.

The problem was, Apollo was picking up on Spence's anxiety, and it was killing him to not be able to do what he was trained to do. Spence didn't even want him riding in the front passenger seat. In case of an accident, the dog could sail right through the windshield. So, until they stopped, Apollo would have to remain in the back seat, as difficult as it might be for both of them.

The security cameras within a two-block radius of the charter office hadn't captured anything of value. Peter's men had probably already scoped out the area before abducting Alyssa and had figured out how to avoid them.

An hour ago, though, authorities had gotten a break. A clerk at a small gas station had reported a message spelled out in toilet paper on the floor of the women's restroom. It had included a vague vehicle description and the first three digits of a tag number.

The clerk had been able to add another detail to "white van." It was a cargo van, the kind that was windowless except for the windshield and two front side windows. He'd seen it pull up, had watched as a man and woman made their way to the ladies' room on the exterior of the building, the man holding the key he'd given him.

He'd been able to give a description of the two people. The man was large, a good ten inches taller than the woman, and far heavier. The long, red hair he'd described on the woman had left Spence no doubt. He'd been looking at Alyssa.

Spelling out a cry for help using toilet paper would be just the kind of thing Alyssa would think of in dire circumstances. She'd always been intelligent in a street-smart kind of way. Intelligent, beautiful, compassionate and witty. Confident, but with an underlying vulnerability that few people ever saw. That vulnerability only endeared her to him even more.

They weren't right for each other, but he loved her with all of his heart. He could no longer deny it.

God, please somehow give me a chance to tell her so.

As soon as he had gotten Jared's call, he'd turned around. Since Alyssa's kidnappers had had a two-hour head start, Spence had no chance of catching them. But being reasonably sure he was heading in the right direction helped his state of mind. He was at least accomplishing something.

Over the next hour, he continued to drive, interspersing a steady stream of prayers with the Christian music he had pouring into the vehicle through the stereo system. Several times, he had to tamp down an overwhelming urge to call Jared for an update. He didn't need to bug his new friend. If there were any developments, he would have already known. Jared would have called immediately.

He heaved a sigh. He'd passed the Alabama/Mississippi border some time ago. How far ahead of him was the white cargo van? Was it even still on Interstate 10? It could have turned off a long time ago and be headed somewhere north of them.

He glanced at the Forester's gas gauge. He was nearing a quarter of a tank. He'd soon have to stop for gas. That would put him ten or fifteen minutes further behind. But running out of gas on the interstate could have him stranded for hours.

For the next several minutes, he searched the exits for signs of well-known truck stops, somewhere he could be in and out in the shortest amount of time. In the distance, brake lights lit up the darkness. He eased off the gas, his pulse picking up speed.

The holdup could be unrelated—an accident or road construction. But chances were good the police had set up a road block. Jared had told him a manhunt involving several agencies was underway.

As Spence approached, the clear night offered great visibility on the straight, flat road. Those brake lights extended as far as he could see. He eased to a stop. He wasn't going anywhere for a while.

He checked the gas gauge again. The needle was now touching the one-quarter line. Traffic crept forward about ten feet and stopped again. Was the white van stuck somewhere in this mess? If so, were the men panicking? Their desperation would put Alyssa in even more danger.

Traffic moved again and he eased onto the shoulder. "Come on, Apollo. Let's go find Alyssa."

He stepped from the vehicle and circled to the passenger side to clip the leash to Apollo's collar. If the van was still on I-10, it would be far ahead of them. After sliding his weapon into his waistband and pulling his shirt over it, he sent another plea heavenward and began moving west at a slow jog, a few feet from the shoulder.

Apollo trotted beside him on his right. On his left, traffic continued to creep forward in its steady start-stop rhythm. His pace, even with his bad hip, was considerably faster than the vehicles next to him.

A good quarter mile ahead of him, a vehicle pulled onto the shoulder. Maybe someone else was low on gas. Instead of stopping just off the road, like he'd done, the driver kept going, off the asphalt and into the grass.

Was the vehicle a cargo van? It was too far away to tell. And now it was growing farther away, moving past the stopped vehicles.

Spence kicked his body into an even faster pace, ignoring the pain in his hip. After about a minute, the vehicle's brake lights came on. Instead of waiting to try to cut back into traffic, it moved even farther from the road, right up against the woods.

As he drew closer, the vehicle crept forward again, wheels turned to the left, and stopped. It was definitely a white cargo van, just like the clerk had described. Moments after the vehicle stopped, it reversed direction, backing up against the woods.

Without slowing his pace, Spence pulled his phone from his pocket and dialed 911. His breath came in pants as he explained the situation to the dispatcher.

"Can you give me your location? A mile marker or nearest exit?"

Oh, man. He should have paid more attention before hitting the traffic jam. "There was an exit about a mile back, a numbered road."

"603?"

"I think that might be it."

"I've got you."

Yeah, she was probably tracking him through his mobile location. "The back door on the van just opened."

"Can you see anyone getting out?"

"No. The door's blocking my view."

"How far away are you?"

"About a football field." Too distant to see beneath the door if someone stepped from the back, especially in the dark. The sky was moonless, and none of the headlights shone that far to the side.

But he didn't need great light to figure out what was going on. Alyssa was in that van. Whatever was happening up ahead, the men weren't going to be caught holding her.

"I'm moving closer."

"Stay back. The police are on their way."

He cast a glance over his shoulder. Flashing blue lights were barely visible on the horizon. "I think I see them, but they're too far away." If the men were preparing to march Alyssa into the woods and kill her, those units would never arrive in time.

He ducked closer to the woods and continued his forward movement, ignoring the dispatcher's commands. The nearby engine noise helped to conceal his footsteps, especially the rumble of the semitrucks.

Her voice once again came through the phone. "Where are the police now?" She'd promised to remain on the line with him until the authorities arrived.

"They're closer." Had the men holding Alyssa seen them yet? When they did, they would likely accelerate whatever plans they had for her.

He dropped his voice to a whisper. "I'm leaving the line open so you can still track my movement, but I'm turning down the volume and dropping the phone into my shirt pocket."

"Sir, you need to let the police handle this."

"They won't get here in time." He'd hissed the words. He would love to step back and let the police handle it, because chances were too good that, for Alyssa to live, he was going to have to kill someone.

Once he silenced his phone and dropped it into his pocket, he pulled his pistol from his waistband. Voices drifted to him.

"Take care of her, and make it fast."

"You got it."

Spence crept closer. The van wasn't more than forty feet in front of him now. A figure was moving away from it, deeper into the woods. No, actually it was two figures—a larger one trying to restrain a smaller one. Sticks crunched under heavy footsteps.

Something else reached Spence, too—muffled sounds of protest, feminine in pitch. The men had gagged her so she couldn't scream.

Suddenly, the man who held her stopped and slid a hand into his pocket. As he withdrew something unidentifiable in the darkness, Alyssa took advantage of the moment and twisted away from him. Her hands were tied behind her back.

She hadn't taken more than two steps before he grabbed her again. He lifted his other arm. A gleam of starlight glistened off something metal. It was the blade of a knife.

Spence raised the pistol.

God, make my aim true.

He pulled the trigger. The shot reverberated through the trees. The man jerked. As his knees buckled, he swung the knife in a wide arc. Alyssa went down and rolled away, coming to a stop against a tree a couple of yards from where the man had fallen. Had he cut her?

With his weapon still trained on the unmoving figure on the ground, Spence gave Apollo a pat on the rump. "Go see Alyssa."

His dog charged over to her while Spence carefully approached the man he had shot. He wasn't moving. The entrance wound was barely visible in the poor light. Spence had shot him in the temple. The man was lying on what was probably a nasty exit wound.

Alyssa's laughter erupted behind him—high-pitched, with a hysterical edge that even the gag couldn't hide. Apollo was showering her face with doggy kisses.

After hurrying toward her, Spence removed the gag and untied her hands. She was still laughing.

He extended a hand. "We need to get out of here."

His gunshot was an announcement to anyone in the area that something had happened. There was still at least one man in the van, maybe more. They would come to investigate, if for nothing more than to make sure their witness was dead.

Alyssa's laughter died as quickly as it had started, and her shoulders shook with silent sobs. In fact, her whole body was shaking. She was probably in shock.

Rustling sounded nearby, growing closer. Spence stiffened, aiming his weapon in that direction. He held up an index finger behind him, signaling Alyssa to stay quiet.

There was more rustling, coming from a different direction. Someone was taking a route similar to the one Spence had taken. Actually, it was several someones. Flashlight beams swept through the trees around them.

The first footsteps he'd heard veered away, the gait fast and heavy. A German shepherd police dog flew past, in hot pursuit. A man's agonized scream followed seconds later.

Suddenly, the woods were swarming with law enforcement personnel. Spence called to one near him. "Check the van. There may be more."

"Others already are."

Spence looked at Alyssa, who was still sitting on the ground, her arms wrapped around Apollo, face pressed against his side. "How many are there?"

At her silence, he hurried over to her and dropped to his knees. "Alyssa?"

She was sobbing louder now and shaking even more violently. He drew her into his arms, and she slowly released his dog. "It's okay. You're safe now."

God, please don't let her be hurt.

He still didn't know if she was injured or bleeding.

Finally, she slid her arms around his neck and took a shuddering breath. "He was going to sell me."

Her words sent a jolt all the way to his toes. "What?"

"He was going to sell me. Peter doesn't fence stolen art. He's a human trafficker. He was taking me to a port to be shipped out." Another shudder shook her shoulders.

Suddenly, she leaned back and looked at him, eyes wide. "There are others."

"What do you mean?"

"Peter talked to someone on the phone a few times. One time he told them to not ship out any of the merchandise until he arrived with me."

Spence motioned one of the police officers to come over and relayed what Alyssa had said.

The officer knelt next to them. "Did he say where this port was?"

Alyssa's arms slid from Spence's neck. "No."

"Did he mention any names or anything that might help us find these people?"

"No, that's all."

The officer rose and radioed in the information.

Spence took both of Alyssa's hands in his. "Did they hurt you?"

She shook her head. "They probably didn't want to damage the merchandise. At least, until they decided they had to kill me."

"When you went down, I was afraid he had cut you."

"No, I tried to step back, caught my heel on a tree root and fell. I knew I needed to get out of the reach of the knife."

"You did good." He wrapped her in his arms again. He didn't know if she still needed his comfort. But he needed hers. He'd come so close to losing her tonight.

She didn't protest. Instead, her arms once again encircled his neck. Judging from the way she was holding on, that was exactly where she wanted to be.

He buried his face in her hair. *I love you.* The silent words never made it past his lips. She was in his arms now. But he couldn't speak for tomorrow or the next day, or the day after that. Now that she was free to go anywhere she wanted to go, no danger, no ties, would she want to settle down? Would she even consider returning to her roots, circling right back to where she'd started? Was that even the right thing to do?

He couldn't answer that. She probably couldn't, either.

But, tonight, he didn't have to think about it.

Because, tonight, he wasn't going to let her go.

Chapter Twelve

Three lit candles rose from a base of greenery in the center of the table, and silverware tinged against porcelain plates.

Kris always set a pretty table, especially when dinner included guests. Although all of today's guests, with the exception of Spence, were family. Kris sat next to Tony, little Gavin on her other side, and Kassie and Jared occupied the other side of the table. Alyssa and Spence completed the circle. Apollo lay in one corner, Bella in the other. The seven of them had just finished attending church together. Actually eight, including Apollo.

Two weeks had passed since Peter and his thugs had abducted her. That night, police had swarmed the Port of New Orleans. As Louisiana's only container port, it had been the most logical starting point. Those efforts had paid off. The authorities had rescued almost four dozen women and children from a container awaiting shipment. Alyssa would likely never meet those trafficking victims, but for the past two weeks, she'd seen them in her dreams—nameless faces, filled with terror then relief as heroes rushed in to snatch them from their fate.

According to Tony and Jared, the authorities had made more

than a dozen arrests since then and the investigation was still ongoing. The operation had been much bigger than Peter and the three men she'd seen him with in the back room.

She was still in awe over how God had heard her cries for help. As the man had dragged her into the woods, she'd been sure she was going to die. First, she'd made sure she was ready to face eternity. Then, like Spence, she'd tried to bargain, promising God that if He saved her, she'd commit her life to Him. At the time, she'd had no idea what that would look like. She still didn't. But she was open to the possibilities.

When she'd heard the gunshot and the man holding her had crumpled to his knees, the last thing she had expected was to see Apollo and Spence step into view. Spence hadn't been just *her* answer to prayer that night. He'd probably been the answer to a lot of other prayers—those of the people in the shipping container, as well as their frantic family members.

The fact her abduction had led to all of them being rescued had made everything she'd gone through during those three weeks worth it. Maybe God would redeem her past mistakes by allowing her to help other girls make better choices than she'd made.

Kassie stabbed a bite of meat and held it up. "This is good. Everything is delicious."

Fifteen minutes ago, the large platter in the center of the table had held roast beef, potatoes and carrots. While they'd been growing up, that had been their traditional Sunday dinner. Early in the morning, their mom would pull out the large roasting pan. She'd brown the meat, sprinkle it with dry onion soup and seasonings, and arrange the potatoes and carrots around it. Then she would put it in the oven and, by the time they'd get home from church, the potatoes and carrots would be tender and the meat would pick apart easily with a fork.

Today's gathering wasn't just to share an after-church meal. It was also Alyssa's farewell dinner.

Kassie continued, the bite still on her fork. "The company

is good, too. We need to go back to making this a Sunday tradition. Not that I'm saying you should feed us every week. We could trade off."

Kris nodded. "I agree."

Alyssa would, too, if she were going to stay. Sunday dinnertime around this table was one of the few good memories she carried from her childhood. Attendance had been mandatory, at least for the three girls—no extracurricular activities and no running off with friends. It was family time, and they were going to engage each other like loving family, which meant no arguing or unkind words. They'd usually managed to comply. The fact they'd spent the morning in church probably helped.

Sometimes their dad joined them—for dinner, anyway. Alyssa couldn't remember a single time when he'd gone to church with them. Maybe the idea of sitting in church on Sunday morning and doing drug running during the week hadn't sat well with him.

Kassie grinned. "My cooking isn't as good as yours, but it's hard to mess up roast, potatoes and carrots." She grew serious and her gaze locked with Alyssa's. "You don't have to go."

Both of her sisters had said the same thing, several times. They weren't just doing lip service, either. They really didn't want her to leave. Coming back home had been one of the smartest decisions she'd ever made. Staying wouldn't be.

"Yes, I do."

"Why?"

"I need to make a fresh start, somewhere nobody has any negative expectations."

"You need your family."

She frowned at Kassie. "I don't need a crutch."

Kris heaved an exasperated sigh. "We're not a crutch. We're a support system. That's something everybody needs."

"I've got to prove to myself I can make it on my own."

Kris pressed her lips together. "That's what you've been doing for the past seven years. We saw how well that turned out."

Alyssa sprang to her feet, slapping her palms down on the table. She'd heard enough. "This is exactly what I'm talking about."

Little Gavin pressed one fist to his mouth and started to cry.

Alyssa's heart twisted. "And now I've upset your little boy. Thank you for your hospitality, but I'm calling a cab."

Kris stood and rushed around the table to stop her before she could escape the dining room. "I'm sorry. I didn't mean it like that. Sometimes my filter doesn't work very well."

Alyssa shrugged. "Don't worry about it. This just proves my point. If my own family can't forget my past mistakes, how will anyone else ever see me as anything but a perpetual mess-up?"

"Alyssa, please. That's not what I meant. I was just stressing the importance of having your family around you. Life's a lot easier when you're not trying to go it alone. After being at odds all of our lives, Kassie and I are finally enjoying the closeness sisters are supposed to share. We want you to be part of that. Our family isn't complete without you."

Alyssa turned to look at Kassie. She was nodding agreement.

She tried to picture what her life would be like if she stayed—working at the charter office, living in the space above, maybe even fixing it up to feel more like a home.

She would have a job, because her sisters chose to hire her. She would have a place to live, because her sisters allowed her to occupy the apartment. Everything in her life would depend on the charity of her sisters.

She didn't just want their affection. She wanted their respect. And the only way she would get it was by proving herself—being a responsible adult, standing on her own two feet, finding her own path to success.

"I'm sorry. I don't have any hard feelings. I'll stay in touch." She forced a smile. "And not just when I need to borrow money. Which I haven't forgotten about, by the way. I'm going to pay you both back for the last time as soon as I get on my feet. But leaving now…this is something I have to do."

Alyssa looked back at her plate, holding a lunch that was only half eaten. The smile she gave her sisters was much more relaxed than the last one. "But I don't have to do it before finishing this yummy lunch."

In fact, she had another hour before she would have to leave for the airport. With Peter gone and his buddies locked up, she could return to Atlanta, but she wanted her fresh start to be somewhere completely new.

So she'd continued with the airline ticket purchase she'd begun the day she'd been abducted. Different date, same destination. A little more effort had gone into her planning this time. She'd found a room to rent in the suburbs for just under a thousand per month. The first month's rent and security deposit wouldn't leave much in her checking account, but she would find a job soon.

Her living arrangements were all set. She'd already passed the background check. She'd made a lot of mistakes over the past seven years, but none of those mess-ups had impacted her adult record.

When they finished eating, Kris stacked the dishes and refused help with cleanup, insisting they weren't going to kill the last thirty minutes of their time together working in the kitchen. Instead, she led them into the family room, where two sets of French doors looked out over the backyard and Bayou Texar beyond.

Alyssa sat on the couch, and Spence eased down next to her. Apollo lay at both of their feet. Several times over the past few days, they had discussed her plans to leave. He'd said much the same things Kris had just said, that she needed the support of friends and family.

Friendship. That was all he'd offered. Not so long ago, she could have agreed. That ship had sailed. Somehow, over the past five weeks, she'd fallen right back in love with him.

Actually, the love had been there all along, stuffed beneath years of anger, resentment and rejection. He had obviously moved on when he'd made his decision to leave eight years ago. She hadn't. Seeing both of her sisters so happy had only made the ache inside even more keen.

Eventually, she would be able to think of Spence as no more than a friend, but it wouldn't happen here in Pensacola—living, sleeping and working right next door to him. No, she would have to leave.

Over the years, she'd had a handful of boyfriends. None of those relationships had worked out. She would have no reason to believe the future would be any different from the past, except from this point forward, she was going to ask God to guide her decisions. She was pretty sure that was a reasonable request. In fact, wasn't there even somewhere in the Bible that said to pray for wisdom?

As soon as everyone was seated, Bella settled down against one of the sets of French doors, and Gavin looked around the room, probably trying to decide which lap to climb into. When his eyes met Alyssa's, a smile climbed up his cheeks, and he made a beeline for her. After stepping around the dog, he held out both arms. "Issa?"

Kris corrected him. "Aunt Alyssa."

Alyssa pulled him onto her lap. "He can call me *Issa.* I kind of like it."

"If you're going to insist on leaving, you've got to at least come back for regular visits." Kris grinned. "If you do this just every seven years, Gavin is going to grow up not knowing his Auntie Issa."

Kassie nodded. "Kris is right. Let's make plans now for Christmas."

"That's less than two and a half months away. I'll be in a new job. I doubt they'll let me off."

"Okay," Kassie said. "Summer vacation."

Alyssa looked around the room, warmth filling her chest.

Everyone was smiling, affection shining from their eyes. This was what family was supposed to feel like.

She hugged Gavin and shifted her gaze to the side. Spence gave the little boy some pats on the back.

Tomorrow was the grand opening of Cavanaugh Music Center. She was kind of sad she wouldn't be around to help him celebrate the realization of his dream. She should have delayed her trip by one more day.

A few minutes later, she handed Gavin off to Spence. "I'm going to order an Uber and say my goodbyes now."

Kassie frowned. "You know, any one of us would be happy to take you."

"I know, but I don't want to walk into the airport all weepy."

She stood, and the others did, too. After hugging each of her sisters, she gave their fiancés goodbye hugs. "I can't tell you how much I appreciate everything you guys have done for me—the encouragement and support, the protection detail, giving me a job and a place to stay. I promise, I'll keep in touch. And I won't stay gone so long this time."

Kassie looked at her long and hard. "It's not too late to cancel that flight."

"I have to do this."

"I understand."

She dropped to her knees for the final two hugs. Gavin wrapped his arms around her neck. "Bye, Issa."

"Bye-bye, sweetie. Auntie Issa will be back."

When Gavin released her, she looked at Apollo, who stood next to Spence, watching the activity. She patted her leg. "Come on, boy."

He trotted over to her, tail wagging, and she cupped the furry face in her hands. "I'm going to miss you, too." He responded with a slurp up one of her cheeks.

She rose to walk to the edge of the family room and then turned back around to face everyone. "Remember, this isn't *goodbye*. It's *see you later*. And *talk to you soon*. I'll let you know when I get to the place where I'll be staying."

By the time she reached the foyer, her eyes burned with unshed tears. *Get a grip*. When she'd arrived five weeks ago, she'd thought the only thing she'd feel upon leaving would be relief. With all the emotions swirling inside her, relief wasn't one of them.

She picked up her backpack from where she'd left it on the Bombay chest against the wall and then stepped onto the porch. Two rockers sat side by side. She eased into one and pulled up the Uber app on her phone.

A few minutes later, the door creaked open beside her. Her sisters and their fiancés were respecting her wishes to do this alone.

Spence wasn't. "Can I wait with you?"

She shrugged. "All right."

He sat in the rocker next to hers, and Apollo lay down in front of him. For several moments, the only sounds were the soft creaks of their chairs and the occasional rumble of a vehicle on one of the nearby roads.

Finally, Spence released a sigh. "I don't want you to leave."

"I have to."

"Why?" It was the same question her sister had asked.

"I've got to get my life on the right track, without people watching, just waiting for me to mess up. We both know that won't happen here. Our trip to Publix proved that."

"You're going to let one crotchety lady run you away from everyone who cares about you?"

"Dorothy's not the only one."

"Who else has judged you?"

"No one else has had a chance, because I haven't been out, except for Gallery Night, and everyone was too engaged with the activities to interact with me." She heaved a sigh. "Look, eight years ago, you needed your fresh start. After all this time, I finally get it. I'm not angry anymore. But now I need you to understand I need mine."

"You can have your fresh start right here. You have family who love you, a job, a place to stay until you're able to get something else." One side of his mouth cocked up in a half smile that looked more forlorn than happy. "A friend who has already proved he'll do anything to keep you safe."

And that was the problem. She didn't need another friend. Not in Spence, anyway.

"I can't make my fresh start here. I need to go somewhere where no one knows the old Alyssa, where no one will judge me for my past mistakes. Somewhere I can heal and grow and develop my newfound faith."

A Toyota Prius stopped at the curb and she stood. "Here's my ride."

He stood, too, and although she had already hugged him goodbye inside, she wrapped her arms around his neck again. His went around her and tightened. For several long moments, he didn't move. The embrace seemed to hold much more than simple friendship. But without the words to back it up, she wouldn't stay.

She released him, picked up the pack and descended the porch steps. When she had settled into the Prius's back seat, she looked toward the house. Big mistake.

Spence was standing on the porch, Apollo next to him. The dog stood stock-still, his tail not moving. Sadness seemed to fill his eyes. Was he really as upset as he looked?

When she shifted her attention to Spence, her heart squeezed. The sadness on *his* face was unmistakable. He might just as well be holding a neon sign.

The driver pulled away from the curb, and Alyssa tore her gaze from her childhood home—and her longtime love—to stare out the front windshield.

She was doing the right thing. She'd even prayed about it.

Maybe not as seriously as she should have, but she was still pretty new to this whole prayer thing.

She wasn't the only one who needed time to heal. Spence did, too. Leaving was the right thing to do. It had to be.

So why did she feel as if she'd just left a piece of her soul on her sister's porch?

Spence sat in the wrought-iron swing, moving it in a steady back-and-forth pattern with one foot. Apollo was curled up next to him, big brown paws hanging over the front edge.

He'd left Kris's house right after Alyssa had, slipping back inside just long enough to offer quick thanks for the meal and abrupt goodbyes. He'd planned to head right to his apartment and had wound up at the park instead.

He'd asked Alyssa to stay, more than once. Each time, her answer had been the same. She needed her fresh start. He understood that part. He'd done it himself. But he'd come back.

He didn't know if Alyssa ever would. Based on what she had told him, since leaving home at eighteen, she'd lived like a vagabond, always running from the past, starting over in one place after another, searching for something she'd never been able to find.

Would her newfound faith make a difference? He hoped so. But it hadn't stopped her from leaving him.

It was all for the best, though. He needed someone stable, someone who would be there tomorrow…and the next month and next year. That wasn't Alyssa.

She needed someone stable, too. Between his nightmares and flashbacks, *stable* wasn't in his vocabulary. Throwing two messed-up people together and hoping a healthy relationship would somehow come out of the mix was being unrealistic. Two broken halves didn't make a complete whole.

Instead, he'd pray she would find a good man, someone who had his act together, someone stable enough to be her rock, whatever the future held. Someone who would strengthen her in her newfound faith, rather than lead her away.

A familiar Kia Sorento drove slowly past, Jared at the wheel. He and Kassie must have left Kris's right after he had.

Spence looked over his shoulder to watch the SUV pull into the driveway behind him. Next to him, Apollo stretched, and Spence rested his hand on his back, making slow circles in the dog's fur.

How many times had he and Alyssa sat on this same swing, talking, sharing their frustrations about their fathers, their dissatisfaction with life in general?

Before her mother had disappeared, her favorite place had been the beach. She'd practically grown up there, on weekends, anyway. Her mother had taken her and her sisters there every Saturday. When he and Alyssa had gotten together, Spence had shared several of those outings.

Then, overnight, Alyssa had grown to hate it. He couldn't have dragged her there if he'd tried. He hadn't. He'd understood. She hadn't wanted the reminders of the mother she'd thought had deserted her. He'd been the only one in their circle of friends who hadn't tried to drag her there with them.

Instead, the two of them had made their round of all the parks in Pensacola. It had been quite a feat, considering there were more than ninety. They'd made a game of it, making a list and checking them off one by one, keeping track of their favorites. This one at North Hill was near the top.

Two paths ran diagonally from corner to corner, creating a large X, a raised bed at the intersection. A playground occupied one end of the park, a gazebo the other. Besides the swing, there were several benches placed in various locations.

Footsteps sounded against the concrete path behind him. A lone adult, judging from the sound. There was something else, too—the soft jingle of ID and rabies tags. Someone was probably walking their dog. Hopefully, the visitor would continue on past. Spence was enjoying the solitude.

The footsteps fell silent and he turned. It was Jared. He had stepped off the path and was moving toward the swing.

Jared smiled. "I thought that was you I saw sitting here."

Apollo jumped down and approached Jared and Justice, tail wagging. Jared knelt to greet the dog with some scratches on the head. When he straightened, Apollo turned to sniff Justice.

Jared walked to the swing. "Do you think Apollo will mind if I take his spot?"

"If he does, he'll get over it. Have a seat." So much for solitude. It probably wasn't the best thing for him right now, anyway.

Jared eased down next to him. "I was really hoping Alyssa was going to stay. Kassie and Kris have been trying to persuade her for the past week."

"Yeah, me, too." His gaze drifted to the round raised bed with its knee-high brick wall, shrubs surrounding the light post rising from the center. The bulb wouldn't come on for several hours yet. Long before then, he and Apollo would be back home in the apartment. Alone.

"Are you okay with her leaving?"

Jared's words jarred Spence from his thoughts. He shrugged. "Not really."

"Then why are you here instead of at the airport?"

"Because if I throw her over my shoulder and forcibly carry her out, I'll probably be arrested."

"Words can be more persuasive than brute force."

"I already tried words. They didn't work."

"How hard did you try? I don't know what you might have said when you followed her out, but throughout the meal and afterward, you weren't exactly acting like she was worth fighting for."

He looked at Jared with raised eyebrows. They didn't even know each other that well. Maybe Jared thought his position as Alyssa's future brother-in-law entitled him to ignore social boundaries.

Jared sighed. "Look, I'm not trying to butt into your business, but I can tell you care for her. I know she cares for you, too."

"We had something years ago. We were both so messed up, what we had wasn't very healthy."

"Do you believe people can change?"

"Of course I do."

"From the little bit Kassie and Kris have said, you certainly have. I gather that Alyssa has, too."

Spence shook his head. "She needs somebody stable."

"And you're not? Let's see. You spent however many years serving your country. You're a few hours away from opening your own music store. You've got what I believe is a strong relationship with God. How much more stability do you think Alyssa needs?"

Spence heaved a sigh. Jared didn't know about all the times he awoke during the night with a scream clawing its way up his throat. Or all the seemingly innocuous things that were triggers for him: crowds, fireworks, shootouts on TV, and sometimes absolutely nothing.

He shifted his gaze to Apollo, who was currently following Justice around the park. "See the vest Apollo's wearing? Do you know what kind of service he provides?"

Jared shrugged. "I'm guessing you saw some stuff that would mess with anybody's mind and he helps you keep it all together."

Spence pressed his lips into a thin line but didn't respond.

"And you think that somehow makes you unfit to be any more than a friend. Hey, bro, we're all broken in one way or another."

Jared stood up and whistled for Justice to join him. When the dog reached his side, he stared down at Spence. "Did you tell Alyssa how you feel? How you *really* feel?"

No, he hadn't. He'd thought it would only make things more

difficult for them if she suspected the depth of his feelings for her.

But Jared was right. Everyone was broken in their own way. Jesus was the only perfect man who had ever lived. Alyssa could find someone else, someone who had never experienced abuse or combat or terror. But the man still wouldn't be perfect.

And whoever this unknown man was, he couldn't possibly love Alyssa any more than Spence did.

Jared shook his head. "The way you look right now, if you don't catch her before she leaves, there's going to be a trip to California in your near future. Do yourself a favor and save some hard-earned bucks. Go see if you can stop her from getting on that plane."

Jared turned and headed back the way he had come, his German shepherd trotting beside him.

Spence watched him walk away. Alyssa had told him she finally understood why he'd had to leave all those years ago. Maybe that meant, after eight years of resentment, she had finally forgiven him. But had she come to feel for him as she once had? Or was she content to remain just friends?

There was only one way to find out.

Spence rose from the swing, and Apollo came to attention. Jared was right. He couldn't let Alyssa leave without telling her how he felt.

He jogged back to the Subaru. The airport was only fifteen minutes away. Depending on how backed up the security line was, maybe he could catch Alyssa before she got beyond where he could go.

After leaving the SUV in the parking garage, he hurried into the airport and scanned the lines of passengers waiting in the security queues. He had almost given up when people near the TSA checkpoint shifted again, offering him a brief glimpse of red hair.

His pulse kicked into high gear. "Come, Apollo."

For the next few minutes, he zigzagged through the line, offering frequent apologies. He got several questioning glances, but only two people voiced protests, which died the moment they noticed Apollo. Maybe the dog made him look a little more official.

Alyssa stepped closer to the checkpoint, one person ahead of her now. She was only about twenty feet away.

"Alyssa!" No reaction. He was close, but not close enough for her to hear him over the murmur of voices and other noises in the airport. He wound his way closer.

She handed her ticket and driver's license to the TSA agent. "Alyssa!"

She turned, scanning the faces around her until her gaze settled on Spence.

"Spence?"

The TSA person handed back her items. "Move on through."

Instead, Alyssa stepped back and motioned the next person to go ahead of her. When she had made her way back to Spence, they both moved as far out of the line as the barrier would allow.

She looked up at him, her eyebrows drawn together in confusion. But her smile said she was happy to see him.

"What are you doing here?"

"I came to ask you to stay."

"I can't."

Yeah, he'd made the request several times, and she'd told him the same thing every time. "That's not the only reason I'm here. I came to tell you how I feel."

She tilted her head to the side. "And how is that?"

"I love you, Alyssa. I don't think I ever stopped. I can't go back to just being your friend. I've come back home, but I realize now that nowhere is home without you in my life. I need you with me, and I hope you'll give me a chance to prove I'll always be there for you, no matter what life throws our way."

Alyssa looked at him with wide eyes and a slack jaw. "But… I *have* to go. I already bought my ticket."

"Turn it in and apply the credit toward the trip I'm hoping we'll both be taking in a few months."

"What trip?"

"Anywhere you want to go…for our honeymoon, if you'll marry me."

Her mouth opened and snapped closed again. He'd apparently put her at a loss for words. Either that or she was trying to figure out the gentlest way to say no.

When he glanced around them, they had the attention of everyone in the immediate area.

He turned back to Alyssa, who hadn't said a word since his awkward proposal. Before he'd joined the army, they had both planned to marry one day. But he could have done a little better with planning the actual proposal.

"Come on, sweetheart." He forced a teasing smile. "You're not seriously going to embarrass me in front of all these people by telling me to take a hike, are you?"

She tilted her head to the side, her lips curving up in a smirk. "Have you cleared this with Apollo?"

"He's the one who suggested it."

"In that case, how can I say no?"

She wrapped her arms around his neck and stood on her tiptoes. He met her halfway.

When his lips met hers, applause broke out around them. Yeah, they had an audience.

It didn't matter. Nothing mattered except the woman he held in his arms. He'd waited eight long years for this moment, without even knowing what he was waiting for.

Alyssa was his, now and forever. They both had healing to do. The road ahead wouldn't be without bumps. But they had love and a shared faith.

He'd thought two broken halves couldn't make a whole. He'd been wrong.

They could, as long as God was the glue binding them together.

Epilogue

The sun shone from a blue sky speckled with fluffy white clouds, and a steady breeze blew across the soft sand. Alyssa stood next to Spence, wearing a tea-length, ivory-colored gown. Kassie was on Spence's other side in an identical gown except in white, Jared beyond. Kris and Tony completed the flattened semicircle, Kris's dress a pale lavender. The men were dressed in suits rather than tuxedos. A dog sat to the left of each couple, wearing a vest and a silk bandana matching its lady's gown.

Behind the pastor, the endless expanse of the Gulf stretched out to meet the horizon. In the middle of May, the temperature was perfect. It had warmed up from the cooler weather of winter, but the hot stickiness of summer hadn't yet arrived.

The triple wedding had been Kassie's idea. With her and Jared planning to tie the knot in early May, and Kris and Tony planning on late May, they'd decided to settle in the middle with a double wedding, which had grown to include the third couple when Alyssa and Spence got engaged.

It was Alyssa who had suggested involving the dogs. Spence was rarely separated from Apollo, and although the nightmares and flashbacks had decreased considerably and they had all agreed on only two hundred guests, she wasn't taking any chances. Her sisters had loved the idea.

Alyssa couldn't remember who had suggested the venue, but she had thought it was perfect. They were at Langdon Beach, part of the Gulf Islands National Seashore, one of their mother's favorite places.

They'd already said their vows and exchanged rings. Gavin had carried Kris's and Tony's forward on a silk pillow and then had taken a seat with Brandi in the front row. Even as well-behaved as he was, everyone involved had decided that, at three years old, forty minutes was a little too long to expect him to stand still.

At the moment, the pastor was charging the six of them to remember the commitment they were making today and to take it seriously, that marriage was harder than people expected.

Behind them, friends and family occupied the white folding chairs lined up on the beach. One of those family members was Spence's father. Shortly after she had decided to stay, Spence had finally given in to the nudge he had tried to ignore for several months. He'd shown up on his father's doorstep one afternoon for what would be the first of many visits.

Alyssa had had mixed feelings about opening those doors. Spence's reconciling with his father had put even more pressure on her to go see hers. Now she was glad she had. His tears and heartfelt apologies had gone a long way in allowing her to let go of the anger and resentment she had carried for so many years.

A week after that visit, he'd succumbed to the cancer ravishing his body. It was as if he'd been hanging on just long enough to make amends with his last daughter.

The pastor ended with a prayer, and a guitarist and soloist stepped forward. Gary and James were both part of the worship team at church. So was Spence. He'd volunteered shortly after arriving back in Pensacola and had been playing with them ever since.

Gary strummed an intro, and James began to sing "I Will Be Here" by Steven Curtis Chapman. Each couple had chosen a song for the wedding. This last one was Spence and Alyssa's.

As James sang, Spence squeezed Alyssa's hand, silently affirming the words of the song. It was his promise to her. She had no doubt—through the good times and bad, through the years, whatever the future held, he would be there.

When the final strains of the song had faded, the pastor prayed a blessing over all three couples and pronounced them husband and wife. "Gentlemen, you may kiss your brides."

Alyssa looked at Spence, head tilted back. Seven months had passed since he had chased her down at the airport, and she still had those occasional moments when she was afraid she was going to wake up back in Atlanta and realize this was all a dream.

Guests applauded, and she pulled away to smile at those gathered. She was now Mrs. Spencer Cavanaugh. Joy coursed through her, along with an overwhelming sense of gratitude.

She wouldn't change a thing. If things hadn't gone the way they had with Peter, she wouldn't have stayed in Pensacola for more than one night. She would have been gone before Spence arrived. She would have had no need for protection. She wouldn't have ended up living right next door to him, and there would have been no middle-of-the-night talks. Those three weeks had been some of the worst weeks of her life, but since that was what had led her to where she was now, everything she had gone through was a blessing.

A recording of "The Wedding March" played through the speaker system, and Alyssa and Spence walked down the center aisle arm in arm, Apollo trailing behind them. Kassie and Jared followed with Justice, and Kris, Tony and Bella brought up the rear, Gavin in Tony's arms.

A tent stood nearby, tables and chairs beneath. A balloon

arch formed a backdrop for the head table, where six places were set, a floral centerpiece in front of each pair of chairs. Pleasant aromas drifted to them from a row of tables holding chafing dishes filled with baked chicken, scalloped potatoes and broccoli in cheese sauce.

Alyssa and Spence stopped at the edge of the tent. The others, along with the dogs, fell in next to them, forming the receiving line.

When Spence's father reached them, he greeted Alyssa with a hug and Spence with a handshake and a smile. After stepping in front of Apollo, he bent over and held out a hand. The dog lifted a paw, and Spence's dad shook it. When he straightened, he was smiling even more broadly. The man had changed a lot over the past few months, becoming a true father to both her and Spence. He was even attending church with them on a regular basis.

Once the last guest had finished congratulating them and stepped under the tent, Spence pulled Alyssa more tightly against his side. "Not a bad ending for a proposal that took place in the security queue at the airport."

Kris grinned. "You did better than this guy." She poked Tony in the ribs with an elbow. "He proposed in a cemetery."

Tony frowned. "Not *in* a cemetery. Right *outside* the cemetery. There's a difference."

Jared laughed. "Looks like I'm the only one who did it right, with a romantic lunch on the water and a ring purchased in advance."

"But we made up for it," Tony said.

Spence nodded. "We sure did. Fancy candlelight dinner, music, the whole shebang."

As they made their way to the buffet, Alyssa looked around at those gathered. They were here for Kassie and Kris, but they were here for her, too. She smiled at her sisters, her nephew whom she'd waited far too long to get to know and the two men who had just become family. Finally, her gaze went to Spence.

Warmth flooded her. This was contentment.

From the time she'd left home seven years ago, she had searched for a new beginning, starting over in one place after another.

But all along, her new beginning was right here.

At home.

* * * * *

Romantic Suspense

Danger. Passion. Drama.

Available Next Month

Colton At Risk Kacy Cross
Renegade Reunion Addison Fox

Canine Refuge Linda O. Johnston
A Dangerous Secret Sandra Owens

LOVE INSPIRED
Searching For Justice Connie Queen
Trained To Protect Terri Reed

LOVE INSPIRED
Wyoming Ranch Sabotage Kellie VanHorn
Hiding The Witness Deena Alexander

LOVE INSPIRED
Lethal Reunion Lacey Baker
A Dangerous Past Susan Gee Heino

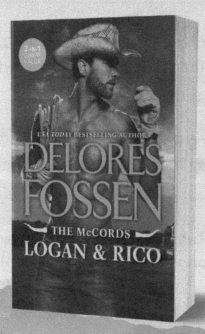

Subscribe and fall in love with a Mills & Boon series today!

You'll be among the first to read stories delivered to your door monthly and enjoy great savings.

WE
SIMPLY
LOVE
ROMANCE

MILLS & BOON

JOIN US

Sign up to our newsletter to stay up to date with...

- Exclusive member discount codes
- Competitions
- New release book information
- All the latest news on your favourite authors

Plus...
get $10 off your first order.
What's not to love?

Sign up at **millsandboon.com.au/newsletter**